ROSEMARY ROGERS

Scandalous Deception

HQN™

ISBN-13: 978-0-373-77250-6
ISBN-10:   0-373-77250-5

SCANDALOUS DECEPTION

www.HQNBooks.com

Printed in U.S.A.

To a new generation of readers
and to my new great-grandson

CHAPTER ONE

Russia, 1820
Tzarskoye Selo

THE JOURNEY FROM St. Petersburg to Tzarskoye Selo was hardly an arduous one during the short summer months when the roads were fair and the brisk breeze held a pleasant scent of wildflowers and rich earth.

Which was precisely why the Emperor had left the Summer Palace two days earlier, claiming that such fine weather was too fleeting not to enjoy a few days away from the pressures of Court.

Lately Alexander Pavlovich would use any excuse to flee his heavy duties, but so far as Lord Edmond Summerville was concerned, it was an Imperial pain in the ass.

Coming over the slight swell in the road, he turned his black charger on the path to Ekaterinsky, the larger of the two palaces that sprawled with a majestic beauty across the Russian countryside.

Catherine the Great's masterpiece was a stunning sight. Over a thousand yards long with narrow wings, it was three stories high and painted a bright blue that contrasted pleasantly with the five golden domes that marked the chapel. Along the front was a line of draped female figures that glowed with a gleaming bronze in the sunlight.

Edmond did not allow his hard pace to slow as he entered the courtyard through the gilded gateway to halt directly before the entrance.

His arrival brought a dozen footmen rushing forward, taking command of his mount and that of his outriders. As the younger son of a duke, Edmond was accustomed to the pomp and ceremony that surrounded royalty and barely noted the scurrying servants as he made his way up the marble stairs and stepped into the vast vestibule.

There he was met by one of Alexander's more trusted companions attired in a dark gold coat and striped waistcoat that would have been perfectly suitable in any London drawing room. European fashions were always preferred among Russian aristocracy.

Herrick Gerhardt was of Prussian descent and had arrived in St. Petersburg when he was barely seventeen. He possessed a gaunt countenance, a thick crop of silver hair, and piercing brown eyes that held a cold, ruthless intelligence.

This was a man who did not suffer fools gladly and had made countless enemies among the Russian court for his brutal ability to see through their treacherous deceits.

His love of his Emperor was unquestionable, but his talent at diplomacy was sadly lacking.

"Edmond, this is a most unexpected surprise," he said in the perfect French spoken by all the Russian nobles, his gaze searching Edmond's starkly chiseled features, the vivid blue eyes that were such a stunning contrast to his thick raven hair and arched brows, and the wide mouth that was missing his usual charming smile.

Despite being the son of an English duke, Edmond possessed the high Slavic cheekbones of his Russian mother, as well as her cleft chin, which had been driving women to distraction since he left the nursery. He also possessed a love for his mother's land that his elder twin brother would never comprehend.

Edmond offered a respectful nod of his head.

"I fear I must beg a few moments with the Emperor."

"Is there trouble?"

"Only of a personal nature." The restless fear that had plagued him since receiving his brother's latest missive clenched at his heart. "I must return to England without delay."

The older man stiffened, his thin face hardening with displeasure. "This is an ill time for you to leave the side of the Imperial Highness," he chided sternly. "It was assumed you were to travel with him to the Congress of Troppau."

"An unfortunate necessity, I fear."

"A great deal more than unfortunate. We both know that there is growing distrust of Metternich and his increasing influence on the Emperor. Your presence would assist in keeping the Prince at a distance."

Edmond shrugged, unable to feel any disappointment that he would be missing the conference of the Quadruple Alliance in Opava. For all his love of politics and intrigues, he despised the stifling formality of diplomatic gatherings. What could be more tedious than watching puffed-up dignitaries strutting about and pinning medals upon each others' chests?

Serious negotiations were best done behind closed doors and far from the public view.

The fact was that without Britain or France in attendance, the Congress was doomed from the beginning.

Not that he was about to mention his doubts in front of Gerhardt. The Emperor was set on this mission, and it was expected that his loyal subjects would cheer his strong determination to squash the revolution in Naples.

"I believe you overestimate my influence," he instead murmured.

"No, I am well aware you are one of the few confidants that Alexander Pavlovich still trusts." Gerhardt regarded Edmond with a fierce scowl. "You are in a rare position to assist your motherland."

"Your confidence in my meager skills is flattering, but your own presence with the Emperor will dampen the ambitions of Metternich far more than my own humble self."

A hint of frustration tightened Gerhardt's thin face. "I must remain here."

Edmond arched a brow. It was rare for the older man not to be at the side of his Emperor at such an important gathering.

"You suspect trouble?"

"So long as Akartcheyeff is left in charge of the country, there is always danger," he muttered, not bothering to hide his distaste of the man who had risen to such lofty ranks despite his lowly birth. "His devotion to his Emperor is beyond question, but he will never learn that you cannot use force to earn loyalty. There is a powder keg beneath our feet and Akartcheyeff might very well be the spark that ignites disaster."

Edmond could hardly deny the danger. He, better than anyone, understood the smoldering dissatisfaction with the Czar that infected not only the masses, but several aristocrats as well.

The last thing he desired was to leave during this volatile time, but there was no choice.

"He is…unfortunately brutal in his dealings with others," Edmond admitted, "but he is one of the few Ministers who have proven his integrity cannot be swayed."

Stepping even closer, Gerhardt pitched his voice so it would not carry to the two footmen on duty beside the door.

"Which is why it is so important that you remain at Alexander Pavlovich's side! Not only do you have the ear of the Emperor, but your…network will learn of any dangers long before any official report is put on my desk."

Gerhardt's delicate mention of the web of thieves, prostitutes, foreigners, sailors and more than a few nobles brought a smile to his lips. Over the past eight years, he had managed to create a connection of spies that kept him aware of brewing trouble the moment it began to stir.

It was an invaluable asset to Alexander Pavlovich. One that he had come to rely upon, as did those who considered it their duty to keep him safe.

"I will ensure that my associates keep in close contact with you," he promised, his expression somber, "but I cannot postpone my return to England."

Realizing that Edmond would not be swayed, Gerhardt stepped back, his brow furrowed with concern.

"Should I offer my sympathies?"

"Not if I can prevent it, my friend."

"Then God go with you."

With a bow, Edmond turned and with swift steps headed toward the Main Staircase, a magnificent work of marble that towered for three stories. For most guests to the Palace it was the extensive collection of Chinese porcelain vases and plates displayed along the walls that captured their attention, but Edmond had always been captivated by the warm glow of sunlight that was reflected in the rich marble. A true architect could breathe life into a building without the fuss of ornamentation.

From there he moved through the Portrait Hall where the painting of Empress Catherine I held a fitting place of glory amid the seeming endless gilded carvings, then through another hall, to at last reach Alexander Pavlovich's private study.

In contrast to the lavish public rooms, Alexander had chosen a chamber that was refreshingly small and comfortable with a view of the beautiful gardens. Ignoring the guards who stood at impassive attendance, Edmond entered the room and performed a deep bow.

"Sire."

Seated behind the rigidly tidy desk, Alexander Pavlovich, Imperial Highness, Emperor Czar, lifted his head and offered that singularly sweet smile that never failed to remind a person of an angel.

"Edmond, join me," Alexander commanded in French.

With his Hessians clicking against the inlaid wooden floor, Edmond moved to settle his tall, lithely chiseled form in one of the mahogany carved and gilded wood chairs, his gaze covertly studying the man who had earned his unwavering love and loyalty since the battles against Napoleon in 1812.

The Emperor possessed the imposing form of his Russian ancestors that had grown a bit stout over the passing years, and the fine, even lines of his mother's countenance. The golden hair had receded, but the blue eyes remained as clear and intelligent as in his youth.

It was the air of weary melancholy, however, that Edmond silently considered. It was growing worse. With every passing year, the once eager, impractical idealist determined to alter Russian's future was becoming a defeated, withdrawn man who was riddled with such distrust, of himself and others, that he retreated more and more from the Court.

"Forgive me for my intrusion," Edmond began gently.

"There are many who I consider an intrusion, but never you, my friend." He waved a hand to the ever-present tray on his desk. "Tea?"

"Thank you, no, I do not desire to keep you from your work."

"Always work. Work and duty." Alexander heaved a sigh, precisely laying down his quill before leaning back in his chair. Like his father, Czar Paul, Alexander possessed a preference for a simple, military-style attire, relieved only by his Cross of St. George. "There are nights I dream of simply walking away from this palace and disappearing among the mobs."

"Responsibility always comes with a heavy price," Edmond readily agreed. There had been more than one night he had dreamed of becoming lost among the crowds. A simple, uncomplicated existence was a rare gift that few appreciated as they should.

"A pity I was not like you, Edmond. I think I should have liked to be a younger son, to have had some say in my own destiny. There was a time I even considered abdicating the throne and living a quiet life upon the Rhine." He offered a wistful smile. "It was impossible, of course, a foolish dream of youth. Unlike Constantine, I had no choice but to accept my duty."

"Being a younger son comes with its own share of troubles, sire. I would not wish my life on anyone."

"Yes, you hide your troubles well, Edmond, but I have always sensed your heart is not at rest," Alexander Pavlovich astonished Edmond by admitting. "Perhaps someday you will share what demons haunt you."

Edmond battled to keep his face impassive. He had vowed never to speak of the raw wound that festered deep in his heart. Not with anyone.

"Perhaps." He wisely evaded a direct response. "But not today, I fear. I have come to beg your forgiveness."

"What is it?"

"I must return to England."

"Has something occurred?"

Edmond carefully considered his words. "I have been concerned for some time, sire," he confessed. "The letters that I have received from my brother over the past months have mentioned a number of…incidents that make me suspect that someone is attempting to do him harm."

Alexander abruptly leaned forward. "Explain these incidents."

"There have been gunshots from the nearby wood that my brother dismissed as poachers, there was a bridge that collapsed just as my brother's carriage was upon it, and most recently a fire was started late one night in the wing of Meadowland where my brother's bedchambers are located." Edmond gripped the arms of his chair until his knuckles turned white as he recalled his brother's latest letter. He intended to kill whoever was stupid enough to threaten his twin brother's life. Slowly, painfully, and without mercy. "It was only because of an alert servant that there was nothing more than a few scorched walls instead of a tragedy."

The Emperor did not pretend shock that someone as powerful as the Duke of Huntley might be in danger. The previous Czar had been assassinated, with scandalous rumors that Alexander himself had been involved. Then, of course, there was rarely a month that passed without some threat to the throne.

"It is understandable that you are concerned, but surely your brother has taken steps to ensure his safety?"

Edmond grimaced. Despite the fact there was less than ten minutes between their births, the two brothers could not be more different.

"Stefan is a brilliant Duke," he said, speaking nothing less than the truth. "He tends his lands with the love of a mother for her child, his business investments have tripled the family's coffers, and he is devoted to the care of those who depend upon him, whether it is his reckless younger brother or his lowest servant." A rueful smile touched Edmond's mouth. As different as they might be, the two brothers were devoted to one another, even more so since their parents' tragic drowning years earlier. "As a man of the world, however, he is extraordinarily naive, completely trusting of others and utterly incapable of deception."

Alexander gave a slow nod of his head. "I begin to comprehend."

"I want more than to keep Stefan safe," Edmond said in a soft, lethal voice. "I want whoever is responsible in my hands so I can choke the life from him."

"Do you know who it is?"

Edmond's body clenched with a fury he could barely contain. Along with his brother's grudging revelation of the odd incidences that had plagued him, had been a passing reference to the fact that their cousin, Howard Summerville, was visiting his mother who lived only a few miles from the Huntley family seat.

Howard was his eldest cousin and the third heir in line to inherit the dukedom if anything were to happen to Stefan and Edmond. He was also a pathetic whiner who rarely missed an opportunity to inform all of society that his family had been ill-used by the Dukes of Huntley.

Who more likely to wish to do away with Stefan?

"I have my suspicions."

"I see. Then most certainly it is your duty to protect your brother," Alexander agreed with a grave nod of his head.

"I realize it is an awkward time to leave, but…" His words were cut short as the Emperor abruptly rose to his feet.

"Edmond, go to your family," he commanded. "When all is settled, you can return to me."

Edmond gained his feet and performed a deep bow.

"Thank you, sire."

"Edmond."

"Yes?"

"Just make certain you do return," the Emperor commanded. "The Duke has given his loyalty to England, but your family owes Russia one of their sons."

Hiding a smile at the thought of what King George IV might have to say at the royal command, Edmond merely inclined his head.

"Of course."

LEAVING HIS SERVANTS AND carriage to follow behind him, Edmond urged his mount to a steady pace from London to his childhood home in Surrey.

Stefan might be a meticulous correspondent, but he tended to devote far too much attention to his crop rotation and newest farm implements. Edmond knew the precise details of the plantings in the north field and very little of how Stefan truly fared.

Still, for all Edmond's urgency, he couldn't halt the overwhelming desire to slow his grueling pace as he entered the familiar wooded landscape surrounding his home.

It was all in perfect order, of course. Everything from the neatly trimmed hedgerows to the recently harvested fields. Even the cottages were brightly whitewashed with fresh thatching on the roofs. Stefan would demand no less than perfection. Which was why he was considered one of the finest landlords in the entire realm.

Edmond was surprised, however, to realize he could vividly recall every curve in the road, every tiny stream that cut through the rolling pastures, and every towering oak that lined the long path to the house. He recalled playing pirates with Stefan on the glittering lake in the distance, having picnics with his adoring parents in the Grotto, even hiding from his tutor in the large conservatory.

His heart clenched with a bittersweet pain that only intensified as he cantered past the ivy-covered tower gate and his gaze fell upon the rambling, stone house that had been the crowning glory of the countryside for two hundred and fifty years.

Perched at the end of a tree-lined drive much of the foundation of the great house was still from the original Norman stonework, a testament to the excellent craftsmanship. There were twelve impressive bays that boasted sash windows and stone balustrades that lined the roof. The previous Duke had added a Portrait Gallery and the woodland gardens had been expanded to include several fountains created for his mother by Russian artists, but the overall image remained one of solid, ageless English beauty.

Behind the main house, the stable block was a handsome structure that maintained much of its rustic beauty with numerous wooden stalls and carved pillars. In the past the stables had housed the local villagers when the plague had swept through the country, providing a sanctuary from the ravaging death. These days, however, the building had been returned to its traditional purpose, housing the extensive collection of Huntley horses that were praised in the *Sporting Magazine* and sought after by foxhunters all over England.

As a youth, Edmond had loved the scent of the stables, often hiding in the hayloft to avoid the tedious lectures of his tutor or, as he grew older, to enjoy a bit of privacy with a willing maid.

Sucking in a sharp breath, Edmond sternly dismissed the memories that threatened to overwhelm him. He hadn't returned to England to dredge up the ugly past. Or to waste his time brooding on what might have been.

He was here for Stefan.

Nothing more.

Edmond angled his horse toward the side entrance, hoping to avoid the fanfare that always occurred on the rare occasions he made an appearance at his ancestral seat. Later he would make sure he managed to greet the large staff he considered more family than servants, but for now he wanted to assure himself that Stefan was safe. Then he needed to find a trust-worthy ally who could tell him the truth of what had been happening here in Surrey.

He managed to slip through the double French doors and make his way through the small study that his brother had confiscated to use for his private art studio. The satinwood furnishings had been shifted to a distant corner, leaving space on the Persian carpet for a stack of canvases and a wooden tripod. Even the pretty green and ivory striped curtains that perfectly matched the wall panels were now folded and stacked on his mother's writing desk. A smile touched Edmond's lips. It was a ridiculous waste of space, considering Stefan had managed to create nothing more than a handful of truly ghastly landscapes in the past twenty years.

With a shake of his head, he crossed through the adjoining music room before being caught by the thin, silver-haired butler who was hovering near the marble staircase, as if sensing someone had invaded his domain.

For the briefest moment, a hint of confusion touched the servant's sharply carved face, as if wondering why the Duke of Huntley would be sneaking through the house like a thief, before realization struck.

Even servants who had known Stefan and Edmond all their lives found it difficult to tell them apart at a glance.

"My lord," he breathed in shock, hurrying forward with a rare smile curving his lips. "What a delightful surprise."

Edmond readily returned the smile. Goodson was a genuine treasure, always efficient, well-organized and in ruthless control of the vast staff. His true talent, however, was his ability to maintain the sense of calm peace that so pleased Stefan.

There was never, ever anything to disturb the serenity of Meadowland. No sounds of squabbling servants, no upheavals from unwanted guests who were firmly, but diplomatically, turned from the door, no awkward unpleasantness during the rare social events that were held at the grand house.

He was, all in all, the perfect butler.

"Thank you, Goodson," Edmond said. "I am shockingly pleased to be here."

"It is always good to come home," Goodson replied, able to hide the least hint of reproach at Edmond's lengthy absence.

The staff would never fully resign themselves to Edmond's preference for living in Russia. To them he was an Englishman, regardless of his mother's blood, and a duke's son. His place was at Meadowland, not some strange, foreign land.

"Yes, I suppose it is. Is the Duke at home?"

"He is in his study. Do you wish me to announce you?"

Of course Stefan was in his study. If his diligent brother was not overseeing the work in the fields he was *always* in his study.

"No, despite my advancing years, I believe I can still remember my way."

Goodson gave a dignified nod. "I will have Mrs. Slater bring you a tray there."

Edmond's mouth watered at the mere thought. He had eaten the food of the most famous chefs in the world, but none could compare to Mrs. Slater's simple English fare.

"Will you ask her to include her famous seed cakes? I haven't had a decent one in years."

"There is no need to ask," Goodson assured him dryly. "The woman will be so delighted to have you returned to Meadowland, she will not be satisfied until she manages to produce every dish you have claimed to prefer since you were in shortcoats."

"At this moment I believe I could eat them all." Edmond turned toward the steps only to sharply turn back toward the hovering servant. "Goodson."

"Yes, my lord?"

"My brother happened to mention in one of his letters that Mr. Howard Summerville was visiting his mother."

"I believe he and his family did stay several weeks with Mrs. Summerville, sir."

There was nothing to be detected in the bland tones, but Edmond did not doubt the servant knew the precise day Howard arrived in Surrey as well as the exact moment of his departure. It would, after all, be the valet's unpleasant duty to ensure the sponger did not manage to slip past his guard and trouble the Duke with his tedious pleas for money.

"How many weeks?"

"He arrived six days before Christmas and did not leave until the twelfth of September."

"Rather odd for a gentleman devoted to the delights of town to leave London for such a protracted length of time, was it not, Goodson?"

"Very odd, unless one believes in village gossip."

"And what village gossip would that be?"

"That Mr. Summerville was forced to close his town house and retrench." The disdain deepened. "It was said that the gentleman could not so much as step out his door without being surrounded by bill collectors."

"It seems my cousin has managed to become an even greater dolt than I had anticipated."

"Yes, indeed, my lord."

He sucked in a deep breath. "Once I speak with my brother I would like to have a word with his valet."

The flicker of surprise was so brief it might have been nonexistent. "I will have James awaiting you in the library."

"Actually I would prefer the privacy of my personal sitting room, always presuming it has not been converted into a nursery or filled to the ceiling with Stefan's farming manuals."

"Your rooms are just as you left them," the servant assured him in grave tones. "His Grace insists that they always be prepared for your return."

Edmond smiled wryly. It was predictable of his brother. And oddly comforting. There was something to be said for always knowing there was a place waiting for you.

"Have James meet me in my sitting room in an hour."

"As you wish."

Knowing that Goodson would not only have James waiting for him, but would do so with the sort of discretion that would avoid any unnecessary chatter below-stairs, Edmond turned and continued his way to the second floor.

Deliberately avoiding the Picture Gallery, Edmond chose the lesser-used Minstrel's Gallery to make his way toward the private rooms of the vast house. A faint smile touched his lips as he realized that the pale blue damask wall panels were precisely the same as they had been when he was a child, as well as the blue and ivory silk curtains that framed the high, arched windows that ran the length of the gallery.

His amusement only deepened as he silently pushed open the door to the large study that was nearly overrun with books, ledgers and farming manuals stacked on every available surface. Only the heavy oak desk was relatively clear of debris, with one ledger book spread open. Stefan was seated behind the desk in a leather chair, quill in his hand.

"Do you know, Stefan, it is nothing short of remarkable how nothing ever changes at Meadowland, including you," he murmured softly. "I believe you were sitting at that precise desk, tallying the same quarterly reports in that same old blue coat the day that I left."

Lifting his dark head, Stefan stared at him in shock for a long beat.

"Edmond?"

"For my sins."

With a choked sound between a laugh and sob, Stefan was on his feet and hurrying to clasp Edmond in a bear hug.

"Dear God, it's good to see you."

Edmond readily returned the embrace. His feelings for

Stefan had never been complicated. His brother was the one person in the entire world he truly loved.

"And you, Stefan."

Pulling back, Stefan allowed a rueful smile to touch the face that was an exact replica of Edmond's.

Oh, the discerning eye might pick up the fact that Stefan's olive skin was a shade or two darker from the hours he spent overseeing the tenants, and that the vivid blue eyes held an expression of sweet trust that would never be seen in Edmond's. But the thick raven hair curled in exactly the same manner, the chiseled features held the same Slavic beauty; even their tall, lean bodies were exactly matched.

The two had spent their childhood taking great delight in switching places and confusing others who could never tell them apart.

Everyone, that is, but their parents and their young neighbor Brianna Quinn. The tiny minx with a wild mane of autumn-hued curls could never be deceived.

"I will have you know this coat is not above three or four seasons old," Stefan assured him as he smoothed his hands over the blue coat.

Edmond gave a soft laugh. "I would lay ten quid your valet would tell me differently."

Stefan wrinkled his nose, his gaze skimming over Edmond's closely tailored mulberry jacket and silver waistcoat.

"Well, I never was as dapper as you."

"Thank God," Edmond said with utter sincerity. "Unlike your feckless brother, you have far more important matters to fill your days than the cut of your coat or gloss of your boots. Not the least of which is allowing me to live in magnificent comfort."

"I would hardly consider being the guardian angel of his Imperial Highness as being feckless," Stefan countered. "Far from it, in fact."

"Guardian angel?" Edmond gave a sharp, disbelieving laugh at the ridiculous words. "You are far off the mark, dear Stefan.

I am a wicked sinner, a rake, and a self-indulgent adventurer who has only avoided the hangman's noose due to the fortune of possessing a Duke for a brother."

The vivid blue eyes narrowed. "You might be able to fool others, Edmond, but never me."

"Because you are always determined to believe the best in everyone, even your worthless brother." Edmond lowered himself into a wing chair near the desk, quite ready to be done with the conversation. "Presumably Mrs. Slater is busily pre-paring a banquet, but in truth I am in more need of a shot of that Irish whiskey you keep hidden in your drawer."

"Of course." With a knowing smile Stefan moved to the desk and pulled out the bottle of whiskey and two glasses. Splash-ing a healthy measure of the amber spirit into each, he handed one to Edmond and took his own seat behind the desk. "Cheers."

Tossing the spirit down his throat, Edmond savored the de-licious burn.

"Ah…perfect." Placing the empty glass on a nearby table, Edmond settled back in his seat and took a deep breath. He smiled at his brother. "This room smells of England."

"And what does England smell of?"

"Polished wood, aging leather, damp air. It never changes."

Stefan polished off his drink and set his glass aside. "Perhaps not, but I find such familiarity comforting. I am not like you, Edmond, always seeking some new adventure. I prefer a more dull and tedious existence."

"There is something to be said for familiarity. I am glad you haven't changed Meadowland. I like knowing that when I return, it will be just as I remembered." He studied his brother, a wicked glint in his eyes. "Of course, once you take a wife you will no doubt be badgered into constant renovations. We might love this rambling old place with its smoking chimneys, leaking casements and sadly dated furnishings, but I doubt a woman of good breeding would be happy to live among such shabbiness."

As always Stefan refused to rise to the bait. "No doubt that is the reason I still have yet to take a wife," he murmured with a placid indifference to his bachelor state. Of course he could be. Everyone knew there wasn't a maiden in all of England, or the rest of the world for that matter, who wouldn't leap at the opportunity to become the next Duchess of Huntley. "I cannot bear the thought of altering my treasured home."

"More likely you are just foolish enough to be waiting for love to strike your heart, and when it does I predict that it will be to some entirely unsuitable miss who will lead you about by your nose."

Stefan arched a dark brow. "Actually I've always assumed that you would be the one to tumble neck deep in love with some spirited lady who will lead you a merry dance. It would be only fair, for all the havoc you have caused among the fairer sex."

There was no need for Edmond to fake his shudder. He possessed a natural desire for a beautiful woman, but never for more than a passing affair.

He would readily share his body and his wealth, but never anything more.

"*Mon dieu,* not even I deserve such a hideous fate," he muttered.

Stefan chuckled, but he didn't appear nearly as convinced as he should have been. "Now, tell me all the news from Russia. You know I hear nothing here in the country."

Edmond leaned forward, his smile fading. "Actually, Stefan, I am far more interested in what has been happening at Meadowland."

IT WAS CLOSE TO TWO HOURS later when Edmond entered his private sitting room. Decorated in soothing shades of cream and sapphire, it possessed a simple elegance. The furniture was fashioned in the solid English style with a satin settee, a mahogany chased ormolu and brass bureau, and a few trellised-backed chairs that smelled of beeswax. On the walls were several Flemish masterpieces that had been collected by a distant ancestor; the floor was covered by a magnificent oriental carpet.

It was the logs laid in the fireplace and fresh flowers arranged on the marble mantle, however, that made his lips twitch with amusement.

Clearly Goodson had not lied. The room looked as if he had never left.

Shifting his attention, he regarded the short, rotund form of his brother's valet who was standing near the arched windows that offered a stunning view of the nearby lake. The servant was neatly attired in a black and gold uniform, his pudgy face settled in lines of stoic patience.

"James, thank you for coming."

"My lord. It is good to have you home." The valet, who had been with Stefan for over ten years, offered a deep brow. Straightening, he dared to allow a hint of disapproval to touch his pale eyes. "His Grace pines for your company when you are gone."

"Well, I am here now."

"So, you are, sir." James covertly glanced over Edmond's elegant attire. "I would be happy to lend you assistance in your chambers whenever my duties with your brother…"

"No, my manservant should be arriving with my luggage before nightfall," he interrupted. "What I need from you is information."

James frowned in confusion. "Information?"

"I want to know every incident, no matter how trivial, that has put my brother in danger over the past year."

"Oh…thank God." Without warning, the servant was moving forward and falling to his knees directly before the startled Edmond. "I have tried to convince his Grace that he is in danger, but he refuses to believe that anyone would want to harm him."

"I assumed as much, which is why I have returned. Unlike Stefan, I am not naive enough to brush aside such obvious attempts at murder. And I can assure you that I will not rest until I discover who is behind these attacks."

CHAPTER TWO

THE TERRACE HOUSE ON CURZON Street was a narrow affair with a wrought-iron railing and unremarkable facade. The interior had once been fashionable, with a cheerful front parlor and long, formal dining room. These days, however, it could claim nothing more than a vulgar collection of Egyptian-inspired furnishings complete with a sarcophagus and mummy that had caused more than one visitor to faint in horror.

Precisely the sort of overblown opulence that marked the owner as one of those encroaching mushrooms with more money than good breeding.

The house did, however, possess a tidy garden in the back that had the added advantage of a small grotto where it was possible to hide from prying eyes.

Standing near the narrow window of the grotto that overlooked the back gate, a young woman pressed a hand to her stomach, which was tied in painful knots.

Standing in the shadows, with her vibrant curls yanked into a stern knot at the nape of her neck and her small, delicate body encased in a heavy black gown more suitable for the depths of winter than the pleasant October day, she should have looked a dowd. That had certainly been her intention when she had left her chambers that morning.

Unfortunately, nothing could manage to dim the finely molded features that were dominated by a pair of slanted, thickly lashed green eyes and a wide, lush mouth. And certainly nothing could dim the vibrant beauty of her auburn hair that held hints of red, gold and a shimmering bronze.

Her nose was dainty and her eyebrows an elegant sweep of color that emphasized the ivory perfection of her skin. Even her cheekbones were carved with exquisite care.

To men, she appeared to capture the very essence and allure of the first Eve, a woman who could tempt a man to barter his very soul to own her.

But in this moment, she would give her sizable dowry to be invisible to men.

At least to one man in particular.

The familiar squeak of the back gate brought a swift end to her dark thoughts, and leaning forward, she gave a low whistle to capture the maid's notice.

"Janet," she called softly. The plump female, attired in a gray servant's gown and white cap covering her dark curls, cast a glance about the seemingly empty garden. "I am in the grotto."

With hurried steps, the maid entered the grotto and pressed a hand to her ample bosom.

"Lord, Miss, ye bout scared the wits outta me."

"Mr. Wade has returned from his club early, I could not risk having him overhear us," Brianna Quinn whispered.

Janet grimaced, her pretty features hardening with distaste. It was an expression most women displayed when speaking of Mr. Thomas Wade.

"Aye, he is always sneaking about, watching you like a hungry cat watching a mouse."

A shiver inched down Brianna's spine before she was sternly lifting her chin and sucking in a deep breath. No, she could not give in to her looming panic. The only means of saving herself was to keep her wits clear and focused on escape.

"He will discover that I am no mouse," she said, fiercely. "I do not care what it takes, I will be rid of my vile stepfather before the week is out."

"As to that—" Janet ducked her head in apology as she

reached her hand into the pocket of her apron and removed the vellum envelope that Brianna had given her earlier that morning.

Brianna frowned in disbelief. She had devoted the past week to sending letter after letter to Stefan's town house. She had been certain when she learned the reclusive Duke was in town that he would be her savior.

But, as day after day passed with no word from her childhood friend, she had at last sent her maid to confront him directly. It had to be that her letters had gone astray or Stefan had not yet had the opportunity to read them. She could not believe he would be deliberately avoiding her pleas for assistance.

"You were unable to speak with the Duke?" she demanded.

Janet made a rude noise. "Not only wasn't I allowed to speak with the Duke, but I couldn't so much as leave yer note for him."

"Why ever not?"

"There was a great, hulking servant what answered the door. Eyed me like a piece of rubbish that had been dropped on his stoop and told me to be on me way without so much as a good day." Janet gave a disgusted shake of her head. Despite the fact she was the same age as Brianna, two and twenty, she possessed a will of iron and was rarely routed by even the most fearsome opponent. Brianna had seen her beat a drunken sailor to near death with her umbrella for no more an insult than a pinch on her backside. "Sodding man wouldn't even accept the letter ye had written for His Grace. Said as his master was in town for business reasons and wasn't accepting visitors. Then he shut the door right in me face. Bastard."

Brianna was frankly bewildered. She knew all of the Huntley staff, since most of them had been with the ducal family since well before Brianna's father had died. Certainly she could not recall such an intimidating man.

"Describe this servant."

Janet gave a lift of her shoulder. "As I said, he was big and burly with a hard face and thick golden hair. I suppose he be handsome enough if ye like 'em big as an ox." Her brow furrowed in thought. "Oh, and he had a funny accent. He was no Englishman, that much I can tell ye."

"How peculiar." With short, determined steps, Brianna paced the confined space of the grotto, her nerves stretched to the point of screaming. "That does not sound at all like Goodson."

"Who?"

"The Duke's long-time butler," Brianna said absently. "In fact, to my knowledge the Dukes have never employed foreigners. Their staff has been with them for years."

"Looks more like a criminal than a servant, if ye ask me."

"I do not understand, Janet." The swish of her black crape dress over the sarsnet slip echoed through the musty air as Brianna continued her pacing, her fingers absently toying with the fichu she had tucked into the modest line of her bodice. "Stefan would never turn away a request from me, not unless he has changed dramatically in the past few years. My father named him as one of my guardians, for God's sake."

"What will ye do? If ye can't speak with the Duke…"

Brianna came to a sharp halt, her hands clenched into fists. "Oh, I will speak with him. Even if I have to storm the gates of his town house myself."

"Ye can't do that, Miss. Not without causing a fearful scandal."

"You think I would not rather endure scandal than be hauled off to a secluded hunting lodge with my stepfather?" Brianna hissed, her entire body revolting at the mere thought of what would happen once Thomas had her isolated and helpless at the lodge.

"Still…ach." Janet caught her breath. "I jest remembered something."

"What?"

"While I was attempting to get into the house, a boy arrived with a package for his Grace."

"And?"

"The package was a domino and mask that the master had ordered to be made."

Understanding slowly bloomed in Brianna's mind, her fading hope returning in a fierce wave.

"So he plans to attend a masquerade."

"And soon. The servant snapped at the boy for his tardiness, saying that it had best meet with the master's approval as it was too late to have it altered."

"Then it must be tonight." Picking up her heavy skirts, Brianna headed for the door of the grotto. "I need to speak with Mrs. Grant. She always knows what social events are occurring about town."

IT WAS NEAR ELEVEN O'CLOCK that evening before the house was at last quiet enough for Brianna to slip from the back door and make her way through the dark streets until she stood in front of the pretentious town house where the Courtesan Masquerade Ball was to be held.

It didn't look the sort of place where gentlemen of the highest society mixed with courtesans, harlots and ladies of easy virtue. Not with its handsome brickwork and Iconic columns that framed the main entrance with a muted elegance.

Mrs. Grant, however, had been quite firm in announcing that the only masquerade ball on this night was Lord Blackwell's annual event.

Brianna gave a small shake of her head as she noted the long line of carriages stretching down the block and masked gentlemen walking through the front door. Obviously, any disapproval of tonight's festivities was exclusively held by female members of society.

"I do not like this, miss," Janet hissed at her side. "I think I should stay with ye in case there's trouble."

Brianna tugged the domino closer about her body as she battled off the urge to shiver. When she had found the black velvet cloak lined with silver and the matching black feathered mask in her mother's old truck in the attic, she had felt as if fate was urging her to take the daring risk. There was even a matching ball gown in a pale pink satin with black and silver ribbons dotted along the hem and threaded through the scooped bodice. It was precisely the sort of frivolous concoction that would be expected at a masquerade.

Now, however, her palms were sweating and her knees shaking as she contemplated the thought of entering the strange town house filled with randy gentlemen and willing whores. What if she were recognized? Or worse, what if she was accosted before she could locate Stefan, even assuming he was in there?

It took more courage than she knew she possessed to reach out and squeeze Janet's cold hand.

"Nonsense, I need you at home to make sure that Thomas does not realize I am not in my chambers."

"This is no place for a lady. Only harlots would be seen at such a ball."

"But, I will not be seen," Brianna said, her voice considerably more steady than her nerves. "Besides, I have heard any number of rumors that there are ladies of fashion who attend such events. Incognito, of course."

Janet sucked in a sharp breath. Servants tended to have a rigid view of how a noble should behave. Far more rigid than the nobles themselves.

"Not *proper* young ladies."

"I can no longer afford to be proper, Janet." Her voice was bitter. "If I am unable to convince Stefan to take me in as his ward, then I shall be forced to flee and make my own way in the world. In that event, I doubt that a risqué ball will be my greatest concern."

Janet chewed her bottom lip, knowing she could not argue the stark truth of Brianna's words. They had three short days before she was to be hauled off to the wilds of Norfolk. Once there, no one would be able to halt her stepfather from forcing her to his bed.

"Jest promise ye'll take care," Janet demanded with a resigned sigh. "The gents are bound to be drunk and in the mood for trouble."

"I will take the greatest care, I assure you." Brianna squeezed her maid's fingers in warning. "But, Janet, I am depending on you. No one can know that I am not in my bed sleeping."

Janet squared her plump shoulders. "Not a soul will get past yer bedroom door, that I promise ye."

"I will return as soon as I have spoken with Stefan," she promised.

"Good luck to ye, miss."

Loosening her clinging grip on her maid, Brianna squared her shoulders and turned her attention to the waiting town house.

"Let us hope I do not need it."

Brianna waited until her maid had slipped away before forcing herself to cross the crowded street.

Feeling as exposed as if she were stark naked, she neared the throng of gentlemen and began to press her way up the sweep of steps. Her logic told her that no one could possibly recognize her in the concealing domino and feathered mask, especially since she had never been able to move among the more fashionable society, but in her mind, she felt as if every eye was staring at her.

And in truth, they were.

Even though she had tightly braided her conspicuous hair and knotted it at the nape of her neck, the color still managed to shimmer with vibrant beauty in the torchlight. And no mask could entirely disguise the exotic slant of her green eyes and the full curve of her inviting mouth.

Keeping her head lowered as she moved forward, she actually made it through the door before a hand clamped on her arm and forced her to a halt.

"And where the devil do you think you're going?" a male voice rasped.

Glancing up, she met the annoyed glare from a uniformed footman. Her mouth went dry and her heart lodged in her throat.

"I…I am going to the ball."

The servant curled his lips in distaste. "Oh, aye, and you

think you can prance in as if you're royalty? Maybe you think to be announced by the butler?"

"I…"

The footman did not bother to listen to her embarrassed apology, instead simply pushing her back down the stairs to make room for the crowd of gentlemen.

"Round to the back with you, wench. Only the gents come through the front door."

Brianna briefly stumbled before regaining her balance and hurrying to the back entrance. Ignoring the dampness that soaked into her embroidered slippers, she found the narrow entrance where she was shown up the servants' staircase by a dour-faced housekeeper into the long parlors that were richly decorated with gilded ceilings, crimson satin wall paneling and gold-veined marble fireplaces. The floor was a polished parquet that glowed with a rich luster beneath the flickering light of the crystal chandeliers. Along one wall, long tables had been arranged to display the lavish buffet and numerous bottles of chilled champagne.

She had reached her objective, but she discovered that finding Stefan was not to be so simple as she had assumed.

There had to be a hundred guests crammed into the gilt and crimson rooms, all of them disguised in cloaks and masks as they threaded their way through the glittering crowd or lounged on the small couches and chairs that were set in shallow alcoves. Somewhere among the melee a string quartet played, but it was nearly impossible to hear what Brianna assumed was Mozart over the laughter and shouts and shrill giggles.

Under normal circumstances, she might have been shocked by the sight of the women who had tossed open their cloaks to reveal they were wearing nothing more than lacy corsets beneath, and the men who openly reached to grope the wares offered. It was hardly what an innocent maiden was accustomed to seeing.

She was far too concerned with locating the Duke of Huntley

to be as shocked as she should be. Or to even question why such a sweet, kind-hearted man such as Stefan would choose to attend such a vulgar event.

Sheer determination allowed her to make her way to the center of the room before she was halted by a large woman with all the full curves that Brianna lacked.

"Hey there, no shoving, there be plenty of gents to go around," she said, her pox-scarred face heavily rouged.

"I am looking for the Duke of Huntley," Brianna said bluntly.

The woman gave a lift of her darkened brows. "Oh, aye, I bet yer are. Think yer fancy speech will impress such a fine toff?"

"Do you know where I can find him?"

The woman gave a lift of her shoulder. "I heard tell he was in the card rooms. Seems he prefers gambling to the ladies."

"Thank God," Brianna breathed.

"What did ye say?" the woman demanded, suspicious.

"I asked where the card rooms are to found."

There was a pause before the woman jerked her head back toward the hall.

"Down the hall. Last door on the left."

"Thank you."

Brianna turned and began the battle back to the door, a choked scream leaving her lips as a large masculine arm wrapped around her waist from behind.

"Here now, where are you going in such a hurry?" a thick, drunken voice demanded next to her ear.

Brianna struggled against the repulsive grasp. "I be meeting another, let go," she said, mimicking the other doxies in the room.

"You can meet him later. I have a desire for a saucy minx, and something tells me you could be very saucy."

A flare of terrified fury raced through Brianna and with as much force as she could muster, she lifted her foot to kick the man directly on his shin.

"I said I have a meeting," she gritted, managing to wriggle loose as he gave a groan of pain and loosened his grip.

"Why, you bitch…"

An opening appeared and Brianna darted toward the doorway, the crowd filling in behind her to prevent her assailant from following.

Giving a silent prayer at her escape, Brianna did not allow her pace to slow as she entered the carpeted hallway and hurried toward the card room.

CHAPTER THREE

STANDING IN THE SMOKY CARD room, Edmond struggled to contain his impatience.

Predictably, it had not been an easy task to convince his stubborn brother that he truly was in danger. For all Stefan's intelligence, he was remarkably reluctant to accept that anyone could possibly seek his demise, especially not his own cousin.

Then, of course, there had been the battle over Edmond assuming Stefan's identity so he could lure the danger to London and away from Meadowland, hopefully flushing the villain into the open. It did not matter how many times Edmond explained that he was far more skilled to discover the truth behind the attacks and that he alone could turn the hunter into the hunted.

Finally, Edmond had been forced to point out that Stefan's stubbornness might very well be endangering the staff and tenants of Meadowland, explaining that a man willing to murder a duke would not hesitate to kill a mere commoner standing in his way. It was only then that Stefan had given in to the inevitable.

Still, it was a full fortnight before Edmond was at last able to leave Meadowland in the disguise of his brother and arrive at Stefan's town house in London. And another week before he could replace Stefan's loyal staff with his own servants. If he were to be bait for a determined killer, he intended to surround himself with those trained to protect him.

It had not taken much effort to track Howard Summerville.

All he needed was to discover the most lewd, offensive event on the calendar, Lord Blackwell's Courtesan Ball.

He had not been disappointed. Within moments he had located Howard in the back card rooms. Now all he needed was his cousin to notice his looming form standing directly in his path.

Over the past twenty minutes, he had walked past the stupid man's seat at the table on a dozen occasions, expecting to be recognized. After all, there were few in society that could claim the height of Edmond and his brother, and none other who wore the crest of Huntley stamped on a gold signet ring.

Everyone else in the smoke-choked room had instantly bowed in his direction, covertly giving way as was only fitting for a duke when he approached them.

Just when Edmond was convinced he would have to give in to his impulse and drag the man away from the table by the scruff of his neck, Howard tossed in his cards, signed his large stack of vowels and unsteadily rose to his feet.

It would be far preferable for the meeting to appear as nothing more than a chance encounter. The last thing Edmond desired was to tip his hand to his cousin. Howard Summerville was debauched, depraved and detestable, but he wasn't a half-wit. He was going to be curious enough that the reclusive Duke of Huntley was seemingly tossing himself into the wicked pleasures of London without adding fuel to the fire.

Weaving his way toward the door, the slender, dark-haired man with a swarthy complexion, small black eyes and pinched countenance nearly rammed into Edmond before he came to a belated halt.

Squinting upward, the red-rimmed eyes took a long moment to focus. At last they widened as Howard sucked in a shocked breath.

"Good Lord, is that you Huntley?"

Edmond gave a stiff nod of his head, as if the meeting were an unpleasant surprise. It was how Stefan would react.

"Howard."

"Whatever are you doing here?" the older gentleman demanded, shoving a hand through his tangled black hair. He looked ghastly. Having dispensed with his mask and domino, his unhealthy pallor was starkly visible, emphasizing the sunken hollows beneath his eyes. Even his expensively tailored evening suit was as creased as if he had been wearing it for days. "Hardly the place for a grand peer of the realm."

Edmond bit back his acerbic words. For the moment, he was supposed to be the Duke of Huntley, and Stefan would never allow his ducal composure to slip, even if it did become a bit frosty when he was displeased.

"I would say that there are several peers of the realm in attendance," he said, deliberately glancing toward the two Earls and a Baron currently seated at the tables.

"Oh, yes, well, I suppose there are," Howard muttered, sullenly. "Still, I have never known you to partake of the more delicious enticements that London has to offer. Come to think of it, I have never known you to partake of any enticements."

"Which is precisely why I am here."

"What does that mean?"

"Edmond returned to Meadowland for a short visit and demanded that I travel to London and take in the pleasures while he attended to the estate duties. He was quite insistent that I was becoming too dull to bear, and when Edmond has set his mind on a course, there is no budging him."

"I can bloody well imagine. That brother of yours is a menace. Damnation, last time we crossed paths, he attacked me. Russia is the proper place for that one—his heart is as cold as Siberia. Of course, now that I think on the matter, your brother was quite right to send you to the city, Huntley. I have always said that you work far too hard. A bit of enjoyment is what you need. I've told Mrs. Summerville that on a dozen occasions."

"Have you?"

"Yes, indeed." Howard stretched his lips in a ghastly smile.

"And now that you are here, I realize that it is quite a stroke of fortune. Almost uncanny."

Edmond folded his arms over his chest, already knowing what was coming next.

"And what is this stroke of fortune?"

"Well, I did attempt to call upon you at Meadowland. On several occasions, as a matter of fact, although that bastard of a butler would not so much as allow me to step across the threshold."

"Indeed."

"Yes." He gave an awkward pause at Edmond's distinctly unenthusiastic tone. "I…it seems that I have had a bit of trouble with those nasty creditors of late."

"Has there ever been a time when you did not have trouble with creditors?"

"Trifling matters." Howard tugged at his drooping cravat. "On this occasion, however, I fear that I am quite undone. Indeed, I have been contemplating a flight to the Continent if my situation does not improve."

Edmond's expression remained coolly indifferent even as his muscles coiled with tension. That Howard was in dun territory was as predictable as the sun rising. Clearly this time, however, he was desperate.

"And yet, here you are squandering your non-existent funds on cards and whores," Edmond accused, knowing it was what his brother would say.

"I had hoped to recoup some of my losses at the table."

"Ah, of course. That is always a sound notion."

Ignoring the mocking words, Howard plunged onward. "If you could just see your way to lending me a bit of assistance…"

"Let me make certain that I am not misunderstanding you, cousin. Are you asking for money?"

"Just enough to cover my most pressing expenses."

"Tell me, Howard, just how deep are your debts?"

Hope flared through the dark eyes before it was abruptly

replaced by a wary suspicion. Not even the kindhearted Stefan was willing to fund this worthless gentleman, knowing he would simply toss the money away in the nearest gambling den.

"Why do you wish to know?"

Realizing that he had very nearly overplayed his hand, Edmond cast a bored glance around the room.

"It is nothing more than idle curiosity."

Howard heaved a disgusted sigh, his suspicions easily dismissed. "I should have known it would be a waste of effort to request your assistance. Your family has always taken pleasure in the misery of my own."

"And you have always held us to blame for your own failures," Edmond said, his voice edged with ice.

"It wasn't failures. I have simply had a string of bad luck. Could happen to anyone…" Howard's whining came to a startled halt as his gaze shifted to someone approaching from behind Edmond. "Hello, what have we here?"

Aggravated by the interruption, Edmond did not bother to turn, hoping whoever dared to intrude on his private conversation would realize that their presence was unwelcome.

"Your Grace, I must speak with you," a low, startlingly cultured female voice demanded as Edmond felt a small tug on his sleeve.

Edmond glared down at the woman in a domino and feathered mask, his expression one of furious disdain.

"Be on your way, I have no interest."

The stubborn wench refused to be intimidated, and against his will Edmond realized that she was a stunning beauty. Even with her disguise, he could determine the finely drawn features and magnificent green eyes. And that hair…that glorious autumn-hued hair, it could not possibly be real.

"But it is most vital that you give me a few minutes of your time," she continued.

Edmond grimly ignored his body's instinctive response to the enticing scent of lavender and sweet woman.

"I said be on your way," he snapped. "There are many here who will give you the company you seek."

"I, for one," Howard intruded, his sallow face pinched with his insatiable hunger. "Unlike my prudish cousin, I possess a fine appreciation for such a beautiful woman."

Ignoring the ready offer of companionship, the woman shifted until she was standing directly before Edmond, her ivory skin pale in the flickering candlelight.

"Please, Stefan, this cannot wait. I…" The slanted green eyes that seemed oddly familiar abruptly widened. "Good God, you're not Ste—"

"*Mon dieu.*" Sweeping his arms around the dangerous woman he hauled her off her feet and covered her mouth in a punishing kiss.

THE KISS WAS INTENDED AS nothing more than a means of keeping the woman silent. Somehow, she knew that he was not Stefan, and until he managed to figure out who the hell she was, he had to keep her mouth otherwise occupied.

Necessity, however, was most certainly a pleasure as he sampled her lush, sensual lips, her breath tasting of mint and pure magic. Tightening his arms around her, Edmond swept her completely off her feet and cradled her tiny, squirming body tight against his chest.

"Here now, Huntley, you said you weren't interested," his cousin protested. "Where are you going?"

Edmond ignored him, just as he ignored the whistles of drunken enjoyment as he turned and headed for the nearby door. He continued the deep, relentless kiss as the crowd readily parted and he made his way down the hall and up the staircase to the bedrooms above.

Entering the first open door, Edmond kicked it shut with his foot and slowly lowered the woman to her feet, his lips never leaving her mouth as he savored the sweetness that had him hard and aching, despite his annoyance with her untimely interruption.

It would damn well be worth having to track down Howard later if he could spread this wench's legs and bury his throbbing erection into her heat. He sensed she could offer him the sort of intense satisfaction any gentleman would sell his soul to achieve.

Reluctantly lifting his head, Edmond wrenched off his ridiculous mask and glanced round the room, swiftly determining that it was one of the numerous bedchambers. The walls were paneled in pale rosewood with a molded marble chimneypiece near the door to the inner dressing room. It was no doubt attractively decorated, but he had no interest in anything beyond the curtained four-posted bed that was visible in the flickering firelight. Ah yes. That would do perfectly.

About to lead his companion toward the far side of the room, the woman halted his fine intentions as she began to struggle in earnest against his hold.

"Stop this," she hissed, lifting her hands to pummel them against his chest. "Damn you, Edmond, let me go."

Edmond stiffened as her commanding words echoed through the room. *Mon dieu.* He knew that voice.

With a sharp motion he ripped off her feathered mask, his eyes narrowing as her mass of vibrant curls tumbled down in a shimmering river of fire.

Brianna Quinn!

He should have recognized her the moment she approached him. They had been neighbors for years, at least until her mother had remarried and they had moved to London. And while it had been ten years since he had last laid eyes upon her, there could never be another with those cat-like green eyes and astonishing curls.

Of course, his memory of her included a small, too thin body and the unformed features of a child. She was usually covered in grime, her gown ripped in a dozen places from having climbed the orchard trees or devoted the morning to fishing with Stefan.

Now she was very much a woman, with skin as smooth as cream and lush lips that begged for a man's kiss.

An exquisite bit of temptation who was leaving him hard and aching with a frustration that did nothing to improve his temper.

"Brianna Quinn," he growled, a grim note underlying his voice. "I should have known. You are always showing up where you are least wanted."

A blush stained her cheeks as she no doubt recalled the number of times she managed to interrupt his various seductions, when she was forever climbing into the hayloft or poking about the Conservatory.

"Perhaps unwanted by you, Edmond, since you were always up to some wicked pastime, but never by Stefan," she retorted, clearly having changed in more ways than just physical. As a young girl, she had been terrified of him, always darting away when he glanced in her direction and stammering when she attempted to speak. He had called her *ma souris:* my mouse. Now she met his gaze squarely, her chin high and her expression stubborn. "Where is he?"

Edmond folded his arms across his chest, not even considering the possibility of a lie. Brianna had been one of the few people who had always managed to determine which twin was which.

"Comfortably tucked into his bed, I should imagine," he drawled. "You know how devoted he is to country hours."

She froze at his words, her ivory skin paling to a sickly white.

"He is still at Meadowland?"

"Yes."

"But…" She scowled in genuine anger. Obviously she was not at all pleased to discover Stefan was not in London. "You are pretending to be the Duke. Why?"

He narrowed his gaze. This woman had already managed to wreck his evening of interrogating his dastardly cousin. On top of that, she had very nearly destroyed his charade—and had stirred the coals of his desire to a fever pitch. It was time that she explained her damnable presence at such a nefarious event.

"Actually, I think the better question is what the devil a sup-posedly respectable young lady is doing attending a Courte-san's Ball," he corrected.

She did not cringe or cower as he had expected. Instead, she planted her hands on her hips and glared at him with flashing green eyes.

"I have no intention of answering any questions until I know why you are pretending to be the Duke of Huntley."

"You are mistaken, *ma souris*." Using his considerable height and weight to his advantage, Edmond backed the tiny woman against the wall, his expression hard with warning. "You will answer my each and every question, and you will do so this moment."

The pulse at the base of her throat fluttered with obvious fear, but she grimly refused to give in to the inevitable.

"You cannot make me," she hissed.

In spite of himself, Edmond could not deny a tiny surge of respect for her refusal to be intimidated. He had made grown men crumble with one withering glare, and yet she stood her ground.

Brianna Quinn might still be intruding into places that she did not belong, but his usual desire to throttle her had become a very different desire.

One that included having her spread naked on that nearby bed as he tasted every inch of her ivory skin.

"Surely you have not forgotten how dangerous it is to chal-lenge me?" he husked, shifting to press the hard muscles of his thighs against her. He choked back a groan at the feel of her delicate, perfectly curved body beneath the heavy cloak. "I can never resist a dare."

She shuddered, her eyes darkening with awareness. "Let me go, Edmond."

A taunting smile touched his lips as he deliberately rubbed his aching erection against the soft swell of her stomach. The realization that she was not indifferent to his touch only inten-sified his surging need to be inside her.

"Tell me what you are doing here, or I will open this door and announce to the entire ball you are in attendance."

Expecting her to falter beneath the threat, Edmond was unprepared when she lifted her hands to give him a sharp shove. He felt it no more than he would the brush of a butterfly, but it was enough to distract him so that she could slide away and walk toward the door.

"Fine, prance me in front of the entire crowd if you desire, I have nothing left to lose," she said, tossing off the cape to reveal the pink ball gown that was cut to expose the soft curve of her breasts. Seeming indifferent to Edmond's heated gaze locked on her plunging neckline, she yanked open the door and turned to glare at his distracted expression. "But be assured that, as soon as I am revealed, I will scream loud and clear that you are no more than an impostor."

It was a bluff. It had to be, Edmond told himself as he stormed to her side and waved his hand toward the door. No woman was foolish enough to willingly toss away her future with such disregard.

"Let us test that theory, shall we?" he said smoothly.

Her chin tilted as she stepped into the hall. "Let's do."

Hearing approaching footsteps, Edmond had no choice but to grab her arm and yank her back into the room. He slammed shut the door and turned the lock, before turning to her with impatient fury.

"Have you taken complete leave of your senses? You will be ruined," he hissed furiously.

Brianna wrapped her arms around her waist, her face pale. "Unless I can convince Stefan to help me, I am already ruined."

"What the devil are you talking about?"

"First, I demand that you tell me why you are pretending to be the Duke of Huntley."

He muttered a foul curse. "Brianna, do not try my patience any further. Confess why you seek Stefan."

"Or what?" she demanded. "You will hit me?"

Edmond slowly narrowed his gaze. He was a gentleman who had developed the sort of skills to obtain the information he desired, whether it was from a cutthroat, a corrupt politician or the beautiful wife of a foreign ambassador.

If one method did not work, he was quite adept at changing his tactics.

The fingers gripping her arm eased to run an intimate path upward, lingering on the pulse that raced at the base of her throat. Heat exploded through his body at the feel of her smooth, silky skin. It was just as it promised: heated ivory.

"And mar that beautiful skin?" he demanded, giving in to the impulse that had been raging through him since he had first kissed those lips. With one graceful motion, he had her off her feet and was crossing to the bed. Ignoring her struggles, he tossed her onto the feather mattress and swiftly followed her down to cover her slight frame with his much larger one. "I have a far better means of acquiring what I desire."

Her eyes were wide, shimmering like the finest emeralds in the firelight, her hair spread over the pillow in a breathtaking cloud of autumn flame.

"Edmond, what are you doing?"

He gave a bemused shake of his head. "When did you become such a beauty, *ma souris?*"

Scowling in fury, Brianna futilely struggled to wiggle from beneath his large body.

"Damnation, this is not funny."

Edmond sucked in a sharp breath at the feel of her squirming against his taut muscles. *Mon dieu,* the minx was driving him mad. How was he supposed to recall that she was currently the enemy when his body was on fire?

Unable to resist temptation, Edmond lowered his head and buried his face in the curve of her neck. He breathed deeply of her lavender scent, shuddering as the tantalizing aroma filled his senses.

This was how a woman was supposed to smell, he realized

in startled pleasure. Sweet and feminine, rather than drenched in the cloying perfumes so many ladies preferred.

"Tell me why you are here, Brianna," he whispered as his lips brushed the hollow beneath her ear.

She gave a soft shriek as her body jerked in reaction to the gentle caress.

"Edmond, halt this at once," she whispered, her hands clenched in the folds of his cloak.

Closing his eyes to better savor her exquisite taste, Edmond trailed his lips down the line of her jaw.

"Tell me."

"No."

He nipped her chin, his hands traveling along the narrow line of her waist and then slowly back up, inching ever nearer the delectable curve of her breasts.

"Brianna, I will not halt until I have the truth."

The green eyes flashed with fury and a darkening awareness she could not entirely hide.

"I came here to speak with Stefan."

He stole a brief, possessive kiss, before reluctantly pulling back to regard her with a narrowed gaze.

"Concerning what?"

"Stefan is my guardian. I need him to assert his rights and take me from the home of Mr. Wade."

"Your stepfather?" Edmond had never met the man who had married Brianna's mother, Sylvia. He knew little more than that the man was the son of a common butcher who had managed to make a fortune in the West Indies, a social-climbing mushroom who was well beneath the notice of most of the ton. Sylvia had been desperate, he'd supposed, to find the means of paying her gambling debts, and would no doubt have married Beelzebub himself if he'd offered. "Why?"

"That is something I would prefer to discuss with Stefan."

"I did not ask what you prefer, *ma souris,*" he growled. "Answer the question."

"Thomas intends to take me to Norfolk on Friday."

Edmond made a sound of disgust. How typically foolish. Was there ever a woman born who did not allow herself to be ruled by flights of fancy rather than common sense?

"And you risked utter ruin because you have no wish to leave London society?" He gave a shake of his head.

Without warning her hands lifted to smack against his chest, her face flushed with fury.

"I do not give a bloody hell about London society, you wretched man," she gritted. "Indeed, if I never had to spend another night in this horrid city I would be delighted."

"Then why the devil are you so desperate to avoid Norfolk?"

She squeezed her eyes shut, almost as if in pain. "Please, do not do this, Edmond," she whispered.

Edmond stilled, realizing that there was far more to this than a mere feminine whim.

"Brianna?"

A shudder wracked her body, before her thick lashes at last lifted to reveal haunted green eyes.

"My stepfather intends to take me to his hunting lodge so he…he can…have his way with me."

"Have his way with you?"

"He intends to rape me," she hissed. "There, are you satisfied?"

"Christ, Brianna," he rasped, shocked to the very depths of his being. "What the hell makes you think such a thing?"

"Because he attempted to force his way into my bed three months ago." Her voice was wooden, but Edmond was not fooled by the lack of emotion. She was so on edge, he knew she was a breath away from shattering.

"I warned him that I would contact Stefan and reveal the treachery if he so much as touched me. I thought the threat would be enough, but two weeks ago he informed me that he had purchased a new hunting lodge in Norfolk and that he intended to take me there. He also made it clear that any servants he hired would be completely loyal to him. So loyal that they would turn a blind eye if Thomas chose to keep me locked in my chambers."

With a hiss, Edmond surged off the bed, a fury trembling through his body. The rotten, sick bastard.

"Why haven't you contacted Stefan before now?" he snapped.

Keeping her wary gaze on him, Brianna slipped off the bed and wrapped her arms around her waist; the bodice of her gown disarranged to reveal a far too tempting glimpse of her creamy breasts.

"I sent a letter the moment that I learned of Thomas's plan to leave London, but Stefan did not respond. After I learned that he had arrived in the city, I had hoped that he had come to assist me." Her tone was accusing. She clearly held him to blame for Stefan's absence. "Of course he never came to call, so I sent near a dozen messages to the town house. I even had my maid deliver a letter—only to be turned away by a huge brute of a man who would not so much as allow her across the threshold."

"I did not hire Boris for his talents in proper London etiquette," he said dryly.

Her eyes flashed, her beautiful hair tumbled about her shoulders. "Well, because of Boris, I was forced to attend this hideous ball in the hopes of speaking with Stefan. And now you have ruined even that."

Edmond was not a gentleman who was chastised by others. Not even Alexander Pavlovich would dare offer more than a mild reproof. And yet, this tiny scrap of a woman stood there and boldly dressed him down, as if he were no more than a disobedient child.

Astonishingly, however, it was not resentment, but fascination that flowed through him.

Brianna Quinn had the sort of spirit that was all too rare among well-bred females. For God's sake, any other woman would have been mindless with fear, or at the very least hysterical, after being threatened with rape by her stepfather. Brianna instead had boldly set upon a course to save herself, even daring to attend the most notorious ball in all of London.

"I will contact Stefan to ensure he knows of your troubles," he promised, not bothering to inform her that he intended to deal with Thomas Wade in his own straightforward, if covert, fashion. "Until then you will stay with a friend. You must know someone in London."

Her lips thinned at his sharp command. "I know several people in London, but none are in a position to prevent Thomas from taking me away. Only Stefan…"

Edmond frowned as her words came to an abrupt halt, her eyes narrowing as if she had been struck with a brilliant notion.

"Only Stefan, what?" he demanded, impatient to return to the ball and Howard Summerville now that he had solved the mystery of Brianna Quinn.

"Only Stefan can protect me." Her chin tilted as a thin, determined smile curved those tempting lips. "And that is precisely what he is going to do."

"I am certain he will, once he discovers your…"

"No, I cannot wait for Stefan to rush to the rescue. *You* are already here, after all, pretending to be Stefan. There is no reason I cannot move into the town house. Tonight."

CHAPTER FOUR

EDMOND'S FEATURES TIGHTENED, his admiration for Brianna's courage being replaced by a dark, seething anger.

Did the woman think he was sweet, tender-hearted Stefan who could be manipulated by every pathetic waif who crossed his path?

Or did she believe his unmistakable lust for her delectable body gave her power over him?

"I can only presume that is some sort of jest." His voice was low and cutting as he stepped to loom over her in a threatening manner.

Her breath rasped loudly in the still air, but she refused to back away.

"Not in the least. All of London believes that the Duke of Huntley is currently residing in his town house. Why would he not invite his ward to come and stay with him?"

"Not even a ward can stay alone in the home of a bachelor. You would be ruined."

"Not if you hire a companion," she retorted stubbornly.

He gave a sharp bark of laughter. "So now I am not only to have my privacy invaded by a pesky, unwanted ward, but also a middle-aged dragon?" he taunted. "You truly have lost your wits if you think I would consider such a ridiculous notion for even a moment."

She hissed in frustration. "You would rather allow me to be hauled off by my stepfather and raped?"

Edmond ignored the tide of black contempt. Thomas Wade

would soon be no more than a forgotten corpse. For now, Edmond was much more concerned with this aggravating minx standing before him.

"I assure you that the matter will be dealt with."

"Forgive me if I do not entirely trust such an ambiguous promise," she retorted, her expression bitter.

"It will have to do."

She remained silent for a brief moment, as if waging some inward struggle. Then, drawing in a deep breath, she met his glittering gaze squarely.

"No, it will not have to do." Her voice wavered before she gathered her nerve and continued. "You seem to forget that I have a means of compelling you to take me into the town house."

Edmond stilled, his predatory nature coiled and prepared to strike as he sensed danger. Reaching out, he grasped her shoulders, hauling her close enough that he was wrapped in warm lavender.

"Take care, Brianna, I do not respond well to blackmail."

She swallowed heavily, but she was wise enough not to struggle against his biting grip.

"You have left me no choice," she gritted. "Either you agree to take me in as your ward, or I will return to the ballroom and inform one and all that you are not Stefan."

Edmond had been a powerful force in politics for the past eight years. He had intimidated, seduced, and at times deceived others into obeying his will.

Now this little wisp of a girl thought to bully him?

His fingers tightened. "You are a fool to threaten me, *ma souris*."

"Not a fool, only desperate. I will not remain another night under the roof of my stepfather."

With a jerk, he had her pressed against the door, his body leaning heavily into her slender form with an unmistakable warning.

"You believe you are any safer under my roof?" His voice

deepened as that growingly familiar heat flowed through his blood. Brianna Quinn might be a stubborn, unruly wench, but she stirred his passions to a fever pitch. To have her sleeping just a few doors away would bring a certain end to her innocence. "I am not the oh-so-honorable Stefan. I do not rescue damsels in distress without expecting some sort of reward."

She trembled, but not with fear. She might be a virgin, but she was vibrantly aware of the sizzling heat that pulsed between them.

"You do not have to remind me that you have always been a cad and a scoundrel."

He arched a raven brow. "Well, then?"

"I do not gain control of my inheritance until my birthday in the spring, but I do have several jewels…"

His husky laugh filled the shadowed room. "I have no need for your money or jewels."

She frowned in confusion, revealing just how innocent she truly was. "Then what sort of reward do you demand?"

Edmond deliberately allowed his heated gaze to run over her ivory features before lowering to rest on the slight swell of her breasts.

"Obviously, you have nothing to barter but your feminine charms."

She attempted an expression of outrage, but Edmond did not miss the darkening of her magnificent eyes. She would never admit it, but she was not entirely averse to the thought of having those charms tasted. Perhaps even devoured.

"You are no better than Thomas," she accused in a shaky voice.

Edmond smiled with cold intent, abruptly stepping back and tugging her from the door. He had wasted enough time. He was here to discover a murderer, not to seduce his brother's ward. Stefan was far better suited to deal with such a mess.

He still intended to kill Thomas Wade. That was a given. But tonight, his priority was Howard Summerville.

"Then I suggest that you remain with your stepfather, where

you belong, or find some other accommodations," he informed her, releasing his hold so he could pull open the door.

"Damn you," she hissed.

Edmond paused to cast a mocking glance over his shoulder. "You are too late, *ma souris*. I was damned years ago."

IT WAS JUST PAST THREE in the morning when Brianna and her maid slipped through the back gate of the Huntley town house and made their way to the kitchen door.

Although only a few blocks away from her stepfather's home, the two establishments could not be compared.

The entire area had once belonged to Westminster Abbey and had been taken into possession by Henry VIII. Later it was developed by the Curzon family, who named the neighborhood Mayfair after the annual fair that had once been held in the open fields.

Unlike many of the grand homes, Huntley House had been built by James Stuart, who preferred a plain exterior of pale stone and wrought-iron fencing to the more elaborate style of Robert Adam. The elegant interior, however, was a lavish display of wealth.

As a child, Brianna could recall entering the home and marveling at the split staircase that led to a formal landing that boasted heavy marble pillars and Grecian statues. A perfect setting for the Duke and Duchess to greet their guests in a truly regal fashion.

The jewel of the house, of course, was the neo-classical drawing room with its series of tall windows that extended the length of the house and overlooked Hyde Park. It was a room that had been near overwhelming for young Brianna, who had been terrified of destroying some priceless work of art.

And now here she was, about to enter the house as a thief.

More unnerved by the realization than she cared to admit, Brianna set down the heavy bags she had carried from her home, and watched as her maid bent over the door knob to study the lock in the faint moonlight.

The two women were currently hidden in the shadowed alcove of the servants' entrance, having slipped through the mews to the back of the grand town house. Behind them, the silence of the sunken rose garden offered the sense of being isolated from the hustle and bustle of London, but Brianna was no fool. Huntley House employed over a dozen servants, any one of which could make an untimely arrival.

"Can you do it, Janet?" she whispered.

Janet straightened, her round face somber. "Aye, it be a simple enough lock."

"Then what are you waiting for?"

"Are ye certain this is a wise notion, Miss Quinn?" the maid demanded, her words abrupt. "The way ye speak of the gent makes me fear that ye are leaping from the frying pan right into the fire."

Brianna suppressed her instinctive shudder.

When Edmond had abandoned her in that bedchamber at the masked ball, she had been momentarily paralyzed with fear, knowing she had no one left to turn to.

It had seemed very much like she was doomed.

And then, gathering her shattered courage, Brianna had squared her shoulders and made perhaps the most dangerous decision of her life.

Edmond might not desire to help her, but it was no less than his duty. He was pretending to be Stefan, so he could bloody well take on Stefan's responsibilities, including his obligation to save her from Thomas Wade.

Her mind settled, Brianna had silently slipped back into her house and awakened Janet, who was sleeping in a chair beside Brianna's empty bed. The maid had not been pleased with the daring notion, but grumbling beneath her breath, she had at last assisted Brianna in shoving what clothing she could fit in her valises.

In less than an hour, Brianna and Janet had been sneaking through the dark streets, avoiding the traffic as the nobles returned home after their night of revelry. There had been a brief stop in the stables to ensure that Edmond had not yet returned before they slipped through the back gate and followed the flagstone path past elegant statues and lavish fountains to the mansion.

If Edmond would not help her willingly, then he would do so unwillingly.

"Edmond is no prize, but he is certainly preferable to Thomas Wade," she muttered.

"But if this man has promised to contact the Duke, then…"

"I cannot take the risk of waiting," Brianna interrupted. "If Thomas should even suspect that I am attempting to flee, he will have me hauled off to Norfolk before I could do a thing to stop him."

Janet heaved a heavy sigh. "I suppose that is true enough."

"I will sell my soul to the devil before I allow that to happen."

"Mayhap that is what yer about to do," Janet muttered, removing a thin strip of metal from her pocket before efficiently setting about tripping the lock.

The maid rarely spoke about her childhood, but Brianna knew Janet had been the child of one of London's most notorious thieves. And that, until she had fled the underworld, she had learned many tricks of the trade. Such talents had come in handy more than once.

There was a faint click and then the tumble of the locks before the door swung open. Brianna heaved out a deep breath of relief. She knew that Edmond would be returning at any moment, and she had to be firmly settled into the house before he arrived.

Lifting her heavy baggage, Brianna brushed past her maid and entered the kitchen. If anyone was to be shot as a housebreaker, it was only fair that she take the bullet.

Thankfully, there was no sound of gunfire as she stepped over the threshold and glanced about the long room.

There was nothing more threatening than the bundles of herbs hanging from the open-beamed ceiling, a stack of gleaming copper pots and the flicker of dying embers from the massive stone fireplace.

With a gesture toward Janet, Brianna silently crossed the stone floor, keeping her gaze trained on the distant door that led to the private servants' quarters. She skirted the long wooden tables, her stomach rumbling at the scent of freshly baked bread and raspberry pastries that had been left to cool. It was tempting to linger a moment and indulge her sweet tooth with one of the delicate tarts, but with a stern effort, she continued onward, ducking through the arched doorway that led to the back staircase.

If she did not find herself in the gutter in the morning, she could enjoy all the tarts she desired. For the moment, only sheer luck would allow them to reach the guest chambers before being caught.

Darkness shrouded the narrow flight of steps, and Brianna cursed softly as she was forced to slow to a snail's pace. Whatever her panicked sense of urgency, she would not risk breaking her neck by charging up the uneven wooden stairs.

Placing her hand on the stone wall, she struggled upward, concentrating on each step. By the time she reached the third floor, her breath was rasping loudly in the silence and her back was aching from the unaccustomed strain of carrying her heavy bags. She paused long enough to fumble with the door, her heart lodging in her throat as the hinges squeaked in protest.

To her fevered imagination, the sound seemed to carry throughout London.

Had she alerted the entire house to her presence?

With Janet pressed nervously against her back, Brianna forced herself to count to ten. When there was no rush of servants, no cries of alarm, she allowed herself to suck in a deep breath of relief and step from the stairwell.

The wide corridor was bathed in the soft glow of candlelight from the nearby candelabra, revealing the vaulted ceiling and fine plasterwork that had been painted a pale ivory. The Persian carpet shimmered with vivid reds and blues and gold, reflected in the framed pier mirrors that lined the walls.

She was attempting to recall which of the numerous doors led to the guest chambers when a hulking shadow detached itself from the wall to reveal a large man with a hawkish face and fierce pair of blue eyes. Brianna froze in shock. Although the man was attired in the Huntley livery, she did not believe for a moment that he was any simple servant. He looked like a soldier.

Or an assassin.

"What is this?" he growled, his thick accent unmistakably Russian. "What do you think to do?"

This had to be the oaf that Janet had confronted earlier, and with that accent most certainly one of Edmond's men.

Damnation. There was nothing to do but brave it out.

"Allow me to introduce myself." Once again dropping the bags, Brianna performed an elegant curtsey. "I am Miss Quinn, the Duke of Huntley's ward. I will be staying here for a few days, as will my maid."

Brows that matched the man's thick golden hair drew together in wary disbelief. "I have been told nothing of a ward. You will leave now."

Brianna tilted her chin to a haughty angle. She may not have royal blood running through her veins, but her father was first cousin to an Earl and she could feign a conceited self-worth when necessary. And sometimes even when it was not necessary.

"I most certainly will not be leaving. This is my home now."

"You will leave, or I will toss you out."

"You would dare to lay a hand on the Duke's legal ward?" she said, her voice pure ice.

"I was told to keep everyone out." The man began to walk toward her. "That is what I will do."

Brianna was quite convinced that the man intended to toss her out. Even if it meant hauling her to the curb screaming and kicking. It was clearly time to reveal her one and only weapon.

"Before you take another step, I must warn you that I have given a note to a friend with instructions that, unless she hears from me first thing in the morning, it is to be posted to the *London Times,*" she said, her voice echoing through the wide corridor with as much courage as she could muster.

At least the menacing servant came to a halt, his pale eyes glittering with the wariness of a seasoned warrior. He clearly sensed that she was not bluffing.

"What do I care of this note?"

She felt Janet move to stand at her side, as if the maid was preparing to protect her from the man—a brave, if rather foolish, display of loyalty.

"The note will inform all of London that it is not the Duke of Huntley who is staying in this town house, but rather his younger twin, Lord Edmond," she said, a smile curving her lips as the man gave a revealing jerk of surprise. "I doubt your master would appreciate such information becoming the source of tomorrow morning's fodder."

"How did you…"

Not about to lose the brief advantage she held, Brianna grabbed her valises and headed for the nearest bedchamber.

"Come along, Janet. We will have to wait until morning to speak with Edmond."

Stepping into the shadowed room, Brianna firmly shut the door in the face of the servant, dropped her bags and fumbled to turn the heavy key in the lock.

"Ye are going to get us strangled in our sleep," Janet muttered in the dark.

"Nonsense." Holding out a hand to keep from banging into the furniture, Brianna searched for the mantle where there would surely be a flint to light the candles. "Edmond might be a coldhearted cad, but Stefan would never forgive him if he murdered me."

Janet heaved a deep sigh. "I would sleep a mite easier if you dinna sound as if ye were trying to convince yerself and not me."

EDMOND LEANED AGAINST the doorjamb and silently studied the female curled in the middle of the vast, canopied bed.

His breath caught at the sight of the morning sunlight shimmering in the lush hair spread across the pillows and warming the delicate ivory features. He'd expected the vision he had carried in his head from the previous night to be tarnished in the harsh light of day. No woman could possibly be as exquisite as he had imagined.

But he was mistaken.

Christ, she was even lovelier.

He battled against the primal urge to pluck her tiny body from beneath the covers and carry her to his bed where she belonged. What the devil was the matter with him? Brianna Quinn might be a beauty, but he was not about to forgive her blatant intrusion into his home.

When he had returned home last eve after futile hours of trying to locate Howard Summerville, he had been stunned to discover from Boris that two females had locked themselves in one of the guest chambers and that one of them had threatened to send a note to the *London Times* naming him as Edmond.

His first thought had been to break down the door and toss Brianna into the nearest gutter. The devilish chit was a distraction he did not need. Unfortunately, while he did not believe her bluff for a moment, he could not be entirely certain that she would not scream bloody murder and waken all of London if he dared to haul her from the house.

Brianna Quinn had been clever enough to outwit him for the moment, but that did not mean she held all the cards.

He had every intention of ensuring she paid, and paid dearly, for daring to cross him.

Straightening from the jamb, Edmond stepped into the room decorated in a delicate French style with amber wall panels and Savonneirie tapestries framed above the carved chimneypiece. The furniture was made of lemonwood and covered with pretty

English chintz that his grandmother had considered *de rigueur* for a London town house.

Closing the door and turning the key he had retrieved from his housekeeper, Edmond approached the bed. Barefoot and wearing nothing more than a dressing robe, he made no sound as he crossed the Persian carpet.

He paused just a moment to savor the delicate lines of her face. The straight line of her nose, the lush curve of her lips, the thick fan of lashes that lay against the pale ivory skin.

A sleeping Aphrodite.

His hand reached out of his own accord to stroke the sleep-flushed cheek, only to pull back as if he were burned. He was here to rid himself of the pestilent woman, not entangle himself even deeper into her fascinating web.

With a sharp motion, he reached to grasp the quilt and jerked it aside to reveal her tiny form covered only by a thin chemise.

Brianna's eyes flew open as she squeaked in alarm, an alarm that only deepened as her wide gaze caught sight of Edmond hovering over her.

"Edmond."

He curved his lips in a cold smile. "Well, well, I see that Boris was not mistaken. My home was infested by little mice during the night."

She reached down to tug at the cover, muttering in frustration when he refused to release his hold.

"For God's sake, are you trying to give me heart failure?"

"Heart failure is the least of your worries," he drawled, not bothering to resist temptation as he slid into the silken sheets behind her reclined form and gathered her trembling body to spoon intimately against his. "I did warn you what would happen if you stayed beneath my roof."

She stiffened in shock as his hands touched her, exploring the slender curves with the confident assurance of a well-seasoned seducer.

"What are you doing?" she gasped.

His head lowered to stroke his lips over the bare skin of her shoulder, brushing aside the narrow ribbon holding up her chemise to taste of her lavender-scented skin.

"Claiming my reward," he murmured, nipping the curve of her neck before soothing it with his lips.

"Stop this. Edmond…" She caught her breath as his hands found the proud curve of her breasts, strumming his thumbs over the sensitive tips. "Dear lord."

"Do you like that, *ma souris?*" he whispered next to her ear, allowing his tongue to trace the delicate shell.

"No, you cannot," she groaned, her hands lifting to cover his own, although they made no effort to halt the soft caresses.

"Perhaps you prefer this." He teased the tender nipples until they hardened to tight little buds, his cock growing thick with need as she moaned in pleasure. "Yes, sing that sweet song for me."

Kissing a path down the curve of her neck, Edmond breathed deeply of her intoxicating scent, one hand slipping down to press flat against her stomach, urging her backside more firmly against his aching erection.

He had started this to frighten the minx into fleeing his home, to prove to her that he would not be cajoled or threatened or manipulated into taking her in. His purpose in joining her on the bed, however, was swiftly being forgotten beneath the searing flood of hunger that pulsed through his body.

He would be driven mad if he did not have her soon.

Still caressing her breast with one hand, Edmond allowed the other to slip over her stomach and down to the delectable heat between her legs. He hissed in pleasure as he felt the dampness through the thin material of her chemise.

She wanted him. Her body could not lie.

Debating whether to simply lift her leg over his hip and enter her from behind or to lay her on her back so he could watch her face as she received him into her body, Edmond was caught off guard as she suddenly began to struggle against his hold.

"No." Squirming with determination, she managed to turn

to face him, although he refused to allow her to break free. The green eyes smoldered with a combination of anger and terrified desire. "Damn you, Edmond. All I ask for is your protection until Stefan can become my legal guardian. Is that too great a burden to you?"

He growled in frustration. "You have no notion whatsoever."

"I promise not to be any bother. You will not even know I am here…"

"*Mon dieu,*" he rasped. "You cannot be that innocent."

Her brows drew together in annoyance. "What do you mean?"

"This."

Without a shred of modesty, Edmond grasped her hand and tugged it beneath his dressing robe. Brianna made a sound of shock as he wrapped her fingers around the hard thrust of his erection.

"Dear God," she breathed, her gaze trapped by the searing heat in his eyes.

"This is what you do to me simply by being near," he growled. "If you remain here, I will have you."

"You do not even like me," she protested, her voice oddly breathless.

His hand remained wrapped around hers, but it was Brianna who began to stroke slowly downward, as if curious in spite of herself at the feel of his throbbing erection. She reached his heavy sack before she moved back to the tip, her thumb brushing the bead of moisture that had gathered. Edmond moaned at the exquisite sensations that exploded through his body. He had nothing more than her fingers on him, but she offered more pleasure than any number of women who had devoted hours to bringing him to climax.

"You are a desirable woman and I am a man who possesses a fine appreciation for such beauty," he managed to mutter, his voice raw as the pressure began to build with a stunning swiftness. "Christ…yes. That feels so good." He shifted, then scattered kisses over her startled face. "Squeeze harder."

She shivered beneath his soft kisses, her breath rasping loudly in the air.

"Edmond, I do not think…"

"Precisely."

"What?"

"Do not think."

Smothering her lips in a demanding kiss, Edmond closed his eyes and allowed himself to savor the bliss of her slender fingers tightening around his cock as his hips pumped forward. He had known the moment he had gazed into those magnificent green eyes that it would be like this. A searing, mind-shattering desire that stripped a man of his thin veneer of civilization.

The next time he experienced this, he intended to be buried deep inside her as she screamed her own release.

Edmond plunged his tongue into the wet heat of her mouth as his hands toyed with her straining breasts, tasting her heady sweetness as his muscles clenched with a sharp, sudden pinnacle of delight.

"Brianna."

With a wrenching groan, he turned onto his stomach to release his seed into the sheets.

CHAPTER FIVE

BRIANNA WAS AN INNOCENT, well-reared maiden who had been
taught that any intimacy should be conducted only between a
husband and wife, and she knew that she should be shocked and
horrified with what had just occurred.

But she could not deny a dark fascination as she watched
Edmond's beautiful features twist with what appeared to be
intense pleasure, a pleasure that she'd briefly tasted as his hands
and lips had explored her body.

For a wild moment, she had wanted to allow his experienced
caresses to continue, to discover precisely where the tingling
sensations would carry her. It was only fear, and a stubborn
refusal to concede so easily to this aggravating man, that had
brought her to her senses.

Now, she could not deny a sense of frustration, as if her body
were determined to punish her for denying it the satisfaction
Edmond seemed to offer.

Dear heavens, what was the matter with her?

She had spent months fending off Thomas's repulsive
touches, even those of her few suitors who attempted more than
a chaste kiss. The mere thought of having their hands on her
breasts had been enough to make her physically ill.

But with Edmond…it was not revulsion that she felt.

Far from it.

With a low, husky laugh, Edmond rolled to face her, his dark
hair charmingly tousled and his face sinfully handsome in the
morning light.

"Now, that is a perfect means to beginning a day, *ma souris*," he murmured, his hand lifting to lazily play with an auburn curl that lay against her cheek. "Of course, I should have preferred to be snugly tucked between your thighs. Next time, I will be deep inside you when I find my release."

Lightning streaked through her body at his casual words, the image of Edmond poised above her as he tutored her in the pleasures of passion all too vivid.

"There will be no next time."

He gave her curl a sharp tug. "Then you intend to leave?"

Something that might have been pain briefly clenched her heart. Ridiculous, of course. The man had no doubt enjoyed the delights of hundreds of women, far more fully than with her. Why would a few meaningless moments alter his desire to be rid of her?

"You've…had your pleasure, surely that has earned me a few days?" she retorted, sharply.

Without warning, Brianna discovered herself flat on her back with Edmond's heavy body pinning her to the mattress. She swallowed a groan as he grasped her hands and tugged them over her head, his mouth skimming down the length of her neck in a path of searing fire.

"So long as you are near, I will want you. And if you do not flee, I will be your lover," he muttered, exploring the line of her gaping neckline. "*Mon dieu.* Perhaps it is already too late for flight."

"Edmond…" The words became choked in her throat as his mouth found the tip of her breast through her chemise. "Oh."

Brianna closed her eyes as her entire body jerked in response. Was this heaven? She had never dreamed such exquisite sensations existed. It was enough to steal the wits of even the most intelligent woman.

His tongue circled her sensitive nipple, drawing low moans from deep in her throat. At the same time, his leg was pressing between hers to part them wide enough for him to settle his hips between her thighs.

Brianna gasped as her chemise was bunched around her hips and the feel of his hair-roughened legs brushed against her. Then, he settled even deeper and the hard thrust of his arousal pressed at the sensitive flesh between her legs.

Oh, this was…wicked. And wondrous. And so amazingly dangerous.

Edmond sucked in a sharp breath, as if he were as shocked by the violent jolt of pleasure as she.

"Damn you," he breathed, his eyes a stormy blue that spoke of his tumultuous emotions.

Uncertain why he was angered, Brianna parted her lips to demand an explanation only to have the words halted as a sharp rap on the door made them both freeze in shock.

"Sir," a muffled voice echoed through the door.

"Go away, Boris," Edmond snarled, his fierce gaze never wavering from her wide eyes.

"We have an intruder," the servant retorted.

"Get rid of them," Edmond commanded, his tone promising severe retribution for the interruption.

"It is Miss Quinn's stepfather," Boris insisted. "He has threatened to call for the constable if he is not allowed to see his daughter."

"Dear lord," Brianna breathed, stark fear clenching her heart. "How has he found me so swiftly? How has he found me at all?"

Muttering what she assumed were foul Russian curses, Edmond lifted himself from the bed and roughly tied the belt of his robe.

"Get dressed."

"No. I will not go back to him." Scrambling off the bed, Brianna pressed herself against the wall, shaking her head in horror. "I will throw myself out the window, I swear it."

"It is too early for such theatrics, *ma souris,*" he drawled, all hint of passion replaced with a shimmering fury. "Get dressed and come downstairs."

"Do you intend to hand me over to him?"

"Either that or I will toss you out the window myself." His gaze ran a grudging path down her slender body barely hidden by the thin chemise. "You are a complication I do not want and do not need."

"If you do this, all of London will know that you are not Stefan," she warned. "You seem to forget that I have a note revealing your true identity written and prepared to be sent to the *Times*."

A smile twisted his lips. "Your maid has been locked in her chamber, with no possibility of escape until I decide to release her. And since I doubt you have had the opportunity to actually deliver a note to anyone else from the time you left the ball until you forced your way into my home, I feel fairly confident that my secret is safe."

Her own ready temper flared. "You are a...a coldhearted bastard. How you could possibly be related to Stefan defies imagination."

With pathetic ease, he grasped her chin and tilted her face upward. His lips covered hers in a raw, demanding kiss.

"Get dressed and come downstairs," he commanded against her lips. "Boris will wait for you. If you try to run, I will order him to tie and gag you and haul you downstairs."

Without waiting for her reply, he crossed the room and yanked open the door. He spoke briefly with the looming giant waiting in the hall before turning to send one last warning glance as he shut the door in her face.

EDMOND WAS LIVID AS HE returned to his bedchambers and forced himself to prepare for his unwelcome guest.

He barely noticed as his valet shaved him in well-trained silence and styled his hair in the manner his brother preferred, although he did rouse himself enough to choose a fitted jacket in a Cambridge blue that was matched with a blue and silver waistcoat. He also took personal charge of the linen cravat that he tied in an intricate mathematical knot.

Still, his thoughts remained consumed with Miss Brianna

Quinn. Damnation. The woman threatened to ruin everything. First with her blatant threats to expose his identity, and now by dragging her troubles into his home.

In a mood that boded ill for Thomas Wade, Edmond made his way down to the front anteroom where the intruder had been left to cool his heels. He paused in the doorway to study the large man with the thick, florid features and heavy jowls of his ancestors. Despite being properly attired in a dark jacket and white waistcoat, Wade still looked more a butcher than a gentleman as he uncomfortably perched on the edge of a delicate Louis XIV chair.

Another wave of murderous fury raced through Edmond at the mere thought of the man's hands on Brianna, his fat, disgusting body heaving above her. Damn, he'd see Thomas Wade at the bottom of the Thames first.

At last realizing he was no longer alone, Wade surged to his feet, his small eyes glittering with a hard anger.

"About time you decided to make an appearance, Huntley," he growled, his accent still hinting of his humble origins. "You are fortunate I am a patient man, otherwise you would have had the constables on your doorstep."

Stepping across the threshold, Edmond allowed his gaze to flick over the man in silent condemnation.

"You are a fool if you believe that any constable would darken the doorstep of a Duke."

Wade curled his hands into tight fists at Edmond's cool, taunting words.

"So you believe you are above the law?"

"Yes, actually I do." Edmond casually strolled closer to Wade, inwardly judging the considerable bulk of his opponent. Perhaps in his youth Thomas Wade might have been capable of holding his own against Edmond, but now he was soft and flabby from years of self-indulgence. He was no more than a bully who hoped to intimidate others with his sheer size. "But that is not the point. If anyone is breaking the law it is you, Wade. By what right do you force your way into my home?"

"The right of any father to retrieve his only daughter."

Edmond narrowed his gaze. "And what makes you so certain that she is here?"

"I have my means."

Moving so swiftly that the older man had no opportunity to react, Edmond had Thomas slammed against the wall, his forearm pressed to the thick throat.

"I asked you a question," he said, his soft, lethal voice making Wade pale in fear.

"What the hell do you think you are doing, Huntley?"

Edmond pressed his arm harder against the man's throat. "I asked you a question."

Wade made a choked sound as he struggled to breathe. "One of my servants heard her sneaking from the house last night and followed her here."

"You are having her watched?"

The beady eyes held a wary glint, as if attempting to calculate just how much the Duke of Huntley might know of his nefarious plans for Brianna.

"What father would not desire to protect his daughter? London is a dangerous place for an innocent maiden," he grunted.

"But she is not your daughter, is she?" Edmond pointed out. "She is only your stepdaughter."

"She is in my care."

"And in mine. As I recall, our guardianship is jointly held."

Wade dropped his mouth in shock. Edmond did not entirely blame him. Stefan had been inexcusably negligent in ensuring that Brianna was secure and happy in her home. If his older brother had done his duty, she would not currently be creating chaos in his carefully laid plans.

"You have never taken an interest in the chit," Wade gasped.

"An unfortunate oversight that I intend to correct immediately," Edmond drawled, disgusted. "It was naive of me to think you could possibly be a man entrusted with the welfare of a young lady."

The wariness deepened. "Are you impugning my honor?"

"What honor, you sick, pathetic maggot?" It was an effort not to snap the idiot's fat neck. "I should do the world a favor and kill you now."

"Dammit, Huntley, what did the wench tell you?" Wade blubbered, genuine fear bringing a layer of sweat to his brow. "Whatever it was, it was a lie."

"Then you do not intend to take her to Norfolk in two days?"

"I…I think it best that we leave town for a short while. Brianna has not entirely recovered from the death of her mother, and the country air will do her good." He forced a hoarse laugh that grated against Edmond's temper. "Of course, like any young girl, she is angry to be taken from her friends and beaus. It is only natural she would do whatever necessary to stay in town."

"So this trip is entirely for Brianna's benefit?"

"Of course."

"You bastard." Abruptly shifting his hold, Edmond grasped the man's lapels and gave him a violent shake. "You are taking her from London so you can force your disgusting attentions upon her."

"No…"

"Do not even attempt to lie to me," he growled. "I know the truth, and all of London will soon learn of it if you do not walk from this house and forget that you even know the name of Miss Brianna Quinn."

Something that might have been desperation twisted the heavy features as Wade realized that Brianna might truly have slipped from his grasp.

"By gads, she is my daughter," he rasped. "You cannot simply take her from me."

"I already have."

"I will petition for her return," Wade blustered, his voice shrill. "Her mother left her in my care."

Edmond frowned at the hectic glitter in the man's eyes and

the spittle forming at the edges of his mouth. *Mon dieu,* Thomas Wade was clearly at the edge of sanity.

At least when it came to matters of his stepdaughter.

"Her mother was a weak-willed fool who cared for nothing beyond the gaming tables. She would have sold Brianna to Beelzebub for a few quid." He needed to make very certain that Thomas Wade understood the price of creating a scandal. Until he had the time necessary to covertly rid the world of the nasty creature, it was vital to keep his mouth shut. "And I would caution you against bringing the smallest breath of attention to Brianna's change in residence. Not unless you wish me to inform the entire ton of what you intended for your stepdaughter."

Wade's harsh breath echoed through the ante room. "It would be her word against mine."

Edmond smiled with the ingrained arrogance of a true aristocrat. "No, it would be the Duke of Huntley's word against a mere son of a butcher. Who do you think they would believe?"

The beefy face turned from purple to crimson as the smooth insult sliced through his pride.

"I am not without influence. Money does have a few benefits."

"Then let me raise the stakes." Edmond smiled with icy intent. "If you make one attempt to try and take Brianna from my care, I will castrate you."

Wade gave a shudder of alarm, then his gaze shifted over Edmond's shoulder and a stark hunger filled his eyes. Edmond did not need to turn to know that Brianna had entered the room.

Suddenly, he wished that he had not insisted that the chit come down.

"Brianna…" Wade attempted to step forward only to be shoved roughly back against the wall. "Damn. My dear, tell this madman to release me."

There was a brief hesitation before Brianna moved to stand beside Edmond, appearing far too tempting in her poppy India muslin gown decorated with small sprigs of gold. Matching ribbons were threaded through the auburn curls she had pulled to a high knot atop her head. Even without ornamentation, she appeared as young and fresh as a spring breeze.

"This madman happens to be my guardian and the Duke of Huntley," she retorted, her expression frigid.

Wade futilely struggled against Edmond's hold, desperate to reach Brianna.

"Please, you must listen to me, my dear. This has all been some terrible misunderstanding," he cajoled. "If you would just return home, we could settle this in private."

Edmond sensed Brianna's shudder of horror as she wrapped her arms around her waist. "This is my home now."

"Brianna, do not be a fool." The older man shot Edmond a venomous glare. "This man is practically a stranger to you. Certainly he has made no effort to claim his right as a guardian before today. He will no doubt marry you off to the first bounder he can convince to ask for your hand, just to be rid of you."

"It would be a preferable fate than remaining with you."

"How can you say that, after all I have done for you and your mother?"

Brianna pressed even closer to Edmond, clearly taking comfort in his presence.

"You destroyed any loyalty I might have felt toward you when you attempted to rape me," she hissed.

"I think that is a fitting end to this unpleasant encounter." Keeping his grim hold on the lapels of Wade's jacket, Edmond hauled him toward the door. "It is time you return to the gutter that spit you out."

Struggling against his inevitable fate, Thomas Wade wrenched his head around to cast Brianna a frantic gaze.

"No, damn you. Brianna. You belong with me, and I will not allow anyone to stand between us."

With a violent shove, Edmond had the man through the vast foyer and out the door held open by his footman.

"Boris, keep an eye on the bastard," he commanded, turning

his back as Thomas Wade stumbled down the steps, followed closely by the massive Russian assassin.

Halting before the mirror, Edmond calmly adjusted his cravat and smoothed his jacket. He had rid himself of one rodent, now he had to decide what was to be done with his beautiful little mouse.

STANDING BESIDE THE TALL window, Brianna watched in a numbed sort of fascination as Thomas climbed unsteadily into his carriage and was driven away.

A part of her wanted to feel relief that she was seemingly safe from her stepfather, who had been well and truly trounced by Edmond. What man would dare to return after such a humiliation?

Her far more sensible part, however, knew that whatever had prompted Edmond to dismiss Thomas with such disdain had nothing to do with assisting her. He cared only for his mysterious reasons for being in London, and if she threatened those plans, she would be offered the same brutal treatment.

If not worse.

A shiver shook her body as she sensed Edmond return. She had no need to turn and confirm his presence. Every nerve she possessed seemed suddenly attuned to him.

It was odd. As a child, she had been overawed by his intimidating presence, at times even frightened by those brilliant blue eyes that seemed to see everything. She never would have thought she could feel anything but unease while in his company. He was nothing at all like sweet, gentle Stefan, who had somehow understood the stark loneliness of her childhood and always made her feel welcome at Meadowland.

She certainly hadn't thought she'd feel this powerful awareness that made her heart jump and her stomach clench in pleasure.

"Why did you not turn me over to him?" she demanded, needing the answer to the question that had haunted her since she had walked down the staircase and heard Edmond threaten to castrate her stepfather.

There was the sound of approaching footsteps as he moved to stand directly at her back. A tingle of excitement trickled down her spine and, stifling a gasp, she turned to confront him.

That, of course, only made matters worse. Her breath caught in her throat. He was so...*beautiful.* The elegant line of his masculine features, eyes the perfect blue of a cloudless sky, dark curls that held the gloss of polished ebony, blended together to create nothing less than a masterpiece.

Edmond studied her with a brooding expression.

"Because I am not yet done with you, *ma souris.*"

Brianna frowned, uncertain what to make of his words, then with an inward shrug, she turned her thoughts back to her most pressing concern.

"Do you think he is gone for good?"

"I do not believe he will dare to attempt to storm this citadel again, but I should be very surprised if he has actually given up his obsession to have you." His expression hardened. "The very fact that you have become inaccessible will only feed his madness."

She pressed a hand to her heaving stomach. Damn Thomas Wade. And damn her mother for leaving her at the mercy of the demented monster.

"I must leave London."

"And go where?"

"You could send me to Meadowland in your coach." Without even realizing what she was doing, Brianna reached out to grasp his arm in sudden hope. Of course. She should have thought of it the moment she realized that it was Edmond rather than Stefan in London. "I would surely be safe with your servants to protect me."

"Why did you not flee to Stefan before now?" he demanded.

"Because I would have been forced to take a stagecoach, and Thomas could easily have overtaken me before I reached Meadowland." She shrugged. "Besides, Stefan never responded to my letters. For all I knew, he might have been away from the estate and then what would I have done?"

He studied her with a hooded gaze. "I do not doubt you would have thought of something. You are a very…" He deliberately allowed his words to trail away as his gaze lowered to the modest neckline of her gown. "Resourceful sort of female."

A blush stole beneath her cheeks, but she refused to rise to the bait. She had done what was necessary. She would not feel shame for that.

She squared her shoulders and pasted a smile to her lips. "Now, however, I can be certain Stefan is there and with your carriage…"

"No."

"Why ever not? You do not want me here and I would far prefer to be with Stefan. It is the perfect solution."

"Except for the fact that, so far as the world is concerned, Stefan is here in London while Edmond is in charge of Meadowland," he said succinctly. "Do you not think it would stir curiosity if I were to send my newly acquired ward to stay in a home with my renowned rake of a brother?"

She dropped her hand and stared at him with a wary confusion. Why was he being so difficult? He could not have made it more obvious that he wanted nothing more than to be rid of her. He should be delighted by the notion of sending her off to Meadowland.

"You could say that I was ill and in need of the country air," she pointed out slowly.

His lips twisted. "Then it will be speculated that I made you pregnant and banished you to Meadowland until the babe is born."

"That is absurd," she choked out, her skin feeling oddly hot and far too tight for her body. "You just arrived in London, how could you possibly have made me pregnant?"

Edmond shrugged, his lightly bronzed features unreadable. "Stefan does come to London to attend his duties in the House of Lords, although he rarely opens the town house. Besides, gossip has no need to make sense."

It was true enough. She had been in London long enough to

know that spreading rumors was the ton's favorite pastime. And the more outrageous and titillating the scandal, the more it was enjoyed.

Still, she found it ridiculous to suppose anyone would believe Stefan capable of seducing and abandoning his own ward.

"Even supposing that a few spiteful tongues wag, it hardly matters."

"It happens to matter a great deal," he snapped, stepping close enough for the heat of his body to sear through her thin muslin gown. "I am attempting to avoid any unnecessary attention being drawn to my visit here in London, a task that has become considerably more difficult, thanks to your interference."

Brianna was effectively trapped as she struggled not to react to the scent of sandalwood and warm male.

"You still have not told me why you are pretending to be Stefan."

"I rarely reveal my secrets to a proven blackmailer."

Stung by his mocking tone, Brianna lifted her hands to shove them against his chest.

"But you are willing to take one as your lover?"

The blue eyes darkened, and without warning, his hands grasped her arms to jerk her against his chest.

"Do you need further proof, *ma souris?* Shall I take you here and now?"

Not at all certain that she could resist the desire to allow him to do whatever he wanted to her trembling body, Brianna gave a desperate shake of her head.

"Please, Edmond."

"Please, what?"

"Please send me to Stefan."

Edmond stepped back, his nose flaring with something that might have been anger.

"Never."

"But…"

"Enough." Turning on his heel, Edmond stormed toward

the door, pausing at the threshold to scowl over his shoulder. "You were foolish enough to force your way into this house. Now you will endure the consequences."

CHAPTER SIX

THE VAST LIBRARY IN HUNTLEY House was Edmond's favorite room.

A long rectangle with floor to ceiling length windows that overlooked the terraced garden below, it was renowned for the carved and gilded doors that had been a gift from the previous King, as well as the painted ceiling that portrayed a distant relative on a chariot bound for the Temple of Zeus.

On either side of the black and gold veined marble chimneypiece were matching English gilt gesso chairs and closer to the windows was a heavy walnut desk that had been in the Huntley family for two centuries.

It was more than the white marble floor or the towering bronze lamps, or even the Gainsborough paintings that his father had collected over the years, however, that called to Edmond's soul.

It was the rich scent of leather-bound books and polished wood that reminded him of evenings spent with his father reading to them of distant travels, or teaching them the finer art of playing chess. Days when life had held nothing but a carefree happiness and the promise of a glorious future.

Days long past.

Storming from the anteroom and Brianna Quinn's disturbing presence, Edmond headed unswervingly to this familiar spot, almost as if his unconscious mind was in need of the peaceful sense of refuge.

Or perhaps it was simply the fine whiskey he knew would be stashed in the bottom drawer of the massive desk.

Tossing his tall frame into the leather chair, Edmond yanked the drawer open and pulled out the spirits, then took a deep drink directly from the bottle.

Damn the wench.

He had just rescued her from the rutting animal she called a stepfather, but had she flung herself at his feet in gratitude? Had she even bothered to thank him at all?

No. All she could think of was her precious Stefan and just how swiftly she could flee to be in his comforting presence.

Well he'd be damned if he wasted his handful of servants and one of his carriages to haul her to Meadowland. Not when he was beginning to realize her aggravating presence beneath his roof might be an actual godsend.

Continuing to take deep pulls on the whiskey, Edmond brooded on the best means of turning the upheaval in his plans to his best advantage, until he was interrupted by the arrival of Boris.

The large, Russian-born man came from a long line of proud soldiers and his heritage was etched into every hard plane and angle of his massive form. But while he possessed the golden blond hair and bluntly carved features of his father, his eyes were the hazel of his English-born mother.

He also possessed an uncanny intelligence that had captured Edmond's attention from the moment they had first met nearly six years earlier. It had taken some effort to convince Alexander Pavlovich that one of his most promising soldiers should be given over to Edmond to assist in his covert activities, but in the end, Edmond had had his way.

Once the door was firmly closed and locked, Boris shed his charade of a lumbering foreign servant to reveal the ruthless, well-trained soldier beneath.

Leaning back in his chair, Edmond set aside the whiskey bottle. "Well?"

Boris gave a lift of his shoulder, an unexpected smile touching his lips.

"The coward returned to a house on Curzon Street." Boris's

voice was deep, but without the thick accent he adopted when in his role as servant. With an English mother, he spoke the language as well as Edmond.

"What is so amusing?"

"The fat fool fell on his face twice as he ran to his door. You would have thought the devil himself was nipping on his heels." Boris snorted.

"Fool he might be, but he is a dangerous fool." With an elegant motion, Edmond was on his feet and moving toward a nearby window. It took only a moment to spot the thin man who was attempting to appear nonchalant as he strolled up and down the cobbled street. "He left a guard to keep watch on the house."

"Good," Boris muttered as he moved to Edmond's side. "I will kill him."

"No, Boris." Edmond gave a regretful shake of his head. "Not yet. Once I have discovered who is attempting to harm Stefan, I will deal with Thomas Wade and his inept servants. Until then, I must not draw unnecessary attention."

"Then why not hand the wench back over to the bastard? That would put an end to this man's interest, and we could concentrate on more important matters."

Edmond abruptly turned and moved to lean against the white marble fireplace, careful to keep his expression unreadable.

"Because I have decided that she will be of use."

"Use?" Boris grimaced. For all his skills, the man was remarkably shy when it came to the fairer sex. "When is a female ever of use?"

"You have spent too much time on the battlefield, Boris, if you have forgotten there is at least one use for a female," Edmond drawled.

Boris muttered a curse beneath his breath. "You can have that sort of use in the nearest alley. No need to bother with the fuss of bringing her into your home."

Heat feathered through Edmond's body at the thought of Brianna pressed against the wall of an alley, her legs wrapped around his waist as he pumped deep inside her. It could hardly compare to a soft bed and hours to devote to her satin heat, but there was a certain charm to a swift, heated coupling.

Grudgingly, he forced the image away.

"On this occasion it is actually her presence that I do need, as aggravating and annoying as that presence might be."

Boris narrowed his gaze, a hint of suspicion in the hazel depths. "Why?"

Edmond stretched his arm along the mantle, his slender fingers drumming an impatient tattoo on the smooth marble. He did not want to explain his reasoning for keeping Brianna at his side. Perhaps because he had not yet completely convinced himself of those reasons. But Boris deserved some explanation. He was, after all, putting his own life at risk.

"It occurs to me that while my presence in London, posing as Stefan, has diverted the danger away from my brother, Howard might be more reluctant to strike," he said, smoothly. "After all, it is far easier to plan an accident on a lonely country road than in the midst of London."

"I thought that was the reason you were so eager to seek him out?" Boris countered. "To prod him into showing his hand."

Edmond shrugged. "I have found a better means to prod him."

Boris's suspicion deepened. "The woman?"

"Yes."

"Why the hell would he care if you have Miss Quinn living with you?"

"He will not." A cold smile twisted his lips. "Not until I allow gossip to spread that she is soon to be my wife."

"Your…" The hazel eyes bulged. Edmond had never made a secret of his grim resolution never to wed. Not even Alexander Pavlovich had been capable of compelling Edmond into cementing his place in the Russian court with an advantageous match. "Wife?"

"Precisely."

Boris took a step forward before forcibly coming to a halt.

"Have you taken a blow to your head, or did the wench simply bewitch you?" he growled.

Edmond's expression hardened.

"It will be a cold day in hell before any woman can bewitch me to the altar, old friend," he snapped, uncertain why he was angry.

"Then it *was* a blow to the head?"

Edmond sucked in a deep, calming breath, his temper clearly strained far more than he had realized by the past few hours.

"Just consider, Boris," he said, his voice deliberately even. "For now, Howard must only be rid of Stefan and myself to gain a vast fortune and grand title. Not entirely impossible, if he is willing to be patient and await the proper opportunities. If, however, he is convinced that the Duke of Huntley is about to wed, he will be forced to take swift measures before Stefan can begin producing a pack of potential heirs."

Boris turned the words over in his mind before at last giving a grudging nod.

"I suppose it might provoke him."

"Suppose?" Edmond straightened from the mantle. "It is a bloody well brilliant notion."

"And one that allows you to keep Miss Quinn near at hand."

This time Edmond merely smiled, his composure under firm control. "Do you have a point?"

"Yes, I have a point," Boris said. "It is not like you to allow yourself to be distracted once you have decided upon a course of action. Especially not by a mere female."

Edmond gave a sharp bark of laughter. "Brianna Quinn is not just a mere female, Boris, she is a force of nature. And I am not distracted. Like any good tactician, I merely have altered my plans to take advantage of the unexpected opportunities presented to me."

"And that is all she is? An unexpected opportunity?"

"Enough." Edmond held up a warning hand. He would not discuss his desire for Brianna. Not with anyone.

Boris heaved a gusty sigh before conceding defeat. "Very well. What do you wish of me?"

"I need you to keep a careful eye upon Miss Quinn."

"You fear she will betray the truth as she has threatened?" Boris demanded in surprise.

"No, but I do believe she is still in danger. Thomas Wade will not willingly allow her to slip from his grasp."

"Damn you, Edmond, I am not a nursery maid. I should be keeping watch upon your cousin. If your scheme is successful, and Summerville is forced to strike in a hurry, then you will be in grave danger."

Edmond hid a smile at the man's offended tone. "Yes, which is why neither of us is capable of keeping a close enough guard upon Howard."

The hazel eyes flashed with irritation. "So now I am not only lowered to being no more than a nanny, but you also intend to insult my skills?"

Once again, Edmond was forced to battle a smile. There was never anyone less suited to play the role of nanny. On the other hand, there was no one more suited to keeping Brianna safe.

"Never that," he assured his companion. "But I can hardly shadow a gentleman who knows me so well and you, old friend, do not precisely blend in with the London natives. Not even Howard is dim-witted enough to overlook such a great brute following him about London. The last thing I desire is to spook the bastard off before he can attempt to kill me." He lifted his hand as Boris thinned his lips with disapproval. "And before you protest, I assure you that this has nothing to do with Miss Brianna Quinn. I made the decision to hire a professional before we ever left Surrey. In fact, I have an interview with a potential candidate this afternoon."

Boris jutted his jaw forward. He clearly wanted to argue, but the expression on Edmond's face halted the words before they could leave his lips.

"So I am just to trail behind a half-sized wench for the next few weeks?"

Edmond chuckled as he moved to the desk and picked up the bottle of whiskey. Turning, he shoved it into Boris's hand.

"Actually, I have a far more dangerous task for you this morning."

Boris had been with Edmond long enough to take a deep, fortifying chug of the spirits before asking.

"And what is that?"

"I need you to release Brianna's screeching maid from the chamber I locked her in earlier this morning."

DESPITE THE NIGGLING VOICE that told her she should be grateful at having escaped the clutches of Thomas Wade, Brianna had managed to work herself into a fine temper by late afternoon.

Damn Edmond. How dare he storm from the room and then disappear for hours on end? He had to realize she would be worried sick about her future.

It was all good and well to toss Thomas from the house and threaten to have him castrated, but what was to come next? He had refused to send her to Meadowland and had certainly made it clear that she was unwelcome here, so what the devil was she supposed to do?

Even worse, she had been unable to locate Janet anywhere in the house. The loyal maid would never have left Brianna unless she had been forced away.

Who knew what had happened to the poor woman?

At last Brianna could bear it no more.

By God, she was not going to helplessly wait for Edmond to make some sort of royal appearance and announce what her fate might be. She had already spent too many years at the mercy of others. She had promised herself that if she ever escaped Thomas, she would willingly walk through the pits of hell to gain control of her life.

And if confronting Edmond was her current pit of hell, then so be it.

Squaring her shoulders, Brianna marched through the state rooms with their silk damask furnishings and walls lined with family portraits and shimmering gilt mirrors. The mansion was eerily empty and not for the first time she wondered why Edmond had seemingly dismissed Stefan's large staff. The only explanation seemed to be that he was up to something nefarious that he feared would be discovered by the servants.

But if that were true, then Stefan must be involved as well. After all, Edmond could never take command of Huntley House and the staff without his approval. And while Brianna was willing to believe anything of Edmond, she could not convince herself that Stefan would ever condone something truly wicked. His sense of honor simply would not allow it.

Finding no trace of her prey in the formal public rooms, Brianna directed her search to various parlors and saloons, even searching the rooftop viewing gallery before concluding that Edmond must be hidden in the library.

She did not allow herself to hesitate as she pushed the door open and stepped into the long, beautiful room. Instinctively, her gaze moved to the heavy desk set near the long row of windows, and she was not at all surprised to discover Edmond seated behind it.

Her heart gave a disturbing leap as she watched his dark head lift to reveal his perfectly carved features. It did not seem at all fair that a man blessed with such wealth and power should also possess the face and form of Adonis.

But then again, life was rarely fair.

Brianna met the fierce blue gaze. Something dangerous, almost possessive, smoldered in the cerulean depths, but it was gone so swiftly she wondered if it was nothing more than a figment of her imagination.

"Brianna." His expression was unreadable as he set aside the quill in his hand. "What do you want?"

Her chin tilted at the unmistakable reprimand in his low, compelling voice.

"I waited for you at luncheon, but you never joined me."

"I did not join you because I am busy. So if you would close the door behind…"

"Oh, no, I am not about to be so easily dismissed. I want to know what you have done to Janet."

"Janet?"

"Do not be deliberately obtuse, Edmond. You know very well that Janet is my maid, just as you know that she is missing. Where is she?"

"Ah, you fear that I had her murdered and flung into the Thames?"

"I would not put it past you."

"What a vivid imagination you possess, *ma souris*."

She took another step forward, wanting nothing so much as to slap that smile from his lips. Her life had been nothing short of purgatory since her mother's death and the only thing that had made it halfway bearable had been the companionship of her maid. She would be damned if she would allow this man to belittle her concern.

"You haven't answered the question."

Edmond studied her tight expression for a beat before his voice softened. "I assure you that she is well and hearty. I merely had a few errands for her to carry out. Now if that is all?"

Relieved, but far from satisfied, Brianna refused to budge. "No, it is not all. I want to know what you intend to do with me."

"Brianna, I am not accustomed to having my commands ignored. We will discuss this later."

"We will discuss this now." She folded her arms over her chest, ignoring the sudden prickles of danger in the air. "You cannot expect me to cower in my rooms while I wait for you to inform me whether I am to be tossed into the nearest gutter or handed over to my horrid stepfather."

Edmond slowly uncoiled from his seat and rounded the desk

with a deliberate step. Unwittingly, Brianna backed away from the stalking form, not halting until she slammed into the bookshelf behind her.

Moving until he was only inches from her stiff body, Edmond regarded her from beneath hooded lids.

"Actually, I can expect anything I please from you, and there is not a damn thing you can do about it."

She sucked in a deep breath, the scent of his warm, clean skin assaulting her senses and making her body tremble with awareness.

"I suppose this is your means of punishing me? You intend to keep me constantly afraid that I might be tossed onto the street or handed over to Thomas." She grasped the shelf behind her. "God, I wish Stefan was here. He would never be so cruel."

Her words seemed to annoy him for some odd reason, and with a muttered curse, he stepped back to regard her with barely concealed irritation.

"Very well," he growled, his handsome features drawn into stark lines. "If you must know, I am making plans for your future even as we speak."

"And what plans would those be?"

He pointed toward the desk. "Read for yourself."

Brianna warily rounded his tense form to make her way to the large desk. Once there, she plucked the top sheet of parchment paper from the glossy surface to quickly scan the elegant note written upon it.

Then she scanned it again and again, unable to accept that she was not somehow misreading the words.

Stefan Edward Summerville, Sixth Duke of Huntley announces his engagement to Miss Brianna Quinn, the daughter of the late Mr. Fredrick Quinn.

At last, she dropped into the leather seat and gave a numb shake of her head.

"Is this supposed to be some sort of jest?"

Edmond folded his arms over his chest, his features ruthless in the late afternoon light.

"Do I seem the sort to jest?"

"No, but I was attempting to be kind."

"Kind?" he demanded.

She waved the paper she held clutched in her hand. "Well, there are only two reasons for you to announce Stefan's engagement to me." She could barely even force the shocking words past her stiff lips. "Either this is some horrid joke, or proof that you are stark raving mad."

"Not Stefan's engagement," he snapped. "The announcement is for the current Duke of Huntley, which happens to be me."

Brianna grimly ignored the strange jolt that raced through her at the savage claim. "Now I know you are mad."

With a visible effort, Edmond eased the tension gripping his large body, a mocking smile touching his lips.

"I am not at all certain that I would argue with you."

"This is ridiculous." Rising to her feet, Brianna tossed aside the announcement and glared at the gentleman who was swiftly becoming the bane of her existence. At least Thomas Wade was a predictable, if extremely loathsome companion. Edmond was making her head swim in confusion. "Why would you announce our engagement?"

"Because it suits my purpose."

"And that is your explanation? Because it suits your purpose?"

"Yes."

"Well, it doesn't happen to suit mine."

"It should."

"Why? Because you believe that every woman is desperate to be your wife?"

"Most of them are."

He leaned against the shelves, his linen shirt thin enough to reveal the sculpted muscles beneath, and his dark breeches molded to the hard thrust of his legs. He looked like an elegant predatory animal who had discovered his prey and was merely biding his time before pouncing.

The thought sent a shiver down her spine.

"Conceited toad," she muttered, refusing to reveal her flare of unease. "I would not have you as a husband if—"

"Fortunate, because hell will freeze over before I ever become *any* woman's husband," he interrupted icily. "This is no more than a temporary inconvenience that I intend to be done with as swiftly as possible."

She stiffened. Well, that certainly put her in her place. She was good enough to use in his disreputable schemes, but nowhere near good enough to wed.

Why the knowledge should trouble her was a mystery.

"Then why do you claim that this engagement should suit me?" she demanded in a stiff voice.

"This is the only means to ensure that, when you at last leave this house, your reputation will not be shredded beyond repair."

So he was doing this all for her? Not bloody likely.

"There is no need to go to such lengths. You could send me to Meadowland—"

"No."

She frowned in irritation at his sharp interruption. Why the devil would he not send her to Meadowland? It could only be that Stefan was involved in the secretive plots swirling about Edmond.

"Then hire a female companion."

Edmond shrugged. "I intend to invite my aunt to visit during your stay. Even as my fiancée, you cannot remain here without a woman to act as guardian."

"Your aunt?" Brianna blinked in shock. It was well-known that Edmond held the majority of his family in disdain. Only Stefan seemed immune to his universal dislike. "Good lord. I cannot believe you are going to this effort simply to keep my reputation untarnished."

"I do it more for Stefan's reputation," he corrected smoothly.

"He would not be pleased to be considered the sort of nobleman who would seduce his own ward beneath his roof."

"That is because he is a gentleman. Something you would know nothing about."

The blue eyes narrowed. "Careful, *ma souris*. Annoy me enough, and I will simply keep you locked in your chambers until I am finished with my business in London."

She wisely ignored his threat. If he decided to lock her away, there was very little she could do to halt him.

"Did you consider the fact that, once this engagement comes to an end, I will still be ruined?" She held up a hand as his lips parted. "While I am quite willing to trade my reputation to be rid of Thomas Wade, a male might be capable of shrugging off a broken engagement, but a female is not so fortunate. There will be endless gossip and speculation as to why Stefan cried off."

A sardonic smile touched his lips. "Perhaps if you were jilted by most gentlemen, but a woman capable of attracting the attentions of the elusive Duke of Huntley, even for a brief time, is bound to be one of the most sought after young maidens in all of London. No doubt, when this is all said and done, you will be able to land a dull, spineless gentleman who will occasionally remember to crawl into your bed to give you a pack of squawking brats."

It was his mocking scorn that made her chin tilt. The jackass! What choice did most women have but to claim a destiny that included marriage and children? It was not as if they were blessed with the same opportunities as the wealthy son of a duke.

Thankfully, she would be spared such a horrid fate.

"There will be no man crawling into my bed for any reason," she charged.

"One already has." The blue eyes abruptly darkened with a near tangible hunger as his gaze ran a slow, thorough path over her slender body. "Or have you already forgotten our morning tryst?"

It was her heated response to that mere glance that had Brianna heading for the door. She at least knew that Janet was safe, and that for the moment, Edmond had no intention of tossing her into the street.

It was enough for now.

Pausing at the threshold, she turned her head to toss her parting words over her shoulder.

"If you truly want to bring me happiness, Edmond, then send me to Stefan."

He jerked, almost as if she had physically hit him, but before he could respond, she shut the door and ran up the marble staircase to her bedchambers. She had a great deal to consider.

Not the least of which was the horrifying knowledge that she was about to become the Duke of Huntley's fiancée.

CHAPTER SEVEN

AFTER BRIANNA FLOUNCED FROM the library, Edmond found himself pacing the marble floor with short, restless steps. Why the hell did he allow the chit to stir his temper? He did, after all, have her completely at his mercy. No matter how much she might squawk and squeal, she had no choice but to obey his commands or leave his protection, something she was clearly loath to do at this point. It was ridiculous to be ruffled by her sharp-edged tongue.

It was sheer willpower that kept him in the library as she stormed from the room. He wanted to tame the damnable she-devil until she admitted that he was her master. And the best method of accomplishing such a feat was to have her flat on her back in his bed.

Mon dieu.

Brooding on the numerous ways to make Miss Quinn his devoted, satisfied slave, Edmond was actually relieved when a footman appeared in the doorway, accompanied by a thin, nondescript gentleman with lank gray hair and the sort of bland face that was easily forgettable.

In his modest cravat and plain dark suit that was a shade too large for his body, the man might have been a banker, a lawyer or one of those endless merchants who scurried about London.

Certainly, he did not make one think of a highly reputable Bow Street Runner.

"Ah, Chesterfield." Edmond smoothed his expression with

a practiced ease, giving the hovering servant a faint nod to stop him backing from the room. "Welcome."

"Your Grace." The man performed a surprisingly graceful bow. Edmond arched a brow, realizing that, in a more elegantly cut suit and with his hair more fashionably styled, the man could easily move through the streets of Mayfair. Even his voice was carefully cultured, although he could no doubt sound like a common chimneysweep if he chose. What finer talent for a Runner than being able to move through the lowest to the highest ranks of society without attracting attention? He could use such a man in his Russian network. "May I say this is a true honor."

"Please, have a seat." Edmond waved a hand toward a Venetian giltwood chair, waiting for Chesterfield to take his seat before taking his own place behind the desk. "Brandy? Or perhaps you prefer whiskey?"

"Thank you, no. I never touch strong spirits."

"A teetotaler?"

"Just a man who prefers to keep his wits sharp and his lips shut, neither of which are possible with a belly full of the devil's brew."

Leaning back in his seat, Edmond smiled. "I see that you are indeed precisely the man I need."

"May I ask how you came to know my name?"

"I wrote to Liverpool before arriving in London requesting his assistance in discovering a suitable employee. He assured me that you are not only the finest that Bow Street has to offer, but that you possess an admirable ability to keep your own counsel."

"Very kind of his lordship," Chesterfield murmured.

Edmond gave a bark of laughter. "Liverpool is rarely a kind man, but he is remarkably shrewd, and for the most part, a wise judge of character. Which is why I requested that you meet with me."

At last the Runner allowed a faint hint of curiosity to touch his bland features.

"How may I be of service?"

"First I wish to impress upon you the delicacy of the situation." He caught and held Chesterfield's gaze, the warning in his voice unmistakable. "It cannot be discovered that I hired you."

Chesterfield did not wilt, nor did he attempt to stammer a nervous assurance as many would beneath Edmond's stern gaze. Instead he offered a somber nod of his head.

"I can promise you that I will do everything in my power to ensure that there will not be a soul who will ever know we have crossed paths."

"It may be necessary for you to hire additional companions to assist you in my task. I do not wish my name to be involved."

Again Chesterfield nodded. "I can call upon several associates who I have known for years. They know better than to attempt to discover who my current employer is."

"Good." Satisfied that Chesterfield was precisely the man needed for the job, Edmond opened the top door of his desk and removed a miniature painting of Howard Summerville. It had been a gift to Stefan from the ridiculous buffoon the previous Christmas. With a smooth motion, he pushed the miniature across the desk. "Take a good look at this gentleman."

Leaning forward, Chesterfield studied the painting for less than half a beat.

"Mr. Summerville."

"You know him?" Edmond did not bother to hide his surprise.

"Only by sight." The Runner shrugged. "I always make it my business to keep track of those gentlemen who are having difficulties with the creditors. You never know when a merchant might hire me to keep track of his customer."

"Why the devil would a merchant want you to keep track of his customer?"

"To make certain they do not slip out of the country without paying their debts."

"Ah."

Chesterfield's lips gave a faint twitch, as if aware of Edmond's distaste at the thought of being spied upon by his tailor.

"Do you wish me to keep an eye on Summerville?"

"More than just an eye, Chesterfield." Edmond leaned forward, folding his arms on the desk. "I do not want this man to sneeze without you being aware of it. I want you to make a list of where he goes, who he meets with, and if possible, who he owes money to. I also want his properties searched and any reference to the Duke of Huntley or Meadowland brought directly to me."

Chesterfield considered for a long moment, clearly caught off guard by Edmond's numerous demands.

"It will take a number of men…"

Edmond once again reached into the desk and pulled out a small leather bag filled with coins.

"Hire as many as you need. Just ensure that Summerville does not realize he is being followed or watched."

With a practiced efficiency, the Runner captured the bag and tucked it beneath his jacket.

"You have my word, he will never suspect a thing. I will keep in contact by leaving a message with the pub keeper at the Drake's Nest near the docks. Do you know the place?"

Edmond's lips twisted. "No, but I do not doubt that my man-servant, Boris, will. He possesses an uncanny ability to locate a vast number of unsavory pubs."

With a nod, Chesterfield rose smoothly to his feet. "Tell him to introduce himself as Teddy Pinkston and he will be given a packet of whatever information I have collected."

Edmond committed the name to memory as he lifted himself from his chair. "What if I need to contact you?"

"Have a red rose delivered to La Russa at the King's Theatre. She will arrange a meeting."

Edmond lifted a brow at the mention of the talented opera singer who had taken London by storm. What her connection to the Runner might be defied his imagination.

"You have clearly done this sort of thing before," he murmured, well impressed by the man's discreet organization.

The faintest smile touched Chesterfield's lips. "That, my lord, is a secret I shall take to my grave."

IT WAS NEARING THE DINNER hour when the door to Brianna's bedchamber was at last thrust open.

"Janet, at last." Rising from the cushioned window seat, she pressed a hand to her heart, realizing just how horridly lost she had felt sitting in the vast, empty house all alone. "I was beginning to fear you had been kidnapped."

"Not far from it."

With a frown, Brianna moved forward in concern. "Are you well? You have not been hurt—" Her words broke off as she neared the door and spotted the boxes piled in the long hallway. "Whatever is all this?"

With a rather mysterious smile, Janet bent down to collect a number of the gaily wrapped packages.

"The bare necessities of what ye'll be needing over the next few weeks," she informed the baffled Brianna, depositing the packages on the bed. "Tomorrow yer commanded to visit the dressmakers and order a new wardrobe seeing as ye'll need to be properly fitted."

Tugging at the silver bows, Brianna opened the boxes to reveal the astonishing bounty. There were shifts made of the finest silk and edged with Brussels lace. There were whale-bone corsets, and stockings that had been embroidered with delicate flowers. There were also a dozen bonnets trimmed with satin ribbons and sprigged net with matching cloaks in all shades and fabrics. Janet busily toted in the remaining boxes that revealed soft calfskin boots and various slippers that Brianna itched to try on.

"Commanded to visit the dressmakers?" Backing away from the beautiful treasures that now consumed most of the bed, Brianna glared at her maid in confusion. "What are you talking about?"

"Oh, aye, ye might look shocked." Janet sank onto the edge of the bed with a gusty sigh. "I near had heart failure when that lumbering ox drug me from my chamber and demanded that I purchase what you might have need of."

Feeling as if she had just stepped into some French farce, Brianna struggled to make sense of her maid's disjointed explanations.

"What lumbering ox?"

"Boris." As Brianna continued to frown the maid gave an impatient shake of her head. "Ye must recall the servant who near tossed us out on our ears last eve?"

"Boris took you shopping?"

"That's what I just said, is it not?"

"It is just that I cannot believe it."

The maid doubled over in laughter. "Oh, lordy, it was a sight to behold, miss. Once I realized I was not being hauled off to have me throat slit or to be sold off to the slave-traders, I 'bout near split me gut watching the great hulk walking down Bond Street with a scowl on his face." She paused to blot the tears of amusement streaming down her face.

Brianna smiled, but she was far too unnerved to fully appreciate the humorous description.

"He must have been ordered by Edmond to take you to Bond Street," she muttered. "But why the devil would the man give a fig about my wardrobe?"

Janet snorted. "Oh, aye, Boris would never have released me from my chamber, let alone step foot near that neighborhood, unless he was being forced."

So why then had Edmond…she gasped as realization struck. Of course. He might not give a damn about Miss Brianna Quinn's wardrobe, but he most certainly did care about his soon-to-be fiancée's attire.

Which meant that he had sent her maid to begin her shopping long before Brianna had grudgingly agreed to his ridiculous charade of an engagement.

Spinning on her heel, Brianna strode toward the bay window that offered a stunning view of the nearby park.

"That man is the most arrogant, high-handed, aggravating creature ever born!"

"'Tis true enough that noblemen are rarely blessed with the wits God gave a flea, but it does seem to me that the man has treated ye well enough, miss," Janet pointed out in a slow, cautious manner. "A sight better than we dared to hope for last eve, I would say."

Brianna hunched her shoulders at the undeniable truth in her companion's accusation. Pretending to be the next Duchess of Huntley was a considerable improvement over fighting off the advances of her disgusting stepfather.

Or even fleeing to the Continent with no set destination and no notion of how she was to survive.

That did not mean, however, she was not furious with Edmond and his determination to use her for his own mysterious purpose. Especially when it would be such a simple matter to take her to Stefan.

"I suppose," she finally muttered.

Easily sensing Brianna's tension, Janet moved to stand at her side, her expression concerned.

"What is it?" Her eyes abruptly widened. "Dear lord, did he force himself…"

"No. No, of course not. I may think Edmond the worse sort of scoundrel, but he would never rape a woman." She gave a short, humorless laugh. "He would never have to."

"True enough. They're few women who wouldn't want to welcome such a gent in their beds." Janet heaved an appreciative sigh before a speculative glint entered her eyes. "Of course, he's a mite too smooth for my taste. I prefer a man who's a bit rough around the edges."

It took a moment before Brianna realized that the maid was referring to Boris, a man definitely rough around the edges.

"Janet!" she breathed in shock.

"What?" The maid planted her hands on her hips. "He's a handsome enough brute, and when he's not stomping about breathing fire, he can be pleasant enough company. And if we're to be stuck here for the next few weeks, there's no reason not to have a little fun."

Brianna grimaced, struggling not to allow her opinion of Edmond to rub off on poor Boris. It could be that, beneath his rather brutal facade, he was a lovely man. Not bloody likely, but possible.

"Oh, we are definitely stuck here, Janet. At least for the time being."

"Has something happened while I was away?"

"It has not yet happened, but it soon will."

"What? What is it?"

Brianna shivered, the words tumbling from her lips without consideration to the impact they might have on her companion.

"Edmond is about to send notice of my engagement to the Duke of Huntley."

A shocked silence filled the chamber, but before Janet could find her voice and demand an explanation, there was the sound of approaching footsteps and what might have been the thump of a wooden cane on the carpet.

"No, no," a soft, but relentless female voice echoed through the silence. "This bedchamber, I believe."

"But, the master…" the rumbling voice of Boris began, only to be overruled by the twittering, unyielding female.

"Lavender is just so comforting, do you not think?"

Brianna hurried across her bedchamber, quite astonished to realize that she recognized that sweet voice.

Of all of Edmond's aunts, Lady Aberlane was by far Brianna's favorite. Oh, it was true she could be extremely annoying when she desired, but unlike most, Brianna was not fooled by the woman's vague, fluttering manner and preference for being dismissed as a silly old woman.

Beneath all the fluff was a rapier wit and an uncanny ability to see to the truth of any situation.

Which made Edmond's decision to call for her as a chaperone exceedingly strange. Surely he must know that the woman would not be deceived by his charade for a moment?

Reaching the door, Brianna watched Boris haul the large chest into the bedchamber across the hall before turning her attention to the tiny woman with a puff of silver hair and a heart-shaped face. Although it had been years since she had caught sight of the elder woman, Lady Aberlane did not appear to have changed a wit with her plain but well-tailored gray gown and large gold locket that held a miniature of her beloved husband. And of course, the ebony cane that she never seemed to actually use. At least not unless it was to smack the leg of some unfortunate soul who stirred her temper.

She had never been a lovely woman, but the faintly olive features were well-formed and there was a sweetness in her expression that more than compensated for any lack of beauty.

Perhaps sensing Brianna's presence, the woman slowly turned, a delighted smile touching her lips.

"Oh, hello, my dear," she breathed, her dark eyes twinkling. "Did I disturb you?"

"Not at all." Performing a deep curtsey, Brianna straightened with an answering smile. "Lady Aberlane, it is a pleasure to meet you again."

"Lovely, lovely Brianna." Lady Aberlane heaved a soft sigh. "So kind of you to remember an old lady."

Brianna chuckled. "Of course I remember. You always brought me the loveliest marzipans."

"A pretty treat, for a pretty girl." She tilted her head to the side, looking precisely like a quizzical bird. "And now, here you are, a grown lady engaged to my beloved Stefan."

"So I am. Quite a surprise for everyone, I would think."

There was a long pause, as if Lady Aberlane were giving the offhand words serious consideration. And no doubt she was. Despite Brianna's best intentions, she found it incredibly difficult to lie beneath that dark, penetrating gaze.

"Not a surprise precisely," she said slowly. "Stefan, after all, has always been very fond of you. Still…" A faint frown touched the wrinkled brow before Lady Aberlane was giving a shake of her head. "Well, never mind." She reached out to lightly pat Brianna's hand. "How delighted your father would have been. Oh, and your mother as well, of course."

Brianna smiled wryly. It had been the deepest wish of her parents that she wed into the Summerville family. Her father because he truly believed that Brianna would be happy and well cared for at Meadowland and her mother…well, Sylvia Quinn's motives had never been quite so honorable.

"Certainly my mother would have been pleased," Brianna muttered, a lingering bitterness in her voice. "It would have taken her at least a few years to have gambled away the Summerville fortune."

"Ah, yes." Lady Aberlane gave a click of her tongue. "Poor Sylvia. Such a beautiful, fragile creature. I always knew she should never have married your father."

Brianna stiffened at the subtle implication that her father was somehow to blame for her mother's despicable weakness. Fredrick Quinn had been the finest, most honorable gentleman that Brianna had ever known.

"He loved her very much," she retorted.

Lady Aberlane offered a sad smile. "Oh, yes…quite, my dear. And Sylvia loved Fredrick. But there are simply some restless souls who should not bind themselves to another. As much as they might wish to settle down and devote themselves to a family they cannot help but feel somehow imprisoned. Really, it is no wonder they seek excitement in unfortunate ways."

Brianna's lips thinned, recalling her mother's brittle gaiety that did not quite hide the discontent smoldering just below the surface. Perhaps Lady Aberlane was correct. Perhaps her mother was one of those people who could not be happy when confined by a husband and family. But that did not excuse the fact that she had gambled away her own fortune and then

Brianna's dowry, before wedding a hideous creature who became a danger to her own daughter.

Nothing could excuse that.

"More than merely unfortunate," Brianna said, sharply.

Once again Lady Aberlane reached out to pat Brianna's hand, her expression faintly dismayed.

"So stupid of me to bring up such a painful subject," she said. "Especially one that is all in the past."

"Yes. Yes, it was long ago." Brianna sucked in a deep breath, thrusting aside the pain of old wounds. It was futile to wish her mother could have been different. And it was most certainly futile to direct her ancient frustration toward sweet Lady Aberlane. "It was very kind of you to come and be my companion."

The elderly woman swiftly returned to her fluttering, although Brianna did not miss the hint of speculation in the dark eyes.

"No, no, my dear, I am deeply grateful for the invitation. I have been living much too quietly," she assured the younger woman. "It will be a wonderful diversion to be surrounded by society again. And of course, I always enjoy the pleasure of your company. We shall have a grand time together."

Brianna smiled wryly, more convinced than ever that the wily old fox missed nothing. She would bet her last quid that Lady Aberlane already suspected this was no simple engagement.

"It should at least be interesting," she murmured.

The woman smiled and gave Brianna a wink. "That it will, my sweet Brianna, that it will."

CHAPTER EIGHT

EDMOND CHOSE TO VACATE the town house and enjoy a quiet dinner and lovely bottle of burgundy at his brother's club. Situated on St. James's Street, the club designed by Henry Holland was a place of comfort with leather chairs and tables set about the Great Subscription Room that allowed a gentleman the opportunity to share a quiet conversation.

He told himself that it was necessary to follow Stefan's routine, not to mention that it would be beyond foolish to remain secluded in the town house when he could be out seeking information about his murderous cousin.

The foremost reason, however, was the necessity of being rid of the unnerving distraction of Miss Brianna Quinn.

How the devil was a gentleman to think clearly when his thoughts were consumed by the memory of satin skin and the enticing scent of lavender?

Unfortunately, distance seemed to do nothing to ease his aggravation, and at last conceding that there was nothing to be discovered at the quiet gentleman's club, Edmond had returned to the town house and the temptations that awaited him there.

The household was abed when he silently slipped through the front door, and climbing the staircase to his bedchambers, he was greeted by a thin, balding servant with a narrow face and shrewd black eyes awaiting his return.

Edmond smiled as the man hurried to assist him with his tightly fitted coat. The son of a Russian scholar, Nikolai was not only a skilled valet, but capable of deciphering the most for-

midable codes. On more than one occasion, he had assisted
Edmond in uncovering a plot intended to bring an end to Alexander Pavlovich's position as Czar.

Perhaps his finest talent, however, was his dislike for meaningless chitchat. Unless he had information to pass on, Nikolai
preferred a stoic silence.

Within moments, Edmond was stripped of his elegant attire
and wrapped in a brocade dressing gown. Pausing just long
enough to ensure that Edmond had no further need of his
services, Nikolai quietly slipped from the room, leaving
Edmond alone with his glass of brandy.

For a time, Edmond considered the wise notion of simply
seeking his bed. It was late, and Brianna was no doubt asleep.
She would hardly thank him for waking her at such an hour.

It was only a brief time, however, and draining the last of
the brandy, Edmond walked toward the far wall of his chamber,
then removed a Reynolds painting to reveal the hidden latch.
With a sharp tug, a portion of the wall opened to reveal the dark
passageway.

Pausing to pluck a lit candle from the mantle, he entered the
passageway and made his way the short distance to Brianna's
chambers. There were a few tense moments as he struggled to
recall the precise spot of the lever, then, after brushing aside the
years of dust, he was at last pushing open the narrow bit of wall.

Edmond made no sound as he stepped into the shadowed
bedchamber and closed the secret door behind him, but almost
as if capable of sensing his presence, Brianna rolled over on
the bed, her eyes snapping open in baffled shock.

"Edmond?" With an awkward motion, she sat up in the
middle of the bed, holding the covers to her chest.

Edmond sucked in a sharp breath at the sight of her.

Christ, but she was exquisite.

Even with her astonishing hair in a tight braid, it gleamed
with autumn glory in the light of his candle. And her face…so
elegantly carved that it appeared to be the work of a magnifi-

cent artist rather than the luck of nature. His attention shifted to the pure green eyes that revealed the relentless spirit that smoldered within her.

A spirit that was as captivating as her beauty.

Blushing beneath his intense scrutiny, Brianna nervously dampened her lips, wrenching a groan from Edmond's throat.

"How did you…"

"Shh," he commanded as he crossed to perch on the edge of the bed, setting the candle on a French lacquered side table.

She pressed herself against the headboard, clutching the blankets even tighter. Absurd woman. As if a tiny bit of space and a few scraps of cloth were going to protect her.

"How did you get into my room?" she demanded again, although in a rasping whisper.

"My grandfather had secret corridors installed during the Reign of Terror in France. I believe he feared that it was only a matter of time before the English peasants instigated a similar uprising." Edmond smiled wryly. "He was quite prepared to flee, rather than stand his ground and have his head lopped off. A wise, if not very courageous, decision."

"Secret corridors? How very convenient."

Before she could guess his intention, Edmond shifted to plant a hand on either side of her hips, not only preventing her escape but bringing him closer to the sweet, lush mouth that had haunted his thoughts all day.

"I had no idea how convenient until tonight," he murmured softly.

He watched her visibly resist the urge to wet her lips again. Clearly, she sensed the hunger surging through his tense body.

"What do you desire?" she asked.

Edmond chuckled, moving forward to steal a kiss before moving back to watch the blush deepen on her ivory cheeks.

"That is a foolish question, *ma souris*. You know precisely what I desire."

"Have you taken leave of your senses? Your aunt is just

across the corridor. If she even suspects you are here, I will be ruined beyond all repair."

"Which is precisely why I used the secret doorway," he drawled. "No one will ever know I was here unless you are foolish enough to attract unwanted attention."

Brianna sniffed in disdain at his logic. "You can use all the secret doorways you like, Edmond, but nothing escapes your Aunt Letty's notice." Her gaze narrowed in suspicion. "You must know she is far and away the most intelligent of all your relatives. She will never believe this farce. Indeed, I doubt very much she will even believe you are Stefan."

Edmond shrugged. "She can be tediously insightful."

"Then why did you choose her as my companion?" Brianna pressed, her brows drawing together as he considered refusing to answer the simple question. "Edmond?"

"Because I knew that you liked her."

"Oh."

Taking swift advantage of her obvious bemusement, Edmond shifted even closer. Close enough to feel the soft curve of her thigh against his hip and the brush of her breath on his cheek.

"You sound surprised."

She struggled to summon her usual prickly nature, but it was obvious she was still caught off guard, and not a little bewildered.

"Why shouldn't I be? You have not devoted much effort to pleasing me."

Edmond breathed deeply of her sweet, lavender scent, his body already stirring in anticipation.

"On the contrary, Brianna, I have exerted a great effort into pleasing you," he retorted, his voice thickening. "It has been you that has halted those efforts."

Edmond sensed her tremble, even as she sought to deny the powerful attraction between them.

"You mean pleasing yourself."

"If that is what you believe, then allow me to prove otherwise."

With a smooth motion he shifted to capture her lips, his tongue urging hers to part and allow him entry into the sweet depths.

She trembled, briefly yielding to his soft ravishment before her hands were lifting to press against his chest.

"Edmond…no. You must not do this."

"Actually, I must." Denied her lips, Edmond allowed his mouth to trail along the line of her jaw to discover the sensitive hollow behind her ear. "I have been aching to touch you again since we were so rudely interrupted by your stepfather."

Brianna sighed softly, her head tilting back to allow him greater access. A part of her, however, refused to surrender to the inevitable.

"I think there has been quite enough touching."

"Oh, no, not nearly enough." He trailed a path of kisses down the curve of her neck, lingering on the frantic pulse that beat at the base of her throat. "As you will soon agree."

"You are so certain of your skill?"

He chuckled at her attempt to sound disdainful. "I am certain of this fire that burns between us. This is not about skill, but sweet—" he lightly nipped her shoulder "—aching…" His tongue traced along the edge of the tiny ribbon that held up her nightgown. "Need."

Her moan filled the air as her hands slipped beneath the robe to lay flat against the bare skin of his chest. Edmond jerked as if he had been burned. And in a way it felt as if he had. As if her mere touch were branding him in some indefinable way.

Ignoring the dangerous sensations, Edmond gently tugged the covers lower. She briefly resisted, but Edmond was swift to distract her with tiny butterfly kisses spread over her face, until he was able to pull the covers away from her shivering body.

It was only when the offending blankets were shoved off the bed that Edmond at last eased back to savor the sight of her.

"Mon dieu," he rasped, his gaze traveling over the slender form that was perfectly revealed within the champagne night-

gown. The bits of lace and satin were barely decent. "Your maid possesses a wicked sense of humor."

"What?" her voice was vague, as if she were having difficulty forming the words.

Edmond smiled, sensing her need was overcoming her virginal reluctance.

"This gown was obviously created to stir a man's deepest fantasies."

Running a reverent hand over the smooth skin of her shoulder, Edmond tugged aside the gold satin ribbon that held the gown in place. It was a simple act, one he had performed on more occasions than he could recall, but never before had he felt the strange vibration that echoed deep inside him. It was as though a perfect symphony was being played between them. A stirring, sweeping tidal wave that was building to a mighty crescendo.

Edmond closed his eyes as he captured her lips in a raw, demanding kiss. This was no time for absurd fancies. Nothing was going to distract him from the beckoning pleasure.

Drinking deeply of her willing lips, Edmond brushed aside the remaining ribbon and lowered her bodice so his hands could cup the gentle rise of her breasts. His shaft instantly swelled as Brianna moaned, his fingers finding the peak of her nipples to tease them into hardened nubs.

Her hands jerkily moved over his chest, as if torn between the desire to explore his flesh and the tentative embarrassment of any virgin. Edmond smoothly shrugged off his robe in silent encouragement, murmuring his approval as her touch became bolder, sliding over his tense muscles and down the flat of his stomach.

Confident the minx was suitably distracted, Edmond eased himself onto the bed, stretching out on the fine linen sheets beside her. His hands compulsively reached out to continue their voyage down the slender line of her body, smoothing the devilish nightgown out of his path and at last tossing it onto the floor. He needed to feel the satin heat of her skin, to drown in the glorious scent of lavender.

Christ, she was so slender, so delicate beneath his fingers. And yet there was a heat in that tiny form that made his blood churn with excitement.

"You are…perfect," he muttered, his mouth skimming over her cheek and down her jaw before make a determined path to the rosy tips of her breasts.

Brianna gasped as he drew one of the nipples between his lips, using his tongue to make her squirm in pleasure.

"Dear heavens," she yelped, her nails biting into his shoulders until they threatened to draw blood.

"Shh, *ma souris,* you must be very, very quiet," he chided, even as a flare of dark satisfaction raced through him.

Whatever else this woman might feel toward him, she could not hide her delight in his touch.

Returning his attention to the puckered nipple, Edmond laved it with exquisite care, savoring her soft cries as his hand moved along the curve of her hip and then over the slight swell of her stomach. Her muscles tensed beneath his questing touch, but she made no effort to halt his caress. Indeed, her hands shifted to plunge into his hair as her ragged breaths filled the shadowed chamber.

Edmond needed no further encouragement. Shifting until he was pressed flush against the side of her body, he covered her lips in a fierce kiss, as his fingers slipped through the silken curls at the juncture of her legs and at last found the damp heat he sought.

Her scream of astonishment would have wakened the dead if Edmond had not captured it with his mouth. Smiling against her lips, he slid his finger through the satin cleft, seeking the tiny jewel of her pleasure with his thumb.

Stroking her with a slow, steady rhythm, Edmond pressed his aching erection against her thigh. He wanted to sheathe himself between her legs. He wanted his cock buried deep inside her when she found her release. But he had made a promise before ever entering Brianna's bedchamber.

Never again would she accuse him of desiring only his own

satisfaction. After tonight, she would understand that the bliss to be found in this bed would be entirely mutual.

Her body began to arch as she wound her arms around his neck. She whimpered softly against his lips, clearly caught in the throes of her rising climax.

Quickening the stroke of his finger, Edmond growled low in his throat, pumping his arousal against her hip. *Mon dieu.* Who knew that stirring an innocent to orgasm could be so... erotic? He was intent on her pleasure, but the moment he felt her stiffen with release, he was overcome with his own orgasm that shook him to his very soul.

Edmond continued to pleasure her, until her body at last melted against his with a lethargic satisfaction. Only then did he pull back to study the sated expression and the rather stunned green eyes.

"That was..."

"Just the beginning," he finished with a wicked smile.

DESPITE HIS LATE NIGHT, and the fact he had yet to deflower his beautiful fiancée, Edmond was in a surprisingly cheerful mood as he made his way down to the breakfast room the next morning.

As expected, he found the pretty saffron and gold room empty except for the two towering footmen who stood at attendance near the long side table. Although Edmond had possessed less than half the staff that Stefan could claim, they were all well-trained and quite capable of keeping the household in perfect working order for at least a few weeks. They were also loyal to a fault, highly discreet and capable of dealing with any danger that might threaten.

Moving to the side table, Edmond filled a plate with slices of the freshly cured ham, eggs, toast and marmalade before taking his seat at the head of the table. The footman moved to pour him the hot coffee he preferred to tea, then placed an ironed copy of *The Morning Post* next to his plate.

With a grimace, he forced himself to skim through the paragraphs of the latest scandals and upcoming events. Although he had hired Chesterfield to keep an eye upon Howard Summerville, he intended to make sure that he soon crossed paths with his cousin. The announcement of his betrothal would be in the newspaper, but a sapskull like Howard could hardly be expected to actually read the thing. It would be Edmond's duty to ensure that the man realized the Duke of Huntley was on the precipice of marriage.

That surely would provoke a swift reaction.

Only paying a brief attention to the various speculations of which hostess had provided the finest refreshments at their soirees and which debutante had been favored by the attentions of Lord Mallory, Edmond nearly overlooked the fleeting mention of a gentleman named Viktor Kazakov arriving in London and taking rooms at Pultney's Hotel in Piccadilly.

It was not unusual for a wealthy Russian nobleman to visit London. Or even for that nobleman to choose to stay at a hotel rather than accept the King's hospitality. But Edmond was well aware that Alexander Pavlovich had ordered Viktor to Siberia after he had been overheard raising a toast to the imminent death of the Czar.

Under questioning, Kazakov had desperately claimed he was drunk and merely jesting, but Alexander had no tolerance for seeds of discontent among his Court. Kazakov had been banished to Siberia under the watch of Alexander Pavlovich's own Foot Guard.

So how did he slip unnoticed from Siberia? Edmond wondered, and what the devil was he doing in London?

Knowing this was yet another distraction that he did not need, Edmond could not resist calling for pen and paper so he could scribble a swift note to the Russian ambassador.

He had just dispatched one of the footmen with the missive when the door to the breakfast room was pressed open and Lady Aberlane tottered into the room.

Swiftly rising to his feet, Edmond smiled wryly as the elder woman crossed the floor, only occasionally remembering to use her ebony cane as she smiled at him with obvious delight.

"Good morning, my dear." She came to a halt at his side, waiting until he had bent downward so she could plant a kiss on his cheek before taking the seat he held out for her.

"Good morning, Aunt Letty." Ensuring she was settled, Edmond nodded toward the footman who began filling a plate with an assortment of food, then took his own seat. "I hope that you have been made comfortable?"

"Oh, quite comfortable. It is always such a pleasure to be invited to Huntley House." She smiled as the footman set the plate on the table in front of her, then with that fluttering charm she abused with ruthless efficiency, she gently cleared her throat. "That will be all for now, you may leave us."

The servant waited for Edmond's grudging nod before giving a deep bow and leaving the room. Once alone, Edmond regarded his relative with a wary unease.

As Brianna had pointed out last eve, his Aunt Letty was not only annoyingly intelligent, but perceptive as well. He did not doubt that he would have to reveal at least a portion of the truth to ease her suspicions.

"Now then." The elder woman studied him with that dark, piercing gaze. "Perhaps you will be good enough to tell me why you are pretending to be Stefan, and why in heaven's name you are risking Brianna's reputation by announcing this ridiculous engagement?"

Edmond gave a short laugh. Perceptive, indeed. And quite prepared to speak her mind.

Pushing aside his empty plate, Edmond gave a small shrug. "It was to save Brianna's reputation that I announced the ridiculous engagement. She could hardly remain beneath my roof, or rather Stefan's roof, without the protection of an impending marriage."

Lady Aberlane glanced toward the delicately carved and scrolled ceiling above them. "And a lovely one it is, but why is she beneath your roof at all? Does she not reside with her stepfather?"

Edmond's expression hardened as he gave a brief, clipped explanation of Thomas Wade and his nefarious attempt to force Brianna to Norfolk. His aunt listened in silence, her lips thinning with utter disgust as Edmond revealed Wade's intrusion into the town house and Edmond's belief that he would continue to be a threat so long as he remained obsessed with Brianna.

"Poor child," his aunt muttered, shaking her head. "I always suspected that nasty man was not to be trusted with such a beautiful young woman." She abruptly banged her cane on the Aubusson carpet. "Whatever was Fredrick thinking? He must have known better than to leave his daughter in the care of Sylvia. She was never fit to be a mother."

Edmond grimaced at the memory of the beautiful, temperamental woman who had made no pretense of her lack of motherly affection. It was little wonder that Brianna had so often slipped from her lonely house to visit Meadowland.

"You will get no argument from me," he muttered, oddly annoyed that Sylvia was dead and out of the reach of his punishment. "But you need not fear Thomas Wade troubling Brianna any further. I intend to deal with him when the appropriate moment presents itself."

She sent him a stern glance at the unmistakable edge of lethal intent in his voice.

"You do not plan anything foolish, do you, Edmond?"

"I am rarely foolish, Aunt Letty."

"No, that is true enough." There was a silence as the woman studied him with that disquieting gaze. At last, she heaved a small sigh and nodded her head, as if accepting that Thomas Wade deserved his inevitable fate. "Well, I must say that I am pleased you have taken Brianna away from that horrid creature, but I do not understand why you insisted on keeping her here. You know you could have sent her to me, or better yet, to Meadowland."

He shrugged, surprised by the dark flare of anger at the mere mention of Brianna being taken from his custody.

"I will merely say that her presence was an unexpected windfall that I was swift to use to my best advantage."

Letty blinked at his clipped, unapologetic explanation. "Whatever do you mean?"

"That I cannot tell you. Nor can I reveal why I am here under the guise of Stefan." His expression was grim. "All I can say is that Stefan is in danger and I will protect him. No matter what I have to do or who I have to use to accomplish my goal."

There was none of the vague fluttering as the elder woman leaned forward with a worried frown.

"Stefan in danger?"

"Yes, I fear so."

She clicked her tongue. "Well, of course, you must do whatever necessary. And you know that you need only ask, if I can do anything to assist you."

Edmond smiled, knowing that his aunt's promise was not just empty words. Not only was her position as Lady Aberlane highly respected among society, but her late husband had been a skilled politician who could claim the friendship of the most powerful gentlemen in the world.

"Thank you." He reached out to give her tiny hand a squeeze of gratitude. "I shall keep your offer in mind."

The dark eyes narrowed, clearly accepting his need to protect Stefan, and yet not entirely satisfied with his treatment of his young fiancée.

"I do hope, my dearest Edmond, that you realize Brianna Quinn is not the hardened, sophisticated sort of female you are used to keeping company with." She tapped a gnarled finger on the table. "She could be very easily hurt."

Edmond abruptly rose to his feet. He might have need of Lady Aberlane's presence, but that did not mean he intended to be lectured as if he were fresh from the nursery.

"It is not my intention to harm her," he said, the words clipped.

"Not your intention, perhaps, but…"

"I fear that I cannot linger this morning, I have several appointments today. If you would be so kind, I would appreciate you accompanying Brianna to the modiste today. I am certain you must know which are favored by the most fashionable young ladies of society."

"Do you intend to take Brianna out in society?"

Edmond looked down at Lady Aberlane, a smile playing on his lips. "It would appear odd if we did not attend at least a few functions, do you not think? Thankfully, Stefan's notorious distaste for London society will allow us to keep them limited."

Her lips thinned. "And what do you intend to do with Brianna once this danger to Stefan has passed? Will you send her to Meadowland where she belongs?"

"And why the devil would you think she belongs there?" he snapped, before he could halt the words.

"Stefan is her guardian."

"Then he should have done his duty and kept her out of the clutches of Thomas Wade."

Something that was strangely close to satisfaction glittered in Lady Aberlane's dark eyes.

"As you have done?"

"As I have done." Edmond offered a stiff bow. "Good day."

CHAPTER NINE

FOR THE NEXT THREE DAYS, Brianna was fitted for the obscene number of gowns that Lady Aberlane insisted were necessary for the future Duchess of Huntley.

Morning gowns that were composed of jaconet muslin, as well as figured silks that were trimmed with lace and braid and ornamental satin flowers. Walking gowns with matching spencers and ermine-lined cloaks. There was a carriage gown in a ruby velvet and deliciously warm muff, not to mention an evening gown in a rich brown with gold buckles and a striped rose silk with a border of double tulle.

And, of course, no wardrobe would be complete without the exquisite satin ball gowns that cost enough to make Brianna's head spin.

Not since her father's untimely death had Brianna possessed such a profusion of elegant, sophisticated dresses.

It was not that her mother wished to keep Brianna in rags, but Sylvia had rarely realized that her daughter might be in need of a new wardrobe, and when she did, she preferred to have her own castoff dresses altered. The precious pin money she received from Thomas was needed to pay her gambling debts.

More than once, Brianna wondered if she should perhaps feel guilty at spending Edmond's fortune with such reckless disregard. Granted he was the one who was forcing her into this charade of an engagement, but she *had* thrust her way into this house.

Such thoughts, however, were easily dismissed as she

slowly realized that for the first time in over a year, she felt… almost happy.

Of course, if she were being perfectly honest, she would acknowledge that it was not the pretty gowns and shawls and feathered bonnets that brought a small smile to her lips as she sat at her dressing table and allowed Janet to fuss with her hair.

No, it was the slow, undeniable easing of the brutal grip of fear that had held her captive since her mother's death. For the first time, Thomas Wade could not reach her. Not so long as she was safely hidden in the vast town house.

Despite the smaller staff, the London mansion was nothing less than a fortress. And since she was not allowed out the door without the hulking presence of Boris, she never had to worry about enjoying her shopping expeditions throughout London. Her stepfather was a fool, but not even he was stupid enough to dare an attempted kidnapping while she was under the constant eye of the ominous guard.

Then, there was Lady Aberlane's pleasurable company. Who would not be distracted from their troubles by the woman's charming prattle? It had been so long since Brianna had enjoyed the company of anyone beyond her faithful maid that it was a genuine joy to simply listen to the latest gossip over a cup of tea.

All quite reasonable explanations for her budding sense of comfort, but deep inside, she could not shake the sensation that it was directly connected to Edmond Summerville.

Ridiculous, of course. She had barely caught sight of the aggravating man over the past few days.

And yet, at the oddest moments she would recall Edmond as he hauled the bleating Thomas from his home, or when he flatly refused to allow her to leave the town house without Boris at her side, or holding her tightly in his arms as she shivered with her first taste of passion….

Brianna brought a sharp halt to her wayward thoughts. It had been three nights since she had tasted of Edmond's practiced seduction. Three nights of dwelling incessantly on the astonishing sensation of his fingers touching her with such intimate skill, of recalling the explosion of pleasure that had left her weak and shaken long after he had retreated through the secret door.

Tonight would be her first to brave London society. She would need her wits firmly about her if it were not to end in disaster.

"There, now," Janet murmured, stepping to the side to admire Brianna's hair, coiled into an intricate knot atop her head with tiny curls brushing against her temple. "Perfect."

"Hardly perfect, but it is a beautiful gown." Rising to her feet, Brianna smoothed her hands down the white lace gown worn over an Indigo-blue sarsnet slip. The bodice was cut far lower than any she had worn before, with full, puffed sleeves set well off her shoulders. At the hem were tiny satin roses matching those threaded through her auburn curls. "Lady Aberlane possesses exquisite taste."

"'Tis not the dress that will be attracting the attention of the ton, no matter how fine it might be."

"That is true enough, Janet. There will not be a soul in all of London who is not avid to catch a glimpse of the Duke of Huntley's fiancée. I shall feel like an animal in the Royal menagerie." She pressed a hand to her stomach. "Let us hope that I shall not do anything to embarrass poor Stefan."

Janet snorted as she studied Brianna with her hands on her full hips. "I meant that ye have never been more beautiful. As lovely as a vision."

"A vision, indeed," a dark voice murmured from the doorway.

With a squeak of surprise, Brianna whirled as Edmond calmly entered her private chamber.

She wanted to believe it was surprise that was causing her heart to leap and her body to tingle with a rash of excitement, but surprise could not explain why her gaze lingered on his tall form, which was shown to magnificent advantage by the white knee breeches and fitted black jacket that had been matched with a silver waistcoat. Or why her fingers yearned to run a path through the satin darkness of his hair. Or why she was wishing that he had entered her bedchambers for something other than escorting her to a soiree.

A blush stained her cheeks as she realized that Edmond's dark, knowing gaze had not missed the emotions flitting over her expressive features, and that he was well aware of her thoughts.

"Really, Edmond, you cannot simply walk into my private rooms," she snapped, annoyed that she was flustered by a mere glance.

The dark gaze never wavered from her flushed countenance. "Leave us," he commanded the hovering maid.

Predictably, Janet refused to budge until Brianna gave a slow nod of her head.

"It is fine, Janet."

Janet offered Edmond an evil glare as she strode toward the door. "Oh, aye. It had best be fine, or you'll be answering to me," she muttered.

A dark brow arched in genuine astonishment. "Did your maid just threaten me?"

"Yes, I believe she did."

"And just what does a female half my size and weight believe she can do to me?"

"Do not underestimate my maid, Edmond. Janet is not only cunning, but she happens to be the daughter of one of the most feared criminal lords in all of London. I do not doubt she could call upon any number of ruffians to do her bidding."

He appeared more curious than terrified by her dire words. "Then why did she not call upon them to do away with Thomas Wade?"

Brianna wrapped her arms around her waist, shuddering at the mention of her stepfather, remembering how terribly tempting it had been to give in to Janet's urging to have Thomas murdered in his sleep.

"Because I refused to allow her to do so," she confessed, her voice hoarse.

"Why?"

"If I desired Thomas Wade's head mashed in, then I should have done it myself. Why should someone else risk the gallows for me?"

"So independent, *ma souris?*" he drawled, prowling forward.

Her chin tilted at his hint of mockery. "I have discovered that it is far too dangerous to be anything but independent. Thankfully I will soon be able to claim my inheritance and I shall never be under the authority of another again." Her gaze was steady. "I cannot wait for that day."

"Your inheritance?"

"Yes." She gave a lift of her shoulder. "My father left a portion of my dowry in funds that could not be touched by my mother. I shall be able to access the money when I turn three and twenty. 'Tis not a large amount by the Duke of Huntley's standards, but it will be enough to allow me to rent a modest home and keep a staff." She sucked in a deep breath. "Janet and I will at last be safe."

The hint of amusement vanished from his dark eyes, almost as if he were annoyed by her response.

"That is absurd," he gritted. "Not everyone intends you harm."

"Perhaps not harm, but everyone is certainly anxious to use me for their own purpose." She deliberately paused. "You included, Edmond."

The aquiline nose flared, the dark eyes smoldering with a dangerous emotion.

"Ah, yes, my nefarious purpose." He pointed a finger toward the chair directly before her dressing table. "Have a seat."

"Why?"

"You are here to do my bidding, are you not?" He stepped closer. "Now, have a seat."

"Fine." Refusing to indulge in a struggle she was destined to lose, Brianna turned to the chair and sat down with an angry flounce. "Someday, Edmond, you are going to encounter someone you cannot bully and—" Her words were wrenched away as Edmond moved directly behind her and she felt a cool weight gliding over her skin. Glancing in the mirror, her breath tangled in her throat at the brilliant flash of gemstones that encircled her neck. "Good Lord." Her gaze lifted to study Edmond's reflection. "These are the Huntley emeralds."

His face was unreadable as his fingers stroked the bare slope of her shoulders.

Her hand lifted to touch the priceless jewels, her heart giving an odd twist of pain. Deep in her soul, she knew that the gems and all they represented were intended for another woman. The sort of woman who could offer the grace and poise that the position of Duchess of Huntley demanded. The sort of woman she could never be.

"No, this is not right. I cannot wear these," she whispered, not comprehending why she should be battling an absurd desire to cry.

His stirring temper flared at her soft refusal. "The setting is a bit old-fashioned, I will grant you, but they are still the finest collection of emeralds in all of England," he said, the lethal edge in his tone stirring the hair on the nape of her neck. "There are few women who would balk at wearing them around their neck. Quite the opposite, in fact."

She grimly refused to wilt beneath the smoldering displeasure. Even as a young gentleman, Edmond had made a habit of bending others to his will by the simple force of his personality. The only way to keep from being swept along the tidal wave of his power was to dig in her heels and refuse to budge.

It was something she was rather good at.

"They are nothing less than perfect, Edmond, as you well know." Rising to her feet, she turned to confront him squarely. "But these are for the next Duchess of Huntley, not some mere pretender. It would be wrong for anyone but Stefan's wife to be seen in them."

"They are stones, *ma souris,* they will hardly care whether you are destined to be the future Duchess of Huntley or not," he mocked.

"No, but all of society will recall seeing them upon me. It would tarnish them for Stefan's future wife."

"Tarnish them?"

"Yes."

"You…" With an obvious effort, Edmond controlled his flare of temper, and with an exaggerated bow, he turned to head for the door. "Since I cannot decide whether to strangle you or bed you, I shall instead leave you to finish your dressing. Please be good enough to join me in the foyer when you are done."

HIDING IN THE SHADOWS of the upper landing, Janet watched as Edmond Summerville settled a beaded cashmere shawl around the shoulders of her mistress.

The lean male body appeared to be tense with a tightly coiled anger, but his hands were remarkably gentle as he stroked Brianna's arms, his head lowered as if attempting to breathe in the scent of his delicate companion.

Janet was well aware that Lord Edmond's manner toward his brother's ward had been overly intimate from the moment they had entered the town house. There could be no doubt he had every intention of trying to seduce her, and judging by Brianna's reaction to the handsome gentleman, he might very well accomplish his goal.

But Janet was more bothered when she witnessed Lord Edmond glare at the footman who stepped forward to assist Brianna when she dropped her painted ivory fan. He was possessive, almost aggressively so, as if he considered her his personal property.

Which was far more dangerous than mere lust.

Wondering if they had managed to leap from the frying pan into the fire, Janet was caught off guard when a pair of strong arms wrapped around her waist from behind and hauled her back from the balustrade.

"And what do you think you're doing spying upon my master?" a rumbling male voice demanded against her ear.

Janet twisted until she could face her large captor, lifting her hand to smack against the hard, massive chest.

"Oh, stop that," she hissed.

Clearly expecting a very different reaction, Boris dropped his arms.

"Stop what?"

"Pretending that ye can barely speak English." She folded her arms over her chest, struggling not to notice the flutter of her heart as the candlelight played over his strong features. Her father had taught her from the cradle never to be swayed by a handsome face or pair of pretty eyes, even if they were the exact shade of a cloudless sky. "I may be from the stews but I ain't stupid," she warned, her lips thinning with annoyance at his attempt to deceive her. "I know an educated gent, especially one who happens to be a soldier, when one crosses me path."

He stilled, his eyes narrowing. "Do you?"

"Aye."

He leaned downward, his breath brushing her cheek in a warm caress. "It can oft times be dangerous to see too much."

"Is that a threat?" she demanded even as she shivered in pleasure.

"Are you frightened?" he asked, his accent not nearly so thick.

Janet tilted her chin with a sniff. "By the likes of you? Bah. I've faced cutthroats that could make you weep in fear. Me own father is one."

His lips twitched with grudging amusement as he straightened and peered down the length of his nose at her stubborn face.

"You did not answer my question," he said. "Why are you spying on my master?"

She saw no reason to lie. "I don't happen to trust Lord Edmond Summerville."

"You question his honor?"

"I question the way he looks at Miss Quinn."

"They way he looks at her?"

"As if he intends something wicked."

"She is a beautiful woman. Of course he intends something wicked."

"If that's meant to be amusing, it falls short of the mark."

His hard features softened as Boris stepped forward and allowed his hands to lightly trail down her arms. "What man would not intend something wicked when he is offered such temptation?"

"Here now, ye watch yer hands or—"

Her brave words were brought to an effective end as Boris abruptly yanked her forward and crushed her lips in a kiss that made her toes curl in sweet anticipation.

EDMOND STUDIED BRIANNA from across the crowded salon, his body predictably hard with frustrated longing. Even surrounded by London's most famous beauties, she managed to glow with a stunning splendor that would steal the wits of any gentleman.

Of course, her newfound sophistication did nothing to soften her prickly personality, he wryly acknowledged, recalling their earlier confrontation.

At the time, he had been besieged by a confusion of emotions that all battled for supremacy. Fury that she would dare to defy his wishes. A sharp, aching desire to pull her into his arms and damn the rest of the world to Jericho.

And a fierce satisfaction at the knowledge that she possessed no deep longing for Stefan's jewels.

It was that last emotion that disturbed him. Fury and frustrated desire were common enough when in Brianna's presence. Christ, they plagued him even when he wasn't in her presence. A fact he had discovered during the past three days of doing everything possible to avoid her company.

But why should he be pleased that she could readily dismiss the undoubted temptations that came part and parcel with the position of Duchess of Huntley?

"Ah, there you are, your Grace."

The curvaceous brunette, wearing a dress of Pomona green

edged in velvet and sparkling with diamonds, halted at Edmond's side. Handsome rather than pretty, Lady Montgomery was the most skilled of all the London political hostesses. Indeed, no one doubted that Lord Montgomery's position in the government was entirely due to her efforts.

Edmond offered a faint dip of his head.

"Lady Montgomery."

The teasing smile on her full lips didn't hide the curiosity that shimmered deep in her eyes.

"I am not entirely sure how I can ever thank you," she murmured.

"Thank me?"

"Your presence at my humble soiree has ensured that my position among society has increased significantly. There will not be a hostess in all of London who is not gnashing her teeth in envy that you chose to introduce your fiancée beneath my roof."

Edmond did not miss the woman's air of smug pleasure at having accomplished such a coup.

"Any gratitude must go to my aunt." He turned his head to regard the elegant woman who hovered protectively at Brianna's side, ready to steer her young charge through the dangerous waters of society with smooth efficiency. "She assured me that Miss Quinn would be made to feel welcome among your guests."

"But, of course, Miss Quinn will be made welcome." Lady Montgomery flashed him a covert glance. "A truly lovely young lady. And such charming manners. 'Tis no wonder she managed to steal your elusive heart, your Grace."

Edmond smiled, enjoying the pleasurable heat that raced through his body as his gaze returned to linger on his fiancée.

"She is exquisite."

Lady Montgomery flicked her painted gauze fan open with a practiced motion. "It is a pity about her mother's marriage to that…" There was a delicate pause. "Nasty tradesman, of course. There are bound to be a few vicious tongues that will remind the ton of *that* unfortunate connection, I fear."

"They would be wise to direct their vicious tongues toward topics that do not include Miss Quinn," he replied, his tone edged with an unmistakable warning. "My family would be most displeased with anyone who breathed the name of Thomas Wade and my fiancée in the same sentence." A layer of ice coated his voice. "Indeed, as far as I am concerned, Thomas Wade no longer exists."

"Ah, yes. Yes, I see." Lady Montgomery appeared temporarily startled by the formidable power that smoldered about the usually placid Duke of Huntley, then she gave a rueful laugh. "For a gentleman who rarely mingles among society, your Grace, you do possess a remarkable talent for comprehending how to bend us to your will."

"My only desire is to ensure that Miss Quinn is judged upon her own fine merits, not upon the unfortunate choices of her mother." His expression unwittingly softened, his gaze sweeping over Brianna's delicate profile. "She has suffered enough for Sylvia's weaknesses."

Something that might have been surprise rippled over Lady Montgomery's handsome features before she regained her practiced smile.

"Quite understandable. It was wise to choose Lady Aberlane to sponsor her into society."

"Aunt Letty would never have forgiven me had I chosen someone else to stand as Miss Quinn's sponsor."

Lady Montgomery gave a charming laugh. "That is true enough." Her head tilted to one side. "But why would you insist on having your cousin included?"

Edmond absently toyed with his brother's heavy gold signet ring, which he had slipped on before leaving the town house. He had known it was bound to create a stir of curiosity when he had sent the note to Lady Montgomery requesting the presence of Howard Summerville at the soiree. Still, it was worth any raised brows for the opportunity to witness his beloved cousin's reaction to his engagement firsthand.

"As much as I regret the notion, they are family," he said, his tone dismissive.

Lady Montgomery was far from satisfied. "Yes, but the estrangement between you has been well-known for years. No one would have thought it odd if you had chosen to exclude him from the guest list."

Edmond gave a vague lift of his shoulder. "My fiancée possesses a far kinder heart than either my brother or myself. She dislikes the notion of a rift in the family."

"Ah."

Having endured enough of the less than subtle probing, Edmond tilted his head toward the thin, swarthy gentleman in a far corner who was drinking the expensive champagne as if it were cheap gin.

"With that thought in mind, I suppose I had best seek out my cousin and extend a hand of peace." He dipped his head toward his hostess. "If you will excuse me?"

Lady Montgomery smiled, although her speculative expression lingered. "Of course."

Shrugging aside the woman's curiosity, Edmond moved smoothly across the pale rose and ivory room, occasionally nodding toward the more powerful gentlemen who circled the room, and firmly ignoring the inviting glances from their wives. Edmond might readily enjoy the delectable attentions of a bored wife; Stefan, however, would never take a married woman to his bed.

CHAPTER TEN

PROPPED AGAINST SATIN WALL panels, Howard Summerville, his dark hair already tousled and his cravat drooping, was blearily eying the passing guests. Edmond frowned as he halted at the man's side, acknowledging that his cousin appeared more pathetic than dangerous.

Of course, looks quite often were deceiving.

He had encountered women with the faces of angels who would happily slide a dagger in his back.

"Good evening, Howard," he murmured.

With an obvious effort, Summerville focused his gaze on the towering Edmond.

"Oh. There you are, Huntley," he slurred.

"So I am."

After a brief struggle with gravity, the gentleman managed to push himself away from the wall, his narrow face flushed, and his dark eyes glittering with a hectic light.

"You have some bloody nerve," he growled. "I have half a mind to plant you a facer."

Ah. Edmond hid a pleased smile. This was the reaction he had been hoping to provoke.

"I should be a great deal more concerned if you were not so cast to the wind you can barely stand, Howard," he mocked.

The flush deepened with anger. "If I am, it is entirely your fault."

"My powers are even greater than I ever suspected." Edmond flicked a dismissive glance over his cousin's rumpled attire. "I had no notion I could force a gentleman into his cups from across the entire width of a room."

"Ha." Howard waved his arm, nearly toppling over a terra-cotta bust of Charles II. "You know quite well why I am furious with you."

Edmond grasped the fool by the elbow and steered him toward the French doors leading onto a narrow balcony.

"Perhaps we should discuss this someplace where we can speak without creating fodder for the rumormongers."

"There is a library…"

"Actually, I prefer the balcony." Edmond continued to chart a ruthless course past the startled guests.

"The balcony." Howard stumbled over his feet, only kept upright by Edmond's firm grip. "Damnation, Huntley, it is freezing out there."

"Perhaps it will help to clear your muddled brain." Edmond cursed as his cousin nearly tumbled them both over a rosewood stool. "Not that it would make a great deal of difference," he muttered.

"What did you say?"

"Nothing of importance. Come along." Pausing to yank open the doors, Edmond shoved his cousin onto the stone balcony that overlooked the small garden, and pulled the door shut behind them.

Both men shivered as the thick fog swirled through the air before cloaking them in its clammy chill.

"Bloody hell." Hunching his shoulders, Howard glared at the torches set on the balustrade, making a dismal attempt to fight back the darkness. "English weather at its finest."

Edmond silently agreed. Even accustomed to the brutal weather that Russia could offer, this clinging dampness was unpleasant to endure. Still, it kept the other guests warmly tucked in the town house and allowed them a few moments of privacy.

Taking a moment to light a thin cheroot with one of the torches, he turned back to study his cousin's petulant expression.

"Perhaps you will be kind enough to explain why you wish to plant me a facer?"

"Ha. You know very well why."

Edmond shrugged, turning so he could watch the dim light play over his companion's shadowed features.

"I presume it has something to do with my recent engagement?"

"By God, of course it does."

"Surely you must have known that I would eventually wed? After all, the most important duty of a Duke is to produce an heir."

Running a hand through his untidy hair, Howard laughed with bitter amusement. "To be honest, I hoped you were the sort who possessed a dislike for women. I mean, you have left it rather late in the day to be littering the world with little Huntleys."

Edmond stiffened at the insult to his brother's manhood. *Mon dieu,* he should toss the bastard over the balustrade and be done with him. Unfortunately he first needed to make certain that Howard Summerville *was* responsible for the attempts on Stefan's life.

"And you thought if I possessed an aversion to women, you might be a step closer to the title?" he grated.

"What? Don't be daft. Even if you never bother to have brats, your aggravating brother is bound to. No one could believe Edmond dislikes women."

Edmond swallowed an exasperated curse. Was the man cunning enough to realize that he was suspected of Stefan's mysterious accidents?

It seemed highly unlikely, but what other explanation could there be?

"Then why are you angered by my engagement?" he gritted.

"Because you made a damned fool of me."

"I beg your pardon?"

Howard swayed, as he tilted back his head to glare into Edmond's face.

"Why the devil did you tell me you had come to London to

enjoy the entertainments? You could at least have given me a hint to your true intentions."

Edmond frowned. "I was not yet prepared to reveal my interest towards Miss Quinn."

"Well, you made me lose a bloody fortune," Howard groused.

"What the blazes are you babbling about?"

"The betting book at White's." Howard struggled to remain upright. "The odds were fifty to one that you had traveled to London to choose a bride. Had you given me even the slightest clue, I should have made a tidy return. As it is, I lost twenty quid."

"That is why you are angry? Because you wanted to bet on my engagement?"

"It was also rude." Howard futilely attempted to smooth his wrinkled lapels. "Whether you choose to acknowledge the connection or not, I am your cousin. I should not be the last to discover you have selected your bride."

Edmond rolled his eyes toward the foggy heavens. "Christ."

BRIANNA WAS PLEASANTLY surprised to discover that, while Lady Montgomery's guests were naturally anxious to meet the woman who had managed to capture the elusive Duke of Huntley, they were polite enough not to crush her in one great stampede.

Indeed, after situating Brianna and Lady Aberlane on a pretty brocade sofa near the center of the long salon, Lady Montgomery had taken care to ensure that no more than two or three were ever allowed to linger before being gently urged toward the refreshment tables.

The carefully choreographed introductions allowed Brianna to easily recall the various responses she had rehearsed over the past few days and to deflect the more impertinent queries. It also left far too many opportunities for her attention to stray toward the dark, magnificent gentleman who moved with such ease among the crowd.

No matter how hard she attempted to put her aggravating fiancé from her mind, she was vibrantly aware of his every movement. It was as if every other person in the room faded to insignificance, leaving Edmond to shimmer with a potent, relentless force that demanded her unwavering attention.

Aggravating wretch.

Of course, it was that inability to ignore his presence that allowed her to track his deliberate path across the room to confront the thin, dark-haired gentleman in the corner of the room. Her brows lifted as she realized that she recognized the obviously tipsy gentleman.

Spreading her fan with a flick of her wrist, Brianna covertly leaned toward Lady Aberlane to whisper beneath her breath.

"Good heavens, is that Howard Summerville?"

Following her glance, the older woman offered a small nod of her head. "Yes, I believe it is."

Brianna narrowed her gaze. Lady Aberlane should be as astonished as Brianna at the man's presence. After all, the entire ton knew that the Duke of Huntley refused to be beneath the same roof as his cousin.

Which begged the question of just how deeply Lady Aberlane was involved in Edmond's nefarious plans.

"I thought the two families were at odds with one another," Brianna whispered. "Something like the Capulets and Montagues."

Her companion gave a flutter of her hands, although Brianna did not miss the swift glance toward Edmond, who was leading the drunken Howard toward a far door.

"Oh, certainly nothing so dramatic," she murmured.

"No?"

Lady Aberlane smiled wryly at the direct challenge. "Well, I suppose it is true that Stefan and Edmond hold little love for their cousin."

"So why are they walking together as if they are bosom buddies?"

"That, my dear, I cannot say."

"Hmm." Closing her fan with a snap, Brianna rose to her feet.

"Brianna, where are you going?"

A smile of pure determination curved Brianna's lips. "It is rather stuffy in here, do you not think? I believe I will step onto the terrace for a breath of fresh air."

Lady Aberlane reached up to lay her hand on Brianna's arm. "Do you truly think you should disturb them, my dear? Your fiancé may have business to discuss with his cousin."

Brianna narrowed her gaze. "What sort of business?"

"The sort he does not desire to be interrupted."

Which meant it was precisely the sort of business that Brianna wanted to interrupt. Or more exactly, the sort she wanted to overhear.

Somehow, someway, she intended to discover Edmond's secrets, and when she did, she would put an end to this ridiculous engagement and be safely on her way to Meadowland.

"Then he should not conduct his business in the midst of a soiree," she quipped, turning and marching directly toward the door.

TOSSING ASIDE HIS CHEROOT, Edmond grasped the cold, damp stones of the balustrade, glaring into the dark shadows of the garden below.

Mon dieu.

Either Howard Summerville was the most cunning villain he had ever hunted, or he truly was the bumbling simpleton he appeared to be.

And the fact that he could not yet tell the truth of the matter was making Edmond damn well furious.

He had devoted years to exposing schemers, conspirators and outright traitors. He had forestalled countless plots against Alexander Pavlovich, simply because he could discern the most subtle warnings and sense when others were lying to him.

Now, when it was more important than ever, he found his instincts refusing to cooperate.

Cursing beneath his breath, Edmond struggled to regain his

badly strained composure when the door to the balcony was pushed open and the enticing scent of lavender filled the night air.

"Brianna." He scowled in annoyance. "What the devil are you doing out here?"

She smiled with a blithe indifference at his blunt lack of welcome.

"I was in need of fresh air." She turned to squarely face Howard Summerville who was hurriedly attempting to smooth his hair and tug down his wrinkled jacket. Howard might be a drunken sod, but even he responded to Brianna's enticing beauty. "Am I interrupting?"

Before Howard could find his tongue, Edmond had moved to stand directly behind Brianna, his arms sliding around her waist so he could haul her against the hard planes of his body.

"As a matter of fact you are," he drawled directly in her ear. "But then, that was your intention, was it not?"

She shivered, but with that courage he was beginning to recognize she refused to be quelled.

"Really, Stefan, you should not tease me in such a fashion," she murmured, her hand shifting so she could covertly pinch his arm.

Ignoring the tiny pain, Edmond deliberately pressed his aching cock against her soft curves.

"No, I have far more pleasant means of teasing you, do I not?" he taunted.

She sucked in a sharp gasp before she was tugging away from his grasp and stepping toward the bemused Howard. With an inborn elegance, she offered a small curtsey.

"Mr. Summerville, this is a pleasure." She held out a slender hand. "It has been far too long."

"Indeed, it has." Bending at the waist, Howard planted a kiss on her knuckles, unaware of the savage fury that lanced through Edmond at the mere sight of another man touching Brianna. "Who could have suspected you would grow into such a lovely woman?"

"I, for one," Edmond snarled, encircling Brianna's shoulders with a possessive arm.

Howard took a hasty step backward, male enough to sense Edmond's prickling air of warning. That did not, however, halt him from attempting to try and take advantage of Brianna's arrival. No doubt he hoped that she would be a far easier touch than Stefan or Edmond.

"And now that you are to be family, we must become better acquainted. Perhaps you would join my wife for—"

The slurred words came to an awkward halt as there was a muffled, but unmistakable sound of a shot being fired from the garden below. Edmond hissed in shock, spinning to the balustrade even as Howard gave a shout of alarm.

He was not certain what he intended to do. He could easily vault over the railing and land in the garden, but with the dark and fog he would be nearly blind. Hardly the best means to confront an armed assailant.

Still, he could not allow his attacker to vanish without even attempting to give chase.

"Brianna, go inside and do not leave until I return," he commanded, his hands on the balustrade as he prepared to plunge into the thick shadows below.

He muttered a curse when she did not respond, turning his head to give her a furious glare. By God, he did not have time to waste....

His heart came to a sharp, agonizing halt, as he met her stunned gaze, belatedly noting the dark blood that welled on her temple before trickling down her cheek in a garish path.

He was instantly pulled ten years back in time, to the young man who had howled in helpless fury when he was told his parents had been drowned as they had taken their yacht from Surrey to London. Back then, he had been incapable of doing more than grimly enduring the loss. He had been so...damnably powerless.

This time, he would walk through the gates of hell before he allowed another in his life to die.

The agonized thoughts seared through his mind even as Brianna began to topple forward. With a hoarse cry, Edmond stepped forward, capturing her in his arms.

As was only to be expected, pandemonium erupted as Howard's cowardly squawks of alarm brought the elegant guests spilling onto the balcony to discover that one of Lady Montgomery's guests had been shot.

Edmond was vaguely aware of Howard's stuttering explanation of the mysterious gunshots, and Lady Montgomery's shocked commands that the entire town house and gardens be searched by her servants.

His attention, however, was firmly fixed on the terrifyingly limp body he held cradled in his arms as he stormed through the town house, barking for his carriage and growling at anyone foolish enough to stand in his path.

A voice in the back of his mind whispered that it would no doubt be wiser to take her to Lady Montgomery's bedchamber and call for the doctor, but Edmond dismissed it with a ruthless efficiency. He was seized by a stark need to have her in Stefan's town house. Only there would she be surrounded by his trained servants who were on constant guard and were loyal beyond question.

It was the one place he knew he could keep her safe.

In that moment, nothing else mattered.

EDMOND GLARED AT THE DOCTOR as he tugged on his coat and adjusted the beaver hat on his thinning, silver hair. He did not particularly care for the arrogance etched onto the man's narrow face, or the cavalier manner he dismissed Brianna's injury as a trifling matter, but Letty had convinced him that the condescending ass was the best doctor in London.

"You are certain Miss Quinn will recover?" he growled as the man continued to fuss with his hat.

"Your Grace, I assure you that the bullet merely grazed her temple. The bleeding has already halted and the wound should be completely healed within a few days."

"Then why is she unconscious?"

"Even the glancing blow of a bullet to the temple would be enough to send a grown man into a swoon, let alone a delicate female." He cleared his throat, his gaze casting a covert glance toward the nearby door. His arrogance was swiftly crumbling beneath Edmond's seething frustration. "No doubt it felt as if she were kicked in the head by a mule."

Edmond muttered a foul curse. The memory of Brianna's wide, pain-stricken eyes before she swooned made his heart twist in horror. Christ, had she moved her head just a fraction that bullet would have…

He refused to allow the thought to form. Instead he glowered at the hapless doctor who was edging ever closer to the door and freedom.

"What of infection?" he demanded.

"There is little likelihood, but I shall return in the morning to ensure that all is well."

"Does she have something for the pain?"

"I left a bottle of laudanum with her maid, although it would be best not to use it unless absolutely necessary."

"And you will return if there is need before morning?"

"Really, your Grace…yes. Yes, of course. I will attend Miss Quinn whenever you desire."

Edmond gave a dismissive nod as he turned and headed up the wide staircase. He had no true need for Haggen's grudging promise. If he was in need of the doctor's services, then he would send Boris to fetch him. At gunpoint if necessary.

His footsteps echoed eerily through the silent house, briefly slowing as he reached the landing. The need to continue up the next flight of stairs to the private chambers trembled through his tense body. The fear that gripped him would not be eased until Brianna was out of her bed and creating her usual chaos throughout his house.

He knew better than to attempt to join the wounded minx, at least for now. Both Lady Aberlane and Janet were hovering over Brianna like rabid badgers who would tear him asunder if he dared to interfere in their fussing and fretting.

Sourly, he stomped his way to the library. Entering the hushed room that was lit only by the smoldering embers of the dying fire, Edmond moved to pour himself a large measure of brandy, tossing it down in one swallow. The finely aged spirit burned a welcome path down his throat, helping to ease the icy fear that had clutched him from the moment he'd turned to discover that Brianna had been shot.

He was pouring his second brandy when Boris joined him. The sturdy soldier paused to add another log on the smoldering fire before removing his heavy coat and leaning against the carved mantle.

The moment that Edmond had returned to the town house, he had sent his trusted servant to Lady Montgomery's in the vague hope that the assailant might have been spotted by a servant, or careless enough to leave some hint of his identity behind.

Handing the half-filled glass to his obviously weary companion, Edmond perched on the edge of the desk.

"Well?"

Boris grimaced as he set aside his empty glass. "There was nothing to be discovered in the garden, but it was too dark for a thorough search. I will return at first light."

"Did you speak with the servants?"

"As many as would talk with a foreigner."

Edmond grimaced. There were some things that were as predictable as the sun rising in the east, and the Englishmen and their inbred disdain for anyone they deemed as foreign was one of them.

"I suppose that none of them had the good sense to notice a stranger lurking in the gardens?"

Boris shrugged. "Most of them had gathered in the kitchens, although there were a few of the more adventurous servants taking advantage of the housekeeper's distraction to slip into the mews and enjoy a bit of privacy." Boris deliberately paused to assure Edmond's full attention. "One of the maids distinctly recalls hearing the sound of running footsteps coming out of the stables and entering the garden just moments before the shot was fired."

"From the stables? Then the shooter was not waiting in the garden?"

"Not if the footsteps belonged to the shooter."

"Is it possible to see someone on the balcony from such a vantage?"

"Yes." Boris gave a sharp nod. "In fact, if I were attempting to keep watch on someone within the town house, the mews would be the perfect location to choose."

Edmond abruptly straightened from the desk, pacing the room as he considered the implication of Boris's discovery.

"So it was sheer fortune for the assassin that I was careless enough to step onto the balcony and offer such a ready target?"

"Your cousin did not request that you join him on the balcony?" Boris asked, troubled.

"No." Edmond stilled, meeting his companion's narrowed gaze. "Actually, he was quite reluctant to brave the chilled night air."

Boris gave a slow shake of his head, his tight expression revealing his frustration at the peculiar attack. A frustration that echoed within Edmond.

Not just the fact that someone was brazen enough to take a shot at him in the middle of London. Or that the bullet had strayed and wounded Brianna. But the seeming randomness of the shooting.

It was hardly a brilliant scheme to lurk about a town house crowded with guests and servants on the off chance that the Duke of Huntley might offer himself as an easy target.

"So, if Summerville had been the one to pay the villain to shoot you, it was not intended to occur on the balcony," Boris muttered.

"Not unless he possessed an inordinate amount of faith in the shooter," Edmond said dryly. "We could not have been more than a few feet from one another when the gun was fired."

Boris shrugged. "Of course, if he were standing at your side when you were murdered, it would give him an unshakable alibi."

"Howard does not possess the wits, let alone the courage to plot such a dangerous scheme. Damn. This was not supposed to be so complicated."

For long moments, nothing but the occasional pop of a burning log broke the silence in the room. Then, awkwardly, Boris cleared his throat.

"You are certain you were the intended victim?"

"Who the hell would waste a bullet on Howard Summerville?"

"It was Miss Quinn who was actually shot."

Edmond stumbled to a halt, his blood running cold. "Christ, Boris, it's bad enough to accept that Brianna was hurt because of me. I cannot even consider the possibility that someone had deliberately attempted to kill her."

"Not wishing something does not make it so."

"No." His stark denial echoed through the vast room. "The only one who could possibly desire to harm Brianna is Thomas Wade, and he is crazed with the need to have her in his bed, not in her grave. He would never attempt to kill her."

"Perhaps not," Boris said, clearly skeptical. "Who inherits her dowry should she die?"

"Enough, Boris."

Boris held up his hands in a placating gesture. "I agree, it is unlikely that the bullet was meant for anyone but the Duke of Huntley, but a wise man once taught me that it is dangerous to leap to conclusions and close your mind to other possibilities."

With an effort, Edmond uncoiled his tense muscles and sucked in a deep breath. Those were his words, of course. It was how he trained all of his employees.

It was far too easy to be blinded by the obvious, or worse, to allow emotion to overcome logic.

"A wise man, indeed." His smile was strained as he conceded defeat. Boris was right. There were still too many unanswered questions to make any assumptions. "Tomorrow, I want you to discover whatever you can of Miss Quinn's finances and if anyone stands to benefit from her death."

Boris offered a ready nod. "What do you intend to do?"

"I have already sent a red rose to the King's theatre to set up a meeting with Chesterfield." Lifting a hand, Edmond rubbed the aching muscles of his neck. "If he is having Howard Summerville watched, as he is being paid to do, then someone must have seen something."

"Yes." Boris's expression sharpened at the realization that there might very well be a witness to the attack. "Perhaps I should visit that pub and see if Chesterfield left a message—"

"In the morning, Boris," Edmond interrupted, his expression uncompromising. "I have Danya keeping watch upon the grounds, but I prefer to have you near at hand in the event the villain decides to finish what he started."

"Surely no one would be foolish enough to attempt to slip into this house?"

"So long as Brianna is beneath this roof, I intend to take no chances."

Ignoring his companion's speculative expression, Edmond turned to leave the library. He had given the women long enough to fuss over Brianna. For the remainder of the night, she would be in his care.

CHAPTER ELEVEN

IT WAS THE SOUND OF THE SOFT, yet fierce, argument that lured Brianna from the clinging sleep. For a long, painful moment, she struggled to recall where she was and what had happened.

She remembered being at Lady Montgomery's soiree. And then following Edmond onto the balcony. But after that, everything was lost in the sensations of being held tightly in Edmond's arms and the sway of the carriage. Now it would seem that she was tucked into her bed in the Huntley town house, with Janet standing guard at her door and Edmond not at all pleased to be prevented from entering the room.

"I said to stand aside, Janet," he snapped.

"Nay." The maid was at her most stubborn. "I will not have Miss Brianna disturbed."

"I have no intention of disturbing her, nor do I intend to stand in this hall and squabble with you. Move aside, or I will move you."

Brianna might have enjoyed the battle between the two obstinate, ruthless opponents, if it did not take her full concentration to hold back the looming darkness.

"Now you look here, sir, I don't be caring how top lofty ye might be, ye don't scare me." Janet was utterly fearless as always. "'Tis yer fault that me mistress was wounded. The least ye can do is allow her to heal in peace."

"You are treading a dangerous path, Janet."

"It is my duty to protect my mistress. Especially when she is unable to protect herself."

Brianna heard Edmond's sharp breath and she forced her heavy lashes to lift so she could witness his hard, faintly outraged expression. She doubted it was often that Mr. Edmond Summerville had his honor questioned by a mere servant.

"What the hell do you think I intend to do with her?"

Janet snorted. "There is only one reason for a man to seek out a woman in her private chambers."

"Christ. I am not Thomas Wade. I have no need to force myself on women. Especially not those who are unconscious."

"Mayhaps not, but—"

Brianna was relieved, as Janet's mulish words came to a startled halt as Boris suddenly appeared in the doorway, a faint smile on his harshly chiseled features.

"Allow me, sir," he murmured before grasping a startled Janet around her waist and tossing her over his shoulder.

"Why, ye devil." The maid smacked Boris in the middle of the back with her clenched fists. "I'll have ye gelded. I'll have your throat slit and yer body dumped in the stews."

"Thank you, Boris," Edmond murmured, chuckling as the large servant headed down the hallway with a struggling Janet.

The threats were abruptly muffled as Edmond closed the door and moved to settle on the edge of her bed. Nestled on the mattress, Brianna shivered despite the blankets that had been piled on her while she slept. Even with his magnificent eyes shadowed with exhaustion and his jaw darkened with a hint of his morning beard, Edmond still managed to flood the room with his raw, restless power.

And to send a disturbing shock of pleasure through her.

Instinctively, she attempted to shift from his looming body, only to be halted as Edmond stretched out beside her and tenderly bundled her into his arms.

Brianna stiffened, watching him with a wary expression as she realized that they were very much alone in her bedchamber, and that he was stripped down to his linen shirt and tight breeches, while she was wearing nothing more than a thin chemise.

"Edmond?"

"Shh. Do not move, *ma souris*," he murmured, his lips stroking close to the wound on her temple.

"What is Boris going to do to Janet?" she demanded.

"I think we should be much more concerned for Boris's welfare," he drawled. "Where the devil did you find that terrifying gorgon?"

She knew she should battle her way from his arms. Even with the thick blankets and his rumpled evening attire between them, she could feel his tantalizing heat beginning to seep into her chilled body. But at the moment, she was too tired to fight the inevitable. And besides, it felt so wonderful to snuggle against him and to rest her head in the shallow dip beneath his shoulder. There was a fierce, relentless strength about him that banished the strange sense of unreality that plagued her.

"She is very protective."

"So I have discovered." His lips brushed down the curve of her cheek, his touch one of comfort rather than seduction. "Tonight, however, she has no need to stand guard. I am here to keep you safe."

"I believe she is convinced that having you here to keep me safe is rather akin to having the fox guarding the chickens," Brianna said dryly.

Edmond shifted so that he could frown down at her pale, pain-drawn expression.

"I do not mind being likened to a fox, but I will be damned to be thought a monster. I do not force myself on wounded females."

Wounded.

Yes. That would explain the fiery ache at her temple. She lifted a hand to discover that a plaster had been placed over her injury.

"What happened?"

"You do not recall?"

She started to frown, only to wince in pain. "I remember stepping onto the balcony and a loud explosion. I think something must have hit my head."

The hard, bronzed features were unreadable. "You were shot, Brianna."

"Shot?" She froze in pure shock, her fingers still pressed to her temple. "A bullet did this?"

"Yes."

"Good heavens," she breathed. "Who would shoot me?"

"Who can say?"

"You," she said, glaring into his guarded expression.

"What?"

She cautiously shifted up on the pillows, just enough so she was not lying flat on her back. "You know something."

"Now is not the time to discuss…"

"Dammit, Edmond, tell me."

"I suspect that it was an accident."

She clicked her tongue. "You think I am stupid enough to believe that someone was just randomly shooting at Lady Montgomery's balcony?"

"No, I do not think for a moment that it was random."

She shivered at the low, feral edge in his voice. For goodness sakes, he claimed it was an accident and yet, was certain it was not random….

"Oh." Her eyes widened as realization struck. "You believe that it was an accident that *I* was the one who was hit by the bullet. You think they were shooting at you."

It was only because he still held her tightly against him that she felt his muscles tense.

"That is one possibility," he hedged.

"Why? Why would someone shoot at you?"

His lips twisted in a wry smile. "Surely you, of all people, cannot be surprised that someone might wish me dead?"

No, she would not be surprised. He was, after all, the sort of arrogant, ruthless bastard who would collect enemies with the same ease that some men collected snuffboxes. Not to mention the fact that he was a renowned rakehell who had no doubt seduced his way through all of England and most of Russia.

The only wonder was that he hadn't already been shot.

The blow to her head, however, hadn't completely scattered her wits.

"But no one in London knows that it is you. Everyone assumes that you are the Duke of Huntley," she pointed out, suspiciously. "This has something to do with you pretending to be Stefan, does it not?"

His lips thinned. "It is late, Brianna. You should be resting."

"No." She made a move to sit up, only to be halted as his arms tightened around her. "I deserve to have the truth, Edmond."

He arched a dark brow. "You *deserve* the truth?"

"I was the one shot."

There was a brooding silence as he studied her stubborn expression. Brianna knew that he wanted to ignore her demands for an explanation. He was a man who gave orders and expected them to be obeyed without question. As his gaze lingered on the plaster stuck on her forehead, his beautiful features hardened with a hint of resignation.

"I suppose that is true enough," he grudgingly conceded.

"Please." She touched a hand to his cheek, the prickle of his whiskers that darkened the line of his jaw pressing into her palm with an oddly pleasurable sensation. "Why are you in London posing as the Duke of Huntley? What secrets are you hiding?"

His eyes darkened at her soft touch before his features tightened and he pulled back to regard her with a hard gaze.

"I am here because I suspect that someone is attempting to murder my brother."

An icy disbelief jolted through her body. She was uncertain what she had expected, but certainly not that.

"No. I cannot believe it."

His lips twisted as he gently touched the plaster covering her injury.

"You have the wounds to make you believe."

"But…Stefan." She shook her head, feeling oddly numb as she struggled to accept the shocking notion that anyone could wish harm upon the Duke of Huntley. "You must be mistaken. He is so kind and good. Everyone loves him."

Edmond's expression was grim as his fingers shifted to trail down the curve of her cheek.

"No matter how kind and good he might be, he is also a powerful nobleman who inherited his own share of enemies."

"I suppose." She sucked in a deep breath. "It still seems…"

"Seems what?"

"Unbelievable," she muttered, unable to come up with a suitable word to describe the sick feeling in the pit of her stomach. She was not so innocent that she did not understand there was evil in the world. Thomas Wade had made certain of that. But it was nearly impossible to think of sweet, gentle Stefan being stalked by a coldblooded murderer. "Who do you suspect?"

Frustration rippled over the lean features as Edmond gave a shake of his head. "Howard Summerville seemed the obvious choice. If both Stefan and I were to conveniently cock up our toes, he would be in line for the dukedom and a rather large fortune that he has made little effort to disguise he is in desperate need of."

"Oh." Her eyes widened. "So that is why you allowed your cousin to be invited to Lady Montgomery's."

"Yes."

She pondered a long moment. "Perhaps he was the obvious choice, but he could hardly have been the one to pull the trigger on this eve. Not unless he is a magician."

"He could have paid someone else to do the evil deed while he was standing at my side. What better means to ensure no one believes he is guilty?"

She blinked at the devious implications. "So you think…"

"At this moment, I do not know what to think." He heaved a sigh of aggravation as he tugged her close to his chest and rested his cheek on the top of her head. "All I know for certain is that I am weary and in need of a few hours sleep. We can finish this conversation tomorrow. Or rather, later today," he amended as he glanced toward the window where the faint hint of a rosy dawn could be detected.

Brianna could not deny a desire to snuggle close to Edmond and rest her aching head for a short while. Despite the vibrant awareness, or perhaps because of it, she felt safe and protected and strangely peaceful in his arms. As if nothing could harm her so long as he held her near.

A sensation that was far more dangerous than mere desire.

"Edmond."

"Mmm?"

"You cannot remain in this bed with me."

"Be at ease, *ma souris*. I trust you with my virtue. At least for the next few hours."

"And what of *my* virtue?"

"It is safe." He smiled deep into her wary eyes before turning to blow out the flickering candle beside the bed. "At least for the next few hours."

BRIANNA AWAKENED TO DISCOVER herself still cradled in Edmond's arms. Not entirely shocking. She had not given more than a token resistance to rid her bed of his presence, and then promptly ruined even that by falling asleep with remarkable ease.

It was rather shocking, however, to discover that sometime during the early morning hours, Edmond had shed the last of his clothes and that she was pressed possessively against his naked flesh.

For a moment, she allowed herself to savor the comfort at waking in a man's arms. Then, with a muffled curse at her stupidity, she cautiously began to shift from beneath the leg that Edmond had thrown over her hips. Good lord, the entire household must be aware that Edmond was in her chambers and that he had slept in the same bed.

What must they be thinking?

Intent on her escape, Brianna had managed to wriggle less

than an inch when the arms wrapped around her tightened with an unyielding force.

"Good morning, *ma souris*. How did you sleep?"

Unable to move, Brianna tilted back her head to discover a slit of brilliant blue shimmering between the thick lace of his lashes. Her heart gave a violent jump at the sight of his lean features still softened by sleep and his dark hair tumbled onto his forehead.

He looked younger, more…vulnerable. As if he might actually possess a heart beneath all that ruthless strength.

"Well enough, considering that you consumed far more than your fair share of the bed," she muttered, her breath oddly elusive as his soft chuckle brushed over her cheek.

"Did I? That is easily remedied."

"Yes, quite easily," she said, tartly. It was all very well for him to mock her embarrassment. He no doubt awoke every morning with one woman or another in his bed. She, however, hadn't the least experience in such matters. "All you need do is move aside so that I can rise…"

Her words ended in a squeak as Edmond rolled onto his back, hauling a startled Brianna on top of his hard, splendidly naked body.

"Is that better?"

Sprawled across his chest, she gazed down at his impossibly handsome face, shuddering as she encountered the smoldering hunger that burned in his eyes. It was a hunger that beat deep within her. She craved his kisses, his skilled caresses. His most intimate touch.

"No, it most certainly is not better."

His smile held a wicked awareness of the delicious sensations assaulting her. Deliberately, he trailed his hands up the curve of her back, his smile widening as she trembled in response.

"How is your head?" He startled her by inquiring, an edge of genuine concern in his voice. "Does it still pain you?"

Brianna licked her dry lips, sensing it would be dangerous

to admit that the pain from the night before had dulled to the point that she had to concentrate to actually feel the vague throb.

"At the moment, what pains me is the fact that the entire household knows you are in here," she murmured. "You must let me go."

"Must I?" His hands smoothed down her back, splaying over her hips. "Why?"

Her breath was wrenched from her lungs as his fingers seared through the thin silk of her chemise.

"Because this is wrong."

"Wrong? The hell it is. This is…perfect." His voice thickened, surprisingly holding a hint of a Russian accent, as if his growing desire stirred the more intense emotions of his mother's ancestors.

Brianna stilled, her hands flat against his chest and her back arched so she could meet his smoldering gaze. Beneath her, his body deliberately shifted to press his swelling erection against her lower stomach.

Her every instinct urged her to part her legs and allow him to teach her the ultimate bliss to be found between a man and woman.

"You will ruin me," she husked, more in an attempt to remind herself of the danger of allowing herself to be over-whelmed by the avalanche of sensations than to halt the caress of his hands as they explored the curve of her backside and ran down the back of her thighs.

With a savage curse, Edmond lifted his head and buried his face against her neck. His lips trailed a searing path down to the pulse pounding at the base of her throat, giving it a sharp nip before soothing it with the tip of his tongue.

"Does this feel like ruin?" he demanded, his fingers pulling the chemise upward until his hands could slip beneath the fabric and stroke her bare skin. Then, without warning, his hands slid between her legs and he was tugging them apart so they fell on either side of his hips. She whimpered as his hard arousal was pressed directly to her moist, nearly painfully sensitive cleft. "Does this?"

It felt like paradise. A wicked paradise that had her heart pounding and her breath coming in small pants.

"What do you want from me, Edmond?"

"You," he rasped, his voice raw. "I want you."

As if he couldn't help himself, he rolled over, trapping her beneath his trembling body. With the late morning sunlight slanting over their entangled forms, his lips explored her face, closing her stunned eyes before they sought her mouth in a kiss that claimed her very soul.

A tiny voice in the back of her mind warned Brianna not to respond. There was still a part of her that understood the danger of giving herself to this man. Not so much the loss of her innocence, although that should no doubt be her greatest concern, but the knowledge that Edmond Summerville could steal far more than her virginity.

The voice, however, was easily drowned beneath the sensual flood of pleasure that raced through her body. Instead of pushing him away, her arms lifted to encircle his neck, her lips parting softly under his.

She felt as if she had been waging a war against fate since the day her father had died. First in her futile attempts to halt her mother's slow, inevitable plunge into disaster, and then her terrified determination to prevent her stepfather's mounting advances.

In this moment, she did not want to fight against destiny. She wanted to lower the ruthless barriers she had erected around herself and for a few hours, just be a carefree young woman who desired a man.

Easily sensing her capitulation, Edmond pulled back to regard her with a restless craving.

"I am not Stefan, *ma souris*. I am not noble or decent or selfless." Holding her passion-darkened gaze, he grasped the bodice of her chemise and, with a fierce jerk, ripped it in two. His breath caught at the sight of her exposed breasts, his fingers moving to gently brush over one rosy nipple. "I want you and I intend to take you. Damn the consequences."

Damn the consequences.

Tangling her fingers into his thick curls, she tugged his head down, groaning as he rewarded her boldness by branding her lips with a fierce kiss. He tasted of fire and sin and wicked temptation as his tongue dipped into her mouth.

Lost in delight, Brianna arched her back, savoring the feel of his hands as they molded and teased her breasts, his lips as they devoured her mouth.

"Please," she whispered as he nibbled his way down the line of her jaw and then the curve of her throat.

"Please, what?" His mouth covered the tip of her breast, suckling her with a growing insistence. "Tell me what you desire."

"I…" She gave a choked cry as his other hand slipped between them to stroke the damp heat between her legs. "I'm not…certain."

Lifting his head, he smiled deep into her bemused gaze with an expression of such tenderness that it made her heart ache in the strangest manner.

"Then we shall discover together, *ma souris,* what it is that pleases you."

Lowering his dark head, he returned to tormenting her aching breasts, those clever fingers finding that tiny pleasure point that sent electric jolts through her body. Her fingers tightened in his hair, tugging the curls as her hips arched off the bed in a silent plea for fulfillment.

She needed…something more.

Almost as if sensing her sudden confusion, Edmond tugged apart her legs so he could settle between them, the tip of his heavy erection pressing at her opening.

Brianna's eyes jerked open in a sudden flare of unease, encountering the brilliant blue gaze.

"Hold on to me, Brianna," he muttered, his dark features flushed and a feverish glow in his eyes. "Hold on to me tight."

She barely had time to absorb his warning when his hips lifted and he entered her with one smooth thrust. She cried out at the sharp stab of pain, her nails biting into his shoulders as her body struggled to accept the raw invasion.

Edmond held himself perfectly still, whispering soft Russian words in her ear as he waited for her tension to slowly ease. Only then did he begin to slowly, carefully withdraw nearly to the tip before pushing back into her.

It was a peculiar sensation at first. A mixture of pain and pleasure. But as the tightness lessened, Brianna found the fullness of his thrusting cock a delectable friction.

"Mon dieu," Edmond groaned in pleasure, his hands framing Brianna's face as he claimed her lips in a kiss of pure possession.

Brianna's own hands slid down the muscles of his back to clutch at his surging hips, her heels digging into the mattress as her entire body bowed with tension. Deeper and deeper he penetrated, her harsh pants the only sound to break the silence.

And then, with a force that she could never have anticipated, Brianna's entire body exploded with a pleasure that ripped a scream from her lips.

It was a moment of pure ecstasy.

Trembling from the force of her release, Brianna wrapped herself tightly around Edmond, relishing the feel of his swift, jerky thrusts and the startled moans that seemed to be wrenched from the very depths of his soul.

Not at all what one would expect of a practiced seducer.

CHAPTER TWELVE

IT WAS LATE THE NEXT afternoon when the message from La Russa arrived, informing Edmond that he could call upon her at his convenience.

Under normal circumstances, Edmond would have been infuriated by the ridiculous charade that Chesterfield insisted upon. After sending the requisite red rose, he had expected Chesterfield to arrive at Huntley House in a dignified manner. Instead, he had been forced to wait hours before receiving a reply that he was expected to travel several blocks to La Russa's town house.

Considering the small fortune he was paying Chesterfield, the least the bloody man could do was rearrange his schedule when Edmond had need of him.

Fury, however, was not what Edmond felt as he joined Boris in his elegant carriage that would carry them the short distance to the recently completed square.

Instead, he futilely attempted to rid his mind of the lingering memory of Brianna spread beneath him.

Mon dieu. He had spent hours in her bed, and still he could think of nothing but how soon he could return to the town house and her lavender-scented temptation.

His potent fascination with the woman only seemed to deepen the more he was in her presence.

Belatedly realizing that Boris was studying him with a smug expression, Edmond gave a lift of his brows.

"May I inquire why you are regarding me with that vaguely annoying smile?" he demanded.

That annoying smile only widened. "I was considering whether to offer you my congratulations or my sympathies."

"And why is that?"

"Miss Quinn is, without a doubt, a beautiful female."

"Without a doubt."

"And extraordinarily spirited."

"Oh, yes, she is indeed spirited. Do you have a point?"

"The point is that she is hardly your usual sort."

"I did not realize that I had a usual sort."

Boris folded his arms over the considerable width of his chest. "You know very well that you have always preferred those sophisticated, some might even claim jaded, ladies who no longer believe in romance. Women who understand your rules of seduction." He deliberately considered his words. "You have never encouraged a dewy-eyed innocent who is foolish enough to presume a few kisses are nothing less than a declaration of love."

"Brianna is not a dewy-eyed innocent."

"Perhaps no longer," Boris muttered.

"Take care, Boris," Edmond warned. "No one is allowed to speak of Brianna, not even you."

"I am speaking of you, Summerville. Innocent or not, Miss Quinn is a well-bred young lady who has not yet learned to protect her heart."

Edmond gave a startled laugh. "Are you attempting to lecture me on seducing a beautiful young lady?"

Boris shrugged. "It is one thing to seduce a chit, and another to make her fall in love with you."

A strange, wholly unexpected heat flared through Edmond at the thought of Miss Brianna Quinn gazing at him with a besotted smile, her arms opened wide to welcome him into his bed or merely seated opposite him at the dining room table, listening to him with rapt adoration.

It was the sort of image that should have made him break out in a horrified sweat, not smile with pleasure.

What the hell could be worse than having some female trailing after him, fluttering her lashes and constantly underfoot as she sought to attract his attention?

Of course, if the woman doing the trailing and fluttering were Brianna, it might be worth the annoyance.

More than worth the annoyance, a soft voice whispered in the back of his mind.

"What if she does believe herself in love with me?" he murmured, an unwitting smile tugging at his lips. "For the moment, we are forced into one another's company. It is far more pleasant to have her as my lover than as my enemy."

"You are willing to break her heart?"

Edmond shrugged. "All young women must endure one broken heart, do they not?"

Boris shook his head, his expression tight with annoyed bafflement. "You detest women who attempt to cling to you."

"Do I?"

"Very well." Boris threw up his hands in disgust. "If you want to play with fire then so be it. It's none of my concern."

Smoothing the cuff of his pale blue coat, Edmond sent his friend a wry glance.

"I would say that you are enjoying your own share of dallying with the flames, Boris. Or do you expect me to believe that you hauled the pretty young maid off to her chambers last eve and left her without so much as a kiss?"

A startling hint of color touched the warrior countenance. "Janet is no innocent."

"No, quite the opposite," Edmond drawled, silently wondering just what the hell was going on between his companion and the maid. "She is a woman who would readily geld a man she felt had done her wrong. And if she did not, then her family would. I would say it is equal odds as to whether you shall have your throat cut by the dangerous maid or by her ruffian of a father."

Boris appeared remarkably indifferent to the undoubted

danger he was courting, leaning to peer out the window as the carriage slowed.

"I suppose this must be the place."

Edmond lifted his brows at the sight of the terraced town house that was surrounded by a recently enlarged garden complete with Grecian statues and marble fountains. Although unable to compare with the Huntley mansion, it was a lovely neoclassical design that was set back from the road and framed by towering marble columns.

"Rather elegant for an opera singer," he murmured, before slanting Boris a somber glance. "Remain here and keep an eye upon the house. I want to know if anyone takes an interest in my presence while I'm here."

Boris frowned. "You intend to go in there alone?"

Edmond patted his jacket where he had a pistol and two daggers stashed. "Never alone, my friend."

La Russa's town house proved to be just as tastefully elegant on the inside as it promised on the outside.

Allowing a uniformed butler to lead him up the curved, double staircase to the upper landing, Edmond took close note of the rare Grecian vases that were set in the tiny alcoves along with the collection of Dutch masterpieces that lined the walls. Although he did not claim his late father's love for art, he fully appreciated the value of such a collection.

Shown into a long drawing room that offered a stunning view of the tiny park built in the center of the square, Edmond was once again greeted by the pleasing combination of classical furnishings and breathtaking works of art. Glancing about the ivory and gold chamber, he realized that there was at least one Rembrandt and two Rubens on the damask walls and a Van Dyke carefully hung above the black marble chimneypiece.

He smiled wryly, accepting that it was not at all what he was expecting. Nor was the woman who rose gracefully to her feet at his entrance.

Tall and slender, she was a traditional English rose beauty. Of course, her glorious blond hair was beginning to show a few strands of silver and there was a network of lines about the blue eyes, but that haunting fragility that had bewitched theatre audiences for the past two decades remained as compelling as ever.

Moving forward, Edmond took the slender hand that she offered and raised it to his lips. "Ah, the exquisite La Russa. As beautiful as the rumors claim." He ran an appreciative gaze over the pale mauve satin gown that was cut low enough to reveal the tempting swell of her breasts and trimmed with a sophisticated silver foil. She wore no jewels, but the purity of her creamy skin needed no ornamentation. "I understand why they refuse to serve dinner at my club until a toast has been offered in your honor."

"Please, call me Elizabeth," she said, her voice a low, husky invitation. "I try to leave La Russa at the theatre."

"Understandable." Edmond straightened, careful to hide his impatience that Chesterfield was nowhere to be seen. "Thank you for agreeing to meet with me."

The rosebud lips curved into a knowing smile. "Nonsense. My humble household is honored to be graced by the presence of such a renowned peer of the realm."

"Not so humble." Edmond glanced toward the Van Dyke hanging above the mantle. "You possess exquisite taste."

"There are some women who enjoy fashionable clothes or flashy bits of jewelry. I am rather more dull in my desires."

Edmond was not fooled for a moment by her ingenuous manner. "You are extremely wise, I should say. This collection is worth a fortune and will only increase in value over the years."

"A lady in my position must always think of the future." As if realizing that Edmond was too perceptive to be deceived by her well-practiced act, Elizabeth offered a genuine smile and moved toward a door nearly hidden behind a large potted palm. "This way, your Grace."

Edmond readily followed in her wake. "You know, I cannot

help but be curious as to how you and Chesterfield became acquainted."

She gave a low, throaty laugh. "I was not always La Russa, your Grace. When I first arrived in London I was Lizzy Gilford, the poor daughter of a blacksmith with empty pockets and a head filled with foolish notions of the great destiny that awaited me."

"One that obviously has arrived," he said dryly.

"Greatness is not singing on a stage or dangling upon the arm of some wealthy gentleman. It is not even acquiring these wondrous works of art, as I have learned from Mr. Chesterfield." She cast a brief glance over her shoulder. "Greatness is never turning a blind eye to the suffering of others."

"Ah." Edmond recognized the wounds that shadowed her eyes. Wounds that might be ancient, but had never entirely healed. "He rescued you."

"Yes." She pushed open the door to reveal a paneled antechamber that led to yet another door. "I had barely stepped off the stage from Liverpool when I was approached by a very elegant, very sophisticated gentleman who promised to launch my career on the stage. A lot of rubbish, of course. After he had thoroughly debauched me, he sold me to a brothel and laughed as I pleaded with him to return me to my father." She briefly paused, as if fighting to keep command of her composure. "He said that the only place for a worthless tart was the gutter."

Edmond grimaced. It was no surprise that a supposed gentleman would pad his pockets by seducing an innocent wench and then selling her to the local brothel. Hell, he'd known gentlemen who would sell their own sister for a few quid.

"I suppose it is too much to hope that he was properly gelded?"

She halted at the closed door, turning to reveal a cold, ruthless expression that was never seen upon the stage.

"He was not gelded, but he was most certainly punished."

Edmond gave a slow nod. He recognized the face of an avenging angel. He did not doubt she had killed the nasty nobleman, the only question was who had helped her to cover the crime.

There was an obvious suspect.

"And Chesterfield?" he asked.

Her expression softened, once again revealing that haunting vulnerability which had made her famous throughout England.

"Mr. Chesterfield has a profound dislike for those who would abuse women or children," she murmured softly, pushing open the door and waving him forward. "Just through here."

Edmond stepped into the narrow chamber, his hand reaching into his pocket so he could grip the hilt of his pistol, his gaze searching the shadows. He had no reason to suspect an ambush, but on the last occasion he had lowered his guard, Brianna had been injured.

He was not about to willingly offer himself, or anyone else, up as a sacrificial lamb again.

As if sensing that Edmond was quite prepared to shoot at the first hint of danger, Chesterfield stepped from the shadows, his hands held high in a gesture of peace.

"Your Grace," he murmured with a bow.

Assured that there were no lurking assassins stashed behind the satinwood writing table or trellis-backed chairs, Edmond removed his hand from his pistol and crossed toward the Siena marble fireplace.

The room was charming enough with the pale green wall panels and molded plaster ceiling, but Edmond presumed it was chosen because it had a pair of French doors that led to the back garden and the mews beyond. It would be a simple matter for a man of Chesterfield's talents to enter and leave the town house without even the servants realizing he was there.

"Chesterfield."

"I will leave you two alone," La Russa said from the doorway. "There is brandy or sherry on the side table, Chesterfield, and your favorite cakes on the tray."

A fond smile touched Chesterfield's nondescript features. "Thank you, my love."

Edmond waited until the door was shut and they were alone in the room before pulling out a cheroot and lighting it with a spill from the mantle.

"A most beautiful and intriguing woman."

"That she is," Chesterfield agreed, something in his voice speaking of a deep, unwavering love for La Russa.

Ah, yes. This was a man who would have walked through the fires of hell to keep the fragile woman from harm.

"And quite a sensible female beneath all that polished elegance, I should think."

Chesterfield chuckled as he moved to pour the brandy, pressing one of the glasses in Edmond's hand before leaning against the mantle and sipping the aged spirit.

"You are more perceptive than others. Most gentlemen cannot see beyond a woman's more obvious charms to what lies beneath."

Edmond smiled wryly. "I have reached an age that it takes more than a pretty face to distract me."

"Yes." Chesterfield slowly nodded, a glint in his pale eyes that sent an unnerving shiver down Edmond's spine. "I should think only a most extraordinary woman could distract you, your Grace."

It was almost as if the man could actually read his mind and know just how deeply Brianna was beginning to disrupt his life. He frowned, annoyed by the intrusion into his inner emotions. He shared those with no one. Not ever.

"Speaking of distractions, I presume you know why I asked to meet with you?"

Easily sensing he had stepped over the line, Chesterfield gave a brisk, businesslike nod.

"The shooting at Lady Montgomery's."

"Yes."

"An unpleasant business." His expression hardened, as if personally insulted by the attack. "I am pleased to know that your fiancée has made a full recovery."

Edmond did not bother to demand how the Runner knew this. It was his business to gather information.

"It was a stroke of fortune that she was not more gravely injured, or even killed." His voice was edged with the cold fury that pounded just below the surface. Someone was going to pay for hurting Brianna. "I do not intend to allow such a thing to happen again."

Chesterfield slowly nodded. "Nor do I."

"You had a man keeping watch on my cousin?"

"Two, in fact," Chesterfield confessed. "Unfortunately, neither of them was in the garden to catch sight of the assailant."

Edmond tossed his cheroot into the fire before slamming his hand on the marble mantle. Until that moment, he had not realized how much he was depending on this man to have some information, anything that might help to steer Edmond in the right direction.

"Damn."

"One of them, however, did catch sight of a carriage racing away from the town house mere moments after the shot was fired. That was why I delayed contacting you. I had hoped to discover more about the carriage and who might have been driving it."

Edmond sternly dampened his instinctive flare of hope. Since his return to England, he had encountered one delay, detour and disappointment after another.

Why should this be any different?

"And did you?"

"Not near so much as I would like." Chesterfield reached into the pocket of his plain black jacket to pull out a wrinkled piece of parchment. "Here."

Edmond frowned at the crude map that had been etched onto the paper. "What is this?"

"Gill attempted to track the carriage through the streets. This is where he last had sight of the vehicle."

"It looks to be Piccadilly." Edmond shook his head. "The villain could have been headed anywhere."

Chesterfield grimaced. "That is why I was delayed in contacting you. I have my man scouring the streets in search of the carriage. He is certain he will recognize it if he sees it again."

"Hardly likely."

"Perhaps not." With a sigh, Chesterfield moved to pour himself another large shot of brandy. "I have also been interviewing Lady Montgomery's neighbors and their servants. It is always possible that they noticed something, although they might not realize that it is of any importance."

Edmond folded his arms over his chest. "What is your opinion of the shooting?"

Chesterfield tossed the brandy down his throat in an impatient gulp. Then, turning, he studied Edmond with a somber expression.

"Before I answer, I would like to know what happened between you and your cousin before the shot was fired."

In a concise manner, Edmond revealed the events leading up to the moment that the shot had been fired.

Chesterfield listened in silence, his scowl deepening. "So it was your notion, not Summerville's, to go onto the balcony?"

"Yes."

"And neither you nor your cousin invited Miss Quinn to join you?"

Edmond's teeth ground together. "Most certainly not."

"Then it does not seem likely that she was the intended victim."

"Of course she was not."

"You sound very certain." Chesterfield set aside his empty glass.

"I—" Edmond came to a sharp halt as he was struck by a sudden thought. He had already dismissed the notion of Thomas Wade being involved in the shooting. The foul beast wanted Brianna alive and in his bed. But he hadn't considered the notion that just being his fiancée might put her in danger. After all, he'd assumed that if someone wanted to bring an end to his engagement, he would be the intended victim. It had never entered his mind that someone would be desperate enough to kill Brianna instead. "Christ."

Chesterfield gave a dip of his head. "Quite."

Edmond pushed from the mantle to pace the cramped room. No. He could not dwell on the thought. Now was no time to be distracted.

"Even if she was the target, no one could have known any of us would be on the balcony."

Chesterfield spread his hands in defeat. "I will agree it makes no sense."

"Do you think Howard is responsible?" Edmond growled.

"No." Chesterfield once again reached into his pocket, on this occasion removing a small notebook. He flipped through the papers, his brow furrowed in concentration. "I have kept a constant surveillance upon him, and he has met with no nefarious associates who might be willing to kill off his relatives."

"He might have other means to contact them. Or he might have given them their orders before you began to trail him."

"True, but from what I can discover, Summerville has no immediate expectations of coming into a fortune." Finding the appropriate page in his notebook, Chesterfield handed it to Edmond. "Quite the opposite, in fact."

Edmond shrugged as he regarded the indecipherable words and numbers scrawled across the paper.

"What is this?"

"It is the name of the ship your cousin has booked passage upon as well as the date it is leaving London."

"The *Rosalind*." Edmond lifted his head to study Chesterfield with a growing sense of frustration. "Where is it bound?"

"Greece. It seems that Howard Summerville's wife has an uncle with a villa near Athens who is willing to offer them sanctuary."

So his cousin was preparing to flee the country. And within the next fortnight.

Did that mean he was clever enough to have an alternative

scheme, should he be unable to murder his way to the ducal fortune? Or more likely, was he simply a spineless creature who was preparing to bolt like the coward he was?

Damn.

He was not one step closer to discovering who the hell pulled the trigger in the garden.

DESPITE THE TEDIOUS LECTURES that she could not possibly be well enough to be leaving the town house, Brianna dressed in a jade gown edged with black gauze and a matching spencer, firmly demanding that a carriage be brought to the door.

What did it matter if Janet trailed behind her with a sulky expression, or that Lady Aberlane did not bother to hide her concern as they set out for Bond Street?

She had to be away from Huntley House, if only for a short time. She could not bear to remain in her chambers, dwelling on the endless hours Edmond had devoted to making love to her, and the astonishing pleasure to be discovered in his arms.

Or at least, that was her hope.

Unfortunately, it did not matter how many shops she visited, or how many bonnets she admired, or how many acquaintances Lady Aberlane halted to chat with, she could not rid her mind of the potent thoughts of Edmond Summerville.

Perhaps it was that way for all maidens. A woman did, after all, lose her innocence once in her lifetime. Perhaps it was only to be expected that she would be obsessed with thoughts of her lover.

Or perhaps she was a weak-willed creature who had not only handed her virginity to Edmond on a silver platter, but her few wits as well.

By God, she had promised herself this would never happen.

She, better than anyone, understood the dangers of allowing herself to become bewitched and distracted by Edmond. Or worse, becoming…attached.

Not when she was so close to achieving the independence she had craved since she was just a child.

At last, disgusted with her inability to control her renegade mind, Brianna called for the carriage and, with Janet and Lady Aberlane, began the return trip to Huntley House.

They traveled in silence, Brianna brooding on her treacherous thoughts, and her even more treacherous body that even now hungered for Edmond's touch, and Janet and Lady Aberlane exchanging worried glances.

Reaching the elegant neighborhood of Mayfair, they had just turned a corner when Brianna was jerked out of her broodings. With a low exclamation, she pressed her nose to the window and craned her head to study the black coach they had just passed waiting in front of an elegant town house.

"Good heavens, that was the Huntley carriage," she said, more puzzled than alarmed. "Edmond said that he was spending the afternoon at his club."

Seated across from her, Janet clicked her tongue in obvious disapproval. "Fah. That ain't no club, I can tell ye that much."

"What do you mean?"

In a flutter of starched wool, Letty reached across Brianna to firmly tug the curtains over the small window, her profile uncommonly stern.

"Do you know, Brianna, I do not believe that was the Huntley carriage at all."

Brianna frowned, a cold unease trickling down her spine. Both her companions were behaving in an extremely odd manner.

"Do you know who resides at that house, Janet?"

"Really, my dear, you are mistaken," Letty insisted. "That was most certainly not the Huntley carriage."

The older woman's protest only deepened Brianna's suspicions. There was something that Lady Aberlane did not want her to discover.

She cast her maid a demanding gaze. "Janet?"

Ignoring the loud sniff from Lady Aberlane, Janet leaned forward, her expression cynical.

"It belongs to La Russa."

"La Russa?" Brianna settled back in her seat, a frown marring her brow. "The name is familiar."

Janet snorted. "It should be. The woman is the most famous tart in all of London."

"Janet, I believe that is quite enough," Lady Aberlane interrupted, icily. "Tell me, Brianna, do you intend to wear the ivory satin this eve? It is so wonderfully flattering to your beautiful complexion."

Brianna barely heard Letty's breathless chatter as a raw, unexpected pain clutched at her heart.

"Oh, my God," she breathed. "La Russa...she is that notorious opera singer. The one who was rumored to have refused an offer of protection from the Duke of Claredon."

Letty reached to pat her arm in a futile gesture of comfort. "Well, my dear, who has not refused an offer of protection from the Duke?"

Brianna slowly shook her head. "Why would he visit the home of such a woman?"

"If ye ask me, there's only one reason for a man to call upon that sort of woman," Janet retorted.

"No one is asking you, Janet, and I must say that I find this all very unsavory," Letty said, her tone sharp. "We should not be speculating on such things. It will only lead to trouble."

Brianna clenched her hands in her lap, her mind struggling to accept the realization that Edmond had left her bed to go to the home of a notorious whore.

It was not so much the fact that Edmond was spending the afternoon with La Russa. What nobleman did not believe he possessed some divine right to have as many lovers as he desired? And Edmond had never made a secret of his insatiable lust for beautiful women. Dear heavens, she had known when she was just a child that he was a rake of the first order.

What disturbed her was the savage, unrelenting pain that was spreading from her heart to the pit of her stomach.

Dammit. She did not want to care what Edmond was doing. She did not want to shudder at the thought of him in the arms of the beautiful, experienced courtesan. She did not want to feel so sick with the sense of betrayal that her stomach threatened to revolt.

This was precisely why she would not allow herself to care for another. And certainly why she would never, ever allow herself to actually to depend on someone else.

Sucking in a deep breath, Brianna grimly forced herself to ignore the perilous emotions. She could not alter the fact that she had given her innocence to Edmond. And in truth, she was not certain she would if she could. For all the man's faults, and there were a number of them, he was a magnificent lover.

What other gentleman could have taught her the endless pleasures to be discovered?

What she could do, however, was suppress the dangerous temptation to see him as anything other than a necessary annoyance that must be endured until she could claim the independence she had waited so long to achieve.

Realizing that her companions were regarding her with obvious concern, Brianna gave a sharp tilt of her chin, allowing an icy resolution to replace the aching pain.

"Yes, you are right, Letty," she said, perfectly composed. "What does it matter if Edmond chooses to devote his afternoons to an aging harlot?"

The older woman frowned. "Brianna…"

"Do you know, I believe that I *shall* wear the ivory satin," she interrupted Letty's protest. "And perhaps my new lace shawl."

CHAPTER THIRTEEN

THE IVORY SATIN WAS JUST as flattering as Lady Aberlane had foreseen.

Although simple in design, it was cleverly cut across the bodice to best flatter her slender curves, and was trimmed with seed pearls sewn into the puff sleeves and blond lace at the hem. When matched with her kid gloves and ivory satin slippers, Brianna had to admit that the soft color contrasted nicely with the vibrant curls that were piled loosely atop her head.

At a glance, she appeared to be precisely what she was supposed to be. A young, sophisticated maiden who was on the precipice of becoming the Duchess of Huntley.

There wasn't the least hint of the brittle tension that hummed just below the surface.

Well, not unless one counted the unnatural pallor of her skin and the hectic glitter in her eyes.

Peering into the mirror of her dressing table, Brianna was contemplating the wisdom of adding a bit of blush to her pale cheeks when the unmistakable sound of a latch clicking had a cold anger rushing through her.

She had no need to turn her head to know that it was Edmond slipping through the secret tunnel. Not only did her body tighten with the familiar awareness, but the warm, sandalwood scent of his soap teased at her senses, causing her stomach to flutter in anticipation despite her best intention to remain indifferent.

At least he possessed the decency to bathe after leaving his whore's bed, she told herself. Deliberately reminding herself of where he'd spent the past hours.

Crossing the room, Edmond halted directly behind her, his hands boldly lifting to caress her bare shoulders as his admiring gaze met hers in the mirror.

"Good evening, *ma souris*. You look…" His gaze lowered to the swell of her breasts revealed by the low cut of her bodice. "Delectable."

With a jerky motion, Brianna rose to her feet, knocking aside his lingering hands as she turned to face him.

"Edmond, can you not at least possess the decency to knock before entering my chambers?" she demanded. "'Tis bad enough you use a secret tunnel to sneak in here…oh…"

Her words were lost in a startled gasp as Edmond reached out to grasp her upper arms and jerk her roughly against his chest.

"But these are not *your* chambers, are they, Brianna?" he growled. "They belong to the Huntley family, just as everything in this town house belongs to us. Everything from the attics to the cellars."

"So now I am just a piece of Huntley property?"

"Not Huntley property." His hands loosened their grip on her arms to run a possessive path down her back to the curve of her hips. "*My* property. You belong to me, *ma souris*. Body and soul."

"Not bloody likely," Brianna rasped, ignoring the tiny flare of panic at the absolute certainty in his voice.

"You seem to forget, my dear," he mocked, "that was the cost for allowing you to remain beneath this roof and away from the clutches of Thomas Wade."

Her hands lifted to press against his chest, a futile effort as his fingers tightened on her hips to yank her even closer. His gesture of pure ownership, however, did at least remind her of the danger of giving even an inch to this man.

"Ah, of course," she drawled. "Giving you my virginity was the payment for not being raped by my stepfather. How stupid of me to forget." She narrowed her gaze. "That doesn't mean, however, I sold you my soul. That, you will never, ever have."

"*Mon dieu.* What is this?"

"What?"

"You are deliberately attempting to rile my temper, why?"

"I merely pointed out that it is common decency to allow me some privacy."

"That is what you truly desire?" His arms wrapped firmly about her waist as he steered her backward, deliberately toward the bed behind her. "Privacy?"

Grimly she remained behind her walls of detached control. She might not be capable of quashing the lust this man could stir within her body, but she would be damned if he would stir anything else.

When he walked away, as he most certainly would, she would feel nothing but relief.

"Yes," she muttered even as Edmond pressed her against one of the heavy walnut bedposts.

His hands skimmed up her back, his hips shifting forward to press his thick erection against her lower stomach. A smug smile curved his lips as she instinctively shivered at the electric sensations of pleasure that shot through her body.

"You can tell as many lies as you want with those pretty lips, Brianna, but your body will always speak the truth."

"And what truth is that?"

"You want me. You want me to strip off your clothes and kiss every inch of that satin skin. You want me to lay you on that bed and thrust myself deep inside you."

Dear God, her blood felt as if it were on fire as it rushed through her body.

"Of course I do," she said, her voice remarkably even. "You are obviously a master at seduction. How could a poor innocent like me possibly resist?"

For some reason, her calm composure appeared to infuriate him. As if he preferred her to be ranting and raving, rather than aloof.

"I see." His expression was dangerously tight as he shifted enough to turn her in his arms, so that she was facing the bed with him pressed against her back. While she was still caught off-guard, he took her hands and placed them against the bedpost, caging her with his much larger frame.

"Edmond?" She struggled to free her hands, not afraid that he would hurt her, but that she would be even more deeply ensnared in his seductive web.

"No," he growled next to her ear. "I am the master, do you not remember?"

"But we are expected downstairs."

"Dinner can wait." His fingers tightened on hers. "Do not release your grip on the post."

"What are you…" She caught her breath as she felt Edmond lower himself to his knees behind her, then with a shocking intimacy, he was beneath the folds of her skirts, his lips coursing a searing path up the back of her thighs, while his hands were firmly tugging her legs farther apart. Brianna's fingers dug into the wooden post as a shudder of sheer delight shook through her. "Oh, dear lord."

"It is too late for prayers," he muttered, nipping at the sensitive curve of her backside before he gave her legs one last tug and he was able to find the damp heat he was searching for.

Brianna gave a strangled scream, her body clenching with shocked joy. There was something extraordinarily erotic in being fully dressed as Edmond made love to her with his tongue and teeth.

Her eyes slid closed as she concentrated on the building tension in the pit of her stomach. She had already accepted she could not be rid of her desire for this man. Why not enjoy what he could offer?

Over and over, his tongue teased at her sensitive peak, occasionally dipping into her opening with a skill that had her swiftly tumbling toward her climax.

Attuned to Brianna's low moans and quickening pants, Edmond abruptly rose to his feet, hiking up the back of her dress and fumbling with the fastening of his elegant breeches.

"Keep a hold on the post," he rasped, his hand tugging her leg up until her foot rested on the edge of the mattress, leaving her feeling open and vulnerable.

Expecting Edmond to lay her on the bed, Brianna glanced over her shoulder in confusion, her heart jerking at the stark determination etched on his dark features. It was as if he were utterly focused on providing her the pinnacle of satisfaction.

"I do not understand."

"You will," he promised, his hand sliding down her inner thigh at the same moment his erection nudged at her slit from behind.

"Oh."

Her head fell back to lie against his shoulder, her neck boneless with pleasure as he thrust deep inside her. Oh…dear heavens. She'd thought he had taught her all there was to know about passion. Obviously, there were still delicious lessons to be learned.

Holding on to the post to help support her weak knees, Brianna groaned as his clever fingers spread her folds, stroking through her damp heat in pace with the fierce, relentless pump of his hips.

Downstairs, Lady Aberlane was no doubt waiting alone in the salon while the servants kept a close watch on the passing time, but at the moment Brianna did not care. Let them speculate on what was keeping her and Edmond absent. Right now, all that mattered was the beckoning release that hovered just on the horizon.

With a rasping moan, Edmond buried his face in the curve of her neck, his mouth branding savage kisses against her damp skin.

"Tell me what you feel," he demanded. "Tell me this is more than passion."

"No."

"Tell me, Brianna." He thrust deeper, faster. "Tell me."

"It is…just…" Her body bowed and she instinctively reached back to shove her fingers in his hair as the shattering bliss clutched at her body. "Lust."

EDMOND LEANED AGAINST the mantle, sipping the tepid champagne and ignoring the speculative glances cast in his direction by Lord Milbank's numerous guests. He knew they were simply curious at the presence of the elusive Duke of Huntley. Stefan so rarely attended these tedious functions, it was bound to stir excitement.

Especially considering he had arrived with a fiancée dangling upon his arm.

So far as he was concerned, they could gawk all they liked. There was nothing to be read on his mild expression. Years of experience had enabled him to master the skill of keeping even his most violent emotions concealed.

And his current emotions were most certainly violent.

Forcing himself to take another sip of the champagne, Edmond slid a brooding glance toward the woman who was entirely responsible for his foul temper.

Mon dieu. He should be utterly, blissfully satisfied.

Not only had he managed to fulfill his insistent desire for Brianna Quinn, but he had demonstrated to the aggravating, stubborn minx that she was incapable of resisting him.

That she *belonged* to him.

It had been proven with each tremble of her body, with the damp readiness she could not disguise as he had penetrated her, and the soft cries of pleasure that he could still hear ringing in his ears.

So why, by God, did he desire to storm across the room and toss Brianna Quinn over his shoulder so he could haul her back to his town house?

Because while he had revealed that she was a willing slave to his passion, she had managed to keep her innermost self hidden behind her guarded barriers.

Damn the wench.

He was not quite certain why he should care. Brianna was nothing more than a pawn to be used in his hunt for his brother's stalker, was she not? And if he was fortunate enough to have the use of her delectable body without the burden of worrying that she might complicate matters with her tedious emotions, well…so much the better, surely?

But it was not for the better. In fact, it was downright maddening.

She should believe herself hopelessly in love with him. Young maidens always confused lust with those ridiculous, tender, sentimental emotions. It was the greatest danger to any practiced rake. And why most wise gentlemen went to such an effort to avoid innocents.

But despite using his every seductive skill, some that would have made the most experienced woman weak in the knees, he had been unable to force her to admit that she felt more than mere passion.

The fact that she could keep herself emotionally aloof was like an aggravating thorn in his side he could not dislodge.

Seemingly unaware of his hooded gaze, Brianna moved among the guests with a remarkable ease. There were few who would ever be able to guess that she had lived such an isolated life with her mother. Or recall that she was in any way connected to a lout like Thomas Wade.

She possessed an innate sense of charm and genuine interest in others that easily allowed even the highest sticklers to forget her unfortunate connections.

And, of course, it did not hurt that she was currently engaged to one of England's most powerful gentlemen.

She was busily endearing herself to Lady Roddick when Edmond grimaced at the sight of his aunt forging a determined path in his direction. There was no mistaking the ominous expression on her elderly face.

Halting at his side, Letty snapped her spangled fan open, practically quivering with disapproval.

"Well, I hope you are pleased with yourself."

Edmond's gaze was ruthlessly lured back to the autumn-haired wench across the crimson and ivory room.

"Not particularly." He battled to keep his expression from revealing his smoldering annoyance. "In truth, it would be difficult for me to be any less pleased with myself at this moment."

"Good," the older woman announced with a faint smile. "I am pleased to hear it."

With a humorless laugh, Edmond returned his attention to Letty. "Is this just an overall pleasure in seeing me tortured, or is there a more specific reason to wish me ill?"

Lady Aberlane lifted a silver brow. "Brianna did not tell you?"

"Brianna is barely willing to be in the same room, let alone tell me anything," he muttered.

"Not surprising, I suppose, considering the circumstances."

He stiffened, his eyes narrowing at his aunt's mysterious manner. It was bad enough to endure Brianna's aggravating, unpredictable behavior. He'd be damned if he would tolerate any more.

"If you have something to say, Aunt Letty, then simply say it. I am weary of puzzles."

The older woman sniffed at his clipped demand. "You desire plain speaking?"

"It would make a refreshing change."

"Very well. As Brianna and I returned from our shopping trip this afternoon…"

"Shopping?" Edmond interrupted, a chilled fear twisting his gut. Taking Letty's arm, he tugged her into a nearby alcove, well aware that not even his considerable control was capable of disguising his furious disbelief. "Do you mean to tell me that less than a day after she was nearly killed, Brianna Quinn was prancing through the streets of London as if nothing had happened?"

Letty's stern expression became one of wariness as she realized the true extent of Edmond's anger.

"Hardly prancing." She frowned. "We visited a few shops and returned home."

"She knows that she is not to leave the town house unless it is in my company, or that of Boris."

Letty searched his harsh expression with a hint of confusion. "For goodness sakes, she is not your prisoner."

"She might very well be in danger, and I will not have her risking her bloody neck with such reckless stupidity," he rasped. "Obviously, she needs a reminder that my orders are to be obeyed."

Edmond turned, intent on reaching Brianna and informing her that she was to be locked in her chambers when he was forced to an abrupt halt as Letty darted directly in his path.

"No, Edmond," she said, her tone low but firm.

"Letty, move aside."

"No." She poked his chest with a bejeweled finger. "You have already humiliated Brianna enough for one day. You will not create a scene among those who will decide whether or not she is to be accepted among society."

Humiliated Brianna enough for one day? What the devil did that mean? Surely the chit had not told Letty of their passionate encounter? And even if she had, it was hardly humiliating. It had been…earth shattering.

He gave a shake of his head. Whatever slight Brianna thought he might have given her would have to wait until later.

First, he intended to make sure she never risked her foolish neck again.

"Society, be damned," he growled. "Brianna will not be allowed to disobey me. Not when I very nearly—"

He abruptly cut off his words, knowing that they would reveal more than he was prepared to admit. Even to himself.

Letty, of course, was too intelligent to have missed his telling admission.

"What? When you very nearly lost her?" she demanded

softly. With a sad smile, she lightly touched his arm. "It was not your fault that Brianna was wounded. The guilt lies squarely upon the shoulders of whoever it was that pulled the trigger."

"It does not matter who is at fault, Aunt Letty." He cut off her words, grimly banishing the guilt that festered deep inside. "Not so long as Brianna understands that she will not be allowed to leave Huntley House until I am certain that the danger has passed."

Something that might have been pity rippled over Lady Aberlane's face before she was heaving a sigh and stepping back.

"I suppose there is no attempting to dissuade you from this ridiculous overreaction, but I do insist that you wait until we have returned home before informing Brianna she is to be put upon such a short leash."

"I told you I do not give a damn about society."

"Well, I do."

He arched a brow. "You fear I will create a scene? Surely you know me better than that."

"Not at all. I would simply prefer to have fewer witnesses when Brianna murders you. She is far too sweet to be hauled off to the gallows."

"Good lord, whatever happened to family loyalty? Should you not be closing ranks with your favorite nephew?"

She snorted as she began to move away. "Whatever makes you think that you are my favorite nephew?"

Edmond chuckled as the spry matron moved toward the clutch of fellow dragons near the window.

How the devil had he allowed his life to become so cluttered with women? He of all men knew the dangers of allowing such complications. They were distractions at best and downright pests at worse.

No doubt if he had the least amount of wits, he would send them packing at the first opportunity.

Ignoring the strangest pang that tugged at his heart at the thought, Edmond started across the room, only to be halted once again. This time by a uniformed servant who performed a deep bow as he reached his side.

"Your Grace."

"Yes?"

"This message was delivered for you."

"Thank you." Taking the folded note, Edmond opened it to swiftly scan the neatly printed words, sucking in a deep breath of surprise. "Please have my carriage brought around," he commanded the waiting servant.

"At once, your Grace."

BRIANNA STIFFENED THE MOMENT she sensed Edmond moving in her direction. For the majority of the evening, he had been content to lean against the mantle, his burning gaze so focused upon her that it was a wonder she had not gone up in flames.

Dear God, how could society not realize that the man posing as the Duke of Huntley was a fraud?

Stefan was so kind, so eager to put the happiness of others above his own. His goodness was a shimmering beacon, while Edmond…even across the room she could feel the potent danger that smoldered about him with a restless energy.

Light and dark. Opposite sides of the same coin.

A renegade excitement tingled through her blood as she felt the heat of Edmond's hard frame halt at her side, his hand possessively landing in the middle of her back.

"My dear, may I have a word?" he murmured, smoothly.

Brianna battled back a jaundiced frown as the elegant ladies who surrounded her heaved a collective sigh of appreciation. What woman would not be enchanted by Edmond's compelling beauty? Or the raw, untamed sensuality that the dark, elegant evening attire could not entirely disguise?

It was impossible not to react.

Gathering the cool composure that was her only defense, she curled her lips into a meaningless smile.

"But of course."

Lady Roddick gave a twittering laugh, leaning forward to lightly tap her fan on Brianna's arm.

"A word of warning, Miss Quinn, it is never wise to always give in to your husband's demands." The older woman slid an undeniably hungry glance over Edmond's chiseled body. The tart. "They are far too likely to run roughshod over a poor maiden who does not possess a bit of pluck."

Brianna forced herself to meet Edmond's smoldering gaze. "I fear his Grace prefers a more spineless creature as his fiancée, is that not so…Stefan?"

"Ah, if only such a creature truly existed," he drawled, his hand firmly propelling her away from the crowd. "This way, my love."

With no choice but to follow his lead or put up a ridiculous struggle, Brianna waited until they were standing near the refreshment table, which offered a selection of lobster patties, potted pigeon, stuffed mushrooms and various custards, before turning.

"What is it you want?"

"To throttle you, for a start," he growled.

"Go right ahead." Her chin tilted. "I doubt anyone would be willing to dare the wrath of the Duke of Huntley to halt you."

For a moment, Brianna feared he might actually wrap his hands around her throat. His anger was a palpable heat that crawled over her skin, making it prickle with unmistakable warning.

In the end, his fierce restraint overcame his temper, and muttering a foul curse, he contented himself with a warning glare.

"I do not have time for this nonsense. We must leave immediately."

"Leave? Why?"

"I have information that the villain who shot you has been discovered."

Brianna accepted the news with a shrug. The small wound on her forehead had induced a great deal of sympathetic interest when she arrived tonight, but she was remarkably indifferent to the knowledge she had very nearly died on that foggy balcony.

Perhaps not so surprising. She had swooned so swiftly that she had little memory of the actual chaos after being shot. And those few memories had been easily burned away by Edmond's intense lovemaking.

And of course, the agonizing sight of Edmond's carriage waiting in front of La Russa's town house.

That was far more painful than any mere bullet.

"So you have not entirely forgotten the reason you are in London?"

"What?" His teeth snapped together as he savagely contained his anger. "Never mind. Very soon, Brianna Quinn, we are going to discuss my dislike for sulky women."

"As if I give a bloody damn."

"You will." Taking her arm in a grip that was a breath away from painful, he began towing her toward the nearby door. "Now, sheathe that lethal tongue and smile while we make our apologies to our hostess for leaving so early."

"There is no need to drag me, for God's sakes," she muttered.

He cast a warning frown. "Just be glad that Aunt Letty convinced me not to toss you over my shoulder and haul you away."

CHAPTER FOURTEEN

THE NOTE THAT EDMOND HAD received from Chesterfield had
been brief. Just a scribbled warning that his employee had
spotted the carriage used by the villain who had shot Brianna
and tracked him to the stables on Piccadilly.

It was enough, however, to make Edmond take the precau-
tion of gathering Boris and three other guards before mounting
his horse and heading out of Mayfair. He was not taking any
chances of having the mysterious attacker slip through his
grasp again.

The sooner he managed to put an end to the threat to his
brother, the better.

Perhaps then he could return to St. Petersburg and to the
lavish, exotic existence he had always enjoyed. It was far preferable to meddle in others' lives than to have his own bedeviled.

He ignored the sharp clench of his heart as he slowed his
mount and regarded the shadowed stables that were conveniently situated near the hotels located on Piccadilly. He hoped
the assailant would put up a fight. He was in a perfect mood to
beat the villain within an inch of his life.

"Those are the stables just ahead," he said, his gaze scanning
the gas-lit street.

Boris moved to his side, his expression hard with anticipation. He was eager for violence, as well.

"Where are you to meet Chesterfield?"

"At the back entrance."

"Wait here while the guards search for any unwanted surprises. Once we are sure there are no traps, we will move into position and I will whistle."

"That is not…"

Boris leaned forward, his considerable bulk hard and threatening beneath his heavy coat.

"Do not move until then."

Edmond lifted a hand of defeat. Boris might be in his employ, but the trained soldier would willingly knock Edmond unconscious, if he thought it necessary to keep him safe.

"Go, Boris, I will wait for your signal," he grudgingly conceded.

Remaining in the cloaking shadows of a nearby building, Edmond absorbed the sounds of the night. The click of horseshoes on the cobblestone streets, the shout of vendors peddling their wares to the passing pedestrians, the muffled voices of grooms as they passed the evening awaiting the return of their employers.

The predictable sounds of a city.

And the predictable odors.

Edmond grimaced at the scent of rotting garbage and sewage that wafted from the gutters. There were certainly times when he understood his brother's violent loathing for London.

His patience was at a snapping point when at last the low whistle filled the air, and Edmond urged his horse into a trot toward the back of the stables. He had barely entered the yard, when a slender form detached from the shadows.

Pulling to a halt, Edmond slid from his horse and tied the reins to a nearby post.

"Chesterfield."

The Runner was attired in the rough clothing of a groom, his face smudged with dirt. A perfect disguise to move about the London streets unnoted, but it was the speculative smile that captured Edmond's attention.

"Now, I wonder why a Duke would hire servants that not only have obvious military training, but the skills more suitable for a master thief than a footman?"

Edmond shrugged, inanely acknowledging it was a stroke of fortune that Chesterfield was on his payroll rather than that of his enemy. The man missed nothing.

"It would be healthier not to wonder about such meaningless things," he said, his voice soft with warning.

Chesterfield shrugged. "Just so long as the Crown Jewels do not go missing."

"Your message said the carriage was discovered?"

"My employee noticed it outside Lord Milbank's mews, but when he tried to slip closer, the carriage took off," the Runner explained. "Thankfully London traffic is such a nasty tangle, it was easy enough to follow it to these stables."

"And the driver?"

"Disappeared into Pultney's Hotel." Chesterfield jutted his chin toward the nearby hotel. "The back suite on the second floor."

"Mon dieu."

Chesterfield frowned. "Does it make sense to you, your Grace? Because it bloody well makes none to me. In my experience, murderers do not take rooms at Pultney's."

"No. But there is something…"

Edmond furrowed his brow in concentration. He was desperate to capture that elusive knowledge that he had been thinking of Pultney's Hotel only days ago. But why? He had been sitting at the morning table, had he not? And he was…ah yes, reading the morning paper. There had been something that had captured his attention. Some ridiculous tidbit of gossip that had seemed out of place.

Viktor Kazakov! The Russian who Alexander Pavlovich had commanded to Siberia and who should never have been in London. Edmond had sent a note to the Russian ambassador, but then had put the man completely from his mind.

A lapse in judgment that had very nearly cost Brianna her life.

With a sharp curse, he turned to gesture toward his watchful servant.

"Boris."

Chesterfield cleared his throat as the man hurried forward. "Do you have a plan?"

"Boris and I are going to call upon the gentleman."

"Do you think that is wise, considering that he wants you dead?" the Runner carefully pointed out.

"It certainly is preferable to having him shadow me through London, taking shots whenever it pleases him," Edmond growled. "Or worse, leading me about by the nose."

"Understandable. But why not allow me to accompany your servant—"

"No."

"Your Grace, have you forgotten that you were nearly killed only a few nights ago?"

"I will never forget, Chesterfield, that much I can assure you."

"Then why take such a risk, when I am willing to offer my protection?"

Edmond's expression hardened. "Because I have duties that demand secrecy."

"I have assured you of my discretion—"

"You might as well give way, Chesterfield," Boris interrupted the Runner's pleading words. "There is no swaying the man, once he has set his mind on a course. No doubt it has something to do with all that blue blood that runs through his veins. It rots his brain."

Edmond cast his companion a jaundiced glare. "Thank you, Boris."

The soldier smiled. "Think nothing of it."

With a shake of his head, Edmond returned his attention to the Runner. "Remain here with your men. I will call if I need you."

Chesterfield gave in with a small grunt. "Very well."

Reaching into the pocket of his greatcoat, Edmond pulled out his dueling pistol and gestured to Boris to follow him down the street to the corner. He would approach the hotel from the servants' entrance.

Boris remained at his side, his gaze darting from side to side.

"Did you discover anything?"

"That I am a fool," Edmond muttered, coming to an abrupt halt at the sight of the two gentlemen standing at the opening of the alley.

It was too dark to make out the features of the men, but there was no mistaking that the low conversation they were sharing was in Russian.

Edmond flattened himself against the wall of the building, tugging Boris beside him. He was not at all shocked when he recognized the deep voice of Viktor Kazakov.

"You understand my orders?" Viktor was demanding.

"I am not stupid," his companion rasped. "I am to leave London by dawn and travel straight to Dover where I am to take the first available packet to France. From there I am to make my way to Moscow."

"Do not return to your rooms here in London and do not speak with anyone," Viktor commanded in cold tones. "And that includes your mistress."

The other man made a sound of disgust. "This is foolishness. I tell you that I was not recognized."

"You said that the servant attempted to approach you. The same servant who tried to follow you after you were stupid enough to take a shot at Huntley on the balcony."

Boris stiffened next to Edmond. He was too well-trained, however, to jump from the shadows and break Viktor's neck. Not without a direct order from Edmond.

A tempting thought, but one that would have to wait until Edmond had the information he needed.

"You commanded me to make Lord Edmond believe his brother is in danger. How better than to lodge a bullet in the Duke of Huntley's heart? And besides, the servant could have been approaching me for any number of reasons," the unknown man grumbled. "Most likely, he wanted to invite me for a pint of that swill that they call ale in this country."

"We are too close to the end of Alexander Pavlovich's reign to make foolish mistakes. Lord Edmond must continue to believe that his brother is in danger."

Edmond clenched his fists as his sickening suspicions became a hard reality. *Mon dieu.* He was an idiot. A dim-witted, thick-skulled lobcock who deserved to be shot.

"And does he believe it?" the irate man demanded, his tone surly.

"He is in England, is he not?" Viktor snapped.

Even in the darkness, Edmond could sense the tension building between the two men. Viktor Kazakov had a brewing revolt on his hands. The treacherous bastard.

"England, but not in London," his companion pointed out, thankfully unaware that it was Edmond posing as the Duke of Huntley. A small mercy. "Perhaps he remains in Surrey because he suspects that something is amiss."

Viktor stepped closer to the other man, his hand in his pocket where he no doubt had a gun hidden.

"So long as he is away from St. Petersburg and the Czar, he can suspect all he likes."

There was a momentary silence as violence trembled between the two. Then, with a grudging gesture of defeat, the unknown man stepped back from Viktor's taller form.

"The Commander will not be pleased to have me sent from London," he muttered. "I was under strict instructions to keep him informed of your progress here."

Edmond smiled grimly, as he could sense Viktor's fury. The conceited, ridiculously pompous fool had always considered himself superior to others. Including his own Czar.

"I am in charge, not the Commander, and if he desires to be kept informed of my progress, then he should leave the comfort and obscurity of the Winter Palace and travel to London." Viktor spat the words in obvious disgust.

"He cannot risk such exposure," he companion argued.

"And why not? He readily demands that we risk far more

than mere exposure. Why should he be allowed to skulk in the shadows and demand that others do the dangerous work?"

"Perhaps you should ask him yourself."

"Perhaps I will," Viktor warned, icily. "Now be on your way, fool."

The man muttered beneath his breath, but obviously trained to obey orders, he at last hunched his shoulders and slunk down the street. Viktor watched his companion's retreat until he was swallowed by the darkness. Only then did he turn to enter the hotel behind him.

EDMOND AND BORIS RETRACED their path toward the stables, waiting until they were well away from the hotel before Boris at last broke the tense silence.

"Viktor Kazakov." The name came out as a curse. Boris, like most of those in Alexander Pavlovich's inner circle, was well aware that the nobleman mouthed the appropriate words in public, even as he stirred the seeds of discontent in private. "He was banished to Siberia. What the hell is he doing in London?"

Edmond struggled to maintain his composure as they slid down the dark street.

"Clearly laying a false trail that was so obvious that the veriest greenhorn should have realized it was nothing more than a trap," he said, his voice raw with self-disgust. "And yet I, who pride myself on being so terribly clever, followed it as if I did not possess the least amount of wits. *Mon dieu.* How could I ever have been so stupid? I should have suspected from the beginning that I was being lured from St. Petersburg."

Boris sent him a worried frown. "You were worried for your brother."

"And we both know that the best distractions are those that touch a person's deepest vulnerability." Edmond smacked a fist in his open palm. He wished to God that it was Viktor Kazakov's smug face. "Christ, I have used them often enough."

"You had no choice but to return to England and ensure the

Duke's safety, Summerville. No one could hold you to blame for your concern."

"I hold me to blame, as I well should. I allowed emotions to overcome my common sense."

"It is impossible to change the past," Boris said with the philosophical acceptance that was purely Russian. "What do we do now? Kill Viktor Kazakov?"

Edmond's lips twitched into a grudging smile at Boris's eager desire to put an end to the nobleman.

"Not yet."

"He is plotting against the Czar."

That much was obvious, even from what little they had overheard. Unfortunately, Edmond knew Viktor Kazakov well enough to realize that he would prefer death to confessing the truth. He was a true zealot in his determination to reform Russia. Something that Alexander Pavlovich had once promised, only to return to the heavy hand of his ancestors when he became disillusioned and weary of battling his countrymen's fear of progress.

"Yes, but we still do not know who his contact in Russia is. The Commander must be a man of importance if he is a guest at the Winter Palace," he pointed out. "We cannot reveal that we are aware of the threat until we know who is involved. Otherwise, the traitors will simply melt into the shadows until they feel it is safe to try with a new plot."

Boris shook his head in disgust. "Bastards."

"My feelings exactly." Nearing the stables, Edmond placed a hand on his companion's arm as he came to a sudden halt. "I want Viktor Kazakov watched day and night. Hire as many men as you need—he is not to visit the outhouse without you keeping me informed. Is that understood?"

"Of course."

"And send one of the guards after the stranger. He should be able to catch up with him on the Dover Road. Tell him to befriend the man, if at all possible, on the ferry to France. It might be that the traitor will reveal some sort of useful information."

Boris nodded, his eyes narrowed. "What will you be doing?"

Edmond grimaced. His loyalty toward Alexander Pavlovich demanded that he remain in London and monitor Viktor. The man had to be in contact with his Russian cohorts by some means, and no one was better at discovering those means than Edmond.

But for once, Edmond had a more pressing concern than the welfare of his Czar. Viktor had already proven he was willing to murder the powerful Duke of Huntley to further his goals. Who was to say he would not consider Brianna a suitable sacrifice as well?

Besides, there was always Thomas Wade lurking in the shadows. If Edmond were concentrating upon Viktor, he would be unable to protect Brianna from the desperate animal.

"I must return to Surrey for a short time," he said, his words clipped.

Boris lifted his brows before an annoying smile curved his lips. "You intend to take the woman to your brother."

Edmond did not bother to confirm the man's astute supposition.

"Do not fail me."

"Have I ever?"

"Never."

Turning away, Edmond was halted as Boris called out softly. "Edmond."

He glanced over his shoulder, managing to hide his impatience.

"Yes?"

"Take Janet with you as well. If there is danger, then she is certain to do something foolish to try and protect Miss Quinn."

Edmond gave a bark of laughter. "As if I could pry her away from her mistress." He paused, his expression somber. "Be careful, Boris. Kazakov plays the part of an arrogant buffoon, but he is a dangerous opponent who would not hesitate to kill you if he realized you are tracking him."

Boris dipped his head in agreement. "You take care as

well. The traitors are keeping an eye on Meadowland. You must be on guard."

"Always."

ALONE IN HER CHAMBERS, Brianna futilely commanded herself to go to sleep, tossing and turning for over an hour before she at last conceded defeat. Rising from the bed, she pulled on a thin robe and gave into the overwhelming urge to pace the floor.

It was just because she was still angry at the knowledge that Edmond had visited a common tart, she told herself. That was the reason her stomach felt tied in knots and her mouth dry. It had nothing to do with the fact that Edmond had charged off into the night after some dangerous maniac.

Of course, the reasonable excuse did nothing to explain why her pacing took her continually to the window to peer toward the dark mews, or why her ears were strained for the sound of Edmond's footsteps in the corridor.

Or why, when she at last heard them, she had to clutch at the mantle as her knees went weak with relief. She leaned her forehead against the cool marble. What the devil was the matter with her?

The door to her chambers was quietly pushed open and then closed. Spinning on her heel, Brianna regarded Edmond in disbelief.

"Edmond, for God's sake, are you deliberately attempting to ruin my reputation? It is bad enough…"

Her words faltered as Edmond stalked forward, his features hard with a lethal intent.

Hastily she backed away, slamming into the wall. Edmond did not halt until he was standing mere inches from her, his hands landing on the wall on either side of her head.

"When I decide to ruin you, Brianna Quinn, you will know," he warned, his breath brushing over her cheek. "For now what I want is for you to pack your bags."

Brianna blinked in confusion. "What?"

The brilliant blue gaze swept restlessly over her face, almost as if his thoughts were not entirely upon their conversation.

"We leave for Meadowland within the hour."

"Meadowland? Why?"

"What does it matter? You have been tediously demanding to be taken there since you stepped foot in this house."

Brianna shivered as the heat of his body warmed her through her sheer peach nightgown.

"And you have pig-headedly refused my demands, if you will recall. So why have you suddenly decided to go in the middle of the night?"

He paused, considering his words. "I have duties to attend to. You will be safer beneath Stefan's protection."

Brianna stiffened. Of course. How stupid of her. He had visited his mistress, had he not? What use did he have for an untried female?

"I see. You have had your fill of me and now I am to be handed off. Only to be expected, I suppose."

"Had my fill of you?" He growled deep in his throat, his eyes flashing fire as he used his hard body to press her against the wall. Brianna shuddered as he buried his head in the curve of her neck, his erection a hard thrust against her lower stomach. "You are a fool."

Brianna clutched at the lapels of his jacket, the feel of his lips caressing the tender curve of her neck sending sheets of fire through her willing body. The exquisite sensations were stealing any resolve to deny the fierce need that she could sense trembling in his taut body. She wanted this. His heat, his desire, his hungry demand that was more arousing than any amount of tenderness.

"On that we both agree." Her eyes squeezed shut as his mouth moved down to capture the tip of her nipple through the thin fabric of her robe.

"*Ma souris.*" His ragged breaths rasped through the air as he tugged her robe upward. "You are driving me mad."

"Edmond…you said we were leaving…"

"Shh." He captured her lips in a silencing kiss, his hands clumsy as he dealt with the buttons of his pantaloons and positioned the tip of his erection at her entrance. "Do you want me?"

Brianna swallowed a groan of frustration. Dear lord, he was so wonderfully close, and yet refusing to enter her completely.

"Please, Edmond."

"Say the words, Brianna," he demanded against her lips. "Tell me you want me."

Reaching up she shoved her fingers into his hair and arched her body against him.

"I want you."

He kissed her with savage satisfaction as he tilted his hips upward and filled her with one smooth thrust.

CHAPTER FIFTEEN

BRIANNA WOKE THE NEXT morning with a sense of bewilderment. It took long moments of studying the cherubs painted on the ceiling for her to recall she was no longer in her chambers at Huntley House, but instead in a pretty gold and cream room at Meadowland.

A glance toward the window revealed that the sun was slanting across the Persian carpet. She had slept far later than usual, but that was hardly surprising given her eventful evening.

After their sweetly furious bout of lovemaking, Edmond had watched in silence as Brianna had packed her bags and descended to enter the waiting carriage. Her hands had trembled as she had folded the various satin and silk gowns into her valise, but her composure had remained grimly intact.

Edmond had chosen to ride beside the vehicle as it had rattled over the turnpike to Surrey, leaving Brianna alone to endure the curious questions of Lady Aberlane and Janet, who had been awakened to join her on the unexpected journey.

Not that she had any answers. She was as confused as her companions as to why they had been forced to leave London in such a rush.

With a disgusted shake of her head at being hauled about with no explanations, Brianna left her bed and rang for Janet.

There was no point in brooding on Edmond Summerville or his autocratic dictates. With any luck, he would have left Meadowland.

Near an hour later, Brianna was bathed and attired in a

striped emerald and white gown that brought out the green of her eyes and the deep red highlights in her hair. She added brown leather half-boots and a cameo that she had threaded through a green ribbon and tied about her neck.

Leaving her chambers, she headed down the long hallway, fondly noting the worn wainscot with carved cornices that had seen better days. The same could be said for the mahogany and gilt chairs that lined the frayed crimson runner. Despite her aggravation with Edmond at having been hustled out of London in the dead of night, she could not deny a flare of pleasure at returning to Meadowland.

Her most cherished childhood memories were here. Memories of sneaking into the music room to listen to the Duchess of Huntley playing the pianoforte, of Stefan teaching her the rudiments of chess, of Mrs. Slater baking her lemon tarts.

This house had been as much her home as her father's. Perhaps more so, since there had always been such a warm feeling of a loving family, a feeling that had been decidedly absent beneath her own roof.

Oh, her father had loved her, but his constant concern for his unpredictable wife ensured that he had little time to devote to his daughter, and her mother had never bothered to take note of her.

Reaching the grand staircase, Brianna made her way down to the lower floor, a smile curving her lips at the familiar male form standing at the bottom.

Stefan was an exact replica of his overbearing brother, but Brianna knew immediately who awaited her. It was in his kind expression and ready smile. And despite his resemblance to Edmond, Brianna realized that he did not stir thoughts of the arrogant, aggravating pain in her neck.

It was with an uncomplicated affection that she stepped into his arms and returned his warm hug.

"Good morning, Brianna."

"Stefan."

Stefan pulled back. "My dear, I am so sorry."

"Why would you be sorry?"

"Edmond has told me of all you have suffered at Thomas Wade's hands. I never liked the man, but I did not dream—"

"You could not have known," she interrupted firmly.

"But I should have, as Edmond has informed me in no uncertain terms. It was my duty to protect you, and I failed miserably." He dropped his hands and squared his shoulders. "I intend to do everything in my power to make it up to you. That much I promise."

"I am just happy to be here. Meadowland has not changed a bit."

"Yes, so I have been told." He glanced around the foyer, smiling wryly. "I begin to wonder if I should halt living in the past and take steps to refurbish the old monstrosity."

"Oh, no," Brianna protested, only realizing it was hardly her place to decide what should be done to the charming estate. "Well, obviously you must do as you please, but I have to admit that I prefer it to remain just as it is. You know, when I was in Thomas Wade's home, I used to close my eyes and pretend that I was at Meadowland. It always made me feel…safe."

"My dear, sweet Brianna." Brianna was once again tugged into Stefan's arms. "I should have brought you home the moment your mother died."

Brianna happily soaked in Stefan's comfort. "I have missed you, Stefan."

"As I have missed you. This place has been far too quiet without your laughter, and I have grown far too dull without your teasing."

"Well, well. What a touching scene."

Brianna and Stefan jerked apart, as if they were two naughty children rather than lifelong friends.

"Edmond." Stefan cleared his throat. "I thought you would be gone by now."

Edmond's cold regard never shifted from Brianna's face. "I have decided to stay until tomorrow morning. If I am not intruding?"

"Of course not. I was about to take Brianna in to breakfast, will you join us?"

Brianna refused to flinch beneath the diamond-hard glare. She had been doing nothing wrong and she would not allow Edmond to make her feel guilty.

"I have some business I must attend to first." His voice could have sliced through stone. "I will join you later."

"Very well." Watching his brother turn away, Stefan slid Brianna a speculative gaze, taking her hand and placing it on his arm. "Come along, my dear."

Allowing Stefan to lead her into the magnificent dining room, Brianna took a moment to appreciate the glossy walnut table that could easily seat two dozen guests and the scrolled sideboard that was set beneath the large window that overlooked the distant lake. The ceiling had been painted during the reign of Charles II; it portrayed the Huntley coat of arms in glorious detail.

It was a beautiful room that still echoed with the laughter of glittering guests.

With a wistful sigh, Brianna moved to take her seat, only to come to a startled halt when she was nearly bowled over by a large dog that bounded around the table.

With an exclamation of delight, Brianna leaned down to rub the floppy ears, her mood lifting as the hound wiggled with open delight.

"Good heavens, this cannot be Puck?"

"Actually it is Puck the Second." Stefan heaved a sigh of disgust, even as a fond smile curved his lips. "He is just as worthless a hunter as his father, but I could not have him put down."

"Of course you could not. You have far too tender a heart."

"Hmm. Should I be flattered or offended, I wonder?"

"Flattered. Most certainly flattered."

Stefan waved aside one of the numerous uniformed servants and held out a chair.

"If you will have a seat, I will fill you a plate."

Brianna took her seat and flashed him a teasing smile.

"Why thank you, Stefan. It is not often that a woman is waited upon by a Duke."

"Think nothing of it," he murmured, moving to rapidly fill two plates with the buttered eggs, toast, kippers and thickly sliced ham. Returning to the table, he placed one of the plates in front of her before taking a seat at her side. "After all, a man is expected to tend to the needs of his fiancée."

"Oh lord, I had almost forgotten about that." She reached to place her hand on his arm. "I assure you, Stefan, it was not my notion. I would never want to put you in such an awkward position."

"I am assuming that Edmond had his reasons, although he has yet to fully explain them to me. And in truth, I do not consider it awkward to have my name coupled with such a beautiful woman. It can do nothing but elevate my reputation in society."

Brianna grimaced. "Hardly that. Do not forget, I shall always have the taint of Thomas Wade upon me."

"Do not say that, Brianna."

"Why not? It is true enough. If it had not been for the power of the Huntley name, I would never have been allowed into society. And who could truly blame them?"

"I do. Your father was an honorable gentleman who was well-respected throughout England. You have every reason to be proud, Brianna."

She briskly thrust aside the threat of tears. "It does not matter. Once you announce that the engagement is at an end, it will soon enough be forgotten."

He studied her determined expression, his eyes far kinder than Edmond's, but no less intelligent.

"There is no hurry." He reached for his fork. "Now tell me, my dear, did Edmond treat you well while you were in London?"

"Well enough." She took a bite of toast, vividly aware of Stefan's gaze. "You know, Stefan, I feel as if I have been gone forever. I simply have to know all the news from Surrey. I heard Sarah Pierce married Sir Kincaid's youngest son. Did you attend the wedding?"

Stefan's expression warned that he was aware that there was something she was hiding. Unlike his brother, however, he possessed enough manners not to press her. Instead, he readily distracted her with the various news he thought might interest her, allowing her to keep her secrets without censure.

Brianna wondered, not for the first time, how two men could look so much alike and be so completely different.

LEAVING STEFAN AND BRIANNA, Edmond stalked through the study to the terrace beyond the French doors. Once away from prying eyes, he shoved his fingers through his hair and sucked in a deep breath.

Mon dieu, when he had walked into the foyer to see Brianna in his brother's arms, his fury had been so swift and so violent he had very nearly lost control. He trembled with the need to charge across the floor and beat his brother for daring to lay a hand on Brianna. She was *his*. And he would prove it in the most basic and savage means possible.

Only the shock of his reaction kept him frozen in place.

Christ, why had he not left at dawn as he had intended? With Brianna and his Aunt Letty safely in his brother's care, there was nothing to keep him from returning to London and his duties.

Nothing but that damnable reluctance to allow Brianna out of his sight.

Once again, that throbbing fury raced through him and Edmond paced the terrace as he struggled to contain the primitive emotions.

As if to prove her ability to torment him, Brianna walked out a side door to enter the sunken gardens directly below the terrace. Edmond stiffened, hungrily drinking in the sight of her slender body as she moved past the marble statues that lined the path, her hips swaying with provocation and her hair shimmering with autumn fire in the morning sunlight.

He was moving down the steps of the terrace before he realized his intent, his chest squeezing in the oddest manner.

"Brianna."

She froze at the sound of his voice, her shoulders tense. Coming to a halt directly behind her, Edmond sensed her desire to flee from his presence and wisely resisted the urge to reach out and touch her. It might very well send her bolting back to the house.

After a long moment, she at last grudgingly turned.

"I thought you had pressing business to attend to?"

"Why were you in my brother's arms?"

She jerked, as if caught off guard by his question. "We have always been close friends, you know that. And it is hardly the first time Stefan has given me a hug."

"You were a child then."

Her lips twisted in a humorless smile. "And you have made very certain I am no longer that child, haven't you, Edmond?"

"Do you hope Stefan will wed you?"

"How dare you!"

"Just answer the question, Brianna."

"Why should I?" She wrapped her arms about her waist, her expression defiant. "It is none of your concern."

"It is very much my concern. Do you truly believe I would allow my lover to marry my own brother?"

"I am not your lover," she stated. "And I am most certainly not the sort of woman who is constantly angling to land a husband. There are a rare few of us who comprehend the benefits of a life that is not confined by the dictates of some man."

Edmond dismissed her words with a wave of his hand. "Even presuming I believe you would not leap at the opportunity to become the next Duchess of Huntley, my brother is not a monk," he muttered.

"What is that supposed to mean?"

"Stefan lives a life of near isolation here. To bring a young and exquisitely beautiful woman beneath his roof is bound to stir temptation."

"Ah, I see." Her anger shifted to outrage. "Because he is desperate and lonely, he might mistakenly believe he is attracted to me?"

"He would have to be dead not to be attracted to you, but my point is that he is vulnerable. And he already possesses feelings for you."

"Unlike you, Stefan is a gentleman of honor. He would never attempt to seduce his own ward."

"No, he would not seduce you. He would insist upon marriage."

"And having me as a sister-in-law is, of course, unacceptable," she mocked.

His breath hissed between his clenched teeth.

"Completely unacceptable."

She turned her head to glare at the pretty fountain that sprayed water from the head of a marble angel, but not before Edmond caught sight of the hurt in her eyes.

"So I am good enough to warm your bed, but not good enough to wed your brother."

Edmond belatedly realized he should never have approached Brianna while he was still raw with anger at having seen her with Stefan. Dammit. He had made a muck of the entire situation and he had no one to blame but himself.

"It has nothing to do with you being good enough."

She turned back in frustration. "Then what does it matter to you?"

"It matters because I will kill him," he bluntly admitted. "Is that clear enough for you, Brianna?"

She stumbled backward at his blatant threat.

"You've gone stark raving mad."

"Perhaps I have." Edmond offered a shallow bow. "Keep that in mind the next occasion you throw yourself in Stefan's arms."

CHAPTER SIXTEEN

AFTER THE SCENE IN THE garden, Brianna knew it would be impossible to return to the house and pretend nothing had occurred. Instead, she continued down the graveled path that led to the pretty grotto that possessed a perfect view of the lake.

It had always been one of her favorite places, and in the past, she had spent hours playing with her dolls or serving Stefan pretend tea upon the marble bench. There had also been a few hours devoted to spying upon Edmond when he had lured one of his numerous ladies into the nearby maze so he could steal kisses, and probably a great deal more.

Brianna paced the marble tiles, struggling to slow the rapid pace of her heart.

Why was he acting like a jealous husband, prepared to attack at the least hint of provocation?

After nearly an hour of brooding, the only conclusion that made the least amount of sense was the fact that Edmond's possessiveness had nothing to do with her and everything to do with Stefan. Although the two brothers openly loved one another, there was no doubting there had always been an unspoken competition between them when they were younger. A simple game of croquet could come to near blows.

The explanation did nothing to ease the smoldering anger. It was hardly flattering to be thought of as a piece of property, but it did help her to restore those fragile barriers that protected her heart.

Whatever this was between her and Edmond was no more

than a passing madness. A brief flame that would burn itself out and leave nothing but fading memories.

The reassuring thought had barely passed through her mind when the sound of approaching footsteps had her swiftly glancing down the path. She had a moment of near panic before it eased, as she realized the darkly handsome male rapidly making his way to the grotto was Stefan, not Edmond.

"Brianna? Am I intruding?"

"Of course not." She managed a smile at his hesitant tone. "Please join me."

Walking up the steps, Stefan stood next to her at the open window.

"You have been out here for a considerable length of time. Is anything the matter?"

"I am just out of sorts." Her attention returned to the glitter of the lake. When she was just a youngster, Stefan had often taken her fishing at the edges of the water, and even taught her to swim despite his mother's chiding that it was hardly seemly for Brianna to be splashing about in nothing more than her shift. A faint, longing ache touched her heart at those carefree days. "'Tis nothing to trouble you."

"I would be a poor host if I were not troubled to have one of my guests so unhappy." His fingers trailed a soft path down the curve of her cheek. "What did Edmond say to you?"

Astonished as much by his unexpected caress as by his words, she turned to meet his searching gaze.

"What?"

"I saw the two of you. In the garden."

"Oh." A heat stained her face at the thought that Stefan had witnessed the ridiculous argument. "It was nothing."

"Brianna, I have been accused of being remarkably dense when it comes to understanding my fellow man, but even I could tell the two of you were fighting."

She breathed out a deep sigh, realizing she could not disguise her lingering anger.

"Edmond has always managed to be the most aggravating gentleman I have ever encountered. Even when I was a child, he made me furious more often than not." Her lips twisted. "Nothing has changed in the past dozen years."

His expression was skeptical. "My dear, it is obvious that something happened between the two of you while you were in London. Do you not trust me enough to confess the truth?"

Instinctively she reached out to grasp his hand. "Stefan, I would trust you with my very life." She held his gaze as she gave his hand a slight squeeze. "You must know that. But…"

"But?"

"This is between Edmond and myself, I would prefer to keep it that way."

His eyes darkened as he regarded her for a long, oddly tense moment, as if he was wrestling with some inner emotion.

"I see."

"I am glad one of us does."

There was another silence, then Stefan squared his shoulders and his features hardened with an unexpected hint of steel.

"Will you sit with me a moment?"

Brianna gave a puzzled dip of her head. "Very well."

Together, they moved the short distance to settle on the marble bench, their hands still clasped, as Brianna waited for Stefan to break the silence.

"I think perhaps it would be best if I explain something about my brother."

"Actually, I know quite enough," she muttered. "He is arrogant, overbearing and utterly ruthless in getting what he wants."

"True enough, but he is also deeply wounded."

"Wounded?" Brianna blinked in shock. "Edmond?"

A hint of remembered pain darkened Stefan's eyes. "I know it is difficult to believe. He is always so careful to appear invulnerable, as if nothing can touch him. Especially not another person."

"He loves you."

"Yes, but he refuses to allow anyone else close to him. He is…frightened of opening himself up to affection."

Brianna warned herself to leave the grotto. To simply stand and walk away.

Edmond had taken her independence, her innocence and most of her wits. He could not have her sympathy as well.

But of course she did not leave.

Instead, she leaned forward and gave in to the treacherous curiosity.

"Why?" she breathed.

"You know that my parents drowned when their yacht sank in the Channel?"

"Of course." The pain of learning the Duke and Duchess had died had been far more devastating than the death of her own mother. They had been more than kindly neighbors who had taken pity on a lonely little girl. They had represented her only proof that true love did exist in the world. The death of the glittering, loving couple had seemed a travesty of devastating proportions. "I cried for a fortnight."

The pain deepened in his eyes. The entire family had been unfashionably devoted to one another.

"What most do not know is that they were traveling to London because Edmond had been caught in some mischief with his friends and hauled before the magistrate. It was not truly serious, but of course, my father was determined to ensure that Edmond was fully aware of his displeasure. They…never made it."

Her fingers tightened on his hand. "Oh, Stefan."

"It was horrible for me, but even worse for Edmond. He blames himself, you see. In his mind, our parents would still be alive if not for his mistakes. I am not certain he will ever be able to truly bury his guilt and forgive himself." He gave a shake of his head. "Until he does, he can't risk allowing himself to care for another."

Her heart twisted with a sharp, wrenching pain at the thought of a young Edmond closing himself off from the world and believing he was to blame for the death of his parents.

How could anyone live with such a heavy guilt?

It would be like a disease slowly eating away at his soul.

Without warning, she recalled his outrage at Thomas Wade's intrusion into his home, his fury when he spoke of Stefan being in danger and the sharp terror on his countenance when she had been shot on the balcony.

"He fears he will fail them. That's why he never allows others close."

Stefan heaved a sad sigh. "I have tried to do what I can, but so far it has not been enough."

"I do not think that Edmond is the only one who carries guilt, Stefan." She reached up to lightly touch his cheek. "I am certain that you have done everything possible to help your brother."

His own hand lifted, covering her fingers and pressing them even tighter against his face.

"Perhaps, but it does not make it any easier to know he suffers."

"No, I suppose it does not."

"In any event, I just thought it might ease the tension between you and Edmond if you understood why he pushes others away."

"I am not certain that anything can actually ease the tension," she said wryly. "And no doubt it is for the best."

"Brianna?"

Strangely comforted by his touch, she offered a smile. "Yes?"

"I want you to know that you always have a home here at Meadowland."

Her breath caught at his soft words. She had been alone for so very long. To know that, whatever the future might hold, she would always have a home was as precious as the finest jewels.

"Thank you, Stefan. That means more to me than you can ever know."

"It is the least I can do after…"

She shifted to press her fingers against his lips. "That is all in the past."

He lightly grasped her wrist, his thumb gently rubbing over the steady pulse.

"And my offer is not entirely selfless, you know." His hand tightened on her wrist as she threatened to pull away, his lips moving against the tips of her fingers. "You have grown into an incredibly beautiful woman, Brianna. So beautiful, you take my breath away."

She stilled, not at all certain how to react to his astonishing words.

"Stefan?"

Maintaining his grip on her wrist, he turned her hand so he could place a gentle, lingering kiss on her palm before releasing her.

"I realize that you have always seen me as a friend, but I am a man as well, my dear. One that is quite capable of appreciating the charms of an intelligent, lovely young maiden. Especially a maiden who has always owned a very large part of my heart. No, do not say anything," he interrupted the words trembling on her lips as he rose to his feet. He gazed down at her with an expression she had never thought to see on his face. The expression of a man physically aware of a woman. "I merely wished you to know that I am here for you, should you have need. I must return to the house. Will you walk with me?"

She gave a slow bemused shake of her head. She could still feel the imprint of Stefan's touch upon her wrist. Not the searing, dangerous sensations that Edmond created, but more a comforting warmth that was not at all unpleasant.

"Actually, I do not think that would be entirely wise," she at last managed to mutter.

"Why on earth not?" he demanded, his brows lifting as a blush crawled beneath her skin. "Good lord. You fear Edmond would be upset?"

She shrugged. "He is being particularly pigheaded today. I would prefer to avoid a scene."

"What did he say to you, Brianna?" His lips thinned at her stubborn silence. "Then let me put it this way, did he threaten bodily harm to you or me?"

She shook her head, feeling weary. "I told you, it does not matter."

"It matters a great deal."

"Please, Stefan." She stepped close enough that she could lay her hand on his arm. "I will not have you and Edmond at odds because of me. Just return to the house and I will follow."

He looked as if he would argue, then, perhaps sensing she was at the end of her tether, he gave a grudging nod.

"Very well." He moved to the door, pausing to glance over his shoulder. "Brianna."

"Yes?"

His gaze rested on the faint shadows beneath her eyes. "I do not fear Edmond, nor will I hesitate to throw him from the estate if he chooses to make a pest of himself. You are not only safe at Meadowland, you are safe with me."

EDMOND HAD PACED STEFAN'S overcrowded office for nearly an hour before his brother at last made a grudging appearance. A fact that did nothing to soothe Edmond's ragged temper.

His brother religiously devoted his evenings to poring over his tedious ledgers or studying the latest farming journal; nothing was ever allowed to distract him from his ritual, not even Edmond's rare presence at Meadowland. But on this eve, Edmond was finally forced to send one of the endless footmen to wrench Stefan from hovering behind Brianna as she played on the pianoforte.

He had suspected his brother was vulnerable, but he had not expected the grown man to trail after a slip of a girl as if he were moonstruck.

Hearing approaching footsteps, Edmond sucked in a deep, calming breath as he peered out one of the windows into the darkness beyond.

The entire day, he had concentrated upon the plot to harm Alexander Pavlovich. He had written a dozen letters to warn his comrades in Russia, he had sent a coded missive to Pavlovich in Prussia, and he had made a list of every known associate of Viktor Kazakov. He did not intend to take any risks.

The tasks should have kept him fully occupied, but instead, he could barely concentrate.

Time and time again he had found himself at the door of the library, barely able to keep himself from charging from the room to track down Brianna, only the sheer force of his desire keeping him from giving in to temptation.

To give in to the weakness would prove he was no longer in control of his emotions. Something his pride would not allow.

Instead, he had hidden away like a coward for the day and then grimly pretended indifference as he sat through the interminable dinner watching Stefan and Brianna chat with obvious delight.

At last, he had been driven to this remote office to await Stefan, his pride intact and his mood black as the night sky.

Stefan entered the room and closed the door behind him. "You wished to speak with me?"

Edmond swallowed the harsh words that trembled on his lips.

"Yes. I thought you should know that my suspicions have been confirmed. Those near accidents that have been plaguing you were not accidents at all. They were quite deliberate."

Stefan leaned against the edge of the desk, appearing more disappointed than shocked.

"You are certain?"

"Quite certain."

"God, it is unbelievable. So Howard actually…"

"No, it had nothing to do with our contemptible cousin," Edmond denied. "A pity, really."

"Then who the devil was it?"

"I am shamed to admit that you were nearly killed for no other reason than to lure me from Russia," he admitted, revealing all they had discovered in London.

Stefan listened in silence, shaking his head in disbelief as Edmond finished.

"It seems an incredibly complicated scheme just to be rid

of you." He studied Edmond with a lift of his brows. "They must greatly fear your abilities."

"As you know, Russians are a superstitious lot." Edmond shrugged. He was well aware his talents were formidable, but he was also wise enough to know that he was far from invincible. "By a combination of luck and skill, I have managed to unmask a great number of traitors. I suspect that I have become something of an evil omen to those who have long plotted to be rid of Alexander Pavlovich. No doubt they hoped their luck would be altered if I was out of the country."

Stefan straightened. "So you intend to return to Russia?"

"Of course. Although Alexander Pavlovich has not yet returned to Russia, I have sent a note warning his guards to be on alert. I sent another to Herrick in St. Petersburg to tell him of the dangers. In the meantime, I intend to travel back to London to keep an eye upon Viktor Kazakov." Edmond clenched his hands at his sides. "The man has devoted the past decade to overthrowing the Romanov rule. He will not be content to remain in England when it is time for the trap to be sprung. He will want to be close at hand to take the glory if they are successful. I intend to be on his trail."

Stefan scowled. "I do not like the thought of you taking such risks, Edmond. Czar Alexander has an entire Court, not to mention thousands of soldiers, to keep him safe. Why will you not stay here, where you belong?"

"Because I do not belong here." Edmond raised a silencing hand as Stefan threatened to interrupt. "No, it is true. I was never intended to live the life of a country gentleman. I do not give a fig about fields or tenants or cows. Within a fortnight, I would be seeking every vice available to ease my boredom. In the end, I would either be shot by a cuckolded husband or a hotheaded greenhorn who lost his allowance at the card table."

Stefan did not bother to argue. They both knew it was more than an age-old guilt that kept him from settling at the family estate.

"So instead, you hunt assassins in the wilds of Russia?"

"St. Petersburg is hardly the wilds of Russia," he said dryly. "Indeed, Russian society has become almost civilized."

"I suppose there is no means to halt you. When do you leave?"

Edmond's smile faded. His duty was unmistakable.

"I must return in the morning," he forced himself to say. "You will be relieved to know that I intend to put off my charade as the Duke of Huntley and return to being the poor younger son."

Stefan waved aside his words. "Is there anything I can do to assist you?"

"I need you to keep a close guard upon Brianna." He at last managed to force the words past his unwilling lips.

"You fear she may be in danger?"

"I fear you both may be in danger. These men are fanatical in their desire to take power from Alexander Pavlovich. There is very little that they would not dare, if they thought it would further their goals."

"She will be safe in my care. That I can assure you."

It was precisely what Edmond desired. With the vast army of servants that filled Meadowland, both Stefan and Brianna would be beyond the reach of Viktor Kazakov. They would be safe and he would be free to concentrate upon the plot to overthrow the Czar.

It was not relief, however, but a dark, ruthless anger that flooded through him at Stefan's solemn promise.

"I do not doubt she will receive the most tender care," he gritted.

Stefan pushed away from the desk. "Was that not your purpose when you brought her here?"

"I bloody well do not know what my purpose was." His lips twisted in a grim smile. "Not an uncommon occurrence lately."

Stefan stepped forward, his expression somber.

"Return to London, Edmond, and your duties," he commanded. "I will take care of matters here."

Edmond turned to grasp the frame of the window. "Do you expect that to comfort me?" he rasped.

"It is for the best."

"I saw you this morning," he said, his fingers biting into the wooden frame until his knuckles were white. "Holding Brianna."

"I did not realize until she returned just how much I have missed her. I was a fool not to bring her to Meadowland much sooner."

Stefan's words did nothing to ease Edmond's temper. "It was certainly your duty, just as it is your duty now to recall that you are her guardian."

"Yes, I am. And being her guardian means more than simply providing her shelter. I must also consider what is best for her future. Such a beautiful, innocent young woman is bound to attract the attention of the most despicable lechers, as Thomas Wade has already proven. Not to mention seasoned rakes."

Edmond turned, his chest so tight he could barely breathe.

"And just what do you consider best for her future?"

Stefan met his accusing gaze without apology. "I have growing hopes that she will be content to remain at Meadowland."

"As your ward?"

"As my wife."

Although Edmond had half expected the words, they still hit him like a physical blow.

Brianna wed to his brother? Always within his sight, but forever beyond his grasp?

"What the devil are you babbling about?" he demanded between clenched teeth. "You have not seen her in a dozen years, and within hours, you have decided you want her as your wife?"

"She is young, healthy and breathtakingly lovely. She also loves Meadowland nearly as much as I do. I can think of few women who would suit me so well." Stefan narrowed his gaze. "You are the one continually advising me that my greatest duty as a Duke is to have an heir to ensure you are never burdened with the title."

"Advice that you have continually ignored."

"I am stubborn, not entirely stupid. I am well aware that I shall have to wed and produce a son. Perhaps several sons and a few daughters."

Edmond quivered as the feral fury pulsed through him, his control a breath away from snapping.

"Have all the children you want, Stefan, but be assured that their mother will not be Brianna Quinn."

Stefan refused to back away. "That is hardly your decision to make."

"Stefan, do not press this issue," he warned, his words slow and careful.

"Why? Because you have seduced her?"

"Because I do not allow what is mine to be stolen, not even by you."

"You intend to claim her?" Stefan demanded.

"I already have."

"No, you have taken what you desired without giving anything. Not even a promise of a future."

Edmond flinched. "Did she complain to you?"

"Not at all. In truth, she was most anxious to ensure that she did not cause trouble between us. She possesses a conscience, even if you do not."

Stefan turned on his heel and headed for the door, almost as if he could not bear to be in Edmond's company.

"Stefan."

Jerking open the door, Stefan paused long enough to cast Edmond a cold glare. "For once, do what is right, Edmond. Brianna is not just another bored noblewoman seeking a brief diversion. She is a young, vulnerable girl who has been a very important part of this family. Surely she deserves better than what you are willing to offer?"

He was gone before Edmond could respond.

But then, what could he say?

What was he willing to offer Brianna? A few weeks, perhaps

months, as his mistress? A handful of pretty jewels to ease his conscience when he was finished with her?

While Stefan was prepared to hand her respect, wealth, position, a family to claim as her own.

Just how selfish a bastard had he become?

Reaching for the ormolu clock set on the mantle, Edmond tossed it against the wall, grimly watching as it exploded into a dozen pieces.

CHAPTER SEVENTEEN

THE EXPENSIVE HOTEL SUITE was comfortable enough. There was an elegant sitting room with solid English furnishings that had been covered in a cheerful paisley along with ruthlessly polished walnut tables. Next door was a large bedchamber that included a four-poster bed and French armoire, and connecting rooms for his servants.

Not that Edmond noticed. He had chosen the rooms because they were convenient to Piccadilly and because the back door led directly to an alley where he could slip in and out unnoted.

In truth, since he had arrived back in London three days ago, the rooms had seemed perilously close to a prison.

He had been unwilling to risk spooking Kazakov by being seen in Piccadilly, leaving his servants to keep an eye upon the traitor. Which meant that he had far too many hours to devote to pacing the floors and savagely regretting that rare moment of nobility that had led him to flee Meadowland in the midst of the night, leaving Brianna behind.

He was not a self-sacrificing, noble sort of man. He wanted what he wanted.

The sound of the door to his sitting room opening was a welcome distraction. Edmond turned to watch Boris enter the chamber and cross to pour himself a measure of the whiskey kept on a side table.

"Well?"

"You were right, of course. Kazakov just returned from booking passage on a ship bound for the West Indies."

"And?"

"And on the same day, he is booked on a ship bound for the North Sea under the name of Ivor Spatrov." Boris lifted his glass in a silent toast before draining the potent spirits. "Just as you said he would be."

Edmond shrugged. It was a common enough diversion. One he had used himself on several occasions. "When does the ship sail?"

"Thursday."

Edmond ignored the heavy emptiness that was lodged in the pit of his stomach. *Mon dieu.* This was precisely what he had been waiting for. He would soon be back in Russia, and once the threat to the Czar was ended, he could continue with the life he had worked so hard to build.

"I presume we have passage booked as well?"

"Of course. You are Mr. Richard Parrish, an importer of Russian furs. I thought you would prefer to travel as a wealthy merchant, rather than among the unwashed masses."

"Wise decision." Although he would have to travel in disguise, he preferred to have a decent cabin to endure the weeks of travel onboard the ship. "Viktor has still not attempted to send a message to his contact in Russia?"

"None that I have managed to discover." Boris set aside his empty glass. "I must be overlooking something."

Edmond shrugged, well aware that his companion was doing everything possible to keep track of Viktor Kazakov's nefarious activities.

"I have every faith in your abilities, Boris."

"Then what troubles you?" Boris demanded. "Your brother is safe, and soon we shall be back in Russia where we will be toasted as heroes for having halted a devious plot to overthrow the Czar."

"We have not halted it yet."

"We will."

Edmond could hardly argue with his confidence. Not

without implying he doubted those who had dedicated their lives to protecting Alexander Pavlovich.

"Yes."

"So why then…"

The unwelcome probing was interrupted as there was a sharp rap on the door. The two men shared a brief glance before Boris was sliding to stand behind the door, in position to hit the intruder from behind the moment he entered the room. Edmond moved to stand directly in front of the door.

"Yes?" he demanded.

"It is Jimmy."

Edmond frowned at the youthful voice. "Who?"

"I work fer Chesterfield."

Edmond reached to jerk the door open, unconcerned that it might be a very clever trap. After returning to London, he had shifted Chesterfield's duties from keeping track of Howard Summerville, who was obviously of no interest, to Thomas Wade. For all the chaos, Edmond had not forgotten the man's desperate desire for Brianna.

A slender lad with rough clothing and a cocky smile strolled into the room, his eyes darting about to locate the various items of worth with the skill of a trained thief. He could not, however, halt his squeak of surprise when Boris's large hand descended on his shoulder.

"Keep your hands in your pockets, scamp," the towering man growled.

Edmond stepped directly before the lad.

"You have news?"

The boy swallowed, doing his best to ignore the terrifying soldier holding him captive.

"I was told to come here if the gent I was watching left town."

"And did he?"

"Aye. Slipped away early this morning."

"This morning? Why the devil did you not come to me at once?"

"I had to follow the carriage to make certain it was actually leaving town, didn't I? And then I had to make me way back here. I nearly broke me bloody neck in me rush."

Edmond did not give a damn what the boy had endured. All that mattered was the fact that Thomas Wade was slipping from his grasp.

"Which direction did he go?"

"South."

Surrey. The obscene bastard was on his way to Brianna. A sharp fear exploded through him as he dug in his pocket and pulled out a coin.

"Here." He tossed the coin to the lad, who caught it with practiced ease. "Return to Chesterfield."

"Pleasure doing business with you, guv," the lad managed to mutter before Boris had firmly steered him out the door.

Edmond barely noticed as he moved across the room to collect his greatcoat and hat. Wade had well over an hour's, perhaps as much as two, head start on him. It would take a near miracle for him to catch the carriage before it reached Meadowland.

He had jerked on his coat and was at the door when Boris halted him.

"Edmond."

With the fear that he might be too late pulsing through him, Edmond barely forced himself to pause and glance toward his companion.

"What?"

"We must be on that boat."

"I will return before Thursday," he snarled, not giving a Tinker's damn at this moment about Viktor Kazakov or his endless plots. He wrenched the door open. "Boris."

"Yes?"

"Purchase another ticket on that damn ship."

"You intend to take Miss Quinn to Russia?"

"I bloody well do not intend to leave her here. The woman possesses an unholy ability to tumble into disaster."

"Which I would think would be a reason not to haul her into the midst of a brewing revolution."

"At least if she is at my side, I can protect her."

"But…"

Edmond tossed his friend his leather purse and wrenched open the door.

"Buy the damned ticket, Boris, and make certain that you keep an eye upon Viktor Kazakov. I do not intend to rectify one bout of stupidity only to allow another."

THE AFTERNOON WAS GRAY AND gloomy with a chilled breeze that whispered of the coming winter. Hardly the sort of day to encourage a shopping expedition to the local village, but Stefan had been insistent and, reluctant to disappoint the man who had offered her nothing but kindness, Brianna had given in to his urgings.

Not that it was a huge sacrifice, she had to admit as they rolled down the narrow lane in the luxurious carriage that was designed for comfort. The village was a charming collection of shops and well-tended cottages with a number of friendly inhabitants that she remembered from her childhood. And despite the nip in the air, it was something of a relief to devote a few hours to something beyond brooding on Edmond.

It was infuriating, she acknowledged. She should be delighted she was free of his arrogant presence. Stefan did not order her about as if she were his devoted hound. Indeed, he treated her with a tender respect that any woman would adore.

At last, she was safe and peacefully settled in a place that felt like home. She had nothing to do but concentrate on planning her future of glorious independence.

Staring out the window, Brianna barely noted the soggy fields and occasional copse of trees. Instead, she was envisioning Edmond comfortably settled in London, perhaps even enjoying the afternoon in the arms of his mistress.

Not until Lady Aberlane leaned forward to lightly tap her

ivory fan on Brianna's knee was she thankfully wrenched out of her painful thoughts.

"Well, I suppose that we cannot hope that the dressmaker can claim the talents of those in London, but the gowns will no doubt be charming," she babbled, deliberately cheerful. "So very kind of Stefan to insist that we visit her."

Well aware that the older woman was making a deliberate attempt to lighten her foul mood, Brianna forced a smile to her lips.

"Very kind, but foolishly unnecessary. I have more gowns than I ever dreamed of possessing."

"Now, my dear, a woman can never have too many gowns." The woman tugged the carriage blanket more firmly around her shoulders. "And perhaps Stefan wished to ensure that the local seamstress would benefit from our visit. It is not often that Meadowland has female guests."

"Yes, that is true enough." Stefan devoted his life to caring for the seemingly endless number of people who depended upon him.

A twinkle entered Letty's eyes. "But then again, maybe he wished to impress you with his generosity."

Brianna's stomach clenched. She had done her best to ignore Stefan's less than subtle attentions, almost as if by pretending they did not exist they would simply disappear. Cowardly, no doubt, but she had no wish to hurt her dearest friend.

"Stefan has no need to impress me, Letty. We have been friends our entire lives."

"My dear, I am old, not blind. I have seen the way he watches you and it is not as a mere friend." She watched Brianna shift on the smooth leather seat. "He is a fine man, Brianna. One of the finest I have ever known. As if being one of the wealthiest Dukes in all of England were not enough."

Brianna grimaced. Good lord, did the older woman not realize that Brianna would give anything to respond to Stefan? She was well aware that her future could be one of blessed ease and security as the Duchess of Huntley.

It was never to be, however. And not only because of her tangled feelings for Edmond.

For all the luxury and protection Stefan could offer, it still came with the chains of ownership. Granted, they might be golden chains, but she had sworn that she would never, ever place herself in the power of another.

"Stefan is a most remarkable gentleman."

A faint hint of disappointment touched the lined countenance. "But you do not love him?"

"Of course I love him. I always have. But…"

"You love Edmond more?" Letty demanded.

"I do not know what I feel for Edmond. Most of the time, I want to slap his smug countenance."

"Ah, my dear."

Brianna stiffened at the hint of pity in the older woman's voice. The last thing she needed was sympathy. She had far more than most women.

"It does not matter. Stefan has promised me a home here at Meadowland for as long as I wish. Once I have my inheritance, I intend to purchase my own establishment."

Letty blinked in surprise. "Do you?"

"Yes."

"And have you told the boys of your plans?"

Brianna gave a startled laugh. Only Lady Aberlane would consider two of the most powerful gentlemen in all of England as *boys*.

"Once I reach my majority, it will be none of their concern. I shall be free to do as I please. It is all I have ever desired."

Whatever the woman might think of Brianna's bold plans was to remain a mystery, because the carriage was suddenly swaying as a passing coach rammed directly into their side.

"Oh, my," Letty gasped, struggling to stay in her seat. "Some drunken buffoon, I suppose."

"At this hour?" Brianna peered out the window. Her heart

stuttered to a halt as she recognized the blue and gold livery of her stepfather's grooms. "No. Dear God, no."

"What is it?"

"That is Thomas Wade's carriage."

The words had barely left her lips when the sound of shots being fired echoed through the air. She threw herself to the opposite seat to wrap the fragile older woman in her arms. Her body reacted on instinct, even as her mind refused to accept what was happening.

It was as if her worst nightmare was coming true. And there was not a damnable thing she could do to halt it.

More terrifying shots rang through the air, and both women screamed as the carriage veered into the ditch and slammed to a painful stop. They did not overturn, thank the good lord, but the abrupt motion managed to toss them roughly against the far door.

"Letty?" Pulling back, Brianna studied her companion with a frantic gaze. "Letty, are you hurt?"

Lady Aberlane lifted a shaky hand to straighten her bonnet. "No, no. Just a bit breathless."

Brianna's relief lasted less than a heartbeat as the door to the carriage was suddenly wrenched open and the ghastly sight of Thomas Wade appeared in the opening.

Bile rose in Brianna's throat at the sight of her stepfather's thick, flushed countenance and pale eyes that glittered with hunger.

"You bitch," he growled, reaching out to grab Brianna's arm in a painful grip. "You thought you could escape me?"

Brianna struggled desperately as Thomas pulled her toward the door, but she was barely half the size of her stepfather and there was no means to battle against him as she was hauled ever closer.

"Have you lost your mind? You could have killed us."

His fat lips twisted in an ugly smile. "I would rather have you dead than out of my grasp." With one last heave, Thomas pulled her out of the carriage and had his hand wrapped around her throat. Brianna had only a brief moment to see that at least two of Stefan's footmen were lying on the ground bleeding and that the groom was surrounded by Thomas's henchmen. "You belong to me, Brianna. Do not ever forget that."

Barely capable of breathing, Brianna lifted her hands and futilely tugged at the fingers threatening to crush her throat.

"So beautiful. I will hide you away where no one can find you," he muttered, almost to himself, loosening his grip on her throat.

Brianna forgot the pain in her throat as horror shuddered through her.

"You…bastard," she hissed. "Stefan will see you hanged."

"He will have to catch us first. My yacht is waiting to take us far away from England."

Without warning, Lady Aberlane appeared in the doorway of the carriage, whacking Thomas on the top of his head with her cane.

"Take your hands off her, you fiend."

"Enough!" Thomas growled, dragging Brianna toward his waiting coach. "We are leaving here."

"No," Brianna gasped. "Please…"

"Release her, Wade."

The words came without warning, halting Thomas in his tracks and making Brianna's knees weak with relief.

"Edmond," she breathed, her eyes filling with tears as he stepped from the trees, the gun in his hand pointed directly at her captor.

Behind her, Thomas stiffened, his fingers tightening on her throat until black spots danced before her eyes. Brianna knew she would be unconscious in moments if Edmond did not do something.

"Stay back, or I swear I will kill her," Thomas growled.

"The only one dying on this day is you, Wade."

"Drop the gun, or I will break her neck." Thomas shook Brianna with enough force to make her head snap back and forth. "Drop it."

Edmond halted, his gaze narrowing with fury. Then he bent slowly downward to place his pistol on the dirt road.

Brianna could sense Thomas relaxing as the immediate threat was overcome, and he even loosened his grip enough that she could suck in a short, painful breath.

"That is better…"

His smug words were cut short as Edmond straightened with a fluid motion, his arm flicking forward as he hurled the hidden dagger through the air. There was a glint of steel flashing through the fog, and then the thin blade grazed past Brianna's cheek.

The fingers briefly tightened on her neck before they fell away.

For a long moment, the world seemed to be frozen in time. She was aware of the cold breeze tugging on her wool cloak, the scent of damp leaves, the distant cry of a bird.

At last, it was Edmond who broke the nightmarish spell as he plucked his gun from the dirt and pointed it in the direction of Thomas's stunned henchmen.

"Toss aside your weapons and move to your master," he ordered.

Not surprisingly, the servants hastily scurried to obey the icy command. But Brianna was oblivious to their frantic efforts. Instead, she was numbly turning toward the man who lay sprawled on the ground.

Her stomach rolled as her gaze skimmed over the lifeless limbs sprawled at odd angles. A part of her warned to turn away, that whatever she might see would give her nightmares for years to come. But another part, the part that had endured months of terror beneath her stepfather's roof, possessed a morbid need to know Thomas Wade's ultimate fate.

Swallowing the lump in her throat, she forced her reluctant gaze to lift ever higher. She caught a glimpse of a blood-drenched cravat and the hilt of a dagger sticking from Thomas's thick neck, before she was yanked around and pressed against Edmond's chest.

"No, Brianna," he growled, his hand cupping the back of her head to hide her face in the hollow of his shoulder.

"Is he dead?"

"Get back in the carriage, *ma souris*," he demanded, steering her across the road, keeping her face hidden in the folds of his coat.

"No, this is all because of me," she protested. The sick sensation remained in the pit of her stomach, but the feel of Edmond's warm, comforting arms was restoring her courage. "I will not leave you to deal with the…the…"

"Brianna." Edmond interrupted her stumbling words as he came to a halt and pulled back, his fingers slipping beneath her chin to force her to meet his hard gaze.

"What?"

"That was not a request." Before she could protest, Brianna was lifted off her feet and into the carriage next to Lady Aberlane. The door was slammed shut and Edmond was stepping back to address the shaken groom. "Take them directly back to Meadowland. Shoot anyone who tries to halt you. Do you understand?"

"Aye, sir."

"Edmond…no."

Brianna reached for the handle of the door, but her hands were trembling so badly she could not work it. Then it no longer mattered, as the carriage gave a violent lurch and they were out of the ditch and flying down the narrow road toward Meadowland.

CHAPTER EIGHTEEN

EDMOND WAS STANDING AT the window of his brother's study when the sound of the door opening had him spinning about to regard Stefan with a lift of his brows.

"Well?"

"They both will survive, thank God, although it will be some time before James can resume his duties," Stefan revealed, speaking of the two wounded footmen. Moving to the desk, Stefan took his seat and reached for his quill. "I must make a note to remember to see to his family. I believe he has a number of children."

Edmond was far less concerned with the wounded footmen than with protecting the woman who had been so nearly stolen away from him. Brianna had endured enough. He would not have her become the subject of unpleasant rumors if it were discovered Thomas Wade had attempted to kidnap her.

"And the doctor?"

Stefan glanced up with a frown, his face pale. "What of him?"

"You told him our story?"

"He is convinced that my carriage came upon Thomas Wade, who was in the process of being held up by a gang of ruffians, and that the footmen were shot while attempting to run them off."

Edmond nodded. The fabrication was not his best, but it was simple, and most importantly, impossible to disprove. Not unless one of the participants was stupid enough to speak out of turn.

"And you are certain that your servants will keep the truth to themselves?"

Stefan stiffened in offense at the question. "Of course. My servants are completely loyal. I am far more concerned with the bastards who worked for Wade."

"They know better than to contradict what I have told them to say," Edmond assured him, his lips twisting as he recalled the servants on their knees as they pleaded for mercy. He did not doubt that they were halfway to France by now. "They understand that I will not hesitate to kill them."

"Nor I," Stefan muttered, shoving himself to his feet as he paced the worn carpet. "Damnation. I will never forgive myself for allowing Brianna to be put in such danger."

Edmond ignored his instinctive annoyance at Stefan's possessive concern. He had no one to blame but himself for leaving Brianna in his brother's care, a mistake he would not make again.

"Stefan, you could not have known that Thomas Wade was desperate enough to risk kidnapping Brianna in broad daylight."

"But you did."

"And I was still very nearly too late. I was a fool to ever allow her out of my sight."

Stefan took a jerky step forward, his hands clenched at his sides. "What the devil are you saying?"

"I intend to take her back to London with me."

"You must be jesting?"

Edmond folded his arms over his chest, his expression settling into lines of grim determination.

"She needs my protection."

"She would be no safer in London. In fact, your enemies pose a far greater danger than Thomas Wade." Stefan narrowed his gaze. "Or have you forgotten she was shot while in your care?"

"Take care, Stefan." Edmond's voice was dangerously soft. He loved his brother more than anyone in the world, but Brianna would be leaving with him. By force if necessary. "Besides, we are not remaining in London. At least not for long. Viktor Kazakov is set to travel to Russia on Thursday, and I will be on the ship with him."

"Good lord. Edmond, you cannot take Brianna to Russia."

Edmond turned back toward the window, refusing to meet Stefan's accusing gaze. A part of him understood the risk he was taking. Not only to Brianna, but to his duty to Alexander Pavlovich. It was the damn reason he had left her at Meadowland to begin with.

Now, however, he had no intention of listening to his common sense. The past three days had proven that not having Brianna within reach was far more a distraction than having her near. There was no way in hell he was leaving England without her.

"We will be in disguise while we travel," he said, offhand. "No one will know her identity."

"And once you reach St. Petersburg?"

"What do you mean?"

Stefan's lips thinned. "Even presuming that you manage to arrive at the Winter Palace without being recognized, were you not the one to claim that the Russian Court is a treacherous pit of vipers who prey upon the weak and stupid? Will you toss Brianna into such a dangerous cesspit?"

"I have no intention of introducing Brianna to the Court."

"No? Do you intend to keep her locked away in your chambers? Hidden even from the Czar?"

Edmond glared at the dark garden below. "Such matters can be decided once we reach the Winter Palace."

"For God's sake, Edmond, you have devoted years to earning a place as Alexander Pavlovich's most trusted advisor. Are you truly willing to risk it all because of some strange obsession with a woman?"

"My decision is made, Stefan."

"An utterly irresponsible decision." Stefan's words echoed his own dark thoughts. "You cannot haul an innocent maiden about as if she were a piece of luggage. At best, her reputation will be in tatters, and at worst, she will be caught in the midst of a plot to overthrow the government." Stepping directly behind Edmond, his brother grasped his shoulder in a tight grip. "This is not like you, Edmond."

"Perhaps not, but I will not be swayed."

There was a thick silence before Stefan dropped his hand and stepped back.

"And what of Brianna?"

"What of her?"

"What if she does not desire to be whisked off to Russia? She has just now become settled at Meadowland."

"She will come."

"Because you intend to force her?"

Turning on his heel, Edmond started toward the door. "Because she belongs to me."

SHORTLY BEFORE SUNSET, Brianna once again found herself in one of Stefan's elegant carriages. On this occasion, however, it was Edmond who was seated across from her, rather than Lady Aberlane, and they were rapidly headed toward London.

Somewhere deep inside, she knew she should be outraged by Edmond's highhanded manner. For heaven's sake, he had stormed into her bedchamber tossing about commands and standing over her as she packed her bags, as if she were a witless child.

It was not anger, however, that held her in the strange sense of numb acceptance as they rattled down the dirt road at a savage pace.

She had known that Edmond would return to her. And that when he did, she would willingly follow him wherever he might lead her.

The past three days had made her realize that she would never have peace until the passion that pulsed between them had burned itself to a cinder.

So long as she remembered that, she told herself, her time with Edmond was merely a temporary madness that would soon pass. Why battle the inevitable?

Seated across from her, Edmond slouched in his seat, his long legs stretched out and his arms folded across his chest as he watched her with a brooding gaze. Despite the chilled air he had discarded his greatcoat and hat, revealing the elegant hunter green jacket and striped waistcoat that molded to his body with unnerving precision.

"Do you intend to sulk the entire trip, *ma souris?*" he drawled, breaking the heavy silence that had filled the carriage.

She ignored his taunting words, instead turning her mind to the question that had haunted her since Edmond had stepped from the fog the very moment she needed him.

"How did you know that Thomas Wade was going to try to kidnap me?"

"I did not know precisely what he intended, but I was having him watched. When he left London, I followed." His eyes smoldered with a lingering fury. "Unfortunately, I did not catch up to him until he had already attacked your carriage."

She gave a slow nod. She should have known that Edmond would have Thomas Wade under surveillance. He was far more than a gentleman of leisure; he possessed a lethal awareness and skills that were usually only found among those men forced to live by their cunning.

"Do you truly think people will believe that Thomas was killed by highwaymen?"

"Who would doubt the word of the Duke of Huntley?"

Her lips twisted at the bland arrogance. "I suppose that is true enough."

Despite their differences, the two brothers had been raised with the unwavering knowledge that they were lord and master of their very large corner of Surrey. It would never occur to them that they would be given anything but absolute obedience.

"You need never concern yourself about Thomas Wade again, Brianna."

"I am glad he is dead."

"It is no doubt a widely held opinion. From what I could

discover, he cheated at business, at cards and upon his wife. There were also rumors that he routinely beat his mistresses. A thoroughly despicable man. I doubt there will be a soul who mourns his passing."

"Certainly not me." She grimaced. "I only wish…"

"You wish what?"

She forced herself to meet his searching gaze. "I wish that I had been the one to kill him."

"So bloodthirsty, *ma souris?*"

"No. I dislike the knowledge that I was forced to depend upon you to ride to my rescue."

"Ride to the rescue? Hmm." A smile teased his full lips. "That sounds rather melodramatic. I do not believe anyone would confuse me with a heroic prince or you with a damsel in distress."

She stiffened in annoyance, her pride pricked by his amusement. "Do not jest. I should be capable of taking care of myself."

His amusement faded, his eyes narrowing at her sharp tone. "What is it that troubles you, Brianna? The fact that you had to be rescued or that I am the one who did it?"

"I want my independence. Is that so difficult to comprehend?"

"For a lady who desires her independence, you did a great deal of complaining when I refused to allow Janet to accompany us."

"Janet is not only my maid, she is my dearest friend. I happen to enjoy her companionship."

"A friend?"

"Yes."

"So what am I? Friend or foe?"

Her teeth clenched. "Do you truly wish me to answer that question?"

Brianna forced herself not to flinch beneath his hard gaze. Not even when he smoothly leaned forward, his fingers capturing her chin in a firm grip.

"Why did you come with me?"

The abrupt question caught her off guard. "You commanded me to, did you not?"

"We both know that I could not have forced you. Had you truly protested, Stefan would have stepped in to keep you at Meadowland."

Brianna readily latched on to his unwitting words. She had, after all, considered Stefan often while she had been packing her bags to return to London. She was not so fascinated by Edmond that she would ignore the gentleman who had offered her nothing but kindness.

"And that is why I did not protest," she said.

"What the devil is that supposed to mean?"

"Stefan is the one person in the entire world that I would never, ever willingly hurt."

His fingers tightened on her chin. "And you think it did not hurt to have you leave him?"

"Not nearly so much as it would have if I had stayed. I...I cannot give him what he desires from me, and it is unfair to allow him hope that I will eventually change my mind."

A dangerous satisfaction smoldered in his eyes. "So you do not intend to become the next Duchess of Huntley?"

"No." She did not have to feign her regret. Only a fool would not realize her life would be far simpler with Stefan as her husband. "Someday, Stefan will meet a woman who will make him realize that what he feels for me is nothing more than friendship and a measure of guilt for leaving me in the hands of Thomas Wade. I could never have made him truly happy."

"Of course you could not have." His fingers eased their punishing grip to stroke the line of her jaw. "You were never meant for the dreary life of bucolic bliss. You possess the spirit of a true adventuress."

"I most certainly do not!"

Her rebuff did nothing more than stir his predatory nature, and with a smooth motion, he was settled on the seat next to her with his arms wrapped firmly about her waist.

"No?" He brazenly stroked his lips over the lingering scar on her temple. "What other woman would have possessed the daring to sneak into a Courtesan's Ball and blackmail one of the most feared gentlemen in all of London?"

Without thought, her hands lifted to clutch at the lapels of his jacket. Her entire body was stirring to exquisite life at his touch.

"It was not daring, it was desperation."

He chuckled as his mouth shifted to explore the sensitive pulse just below her ear.

"Why will you not admit that you have a taste for excitement?"

She hissed softly as a jolt of pleasure nearly sent her tumbling off her seat. It would be so easy to drown in the sensations that were flooding through her.

Too easy.

"Good God, Edmond, my mother ruined my life in her quest for excitement," she managed to mutter. "Do you truly believe I would want to walk in her path?"

His hands trailed down to softly cup the curve of her back, his tongue circling the shell of her ear.

"Your mother was a vain, weak woman who indulged her selfish whims without regard to who she might hurt. You could never be like her." He gave her lobe a sharp nip. "You possess courage." His lips trailed over her cheek. "Intelligence." He nibbled the corner of her lips. "Strength."

Brianna fiercely ignored the flutters in the pit of her stomach. She desperately wanted to close her eyes and allow herself to drown in the heat that Edmond offered, but the mere mention of her mother was enough to harden her resolve. She would not be ruled by her passions.

Not ever.

"Edmond."

His tongue teased her mouth, urging her lips to part. "Mmm?"

Brianna planted her hands on his chest and arched away from him.

"You said we would be leaving for Russia," she said, seeking the first distraction that came to mind. "Why?"

"Does it matter?"

"Of course it does." For the first time since Edmond had casually tossed out the information that he intended to haul her to Russia, she actually considered the ramifications of such a trip. She frowned at the realization of how her presence would be perceived in society. "I will not be pranced through the Czar's Court as your mistress."

"Why not?" He appeared genuinely curious. "If you are determined to shun marriage and live in solitary splendor, then what does it matter if the world knows that I have taken you as my lover?"

Her blood froze at the mere thought of the whispers and finger-pointing that would forever follow in her wake. It was bad enough that she would inevitably be known as the woman jilted by the Duke of Huntley. To add the notion that she had been tossed aside by Stefan to end up in the bed of his younger brother…

She would be as notorious as Lady Caroline Lamb.

No. She pressed a hand to her tightly clenched stomach. She could not bear it.

"Being a lady of independence does not necessarily mean a tart with no morals. I should like to maintain a shred of respect among society." She stiffened as his low chuckle filled the carriage. By God, satisfying this stupid bout of lust was not worth sacrificing her last shred of dignity. She would remain at Meadowland before she would return to being a source of mockery to others. "Edmond, I am quite serious. I have already endured the shame of being related to Thomas Wade, I could not…"

"No one will even know you are in my company." He abruptly grimaced. "Well, perhaps Alexander Pavlovich, if he returns to St. Petersburg while we are there. He has become increasingly suspicious of others, and he does not take kindly to those who keep secrets from him, no matter how harmless they might be. I cannot afford to stir his ire during such dangerous times."

She ignored the unnerving thought of being introduced to

the Imperial Highness as well as Edmond's reference to dangerous times. Instead, she concentrated upon the ridiculous notion that she could somehow become invisible.

"And how do you intend to hide my presence?"

"Quite simple. We shall both travel in disguise."

"Disguise?"

"I am to be a wealthy merchant and you will be my devoted wife."

"*You* a wealthy merchant?" She gave a short, disbelieving laugh. Edmond was a nobleman, from the top of his glossy curls to the tips of his champagne polished boots. He could be attired in rags, and no one would believe he was anything less than an aristocrat.

"This is absurd. You cannot travel about in disguise…" Her words trailed away as she was struck with a sudden thought. This had nothing to do with protecting her honor and everything to do with his mysterious determination to rid himself of her presence three days earlier. She had known that there was something afoot. "Oh, of course. What the devil are you scheming?" She narrowed her gaze as his lips parted to deny her question. "And do not try to convince me that you are willing to risk traveling about in disguise simply to have me with you. There is something you are hiding."

His lips twitched as he reached out to part her cloak so he could run a teasing finger along the neckline of her French gray carriage dress.

"I am willing to bare all my secrets if you are."

Her nipples hardened in anticipation as his finger slipped beneath the Brussels lace that edged her camisole. Oh, the man had surely bewitched her. How else could he manage to make her melt while they were rattling over the rutted road in a freezing carriage?

"No, I will not be distracted." She reached to tug his fingers from her aching breasts. "Tell me why we are going to Russia."

He heaved an exaggerated sigh. "You are a hard woman, Brianna Quinn."

"Tell me."

TOSSING HIMSELF BACK INTO the soft leather seat, Edmond grudgingly accepted he would have to confess at least a portion of the truth.

With a minimum of fuss, he revealed what he had discovered over the past few days and his plans to follow Viktor Kazakov back to Russia. Brianna listened in silence, but even in the fading light, Edmond did not miss the scowl that marred her brow. Predictable, of course. He could never be so fortunate as to have her simply fall in with his plans without questions or complaints.

"I understand your need to warn the Czar of his danger," she said slowly, as if still sorting through his unexpected confession. "It is the duty of any citizen to protect their monarch. But why do you consider it your responsibility to put your life at risk by actually following this Viktor? Surely there are authorities that would be better suited to take command of the situation?"

Edmond grimaced. "There are an endless horde of authorities, *ma souris*. Unfortunately, Russian officials tend to be plodding, unimaginative souls who would not accept that there was a traitor in their midst, unless they actually witnessed the Czar being murdered."

"Then what of the Emperor's guards?"

"Those that are trustworthy are at his side as he travels to Prussia. Unfortunately, it is far more likely that the traitors will attempt to stir up trouble in St. Petersburg, where Alexander Pavlovich's ministers are not quite so loyal as one would hope."

"Good lord."

He smiled wryly at her naive shock. How many years had it been since he believed that those in power were noble, self-sacrificing creatures who were blessed by God to protect the masses and that all who surrounded them were loyal to the death?

"Politics is a treacherous business that is practiced behind closed doors, *ma souris.* What the public is allowed to witness is a well-staged show that is orchestrated by powers that prefer the shadows," he admitted. "And in truth, there are times when the Russian Court is embarrassingly similar to a nursery filled with vain, boorish, squabbling children."

Her magnificent eyes were suddenly lit with an unnerving glitter of comprehension. "And you are one of those shadowy powers?"

Wondering why she looked like someone who had just grasped the answer to a particularly perplexing puzzle, Edmond shrugged.

"I have earned a place in Alexander Pavlovich's most trusted circle because I have developed a vast number of associates who keep me informed of those who would desire to topple the Russian government," he revealed, surprising himself. He never discussed his secretive work for the Czar. Not even with Stefan.

"Are there so many traitors, then?"

"Every country has its share of traitors. The radicals, the power-hungry, and those who are simply mad." He gave a slow shake of his head. He was honest enough to admit Russia's numerous faults, but it did nothing to diminish his love for his mother's homeland. Or his determination to thwart those who would see it destroyed. "Russia, however, is in a state of transition between those who would keep it locked in ancient tradition and those who are determined to see it forcibly altered to resemble its European neighbors. The state of upheaval offers ample opportunity for treachery."

She tugged her cloak tighter with a small shiver. "It hardly sounds a comfortable place to choose for your home. Why not remain in England?"

He reached out to flick a finger over her pale cheek. *Mon dieu,* she was a beautiful creature. Even in the gathering dusk, her hair glowed with an astonishing fire, a handful of curls framing her delicate ivory face.

"Like you, I possess a love for adventure. I could not bear the placid life my brother holds so dear, nor could I spend my days prancing about London," he murmured, his finger shifting to touch the corner of her full mouth. "Besides, I am half Russian. My mother would be pleased to know that her son is dedicated to the welfare of her homeland."

Her expression abruptly softened. "That is why you put yourself at risk. For your mother."

Edmond stiffened, belatedly realizing he had revealed far more than he intended.

Christ. He should hire the woman to become one of his spies. She could seduce the secrets from the most hardened scoundrel.

"Do not endow me with any sense of nobility, *ma souris,* you will only be disappointed," he deliberately mocked, ignoring the pang of regret as her expression swiftly hardened and she pulled back from his lingering touch.

"So we are to follow the traitor to Russia and then what?" she demanded, ice coating the words.

He shoved his fingers impatiently through his hair. It was that, or grabbing Brianna and hauling her onto his lap so he could soothe her wounded sensibilities in the only manner he felt comfortable with. In this moment, she would no doubt reward him with nothing more than a slap to the face.

"Eventually he must meet with his associates," he said, restlessly shifting on the seat. He did not want to be discussing Viktor Kazakov or traitorous plots or even their upcoming journey to Russia. "Once I am convinced that we have identified the majority of the villains, I will turn them over to Alexander Pavlovich and allow him to bring them to justice."

"Somehow, I doubt it will be quite so simple as you make it sound."

His lips twisted at her tart tone. "There is no need to be frightened, *ma souris.* I will keep you safe."

"I am not frightened, but I am confused."

"Confused about what?"

"Why do you insist that I accompany you?" she demanded. "I have no experience in hunting traitors."

His brows arched at her ridiculous question. She could not be that naive.

"I cannot hunt traitors every moment," he pointed out.

"So I am to be a bit of fun when you have the time to spare? Lovely."

Edmond stilled, startled by the edge of bitterness in her voice. "Are you suggesting that you desire to be more than my mistress?" He reached out to grasp her chin and forced her to meet his searching gaze. "Brianna?"

"Of course not."

"Then what do you want from me?"

"Nothing."

On this occasion, Edmond refused to be put off by her instinctive retreat.

"Liar." He leaned close enough that her swift, unsteady breaths brushed his cheek. "I have promised you will not be a source of scandal among society. What else could trouble you?"

"I…" Her tongue peeked out to wet her lips, sending a raw flare of heat through his body. "I am simply surprised that you do not already have a mistress awaiting your return to St. Petersburg. Or perhaps you do."

Edmond was genuinely astonished by her accusation. "You think I would be spending time with another woman when I have you waiting in my bed?"

The green eyes flashed. "It would not be the first occasion."

"What the devil is that supposed to mean?" he snapped, his fingers tightening on her chin as she attempted to duck her head. "Oh, no, *ma souris,* I will have an answer."

Her expression settled in stubborn lines, but when Edmond refused to allow her to escape his piercing gaze, she heaved an aggravated sigh.

"I am well aware that you visited La Russa while we were in London."

"Mon dieu," he breathed in shock. "How could you…" He halted his words and gave a shake of his head. What did it matter how she had discovered his brief visit to the famous opera singer? All that truly mattered was the realization that Brianna was clearly disturbed at the thought of him spending time with another woman. The restless tension that gripped him began to fade beneath a flare of startling satisfaction. His fingers eased their tight grip to stroke up her cheek. "Brianna, I am no saint, but I do not keep a string of mistresses. Not only are they expensive, but I do have responsibilities beyond the bedchamber."

"You can say whatever you like, Edmond. I saw your carriage parked in front of her house."

He chuckled softly. "I begin to understand why you were so cold that night. Well, until I managed to thaw your frosty temper. You were jealous!"

He felt her skin warm beneath his caressing fingers… whether from anger or embarrassed memory of their heated coupling against the wall of her bedchamber was impossible to know.

"I most certainly was not."

His hand cupped the back of her head as he gently tugged her closer. "Do not fear, Brianna. My visit to La Russa's was purely one of business."

Her nose flared with distaste, but she made no effort to pull away. Indeed, her body quite readily arched closer to his aching body.

"I am well aware of La Russa's *business*."

"Brianna, I was at her town house for the sole purpose of meeting with a Bow Street Runner who was keeping watch on my worthless cousin," he said, barely concentrating on his words as he wrapped his arm about her waist and shifted her onto his lap. "I do not need a courtesan to satisfy my pleasure. Not when I have a warm, spirited, exquisitely beautiful woman only too eager to please me." He buried his face in the curve of her neck, breathing deeply of her sweet scent. A shudder wracked his body. How had he ever been so stupid as to believe he could leave her at Meadowland? This is where she belonged. Where she would always belong. "Allow me to prove my point."

Her arms encircled his neck as he planted heated kisses up the curve of her neck.

"Edmond, we…"

"Later," he rudely interrupted, covering her mouth in a kiss that revealed the savage need pulsing through his blood. "We have all the time in the world."

CHAPTER NINETEEN

THE JOURNEY FROM LONDON TO St. Petersburg was made on a British two-decker that was constructed from sturdy timber and offered windows in the quarter galleries, as well as a wide deck for those who desired a refreshing stroll. The icy weather kept most passengers in their private cabins for the majority of the sea passage, and even on the few days that the North Sea was not churning with a vengeful fury, the incessant rain prevented nothing more than a hasty breath of fresh air.

Following the grueling sea voyage were endless days traveling from the coast in a cramped carriage as they pursued Viktor Kazakov through the blinding snow storms.

Brianna, however, had never ventured farther than from Surrey to London, and despite Edmond's constant warnings that she was not to leave the carriage without a heavy veil to cover her face, discovered herself enjoying the unfamiliar surroundings. There was a sense of building anticipation as they raced through the foreign land.

Or at least she convinced herself that it was anticipation that made her waken with a smile upon her lips and added a decided bounce to her steps. Otherwise, she would be forced to consider the notion that it was Edmond's near constant presence that was responsible.

She was quite prepared to accept that she craved his masterful touch during their long nights together. And was even developing a grudging respect for his quick wits and startling displays of humor. But she refused to concede that he was relentlessly creeping his way into her wary heart.

That would be madness.

Thankfully, any unease at the strange, almost giddy sensations that plagued her was forgotten once they arrived in St. Petersburg.

Barely more than a century old, the vast, beautiful city was built on the Neva River that fed into the Gulf of Finland.

It was said that the numerous canals that sliced through the marshland had inspired Peter the Great to build his capital in the image of Venice, and that with ruthless disregard for the misery of his people, he had demanded that forty thousand peasants be sent every year to complete his masterpiece.

And it was a masterpiece, she had to admit, as the carriage carried them down the Nevsky Prospect.

She had never seen so many golden spires and domes glittering against a pure blue sky, all adding an exotic contrast to the bronzed statues and monuments to Peter the Great.

She had only a passing glimpse of the sea-blue and white Winter Palace, with its profusion of columns and pilasters and its golden dome above the Palace Cathedral, before they were headed past the Kazan Cathedral with its exotic onion dome and onto a narrow street with a collection of small shops that Edmond informed her was Gostinny Dvor.

The carriage at last slowed at the Fontanka Embankment, near the baroque palace known as Sheremetev House, then turned to the left, traveling the crescent street back toward the Neva.

A frown touched her brow as they halted before a vast town house where a number of elegant guests appeared to be arriving despite the fact that it was decidedly early for callers.

"What is this place?" she demanded.

Edmond tugged his hat low onto his brow and pulled on his gloves. "It is the home of a friend."

There was an unmistakable hint of fondness in his voice, and Brianna clenched her teeth. "Is she beautiful?"

"She is exquisite." He chuckled softly as he watched her eyes narrow. "She also happens to be old enough to be my mother."

The sharp surge of relief was nearly as annoying as the smug glint in his eyes.

"I thought you were intending to keep your arrival in St. Petersburg a secret?" she snapped, her gaze returning to the grand house that bustled with activity. "This hardly looks a clandestine setting."

"Quite the opposite," he easily agreed. "Vanya Petrova is well known to entertain with lavish style. It is rare that her home is not overflowing with guests." He wrapped a scarf about his neck, covering the lower half of his face in the process. "Which means that the addition of two more will hardly be noticed."

"What of the other guests?"

He shrugged. "The crowd that attends her literary salons is discreetly kept confined in the public rooms, and she has promised to rid herself of all but those who can be trusted to remain as houseguests. They will not breathe a word of our presence."

Brianna turned back, her lips parted to inform the ridiculous man that spreading gossip was the favorite sport of every houseguest, when she was struck by a sudden realization.

"Oh…this Vanya Petrova is one of your associates, is she not?"

He paused, clearly considering how much of the truth to reveal.

"Actually, it would be more accurate to say that I am one of her associates," he at last replied. "Vanya has been one of Alexander Pavlovich's staunchest supporters since he took the throne. She approached me after my arrival in St. Petersburg to assist her in her efforts to keep the jackals at bay."

Brianna discovered her annoyance melting beneath a tide of fascination. Good heavens. What would it be like to know that the fate of an entire country was dependent upon your efforts? That each day you made a difference in thousands and thousands of lives?

For so many years, she had been obsessed with her own

needs and desires, while Edmond had devoted himself to others. Who could ever have suspected?

Of course, the fact that he would be the last gentleman suspected of caring about his fellow countrymen was no doubt precisely why he was so successful.

"Why would she approach an Englishman to help protect the Czar of Russia?"

Warmth glowed in his eyes, his affection for the older woman clearly evident.

"She was a close friend to my mother when they were young." He gave a wave of his hand. "And perhaps unwisely, Alexander Pavlovich has always preferred to surround himself with foreign advisors. It made it a simple matter for me to earn a place among those most intimate with the Emperor."

Brianna grimaced. She had always envied those in power. To a young girl who was too often at the mercy of others, it seemed nothing could be better than to be in a position of command with no need to bow to the authority of anyone.

Now she realized that power came with a terrible price.

"Do you know, I feel sorry for the poor man." She shivered. "How could anyone bear to exist with the knowledge that there were traitors lurking in every shadow just waiting for the opportunity to take his place, or even kill him?"

"It is a burden he wears with a heavy heart. There are times that I fear…"

"Fear what?"

"Nothing."

Knowing Edmond would reveal no more, Brianna glanced toward the lavish mansion, her courage suddenly elusive.

"What have you done with Boris?" she demanded, wishing for the steady companionship of the silent warrior. Over the past weeks, she had come to rely upon his steadfast presence.

"He is remaining on the trail of Viktor Kazakov. I presume that his destination is St. Petersburg, but I will not be caught off-guard again. I intend to keep a vigilant watch on the traitor."

His lips twisted. "Besides which, I am weary of his incessant complaints of being denied the company of Janet. Your maid has a great deal to answer for."

"I did warn you to bring her with us."

"And be denied the pleasure of helping you undress? Do not be a fool."

Her cheeks reddened. "Edmond."

Reaching out, Edmond pulled the veil of her bonnet over her face and shoved open the door to the carriage. "Come, Vanya will begin to worry."

THEY ENTERED THROUGH THE front door, but they had barely stepped into the marble foyer when a uniformed servant was whisking them toward a side staircase and up to the top floor of the vast mansion.

More surprisingly, Brianna was firmly escorted to a set of private chambers, despite Edmond's protest.

With a smile, Brianna closed the door in his outraged face and explored the beautiful rooms with a sense of pleasure.

The parlor was decorated with a hint of European influence in the satinwood furnishings that included a brass inlaid library table and armchairs embroidered with velvet covers as well as lilac wall panels, but the Russian love for lavish excess was obvious in every gilded cornice and jewel-encrusted figurine.

Even in the bedroom, there were dozens of enameled snuff boxes and gilt bronze clocks set upon the marble mantle. Any one of them would have fed most families for an entire year.

Removing her cloak and bonnet, Brianna was standing before the porcelain stove warming her chilled hands when the door was pushed open and a tall, curvaceous woman with silver hair and striking features stepped into the room.

Brianna dropped a hasty curtsey, realizing this must her hostess.

"My lady."

Attired in a gown of apple-green silk with silver stripes, the woman moved to take Brianna's hand, leading her to one of the small sofas before she at last spoke.

"Please, you must call me Vanya," she murmured in perfect English, her pale blue eyes studying Brianna with an unnerving intensity. "I hope that the rooms are to your liking?"

Brianna smiled. Although the lilac and gilt décor was rather flamboyant, it possessed a stylish elegance that had been decidedly absent in Thomas Wade's home.

"They are astonishingly beautiful," she said with absolute sincerity.

Vanya chuckled, obviously pleased with Brianna's response. "Ah, a woman of exquisite taste. Edmond, of course, is furious with me. He insisted that you share his bedchamber, but I informed him that a woman has need of her privacy upon occasion."

A blush stained Brianna's cheeks. "I suppose you must wonder why I…why I am traveling alone with…"

"*Sacre bleu*, what is there to wonder?" Vanya interrupted with a charming smile. "Edmond is an uncommonly beautiful man. If I were ten years younger, I would be battling you for his attentions. Of course, my bed is quite full at the moment, and while there is something to be said for a young, virile lover, I have come to appreciate those older gentlemen who are not nearly so inclined to desire exclusive rights. Variety is, after all, the spice of life." A twinkle entered the blue eyes as Brianna's blush deepened. "Have I shocked you?"

Brianna swallowed a nervous laugh. It was not the thought that the older woman kept a string of lovers that caught her off guard. The ladies of London society were rumored to enjoy the attentions of any number of gentlemen once they had produced the necessary heir. Indeed, Brianna would not be at all surprised to discover her own mother had indulged in affairs.

But no matter how questionable their morals, an English woman would never dare to reveal her peccadilloes.

"No…" Brianna cleared her throat. "No, of course not."

Vanya patted Brianna's hand. "You will discover, *ma petite*, that while I am considered unconventional and eccentric, I am no hypocrite. I live my life as I choose and I never judge others."

Brianna found her embarrassment melting beneath Vanya's firm assurances. There was such ease and charm about the woman that it was impossible not to feel comfortable in her presence.

It was obvious Vanya Petrova had a life filled with freedom and adventure and a rare purpose. Precisely what Brianna had always desired for herself.

"Thank you."

"And even better, I am a woman of the world who is quite willing to tutor you in the best means of handling a difficult man such as Edmond."

"Does the best means include a horse whip?"

Vanya heaved an exaggerated sigh. "A tempting thought, but it would no doubt only make him more stubborn. It is best to use a more subtle approach." She waved a heavily bejeweled hand. "Which is precisely why I insisted that you have your own rooms."

"I fear I do not understand."

"It never does to allow a gentleman to take you for granted," the older woman explained. "If Edmond wishes to join you in these chambers, then he must ensure he does nothing that will persuade you to lock your doors."

Brianna gave a sudden laugh at the thought a mere lock could keep Edmond out of anywhere he wanted to be.

"You are presuming that he would not simply break down the door."

Vanya paused a long moment, as if considering Brianna's words. "I will admit the thought did not enter my mind. Edmond is hardly a man to go to such an effort for a woman." A slow smile curved her lips. "Not until you, *ma petite*. He has never allowed a woman to travel with him. Nor to stay beneath the same roof. I do believe he might charge through any number of locked doors to be at your side."

Brianna's heart gave a dangerous flutter before she was sternly quashing the reaction.

She wanted to accept their relationship with a cool composure that would allow her to walk away with nothing more than pleasant memories.

It was, no doubt, how Vanya Petrova conducted her affairs.

"Only because he believes me to be a challenge. And because he cannot bear the thought that anyone else might have me."

Without warning Vanya tilted back her head to laugh with rich amusement.

"Good heavens, you are innocent."

"Believe me, Vanya, Edmond may be…" She struggled for the appropriate word. "Fond of me, but he will never feel more than that. He would rather slit his own throat than allow anyone close to him. I might be innocent, but even I understand that lust and love are two completely different emotions."

Vanya's lips parted, as if she intended to argue. Then, meeting Brianna's unwavering gaze, she heaved a small sigh.

"I suppose that is true enough. The poor boy. I wish that he would realize that his parents would never have wanted him to blame himself for their deaths. It was nothing more than a tragic accident."

Brianna grimly ignored the pang of sympathy for Edmond. He desired nothing from her but her body, and that was all she intended to offer.

Her chin tilted in an unwitting gesture of pride. "Besides, I have no desire for anything more than a temporary affair."

Vanya blinked, caught by surprise by the stark declaration. "Really?"

"Yes, really."

There was a moment of silence before the older woman gave Brianna's fingers a squeeze. "*Ma petite,* it is not often a woman is fortunate enough to earn the attentions of such a handsome and wealthy man. You would be foolish to toss him aside without giving thought to your future."

The advice was obviously well-intentioned, but Brianna shuddered at the mere thought of trading her body for security.

It would not matter how much she might desire Edmond. Or any other man.

"I have an inheritance that I intend to use to establish my own household," she said, her voice soft but filled with an unshakable dignity. "I will never depend upon a man for my comfort."

The striking features lightened with a smile of pleasure. "Ah, a woman of independence. My very favorite sort. We really must spend some time together, *ma petite*. I can tell you…"

"Perhaps it would be best if you kept your advice for your less innocent guests, Vanya," a dark male voice intruded. "I would prefer Brianna not to be entirely corrupted during our stay."

Both women turned as Edmond's tall form crossed the room to stand directly before the sofa. In their short time apart, he had changed into a plain gray waistcoat, black breeches and gleaming Hessians. The severe style emphasized the hard perfection of his body and dark beauty of his countenance.

"Ah, Edmond." Vanya Petrova rose to her feet and greeted him. She held out her hand for him to kiss. "I thought you were leaving to meet with Herrick Gerhardt?"

"In time." Brushing his lips over Vanya's knuckles, he dropped her hand and straightened with an elegant motion. "First I wished to assure myself that Brianna was comfortably settled."

The older woman lifted a silver brow. "And to assure yourself that I am not busily convincing her that she would be far happier with a more considerate lover?"

The very air froze, as Edmond's features hardened with a lethal anger.

"Vanya, I love you dearly, but if any of your male guests is stupid enough to try to enter these rooms, I will put a bullet through his heart." The sheer lack of emotion in his flat tone was disturbing. "You might wish to pass along my warning. I should not desire any unpleasant mistakes to occur."

Brianna instinctively rose to her feet, but Vanya merely smiled. Clearly the woman possessed a taste for danger.

"Good heavens, my boy, you sound positively stodgy." There

was a short, deliberate pause. "Indeed, you very nearly sound like a husband."

Brianna gave a strangled gasp. Good lord. Did the woman possess no fear?

Or sense?

Thankfully Edmond did no more than narrow his gaze in warning. "Do you not have need to tend to your guests, Vanya?"

With a chuckle, Vanya obligingly moved toward the door, pausing to cast Edmond a last glance. "I will go, Edmond, but do not forget that I am mistress of this house and my sympathies will always go to my fellow women. If I decide you are not treating her with the proper respect, I will have you thrown out."

Waiting until the door closed behind the older woman, Edmond ruefully shook his head.

"This seemed like a good notion when we were in London. Now I begin to wonder if I have made a mistake."

With an effort to appear casual, Brianna wandered toward the ormolu and marble table that held a collection of jade figurines.

"Why?" she demanded. "I like Vanya."

"I am not at all surprised," he muttered. "The woman is convinced that men should be kept as trained pets that she can toss in the gutter when she wearies of them."

"And what is wrong with that? That is how women have been treated for centuries."

Without warning, Brianna found herself pressed to the nearby wall, Edmond's hard body leaning heavily against her.

"Edmond…"

"I was not jesting, *ma souris,*" he rasped, his hand cupping her chin. "I am no hound on the leash, and Vanya's household is unconventional to say the least. Any number of gentlemen will be eager to have such a young and beautiful woman within their reach. I will not tolerate having them make advances toward you."

Brianna cursed her flare of satisfaction at the dark possession in his voice.

"For God's sake, Edmond, it is not the Middle Ages," she forced herself to say. "I am not your chattel."

He covered her lips with a savage kiss, his fingers tugging at the buttons of her gown.

"Chattel or not, you *are* mine," he whispered against her lips. "Do not ever forget that."

Brianna gasped as her bodice was jerked open and his fingers slipped beneath her corset to tease her breasts.

"You make it difficult to forget," she muttered, her lids sliding downward as his mouth nuzzled a path of fire down her throat.

"Difficult?" He pressed his lips against the frantic pulse at the base of her neck. "I intend to make it impossible."

THE SNOW THAT HAD BEEN threatening the entire day was beginning to fall in earnest as the elegant sleigh carried Herrick Gerhardt and Edmond away from the bustle of St. Petersburg. Not that the chill air was allowed to penetrate the heavy furs that lined the interior of the sleigh, or the slick roads to slow the dozen outriders that served as guards.

Herrick often conducted his most confidential business far away from the prying eyes of the Winter Palace and was wise enough to ensure his guests were made comfortable.

Leaning back in the wide seat, Edmond sipped the perfectly aged brandy and forced his thoughts from the woman he had left tucked in her bed at Vanya Petrova's.

Christ. Their furious bout of lovemaking had left even him shaken. Not out of fear he had hurt Brianna in any way. Hell, she had whispered encouragement with every frantic thrust.

No, it had been his overpowering urge to satisfy her so completely that she could think of no one but him, desire no one but him.

As if he could actually brand her with his passion.

Which was as ridiculous as it was disturbing.

"Edmond?"

With a shake of his head, Edmond drained the last of his brandy and turned his attention toward the gentleman seated across from him.

"You managed to join Boris and follow Kazakov from the ship?"

A silver brow arched at the question. Herrick rarely made mistakes. And even more rarely had his considerable skills doubted.

"Of course. As you suspected, he traveled directly to his cousin's home."

Edmond grimaced. Fedor Dubov was a feeble imitation of his elder cousin Viktor. He would never possess Viktor's position or wealth or even charisma, but he was a dependable toady who was readily used by others.

"Bastard."

Herrick held up a gaunt hand. "There is more."

"What?"

"I have never trusted Fedor Dubov's seeming acceptance of Alexander's refusal to consider him a member of his council."

Edmond laughed sharply at the mere notion of offering the fool a position of trust.

"*Mon dieu.* The man claimed that Alexander murdered his own father. Did he think that would be forgotten?"

Tugging his fur-lined cape tighter around his body, Herrick shrugged.

"Many others said the same, some of whom are even now in places of power among the government."

"They were at least wise enough to whisper their suspicions in private, not publicly announce them before the entire Russian Court. He was fortunate not to face the firing squad."

Herrick reached beneath his cloak to pull out a folded piece of parchment that he handed to Edmond.

"His fortune may have just come to an end."

Edmond smoothed open the parchment with a frown. "What have you discovered?"

"That message was sent to the Winter Palace only moments after Viktor Kazakov's arrival in St. Petersburg."

The handwriting was rough, nearly illegible, but Edmond managed to make out the Voltaire quote, along with a short message at the end.

"All murderers are punished unless they kill in large numbers and to the sound of trumpets. The time is upon us...I await your call."

His blood ran cold.

"How did you come by this?"

"As I said, I have never trusted Fedor Dubov, so I have been paying a number of his servants to keep me apprised of his movements and of those who visit." He pointed toward the note in Edmond's hand. "One of them was quick enough to copy the message before it was sent. I received it only moments ago."

Edmond cursed beneath his breath. Kazakov clearly had no desire to waste even a moment before claiming the power he always felt his due.

"Who was the message being delivered to?"

"I fear the servant did not know. Kazakov sent his personal valet to the palace and the man is annoyingly loyal." The shrewd brown eyes narrowed with a grim determination. "I have commanded those who are keeping a watch upon Fedor Dubov's home to follow the valet upon the next occasion he leaves the house."

"Mon dieu." Crumpling the note, Edmond tossed it onto the floor of the sleigh. It was as if he were standing before an avalanche that he was powerless to halt, an unbearable sensation that he had not endured since the death of his parents.

Herrick's gaze was knowing as he studied the frustration that tightened Edmond's expression.

"We will discover who is behind this treachery."

Edmond reached for the brandy bottle that was kept in a small compartment next to his companion. With a smooth motion, he lifted it to his lips and took a deep swig. The welcome burn of the fine spirits helped to ease the chill that was settled in the pit of his stomach.

"Have you had word from the Czar?"

Herrick dipped his head. "He is safe and well-guarded."

"I will not deny I am relieved that you returned to St. Petersburg rather than remaining with Alexander Pavlovich. I fear you are more greatly needed here."

"The treaty was signed and the formalities observed. I had no reason to linger. In truth, I sensed that there was trouble stirring."

Edmond snorted. "A pity that the Emperor did not share your urgency. Although I would not wish him in danger, his place is here among his people. Perhaps then, his enemies would not grow so bold."

Herrick instinctively smoothed his expression. He might trust Edmond with his life, but he would never reveal his most private opinion of his Czar. His loyalty was as constant and unshakable as the vast pyramids of Egypt.

"We both know that the crown sits uneasily upon Alexander's head. He finds peace in his travels."

Edmond shook his head in a gesture of frustration. It was not that he did not sympathize with the Emperor. Alexander Pavlovich had sought reform only to be undermined by his own people, and now, when his rule had returned to the rigid repression of his forefathers, there had been the constant threat of revolt. No matter what his efforts, he could not seem to win the love of his citizens.

Still, he possessed a duty he could not continue to ignore.

"His people have need of him."

Herrick held up a thin hand, his expression revealing a hint of sadness.

"We all do the best that we can, my friend. It is all we can ask."

Edmond wanted to protest. Alexander Pavlovich needed to do more than just his best. He needed to rise from the ashes of his insecurities and become the strong, decisive leader that Russia so desperately needed.

"I will speak with my associates," he said, swallowing his desire to demand that Herrick send for the Emperor. Alexander would return to St. Petersburg only when it suited him. "Perhaps they have information."

"You will let me know."

"Of course."

Herrick leaned to glance out the frosty window, giving a hand signal toward the nearby outrider that resulted in the sleigh turning back toward the city.

For a time, the gentlemen rode in silence, both consumed with their dark thoughts. Then, with an obvious effort, Herrick attempted to lighten the atmosphere.

"So tell me of this woman."

"I beg your pardon?"

"Boris has told me that you have brought an English companion to Russia."

"He should learn to keep his mouth shut."

"Is she beautiful?" Herrick clicked his tongue. "A foolish question. Of course she is beautiful. When have you ever chosen a woman who is not exquisite?"

"She is beautiful, but for once it would not matter. My fascination has nothing to do with the curve of her cheek or the delectable line of her lips."

Herrick gave a startled cough. "A dangerous admission, my friend."

It was dangerous, of course. When a gentleman began to discuss a woman as something other than a tasty morsel to be enjoyed and forgotten, it usually meant that he was about to do something incredibly stupid.

"Denial has done little good," he grudgingly admitted. "I have hopes that proximity will prove more effective."

"You believe you will grow weary of her companionship?"

"It is the inevitable conclusion of all affairs."

Herrick tilted his head to one side, his expression curious. "And if you do not grow weary?"

Edmond ignored the mocking voice in the back of his mind that assured him that he had been well and truly bested by a slip of a girl who could alter his entire mood by nothing more than a smile.

"Then she will remain my lover," he growled. "Forever."

CHAPTER TWENTY

EDMOND COMMANDED THAT Herrick leave him near the Cathedral of our Lady of Kazan. The church had been commissioned by Emperor Paul I and built in a similar style to St. Peter's in Rome. The name was given by the Icon of Our Lady of Kazan who was supposed to have miraculously saved Moscow in 1612.

It was not the beauty of the dome or the colonnaded arms that swept outward in a graceful arch that lured Edmond to its steps. It was, instead, its proximity to the Nevsky Prospect and the Gostinny Dvor.

Keeping his hat pulled low and the heavy scarf wrapped around the lower half of his face, Edmond carefully traversed the snow-packed street toward a small coffeehouse near the busy shops. He entered the smoky warmth, and keeping his head low, weaved his way through the gathered crowd to a private room at the back.

He had barely managed to rid himself of his snow-dusted greatcoat and hat when a large, burly man with dark hair and eyes stepped into the small room that was barren except for a desk and wooden chair, closing the door behind him.

"Welcome home, Commander," he rumbled, crossing the room to pull Edmond in a rough hug of welcome.

Edmond laughed as he disentangled from the thick arms that threatened to crush his ribs. Sergey had served with Edmond during the war and had proven his loyalty by taking a bullet to the shoulder that had been intended for Edmond. When Sergey had been forced to leave the military, Edmond had purchased this coffeehouse for the man, knowing the overly proud soldier would never accept his money.

"Good lord, I had no notion that a coffeehouse could attract such a crowd. I feared I might be trampled by the stampede of customers."

Sergey ran his beefy hands down the expensive fabric of his jacket. "Ah, well, the citizens of St. Petersburg are wise enough to recognize a fine establishment."

"They are indeed." Knowing the gregarious man could talk the entire day, Edmond considered how best to come straight to the point of his visit. "Tell me what you have heard."

The jovial expression faded from Sergey's face to be replaced by a weary concern.

"The rumblings on the streets are as bad as I have ever heard them, Commander."

Edmond frowned. "What do they say?"

"The usual complaints of the nobles squandering their wealth while their serfs starve. The peasants are poor, they are not blind. Their voices grow louder with each passing day."

"Understandable, but as you say, all too common."

"There is also a growing anger among the local merchants," Sergey continued. "They resent the fashion of importing foreign goods rather than purchasing their wares from local craftsmen. The European ships clog our port and flood the markets with their wares."

Edmond shrugged. It was more or less what he had expected. Too many lived in squalor, while a small handful displayed their wealth with gaudy splendor. For the moment, however, they were powerless.

"Viktor Kazakov would not seek serfs or merchants to assist him in overthrowing the Czar." He shook his head. "They may mutter treason beneath their breath, but they are too fearful for outright revolt."

Sergey folded his arms over his massive chest. "No doubt the French government was similarly confident."

"Perhaps, but the Russians do not possess a Rousseau who is capable of stirring the masses to bloodshed." Edmond's stomach clenched at the mere thought. As much as he desired a better existence for the serfs, he would do everything in his power to avoid a bloody revolution. "At least not yet."

"True enough." The soldier's brown eyes hardened with hatred. "They would never follow Viktor Kazakov. His brutality to his serfs is well-known."

Edmond knew an answering hatred was echoed in his eyes. Viktor had long been rumored to treat his serfs as animals, raping girls no older than nine and beating more than one worker to death. Edmond would see him dead before he could claim power.

"Precisely."

"You have your suspicions of who is prepared to assist Viktor Kazakov?"

"More a…vague fear."

"Do you intend to share these vague fears?"

Edmond hid his smile at the clipped command. It seemed that once an officer, always an officer.

"Gather any associates that you still have in the military and question them closely. I want to know precisely what is being said and felt in the barracks."

Sergey sucked in a sharp breath. "Good God."

Edmond held up a warning hand. "I have no logical reason for my unease. Just a gut feeling that Viktor Kazakov is wise enough to know this will be his last opportunity to grasp the power he has always craved. If he fails, his life is forfeit." His hands clenched at his sides. "He cannot hope for a dubious uprising among the serfs that might never occur. He will have to strike hard and fast at the very heart of the government."

"A military coup," Sergey breathed.

"Not if we have anything to say about it, Sergey."

His companion lifted a clenched fist. "I happen to have a great deal to say, my friend."

BRIANNA SLEPT NEARLY TWO hours after Edmond left, but rising from the bed, she discovered she still felt oddly lethargic with a hint of queasiness. She fully blamed Edmond and his intense bout of lovemaking. It was a wonder she was able to even leave her bed, she told herself as she slipped from beneath the covers and swiftly dressed in a round dress of rose figured silk. It was a struggle to pin her thick curls atop her head without the assistance of Janet, but she was reluctant to disturb Vanya's servants. From the noisy echo of voices floating from the public rooms, it sounded as if there were enough guests to keep them occupied.

Pulling open the door, Brianna left her chambers, hoping to rid herself of the clinging lassitude. She avoided the wide staircase that led to the more public area of the vast house, and instead wandered down the corridor until she stumbled across what appeared to be a music chamber.

She smiled at the glossy parquet floors, the light lemonwood furnishings and the priceless tapestries framed upon the walls. There was an intimate comfort to the atmosphere, but she was willing to bet it cost a fortune in rubles to achieve.

Bypassing the gilded harp, Brianna moved to the window seat that overlooked the shallow garden. The air was chilled next to the tall windows, but it seemed to ease her unsettled stomach, and wrapping the heavy cashmere shawl she had brought with her around her shoulders, she watched the snow drift down in a soft, hypnotizing pattern.

She lost track of time, her brow pressed against the frosted window, as she allowed her mind to drift. It was the first time she had been completely alone in weeks, and the hushed silence was a relief.

Of course, the peace could not last forever. Eventually there was the sound of approaching footsteps, and before Brianna could think to retreat back to her chambers, a tall stranger entered the room and regarded her with a quizzical smile.

He was a distinguished gentleman with a handsome face and dark hair heavily threaded with silver. His elegant mauve coat and gray breeches marked him as a gentleman of wealth, as did the large diamond that shimmered in the folds of his cravat. But she had no way of knowing if the man was one of Vanya's trusted guests, or a stray visitor who would question her presence in the house.

"Ah, you must be Miss Quinn," he murmured, his hand lifting at her wary expression. "Do not fear. I am under strict orders to tell no one of your presence in Russia, and believe me, when Vanya issues an order, a wise gentleman is swift to obey."

Her unease became surprise as he halted directly in front of the window seat.

"You are English."

"For my sins." He performed a deep bow. "Mr. Richard Monroe, at your service."

She studied him for a long moment. There was unmistakable nobility carved into his handsome features, but the dark eyes held a kindness that instinctively eased her tension.

"What are you doing in St. Petersburg?"

"The truth?"

Brianna blinked in confusion. "If it is not a secret."

"No, no secret." His smile twisted with a self-derisive motion. "Vanya visited London near a decade ago, and I was foolish enough to tumble into love with her. Since then, I have been following her like a faithful hound, awaiting her to concede defeat and agree to become my wife."

"Ten years?"

He chuckled at her expression of disbelief. "Astonishing, is it not?"

"I…yes, quite astonishing."

"Miss Quinn? Have I said something to trouble you?"

"Ten years is a rather long time. You must be a very patient gentleman."

He heaved a rueful sigh. "On occasion, I lose hope and travel back to my brother's estates in Kent, but I always return."

He gave a lift of his hands. "My life is gray and tedious without Vanya to brighten it."

Brianna tugged her shawl tighter as a shiver wracked her body. It had to be the chill in the air.

It had to be.

"Do you live in this town house?"

"No, I have rooms in the Winter Palace, which of course is the reason Vanya continues to encourage my companionship."

"I do not understand."

The gentleman shrugged. "My place in the Royal household ensures that I can keep a close guard upon those who are closest to the Emperor."

Brianna sucked in a sharp breath. Surrounded by such ease and luxury, it had been easy to forget that Vanya was deeply involved in the dangerous, potentially lethal world of Russian politics.

"Oh. Of course." She regarded her companion with a hint of curiosity. Mr. Richard Monroe was obviously a man of enormous wealth and power, and not even she was impervious to his potent charm. The man could have his choice of the most sought after debutantes London or St. Petersburg had to offer. So why would he toss aside everything for a woman who not only refused to wed him, but openly declared her preference for numerous lovers? "Does it not trouble you?"

"That Vanya only sees me as a weapon to be used in her private war to keep the Romanovs in power?"

"Yes."

Something flashed through the dark eyes. Not pain, but more a wistful longing.

"At times, but as a rule I am far too happy to have any place in her life, no matter how small it might be."

"You must love her a great deal," she said softly.

He tilted his head to one side, a strange expression on his face.

"Is there any such thing as a small love? Either you love or you do not." Before Brianna could respond, the man gave a shake of his head and squared his shoulders. "Now, enough of my sad tale. I am far more interested in you. Tell me of yourself, my dear."

"I fear there is not much to tell. I have always lived a very sheltered life."

He eyed her with a wry expression. "Not too sheltered, if you have been whisked from your home by one of the most powerful gentlemen in all of England and tumbled directly into the midst of a brewing Russian revolt."

"Edmond does certainly possess a talent for making a woman's existence a trifle more exciting."

Richard chuckled. "More than a trifle, I should imagine. Edmond is much like Vanya, despite the fact that they are not related by blood. They both possess that fascinating allure that is so fatal to us poor, benighted souls."

Her chest felt suddenly tight. No. She would never be like Mr. Richard Monroe. She would not spend her life nursing an unrequited love.

"I suppose," she at last managed to mutter.

Easily recognizing her unease, Richard narrowed his gaze. "You do not sound particularly pleased." He studied her for a long, unnerving beat. "You were not brought here against your will, were you?"

"No." She blinked in shock at the unexpected question. "No, of course not."

The older gentleman did not appear entirely convinced. "Miss Quinn, I want you to know that, if you have need of a friend, you can depend upon Vanya or my own humble self. You may be far from home, but you are not alone."

"You are very kind, but…"

"I possess great admiration for Edmond, but I am not indifferent to his ruthless habit of forcing others to his will," Richard gently, but firmly, overrode her words. "A young, innocent woman would have no ability to withstand his considerable resolve."

Brianna could not help but chuckle as she remembered the manner she had blackmailed Edmond into allowing her to remain at Huntley House, and even demanded that he procure a companion for her.

"I assure you, Mr. Monroe, Edmond did not force me to accompany him. It was entirely my choice to travel to St. Petersburg."

Without warning, he reached out his hand to brush a finger down her chilled cheek.

"Then why do you look so pale?"

She gave a slow shake of her head. "I am not feeling terribly well. I think the journey was more draining than I realized."

She had barely finished speaking when he was crossing the room to pour a glass of a dark liquid from the pitcher set on the porcelain stove. Returning to her side, he settled his tall form on the window seat and pressed the glass into her hand.

"Here."

The glass was warm against her skin and filled the air with the scent of cloves.

"What is it?"

"Nothing more than spiced punch. It will warm you." Cupping her hand with his own, he lifted the glass to her lips. "Drink slowly."

She took a cautious sip, nearly groaning in relief as the punch slid down her throat with welcome warmth, soothing the nausea.

Oh…it was delicious.

Savoring the heat spreading through her body, Brianna failed to notice they were no longer alone. Not until a choked cough filled the room.

Brianna turned her head to discover Vanya standing in the center of the room, her countenance carefully expressionless as she regarded the unwitting intimacy of the two seated on the window seat.

Despite the innocence of their position, Brianna felt a blush touch her cheeks. Perhaps it was because she sensed the older woman was far from indifferent beneath her demeanor of calm composure.

"Here you are, Richard." The older woman smiled, her hands smoothing over the mulberry velvet of her gown. "I see you have introduced yourself to my beautiful young guest. Is anything the matter?"

Indifferent to the tension that suddenly filled the room, Richard lowered his hand and slowly lifted himself to his feet.

"Miss Quinn was not feeling well."

Vanya's expression softened with concern. "Oh, *ma petite,* how terrible. Are you in need of a doctor?"

"No, no. Please, it is nothing." Embarrassed that her silly bout of nausea was stirring a fuss, Brianna gave a firm shake of her head. "I am feeling better already."

Vanya moved forward, her worried gaze on Brianna although her feet instinctively seemed to carry her to Richard's side. She even went so far as to lay a possessive hand on his arm.

"I will have a hot bath carried to your rooms. There is nothing more refreshing."

"Oh, that sounds lovely." Brianna did not have to pretend her gratitude. It had been too long since she had the pleasure of more than a swift wash in cold water. Rising to her feet, she dipped a small curtsey. "It was a pleasure to meet you, Mr. Monroe."

He offered his sweet smile. "The pleasure, Miss Quinn, was entirely mine."

Vanya shifted her attention to the gentleman at her side, an oddly somber expression settling upon her beautiful face.

"Do not pay him the least attention, *ma petite.* He is an incorrigible flirt," she murmured.

"How can you say such a thing?" Richard protested, lifting Vanya's hand to press a lingering kiss upon her fingers. "You, my love, are a master of flirtation."

Her body arched toward him with the ease of long-time lovers. "Never with you, Richard."

His expression held enough tenderness to twist even the most hardened heart.

"Yes," he murmured softly, "that is what continues to give me hope."

Feeling decidedly *de trop,* Brianna slipped from the room and silently made her way back to her chambers.

A wry smile touched her lips as she entered the lavish parlor and pulled the door closed behind her. Whatever Vanya's bold words of endless lovers and glorious independence, it was obvious she was deeply attached to Mr. Richard Monroe.

Perhaps more than just attached.

Obviously, however, the woman was simply too stubborn to admit her feelings. Even to herself.

It was a knowledge that sent a chill down her spine.

CHAPTER TWENTY-ONE

THE SUN WAS DIPPING TOWARD the horizon when Brianna heard the sound of Edmond's voice in the corridor.

Not at all certain that she was prepared to face him, she waited until she heard the door to his chambers close before slipping on a heavy, ermine-lined cloak that Edmond had insisted she purchase prior to leaving England along with a heavy muff. With the hood raised, her face remained in deep shadows, and leaving behind the veil, she left her rooms and made her way to the small garden below.

Even prepared for the cold, Brianna's breath was wrenched from her lungs as the frigid air clawed at her. For a moment, she debated the wisdom of scurrying back to the warmth of her rooms. As refreshing as the cold might be, it was edged with a brutal chill that threatened to freeze her to the bone.

Then her gaze caught sight of the nearby Neva River and all thoughts of returning inside were cast aside.

Bewitched by the near fairytale sight of ice skaters, sleighs, vendors and pedestrians moving along the frozen river, Brianna walked to the edge of the empty garden. Despite the cold, there were hundreds of people mingling together, the echo of laughter reaching the garden and bringing a smile to her face.

From behind her, she heard the sound of the terrace door opening, and the crunch of footsteps crossing the ice-crusted snow.

She did not bother to turn around.

"Brianna?"

Still she did not turn. "Hmm?"

"What are you doing out here?"

In truth, she was not certain. It had not entirely been due to a need to avoid Edmond. She had known the moment she had left her rooms that he would come in search of her. If she truly desired to avoid the stubborn man, she would have to travel a great deal further than the garden.

At last, she grasped the most convenient excuse that came to mind. "I needed some fresh air."

"Fresh? It is freezing." Placing his hands on her shoulders, Edmond firmly turned her to meet his searching gaze. "Come back inside where it is warm."

"In a while."

The dark brows drew together at her refusal to jump at his command, but surprisingly, he seemed more concerned than angry.

"Vanya said that you were not feeling well."

"I am fine." She smiled ruefully as he continued to regard her as if she might swoon at any moment. "Truly, I am, Edmond. It was nothing more than a passing queasiness."

He stepped closer, lifting his hand to lightly touch the shadows beneath her eyes.

"You are not accustomed to such hard travel, *ma souris*. You need to rest over the next few days."

"I have been doing nothing but resting the entire day. It feels good to be out of the house." Oddly unnerved by his fussing, Brianna sought to divert his attention. Pulling from his grip, she turned back toward the wrought-iron fencing and pointed toward the island in the center of the frozen river. "What is that?"

There was a brittle silence before Edmond shifted to stand directly behind her, wrapping his arms around her waist and pulling her firmly against his hard body.

"That is the Petropavlovsky Cathedral." He murmured. "It is the burial place for the Czars of Russia."

"There are so many trees. Do they have some religious significance?"

He chuckled softly. "Actually, they were left to grow on the island out of the very real possibility that the soldiers would need firewood if the fortress surrounding the cathedral was ever under siege. Once I have dealt with the traitors, I will take you to visit the island. There are not only the Czars' tombs to see, but a treasury mint and the Governor's House."

Brianna tilted back her head to regard him in surprise. "You intend to take me sightseeing?"

"Of course. I also intend to take you ice skating on the Neva."

"Ice skating? You?"

He leaned down to kiss the tip of her nose. "Why do you look so shocked? I happen to be a fine ice skater."

Sharply turning her attention to the skaters skimming down the river with elegant ease, Brianna easily imagined Edmond among them.

"Of course you are," she said, dryly.

His arms tightened about her. "Or if you prefer, we can simply mingle among the vendors that arrive daily to do business on the river. You have never tasted anything so fine as their fresh gingerbread."

"It seems odd to watch the sleighs travel over the river as if it is just another road."

She felt him shrug. "During much of the winter, it is the most important road in all of St. Petersburg, since most of the bridges are removed once the river freezes over. Ah."

"What is it?"

"Watch the sky," he commanded.

"Why?"

"Just be patient."

Wondering if there were about to be a fireworks show over the city, she obligingly tilted back her head, waiting for the explosions. What she witnessed instead was a slow kaleidoscope of colors spreading across the sky as the sun sank behind the horizon. From pinks to lavenders to the deepest mauve, the beautiful palette brushed over the spires and domes of the city, making Brianna catch her breath in wonderment.

"Oh…I have never seen anything so exquisite."

She felt his chest expand as he breathed out a soft sigh. "Neither have I."

Turning her head, Brianna realized that Edmond was gazing at her profile, not the spectacular sunset. Her heart slammed against her chest as a thick, ready awareness heated the air between them. With a soft groan, he lowered his head to capture her lips in a sweetly savage kiss.

Brianna allowed herself to savor the taste of brandy on his lips, the potent pleasure of his tongue as it dipped into her mouth, the strong hands digging into her waist as his body hardened with need.

At last, it was the belated realization that they were in full view of the house that made her pull back with a small gasp.

"Edmond, someone will see."

Denied her lips, Edmond pushed her hood back far enough to skim his own lips down the curve of her cheek.

"Let them watch. I do not care," he rasped, his breath scalding against her chilled skin. *"Moya duska."*

The unfamiliar Russian words managed to penetrate the intoxicating sensations tingling through her body. Her fingers dug into his arms as her knees threatened to buckle.

"What did you say?"

"I said that, if you think the winter sunset is beautiful, just wait until the summer and the white nights," he easily lied, clearly unwilling to reveal the meaning of his husky words. "The Emperor will no doubt invite us to his yearly celebration on the solstice."

Turning in his arms, Brianna jutted her chin upward and forced herself to meet his brilliant blue gaze.

"No."

"Brianna, you cannot ignore an invitation from Alexander

Pavlovich, no matter how tedious his formal affairs can be," he chided. "They are very much a royal command."

"It has nothing to do with the invitation."

"Then what is it?"

"I cannot remain in Russia until summer."

Edmond dropped his arms and stepped back, his expression as cold as the air that cut through her cape with a sharp fury.

"Why not?"

She shivered, although not entirely from the cold. "I will reach my majority in May. I must be in London to sign the papers and receive my inheritance."

"That can be dealt with by a solicitor."

She narrowed her gaze. "You know how important this is to me, Edmond. I wish to handle the business in person."

Edmond's jaw tightened as he struggled against his urge to toss out a command and have it obeyed.

"Very well. We can travel back to London for a few weeks. Spring is the one bearable season in the city, and Stefan is always pleased when I return for a visit."

Brianna could not deny a flare of astonishment at his concession. As Mr. Richard Monroe had so recently pointed out, Edmond was a gentleman accustomed to having his way. In everything.

Still, there was a tiny voice in the back of her mind warning her not to waver on her impetuous declaration. Mr. Richard Monroe had pointed out more than Edmond's innate arrogance. His mere presence in St. Petersburg revealed the future of anyone foolish enough to allow their passions to rule their heads.

A future that Brianna was determined to avoid. What better way than setting a firm date to put Edmond out of her life?

"I intend to remain in London, Edmond," she said, wrapping her arms about her shivering body. "With my inheritance, I will be able to buy a small home and begin to build the life I have always desired."

His eyes smoldered with a dangerous fury. "Are you attempting to stir my temper, *ma souris?*"

She smiled wryly, despite the prickles of alarm that raced over her skin. "I seem to stir your temper whenever I express my own opinions. Perhaps, Edmond, you would be happier with a woman who is a great deal more biddable than I am."

"I would be happier with a woman who was not forever battling against her desire to be with me." He reached to grasp her chin in his fingers. "You want me. You want to be with me. Why do you try to deny it?"

"I have never denied that I…desire you," she muttered. "But that does not mean I shall devote the rest of my life to being your mistress. There are other things I wish to accomplish."

"What things?"

Feeling distinctly harassed, Brianna jerked from his grasp and turned to glare at the gas lanterns that were being lit along the icy streets.

"I have yet to decide," she grudgingly admitted. Perhaps she would never alter destiny, but London was littered with the poor and defenseless. There had to be any number of charities who were desperate for assistance. "But I will."

She heard his breath hiss between his clenched teeth. "So you intend to leave me so that you can live in a cramped house in the midst of London with no family, no friends and the hope of achieving some vague accomplishment?"

She hunched her shoulders. He made it all sound so…lonely. Almost pathetic.

Dammit. She could be happy, even fulfilled, without this man in her life.

She could.

"I will have Janet," she said, more in an effort to comfort herself than convince him of her wonderful future.

"Are you so certain?" he demanded. "I believe Boris might have something to say about that."

She stabbed him with a frustrated glare. "Fine, then I will live alone. It is better than…"

"Better than what?" He muttered a dark curse as she remained stubbornly silent. "*Mon dieu,* what did Vanya say to you?"

She lowered her lashes over her eyes. Let him assume that Vanya had convinced her of the delights to be found in a life of independence. It was far better than admitting she was terrified of becoming some sort of faithful lapdog, incapable of leaving him.

"Nothing."

"Brianna…"

The sound of a nearby door being opened was like a godsend and Brianna heaved a covert sigh of relief as Vanya's voice floated on the icy air.

"Edmond."

The hard blue gaze never shifted from Brianna's wary face. "Not now, Vanya."

"Forgive me for intruding, but I just received a message from Richard." Vanya firmly refused to be dismissed. "He has all in place, but you must leave now if you are to slip into the palace unnoted."

Brianna sucked in a sharp breath, her heart clenching with concern. "Good lord, you intend to sneak into the Winter Palace?"

He shrugged in a dismissive fashion, an oddly arrested expression on his face as he studied her anxious eyes. As if he were pleased by the knowledge she was disturbed at the thought of him being in danger.

"It will not be the first occasion I have done so."

The fact that she was not at all surprised by his confession did nothing to ease the knots in the pit of her stomach.

"What of the guards?"

He grimaced. "Unfortunately, the palace is far too vast to protect against intruders. Especially an intruder who has an accomplice within."

The accomplice had to be Mr. Monroe.

"What is so important that you are willing to risk exposure?"

"Fedor Dubov has received an invitation to dine. I intend to discover who he speaks with while he is there." A cold smile of anticipation twisted his lips. "It never matters how careful a traitor believes themselves to be, they always give away some hint, even if only by the manner they so obviously avoid another guest."

"Surely Mr. Monroe is capable of such a task?" she demanded, her tone sharp.

Edmond flicked a brow upward, but before he could respond, Vanya moved to stand at Brianna's side.

"Edmond is convinced that he alone is capable of recognizing a conspirator," she said dryly.

"It is not that at all."

Vanya regarded him with patent disbelief. "No?"

"Monroe will be among the diners. It would be impossible for him to keep a constant watch upon Fedor Dubov without arousing suspicion."

Struck by a sudden notion, Brianna frowned in confusion. "And where do you intend to be?"

His expression eased as a slow, wicked smile curved his lips.

"You cannot expect me to reveal all my secrets, *ma souris.*" He cast an intimate glance down the length of her body. "Who is to know when I might need to keep an eye upon you?"

She stiffened, her cheeks flaring with color at Vanya's soft chuckle. Good lord, he was staring at her as if she were standing there stark naked.

"If you dare to spy upon me I shall…"

"You shall what?" he taunted.

"You cannot expect me to reveal all *my* secrets," she said, tossing his own words back in his face.

Vanya's laughter rang through the garden. "*Touché,* Edmond."

He glanced toward the older woman. "You tread a dangerous path, Vanya."

"Not nearly so dangerous as you, *mon ami,*" she said, a

smug smile on her lips as she turned back toward the house. "I will send word to the stables that your mount is to be saddled."

ENTERING VANYA'S STABLES, Edmond was unsurprised to discover Boris awaiting him with a sour expression. The large warrior had not been pleased to discover he was not to join his employer. His life was devoted to hunting traitors.

Now he stood blocking the stall with his considerable bulk, his arms crossed over his chest.

"I should be with you."

A swift glance about the hay-scented darkness assured Edmond that they were alone.

"I need you to keep an eye upon Kazakov. He dare not show his face in the streets of St. Petersburg, but that does not mean he is not up to some mischief. If he has a visitor, I wish to know."

"That is surely Gerhardt's duty?"

Edmond grimaced. "He was unable to avoid the Prince's demand that he make an appearance at the Winter Palace, at least not without revealing the truth. Something he is loath to do, even to the Prince."

"Do you suspect that the conspiracy is so well-connected?" Boris demanded.

"There have been rumors that would make such a claim, but no, I do not believe that the Romanovs are involved." There was a pause. "At least, I hope they are not. I do not believe that Alexander Pavlovich could recover from such treachery."

"So I am to spend the night standing on a cold street, keeping watch on a gentleman who dare not leave his house?"

Edmond clapped his companion on the shoulder. "You know it could be worse, my friend."

"Worse?"

"You could be dining at the Winter Palace."

Boris turned to stomp toward the nearest stall, his foul curses filling the air.

To MOST VISITORS, THE VAST Winter palace was an overwhelming maze of marble and gilt and polished wooden floors. Even within the public rooms, it was an easy matter to become lost among the endless galleries, chambers and staircases. Thankfully, Alexander Pavlovich possessed a large battalion of uniformed servants who stood at every doorway, prepared to assist the flood of guests that arrived each evening.

Edmond, however, had long ago memorized the complex floor plans, including the Czar's private antechambers and the servants' narrow hallways.

Attired in a gray and mauve uniform that marked him as one of Richard Monroe's personal footmen, Edmond managed to slip into the palace and to his lordships' rooms without drawing attention. Not a difficult feat, considering Monroe had deliberately chosen chambers that possessed a private terrace with stairs that led directly to the back gardens.

Entering the sitting room decorated with Russian birch furnishings and plaster walls painted in a delicate ivory, Edmond crossed the inlaid wood floor to where Monroe leaned against his cluttered desk, looking every inch the aristocrat in his formal attire.

Although he had no official capacity, Monroe was the voice of England in those issues too delicate for an official ambassador to become involved. His shrewd intelligence, his calm ability to reason under pressure and his skills in negotiation made him an invaluable asset for King George.

There were few gentlemen that Edmond held in greater esteem.

Halting in the middle of the room, Edmond ran a hand down the jacket of his uniform, his smile wry.

"I must thank you for having my new attire delivered to me, although I believe the buttons are a trifle understated." He touched one of the plain gold buttons. "Surely you should have your insignia stamped upon them?"

Surprisingly, the older gentleman's expression remained grim as he studied Edmond.

"The uniform will fool others from a distance, but your face is too familiar not be recognized. You must remain out of sight."

Edmond's gaze narrowed at the unexpected words of warning. No matter how well-intentioned, he did not appreciate being told how to conduct his business.

"Is there a reason you are lecturing me as if I am a school-boy fresh from the nursery, Monroe?" he said, the warning in his voice clear.

Monroe straightened from the desk, his gaze steady. "Because gentlemen who are distracted are inclined to make dangerous mistakes."

"Distracted?"

"I was fortunate enough to encounter Miss Quinn this after-noon." Monroe made no attempt at subtlety. "She is exquisite."

Edmond took a step closer. Logically, he might understand Monroe's concern, but the thought of any man, no matter how close a friend, attempting to interfere in his relationship with Brianna managed to stir his anger.

"Yes, she is. Do you have a point?"

"In all the years I have known you, this is the first occasion you have revealed your secrets to a female. You would never have done so if she were not important to you."

"My relationship with Brianna is no one's concern."

"That is not entirely true." Monroe absently adjusted the cuff of his black jacket. "By bringing her to Vanya's you put us all at risk."

With a muttered oath, Edmond stepped forward.

"Are you implying that she is a traitor?"

Monroe held his hand up in a gesture of appeasement. "Be at ease, Edmond. I am merely pointing out that you have ob-viously judged her to be worthy of your trust. An honor you have never before offered to any woman beyond Vanya."

Realizing that his melodramatic reaction had revealed far more than he desired, Edmond gave a restless shrug.

"I have known Brianna Quinn since she was born. That aggravating chit may be stubborn, annoyingly independent and incapable of admitting that I know what is best for her, but she would never betray me." His voice held an absolute faith. Brianna Quinn might be the most maddening woman alive, but he would readily trust her with his very life. "She is incapable of such treachery."

"A woman of worth, then."

"Yes, she is."

The dark eyes held a knowing glint. "As I have said…a distraction."

"Surely it is time that we were on our way to dinner?"

Moving forward, the older gentleman placed a hand on Edmond's shoulder.

"Just be on your guard, Edmond. There is a tension in the palace on this night." He shook his head as Edmond's lips parted. "And before you ask me to explain, I cannot. It is nothing more than a feeling in the air. As if lightning were about to strike."

"Or a powder keg about to explode," Edmond murmured, recalling Herrick's words months earlier.

"Precisely."

WAITING UNTIL SHE WAS certain that Edmond had left for the Winter Palace, Brianna pulled on a night robe and climbed into her bed with a sigh of relief.

Perhaps a part of her should be annoyed that she was banned from the public rooms as if she were some shameful secret that must be hidden away, but in truth she was simply relieved that she would not be expected to attire herself in a fine dress and mingle among a crowd of strangers. Her stomach was once again tender and her body so weary that she wanted nothing more than to curl beneath the heavy covers and sleep for the next fortnight.

It was near an hour later when there was a light tap on her door and Vanya peeked her head into the room.

"May I enter?"

Feeling embarrassed to be caught taking to her bed at such an early hour, Brianna shoved herself into a seated position.

"Of course. I would love the company."

Pushing the door wide, Vanya stepped over the threshold, holding a silver tray in her hands.

"I have brought you a small surprise."

Brianna's embarrassment only deepened. "Good heavens, you have no need to wait upon me, Vanya."

The older woman merely smiled as she crossed to settle on the edge of the bed, placing the tray across Brianna's legs.

"I enjoy ensuring that my guests are comfortable."

"But your maid already sent me a dinner tray," Brianna protested as Vanya poured a cup of the hot tea and added several small spoons of sugar to the steaming liquid.

"One that you returned without even having taken a bite," Vanya retorted. "My poor cook was nearly in tears."

"Oh." Brianna winced as she recalled the plates of exquisite food that had been delivered and returned. Just the scent of roasted duck and rich lobster in butter had made her stomach heave in protest. "Please assure your cook that the food was perfectly lovely, but my stomach seems to be off today."

Vanya removed the white linen napkin from a plate on the tray to reveal the fresh gingerbread biscuits. "Perhaps a cup of tea and a biscuit will help."

Brianna breathed in deeply, relieved when she felt nothing more than a faint pang of hunger.

"Actually, it does smell wonderful," she murmured, taking a bite of the gingerbread before sipping the tea.

Vanya watched Brianna with an odd expression as she polished off two of the biscuits and drank the tea.

"Better?"

"Yes." Leaning against the headboard, Brianna heaved a satisfied sigh. "It is so silly. I am never ill. My mother always claimed that I had the constitution of a horse."

Vanya plucked the tray off Brianna's lap and set it on the bedside table.

"Have you thought that there might be a reason for your current...discomfort?"

Brianna shrugged. "I presume I must have caught a chill on the journey. It was rather a grueling voyage."

"Perhaps."

The older woman sounded far from convinced and Brianna frowned in confusion. She sensed that something was troubling Vanya, and that whatever it was concerned Brianna.

"Vanya?" she prompted, softly.

With a jerky motion Vanya was on her feet, her hands nervously twisting the priceless jewels on her fingers.

"I think that you should consider the possibility that you are with child, *ma petite*."

CHAPTER TWENTY-TWO

STANDING IN THE SHADOWS of the anteroom that offered a perfect view of the dining room, Edmond attempted not to fidget as he watched the guests seated about the small round tables with live orange trees growing through the center. Even without Alexander Pavlovich's presence, a dinner at the Palace was always a formal affair with endless dishes served by Mameluke servants who moved through the vast room with a silent dignity.

From his vantage, it was a simple matter to keep sight of Fedor Dubov as he shared a table with the lesser dignitaries at the edge of the room. The short, rotund gentleman was flashing his practiced smile, hiding his undoubted annoyance at being seated so far from the Czar's younger brother, Prince Michael and the royal family, but Edmond's practiced gaze did not miss the nervous twitch of his hands as he smoothed his cravat, or the manner in which his eyes darted about the room.

Fedor had never possessed Viktor's smooth ability to kiss the cheek of his enemy while sliding a dagger into his back. If any of the conspirators were to make a mistake, he was Edmond's best hope.

At precisely ten o'clock, the few royals in residence rose from their table and headed out of the room, signaling the end to the meal. Edmond melted farther into the shadows, a smile curling his lips as Fedor signaled someone with a covert nod of his head and then strolled casually toward the side door that would lead toward an empty ballroom.

With swift movements, Edmond was slipping from the antechamber to the nearest staircase, relieved that the servants would be distracted by the crowd of guests being led toward the Hermitage for the evening concert.

Reaching the upper gallery, he was careful to avoid the splashes of candlelight as he hurried to crouch in the shadows of the marble balustrade that overlooked the short corridor leading to the ballroom. He had barely managed to catch his breath when Fedor stepped through the door, followed shortly by a large gentleman who was attired in the uniform of the Semyonoffski regiment of the Foot Guards.

Edmond sucked in a sharp breath. Grigori Rimsky had been known in his younger years to possess sympathies for the Polish independence movement, but since transferring to the regiment that Alexander Pavlovich claimed as his own, he had proven to be a courageous commander who had risen swiftly through the ranks during the war with Napoleon. Edmond had never suspected his loyalty for a moment.

Which made him the most dangerous sort of traitor.

The highly decorated officer glanced about the seemingly empty corridor before giving the nervous Fedor a furious glare.

"Have you no sense?" he growled, his low voice easily carrying up to the gallery above. "We cannot speak here. If we are seen together…"

"I cannot risk another note," Fedor interrupted, withdrawing a handkerchief to blot the perspiration from his round face. "My house is being watched."

Grigori snapped to attention. "By whom?"

Fedor shrugged. "Gerhardt, no doubt."

"So, by now he knows that Viktor Kazakov has returned to St. Petersburg?"

"It will hardly matter in a few hours."

Edmond choked back his shock. A few hours? *Mon dieu.* As much as he longed for this nasty business to be done with, he was woefully unprepared to halt the mysterious revolt. He needed information. And he needed it swiftly. Even if it meant tipping his hand and hauling these two traitors to the nearest dungeons. Grigori might possess the courage to face death rather than expose their nefarious plot, but Fedor's spine was not nearly so stiff. A few lashes with a horsewhip and he would be begging to confess all.

"Besides," Fedor continued, "Gerhardt is not our greatest concern."

"What do you mean?"

"Lord Edmond is here."

Grigori hissed at the same time that Edmond stiffened in shock. Christ. How had they discovered his presence?

"In St. Petersburg?" Grigori barked.

"Yes." Fedor wiped his face again, his tension palpable in the air. "Viktor has a spy within Vanya Petrova's household."

Edmond silently swore to personally interview each and every one of Vanya's staff. By the time he was done with his little chat, they would be praying that the Czar's guard would arrive and haul them to the dungeons.

Grigori paced sharply toward an elegant Grecian statue, his hands clenched at his side as if his stoic composure were threatening to crack.

"Viktor promised me that Lord Edmond Summerville would be too occupied protecting his brother to trouble us."

"It seems that my cousin was mistaken."

Grigori turned and glared at the younger man.

"Do not make light of this, Fedor. Your family is obviously incapable of performing your roles, no matter how simple they might be, and somehow allowed the bastard to realize that the danger to the Duke of Huntley was no more than a ruse." He gave a sharp bark of laughter. "God, I should have known better than to trust any of you. You have put us all at risk."

Fedor blanched, his weak chin trembling. He might be a coward, but he was not stupid. He easily realized that the furious soldier was quite capable of breaking his neck.

"Lord Edmond will not be a problem," he stammered.

"And how can you be so certain?" the older man demanded. "He has thwarted us on too many occasions."

Fedor swiped his face with his handkerchief. "In the unlikely event that he manages to discover our plans, Viktor and I have ensured that he will not interfere."

Edmond frowned even as Grigori made a sound of disgust. "Indeed? Will you put a bullet through his black heart?"

"A charming notion, although I am not foolish enough to pit my skills with a dueling pistol against the man," Fedor muttered. "It is said that he has killed at least a dozen opponents."

"I do not care if he has killed a thousand. How do you intend to keep him from bringing us to ruin?"

"Lord Edmond did not come to Russia alone. He brought his brother's fiancée."

"His brother's fiancée?" Grigori scoffed. "You are mistaken. All know that the man is a ruthless bastard, but that he would do anything for his precious brother. That is the reason we decided to make the fool believe the Duke was in danger."

"Which means that he must be desperate for this woman," Fedor said, his voice shrill with nerves. "And willing to do anything to protect her."

"You have her?" Grigori demanded.

"I received a message during dinner that Viktor is preparing to collect her from Vanya Petrova's as we speak."

"Preparing to collect her and managing to do so are two very different things. She will not be unprotected."

"Viktor said in the message that he had caught Summerville's servant, Boris, skulking outside my house and has him tied in the wine cellar until I can return and discreetly dispose of him. She is not nearly so protected as some might believe."

"Where…" The soldier broke off his words with a muttered curse and, grasping Fedor by the arm he hauled him toward the nearby door. "Someone is coming. Join the others in the Hermitage. I must set matters in motion."

"Now?"

"Lord Edmond will not be allowed to interfere this time." Grigori marched from the hallway, but his words floated through the air. "I *will* have my throne."

Above the two men, Edmond lowered his pistol to the ground as he struggled to breathe.

A very small part of him realized that it was his duty to follow Grigori from the Palace and discover the remaining traitors so they could be rounded up by the guards to await Alexander Pavlovich's judgment. The intrigue was about to be unleashed, and God only knew how many innocent people would be hurt if it were not halted.

That small part of him, however, was no match for the stark panic that clutched at his heart.

Brianna.

That bastard Viktor Kazakov intended to sneak into Vanya's home and put his filthy hands on…

No. Oh, no.

He would kill him.

He would kill him, and then he would rip his heart from his chest and feed it to the vultures.

BRIANNA'S QUEASINESS returned with a brutal force, but feeling as if she were suffocating, she struggled to wrench aside the heavy blankets and stumbled from the bed.

"No." She pressed a hand to her stomach as she paced toward a heavily scrolled armoire. "It…it is impossible."

Vanya remained standing beside the bed, her strong features lined with concern.

"Are you certain? Absolutely certain?"

Brianna forced herself to think past the panic flooding her mind. The past weeks had been a blur and it was hardly surprising that she had paid little heed to her body's usual functions.

So, how long had it been since her last bleeding?

The answer came with shocking swiftness.

Too long.

With shaky steps she made it to a nearby chair before her knees gave way. "Oh, my God."

"Brianna." With a rustle of silk, Vanya was standing at her side, her hand gently patting her shoulder. "Please do not distress yourself."

"Not distress myself? What if it's true? What if I am carrying Edmond's child?"

"Then you will sit down with Edmond and discuss what you desire for your future," Vanya said, her tone matter-of-fact.

Brianna shied from the mere thought of telling Edmond that she was with child. Instead, she concentrated on dark panic that squeezed her heart so tightly she feared it might halt altogether.

"What future?" she whispered, pressing her fingers to her throbbing temples. "Dear lord, it was going to be difficult enough to return to London and establish my own household without being utterly shunned by society. Now it will be impossible."

"You are always welcome to remain here with me until the babe is born."

Brianna lifted her head to meet Vanya's steady gaze. "And then?"

"Then you could foster the child to a good family and return to London with no one ever knowing."

Foster? Brianna abruptly surged to her feet, her mind-numbing fear oddly giving way to a surge of shock. No, it was not precisely shock. It was more…distress.

"Give up my baby?"

A wistful smile touched Vanya's lips. "It is hardly an unusual situation, *ma petite*."

"It is bloody well unusual for me," Brianna muttered, startled to feel a tear trickle down her cheek. "Damn."

"Brianna." Vanya wrapped a comforting arm around Brianna's shaking shoulders. "We know nothing yet. It might very well be that this illness is no more than a common chill."

Brianna, however, was not about to latch on to the vague

chance that this was nothing more than a passing illness. Her mother had been willing to bet her future on nothing more than a hope and prayer. Brianna was far too practical for such nonsense.

With an annoyed motion, she brushed away the tears and squared her shoulders.

"I am not an utter fool, you know," she said, her voice thick with emotion. "I realized that there were bound to be complications when I became Edmond's lover. But I somehow assumed that our affair would be so short-lived that there would be no time for…for a child." Her lips twisted in a humorless smile. "My mother was wed near ten years to my father before I was conceived, and there was no child between her and Thomas Wade."

Vanya gave her shoulders a squeeze. "Every woman is different, as each gentleman is different."

Brianna was once again aware of that wistfulness that had settled about the older woman and she was struck by a sudden thought.

"What of you?" she demanded, softly.

"I beg your pardon?"

"Have you…"

Vanya's arm abruptly dropped, her eyes darkening with a raw, smoldering pain before she managed to regain her smooth composure.

"I have a daughter," she said, her voice carefully even. "She just turned nine."

"Oh." Brianna regarded the older woman with a frown. She was not precisely shocked that Vanya had produced a child. It was rather inevitable considering she had enjoyed a string of lovers. What she had not expected was the aching wound that the woman could not entirely disguise. "Does she live here with you?"

"No." Vanya absently tugged on a gold locket she had pinned to the bodice of her gown. "I placed her with a nearby solicitor and his wife who were unable to have children. Naturally, I assist in paying for her upkeep and schooling. They named her Natasha."

"Does she know that you are her mother?"

Vanya flinched, although her countenance remained set in stoic lines. Her defenses had been honed to grim perfection.

"When I had her, I thought it best she never know the truth. Even with a comfortable home and plenty of money, it would be difficult to overcome the scandal of being born a bastard." Vanya sucked in a shaky breath as Brianna reached out to lightly touch her arm. "She has always believed she is the true daughter of her parents."

"That is no doubt for the best," Brianna said, her words ringing false even to her own ears. Something had obviously died within Vanya at the loss of her daughter. Something precious.

Realizing that she had not managed to fool Brianna with her pretense of indifference, Vanya allowed her stiff expression to soften to one of boundless yearning.

"For her, I believe it has been for the best. For me...it has been difficult. To have her so close and yet never be able to truly know her as my daughter. At least I am allowed to see her from a distance, and her parents are good to send me small tokens that make me feel a part of her life." With awkward motions, Vanya unpinned the locket from her bodice and flipped it open to reveal the tiny portrait of a pretty girl with dark hair and laughing brown eyes. "This is Natasha."

"She is beautiful." Leaning forward for a better look, Brianna froze. The portrait was a miniature, but the master-strokes clearly revealed the strong line of the girl's jaw and the unmistakably sweet curve of her lips. Features that were easily recognizable. "Oh."

Vanya's lips twisted at the color that flooded Brianna's face. "Yes, Richard is her father."

"Does he know?"

"No." Vanya clenched the locket tightly in her hand. "When I discovered I was with child, he was traveling back to England. At the time, I thought he would never return."

Brianna recalled Richard's wry confession that he occasionally fled Russia for his brother's estates in England and her heart twisted with a wrenching sense of pity.

Whatever pain Vanya had endured in giving up her daughter, it was nothing to Richard's loss. He had never been allowed to know he had a precious daughter. Never given the opportunity to watch her from a distance or to carry her picture in a tiny locket.

Surely it was a betrayal for a gentleman who was so desperately alone?

Brianna gave a slow shake of her head. "Why have you never told him?"

With short, restless steps, Vanya paced toward the window, her expression tight with pain.

"Because he would never forgive me for having given her up," she said, her voice laced with ancient regret.

Brianna swallowed a gasp.

"I do not claim to know Mr. Monroe well, but he loves you and there is nothing that love cannot forgive," she said softly.

"Perhaps if I had been honest when he first returned." Vanya gave a sharp shake of her head. "But by the time I realized that he…well, it is too late."

Brianna was struck by a sudden thought. "That is why you have refused to wed him all these years? You feared he might discover the truth?"

"Yes."

"Vanya, it is not too late…"

Brianna's words of comfort were abruptly cut off as a lean, dark-haired stranger stepped through the bedroom door, his arm raised to point a pistol directly at the older woman's heart.

"Ah, Vanya Petrova, forgive my intrusion, but you have something I need."

TOSSING CAUTION TO THE DEVIL, Edmond charged down the gallery, his mind so focused on reaching Brianna that he nearly missed the tall form that stepped from the shadows as he darted toward the nearest door.

"Edmond, I was waiting…"

Herrick gave a startled grunt as Edmond swept past him, grabbing his arm and hauling him toward the narrow door that would lead to the long terrace.

"Come," he barked, not surprised when the older man easily fell into step beside him. Herrick was a gentleman who adapted with a calm efficiency to any crisis.

"Where are we headed?"

"The stables." He ignored the hovering servants who melted back into the shadows at the sight of Herrick, refusing to slow his mad dash as he burst through the door onto the icy terrace. "You must have Grigori Rimsky arrested. He is the leader of the conspirators."

"Rimsky?" Herrick briefly stumbled, his expression shocked. "You are certain?"

Edmond leaped down the shallow marble steps to the frozen garden. "I overheard him with Fedor Dubov."

Muttering curses beneath his breath, Herrick struggled to keep pace as Edmond angled a direct path to the stables.

"Does he have the military behind him?" the older man demanded, as always capable of distinguishing the most potent risk of having powerful officers in command of the rebellion.

"He must be convinced that he has some who will follow his lead."

"Rimsky. Which regiment does he serve?" Herrick muttered, his breath creating an icy cloud in the moonlight as Edmond shoved open a wrought-iron gate set in the high hedge. Together, they stepped into the cobblestone stable yard, the older man sucking in a sharp breath as realization at last struck. "No. The Semyonoffski Regiment would never betray Alexander Pavlovich." Without warning, Herrick grasped Edmond's arm and forced him to a halt. "He is their chief."

"A chief who has not set foot in St. Petersburg for months and who left his Regiment in the control of that brute Araktcheyeff," Edmond rasped, shaking off Herrick's hand as he continued toward the stables. At the moment, he was too concerned with reaching Brianna to spare much thought to the conspiracy. Or Alexander Pavlovich's sense of betrayal if his Regiment were proved to be a part of it. "We both know that, as painful as it might be to admit, they are ripe for revolt."

"Damn," Herrick muttered, grimly waving away the anxious servants who watched as Edmond grabbed the reins of the nearest horse and vaulted into the saddle.

"Take enough men to capture Rimsky, but not enough to attract the attention of Araktcheyeff or, God forbid, Prince Michael. The more discreetly we can capture the conspirators the better," Edmond commanded, his voice a mere whisper. The traitorous soldier could not be far away. "And send a few soldiers to Fedor Dubov's house. They will find Boris being held captive in the cellar. You might warn them to take care when they untie him. He's bound to be in a dangerous mood, and I would not wish any accidents."

Herrick's brows snapped together. "You are not joining me?"

"No. I must get to Vanya's."

"Why?"

"Viktor Kazakov intends to kidnap Brianna."

"How did he know…" Herrick's words were brought to a sharp halt, as he pulled a dagger from his jacket and turned toward the nearby door. At the same moment, Edmond had his pistol in his hand, his eyes narrowed as he watched the tall gentleman rush through the entrance.

Indifferent to the danger of forcing his way into Edmond's private conversation, Richard Monroe did not halt until he was standing beside the horse Edmond was attempting to steal.

"What is happening?" he demanded, clearly having followed them from the Palace.

"Herrick will explain, I must reach Brianna."

"Wait…I am coming with you."

Ignoring Monroe's hasty efforts to retrieve a horse, as well as Herrick's shouted commands for the nearest guards, Edmond dug his heels into the flanks of his nervous mount and bolted from the stables to the biting wind that swirled through the frozen streets.

A distant part of him was aware of the passing guards who hurried toward the stables, the sharp clatter of horse hooves from behind as Monroe followed his trail, and even the flickering gas lanterns that spilled dashes of light over the thick snow. His mind, however, was focused solely on reaching Vanya's before Viktor Kazakov could arrive.

Managing to traverse the slick streets without breaking his neck, Edmond halted before Vanya's doorway, vaulting from the saddle without caring if the nervous horse bolted.

There was a brief moment of tension as he burst through the door and a number of servants scrambled to halt him. Only the barked command of the butler prevented bloodshed as Edmond shoved aside the baffled footmen and rushed up the staircase.

His hectic charge, however, faltered as he realized that the door to Brianna's chamber was wide open and a uniformed guard was standing just over the threshold.

A cold, savage fear clutched his stomach as he forced his way past the servant, his narrowed gaze sweeping over the sitting room before landing upon Vanya, who was pacing the floor with nervous steps. He did not need to be told that Brianna was gone. He could feel it in the heavy emptiness that filled the room. In the dull ache that pulsed in the center of his chest.

"Brianna."

With a tiny gasp, Vanya turned to regard him with a startled gaze. "Edmond."

"Where is she?"

The older woman pressed a trembling hand to her ample bosom. "Viktor Kazakov took her."

"Where?" He was not even aware he had moved until his hands were grasping Vanya's shoulders and he was glaring into her pale face. "Where did he take her?"

"Easy, Edmond." There was the sound of footsteps behind

him and then Richard Monroe was moving to stand behind Vanya, his face carefully set as he tugged the older woman from Edmond's tight grip. "We are as anxious as you to ensure Miss Quinn's safe return."

Edmond swallowed his furious words at Monroe's unwelcome interruption. Vanya was clearly rattled and in need of the older man's steady comfort. It would no doubt make his questioning easier if she had the man to lean upon.

"Tell me what happened."

With an effort, Vanya sucked in a deep breath and composed her panicked thoughts.

"He…he just appeared in the doorway to Brianna's rooms with a gun in his hand. He demanded that Brianna accompany him." Vanya held out her hand to reveal a crumpled piece of parchment. "He left this for you."

Smoothing the paper open, Edmond read the neatly printed words aloud:

A sacrifice is not worthy unless it is paid in blood. It is for you to choose. Your heart or your soul. Your lover or your country. One or the other will bleed.

Richard grunted in disgust as Edmond cursed and tossed the note onto the floor.

"How tediously melodramatic Russians tend to be."

Under other circumstances, Edmond might have laughed at the flowery threat. Even for Viktor Kazakov, the words were absurdly theatrical, as if he intended to have them read upon a stage or shouted from the rooftops.

And perhaps he did.

Christ. Edmond shoved his fingers through his tousled hair. No doubt Viktor was already envisioning the days when he was in power and the events of this evening would be celebrated as some grand victory over tyranny. The idiot was just pompous enough to have written the note with the thought it would be framed in a museum someday.

"If he so much as leaves a bruise on Brianna I will choke

the life from him," Edmond muttered, his hands clenching as the black fury pounded through him. "Slowly."

With a small, wounded cry, Vanya moved forward, her fingers clutching the tense muscles of Edmond's forearm.

"Oh, Edmond, forgive me."

"What is it, Vanya?"

"I should have done something to stop Viktor," she breathed, her cheeks damp with tears. "I have always thought myself so brave, and capable of dealing with any situation. But I feared he might become violent if I called for the servants and so I let him take her away without so much as lifting a hand in protest. What a damnable coward I am."

Knowing the older woman would torture herself for failing to have kept Brianna from harm, Edmond tugged her into his arms and gave her a swift hug.

"Hush, Vanya, it is all right," he muttered. "I will soon have Brianna home safe and sound."

"How?" Tilting back her head, Vanya regarded Edmond with a terrified expression. "Dear God, Edmond, how will you ever find her?"

CHAPTER TWENTY-THREE

PRESSED IN A CORNER OF THE elegant carriage with her arms wrapped about her shivering body, Brianna struggled against the panic that threatened to consume her. Giving in to terror would achieve nothing, she told herself over and over. Not so long as Viktor Kazakov was seated across from her with a pistol in his hand and an eagerness for violence shimmering in his dark eyes.

No, becoming hysterical would solve nothing. Instead, she bit her inner lip until she drew blood and forced herself to consider the situation with as much logic as she could summon.

She did not believe for a moment that it was sheer chance that this gentleman had entered Vanya's house on this eve. Or that she was chosen to be abducted out of the numerous guests. He had to know that Edmond had followed him to St. Petersburg and that she was his current mistress.

Which could only mean he had taken her captive in an attempt to coerce Edmond. Or worse, lead him into a trap. Neither of which she would allow to happen.

Brianna remained silent as they thundered out of St. Petersburg and headed south. She knew it would be futile to try and escape. Not only could Viktor Kazakov easily overpower her, but there was no mistaking the echo of hoofbeats behind them. There were at least two, perhaps more, outriders following in their wake.

And she would not dare risk throwing herself from a moving carriage into the frigid snow. Not when there was even the least chance that she might actually be carrying Edmond's child. There were some sacrifices she was not willing to make.

Her only option appeared to be in convincing her captor that her presence was not nearly so valuable to Edmond as he presumed.

"You are astonishingly calm for a woman who has just been taken hostage," Viktor at last broke the frigid silence, his dark gaze narrowed as he studied her unreadable face.

Maintaining her seeming calm, Brianna gave a faint shrug. Although the man was sprawled negligently against the leather seat, she did not miss the ease with which he kept the pistol pointed at her heart or the tension in the line of his jaw. Viktor Kazakov would pull that trigger without hesitation.

"Would you prefer that I wail or gnash my teeth or swoon in terror?" she demanded, pleased that her voice revealed none of the panic she was barely keeping at bay.

"It would be a far more predictable reaction for a gently bred maiden who discovers herself in such a predicament."

His mockery helped to stiffen her spine. "I may be gently bred, sir, but I can assure you that the past year has stolen any ability to swoon." Her lips twisted, allowing her thoughts to flit from Thomas Wade to Lord Edmond Summerville to Viktor Kazakov. All three gentlemen had desired her for one purpose or another, none of which had anything to do with pleasing her. "I am quite accustomed to gentlemen storming into my life and using me for their own purpose. If I feel anything, it is resignation."

"Indeed?"

"And perhaps a bit of annoyance that you chose such a miserable night for this abduction," Brianna continued with a dramatic shiver. She had been forced from Vanya's home wearing nothing more than her robe and delicate embroidered slippers.

With a low rasp of laughter, Viktor Kazakov reached for a blanket that was folded on the bench beside him, tossing it toward her with a casual flick of his wrist.

"You are not at all what I was expecting," he said, watching beneath hooded lids as she wrapped the blanket about her shuddering form. "It is little wonder that you have managed to capture Edmond's fancy."

Brianna tugged the blanket up to her chin, as much to hide her body from Viktor Kazakov's heated gaze as to ward off the savage cold.

"Hardly a stunning accomplishment," she muttered. "Anything in skirts would capture his fancy."

"No. As much as I dislike the man, not even I can deny he has always possessed a fastidious refusal to take any mistress who is not utterly exquisite. His taste is—" he deliberately allowed his gaze to roam over her thick curls tumbling about her shoulders "—faultless."

Brianna's fingers tightened on the blanket at his intimate gaze, but she was more determined to convince the man that she held no importance to Edmond than to chastise him for treating her as a common tart.

"I shall have to take your word for it. In truth, I know very little about Edmond." She lowered her gaze, as if in embarrassment. "Well, very little beyond the obvious. It is not as if we spend our time together actually conversing."

Brianna heard a faint rustle, then a slender finger was slipping beneath her chin and tilting her face up to meet Viktor's dark, penetrating gaze.

"I am quite certain that you possess many skills, Miss Quinn, but deceitfulness is not one of them."

She resisted the urge to jerk from his touch, sensing he would be pleased to know he disturbed her.

"I beg your pardon?"

His thumb brushed her lower lip. "You are a terrible liar."

Her heart jolted with fear. His touch was soft, but she did not doubt for a minute those slender fingers could wrap around her neck and squeeze the life from her.

"I haven't the least notion what you mean."

"You are far more than just another mistress." His thumb pressed against her lips as they parted. "And before you attempt to convince me of your utter lack of importance to Edmond, allow me to inform you that I have devoted months to studying the damnable man until I know his habits better than my own."

"A rather tedious means to spend your time."

"But necessary." A cold smile flickered through his dark eyes. "The only means to defeat an enemy is to study both his strengths and weaknesses. And you, *ma belle,* are most certainly one of his weaknesses."

"Absurd. I am nothing to him."

There was a long, unnerving silence as Viktor studied her pale features. Then, with a smooth motion, he settled back in his seat, slipping the pistol into the pocket of his greatcoat. It was a blatant motion intended to reveal that he was in utter command of the situation and there was not a damnable thing she could do about it.

"I am intrigued to know how Stefan has reacted to his brother's treachery," he drawled. "They have been notoriously devoted to one another, but I should think that having Edmond seduce his fiancée would strain even Stefan's mild temper."

Brianna grimaced. The devil take Edmond and his insistence that they pretend they were engaged while he posed as the Duke of Huntley. She had known it was a bad notion from the beginning.

She would endure whatever gossip might tarnish her name, but Stefan deserved better. Far, far better.

"What do you want with me?" she demanded.

"Nothing more than the pleasure of your company." A smug, unpleasant smile twisted his thin lips. "Oh, and of course, the assurance of Edmond's good behavior."

It did not take a great deal of skill to realize that Viktor Kazakov's pleasure in the thought of besting Edmond was far more than just the satisfaction of one opponent outwitting another. It was too fierce, too personal.

For the moment, however, Brianna was more interested in discovering precisely why she had been taken hostage.

"Good behavior?"

"As I am sure you know, Miss Quinn, your lover has made a tedious habit of interfering in matters of the Russian Court that are none of his concern."

"Matters such as treason?"

His self-satisfied smile never faltered. "'Tis only treason if we fail. Once we succeed, we shall be named liberators."

She resisted the urge to roll her eyes. The man certainly possessed enough arrogance to place a crown on his own head. Always presuming he could discover one large enough to fit.

"And you believe that by holding me hostage you will succeed?"

"It will at least prevent Lord Edmond from interfering in our plans."

She bit back a curse as the carriage skated around a sharp corner, tipping precariously before jarring back onto four wheels. It seemed quite possible that she would end up in the ditch with a broken neck before the night was done.

"Good lord, I thought you claimed that you had studied Edmond. If that is true, then you are a singularly inept observer," she said, not having to pretend her derision. Surely he must know that whatever Edmond's instinctive need to protect others, his loyalty would always belong to his Czar.

The dark eyes flashed with fury. "There is a difference between boldness and stupidity, Miss Quinn. You try my temper at your peril."

She forced a stiff smile to her lips, knowing that she dare not provoke Viktor any further.

"I am merely pointing out that Edmond has made it his life's purpose to protect Alexander Pavlovich from harm," she said. "He would never allow any threat, including my kidnapping, to prevent him from carrying out his duty."

"No," he at last growled at the unshakable sincerity in her

voice, refusing to believe he could have miscalculated. "Edmond has risked everything he holds dear, including his brother, to keep you at his side. Besides, I witnessed the two of you in the garden."

She shivered beneath the blanket. "You were spying upon us?"

"Of course." The smile returned to his mouth. "And I must say, I was quite amused by Edmond's rather anxious expression as he fussed over you with such touching tenderness. It is obvious that he is still befuddled by his emotions for you."

Brianna was swift to quash the warm tingle that fluttered through the pit of her stomach. What did it matter if Viktor Kazakov was foolish enough to confuse lust with tenderness? She most certainly was not.

"Befuddled or not, he will never allow himself to be distracted from his responsibilities," she said, more sharply than she intended. "He is incapable of allowing himself to fail."

A dangerous anger tightened his countenance. "You had best hope for all our sakes that you are mistaken, *ma belle.*"

Brianna bit her lip, her stomach sick with dread. She knew better than to press the argument. Viktor Kazakov was convinced that he had halted Edmond from interfering in the looming revolution, and it would only anger him to suggest that his efforts of abducting her were worthless.

And in truth, she was not at all certain what was to happen to her when the man was forced to accept that his plot had failed.

Nothing good, she was certain of that.

Trembling with a combination of fear and cold, she cleared the lump in her throat.

"Where are you taking me?"

A cruel smile touched his lips, as if he were pleased by the apprehension she could not entirely disguise.

"It is a question that has plagued me the greater part of the day," he drawled. "Despite your modest refusal to accept that Edmond is utterly enthralled, I do not doubt for a moment that he will come in search of you. I promised my…friends that I would lead him away from St. Petersburg, perhaps even as far as Novgorod."

Brianna swallowed her groan of despair. Dear lord, how far away was Novgorod? An hour? A day? A week?

And more important, how would she ever make her way back to St. Petersburg? That was presuming she managed to free herself from Viktor Kazakov before he...

No.

She would not give in to despair.

With a grim effort, she unclenched her teeth and considered her options. They were pathetically few, but not nonexistent, she sternly reminded herself as she frantically attempted to recall everything that Edmond had said of this traitorous gentleman.

She recalled that Edmond had claimed the man was cunning, powerful and obsessively dedicated to overthrowing Alexander Pavlovich.

He also said that he was vain, selfish and desperate to claim glory for himself. Which surely meant that he had to be less than pleased with his role as decoy while others were publicly leading the revolt.

"So far?" she murmured softly, her brow wrinkled with a feigned hint of puzzlement. "I would have thought your presence would have been essential during such a momentous event."

His smile remained, but in the flicker of the carriage's gas lights Brianna did not miss the darkening of his eyes.

"My efforts have ensured that all is set into place."

"I...see." Her voice was filled with doubt. "So you are not the leader of the conspirators?"

A flush touched Viktor's high cheekbones. Whether it was anger toward her probing or annoyance at not being able to claim ownership of the revolt was impossible to determine.

"I will not deny I am...disappointed not to have the pleasure of watching the final, glorious destruction of the Romanov rule. It is, after all, what I have struggled to achieve since Alexander Pavlovich murdered his way to the throne."

"Yes, it hardly seems fair that you should be trapped in a miserable carriage, while others are celebrating your victory," Brianna murmured. "And perhaps doing more than merely celebrating."

The dark eyes narrowed. "Precisely what are you implying, *ma belle?*"

She did not have to feign her shiver. Despite the heavy blanket, she felt as if the frigid air was freezing the blood in her veins. She had not been so cold since she had been a child and managed to lock herself in her father's icehouse. She shivered again as she recalled that it had been Edmond who had heard her screams for help and rescued her.

On this occasion, she would have no one to depend upon but herself.

Astonishingly, the rather dark thought helped to stiffen her spine.

"If you do manage to overthrow the throne, then there will be a mad scramble for power, will there not? You can hardly claim your share if you are in Novgorod." She abruptly widened her eyes, as if struck by a sudden thought. "Oh. But then, that is no doubt the reason you were urged to take me there in the first place."

"You know nothing of my compatriots. I would trust them with my very life." His hands curled into fists as they lay on his lap, belying his determined air of nonchalance. "And there will be no mad scramble, as you so charmingly claim. The throne will be handed to the one best suited to lead."

"And who is that?"

"Such an important matter will be decided by the Russian nobles, of course."

His words were smooth enough to reveal he had practiced them on several occasions, but Brianna sensed the dark hunger behind them. Viktor Kazakov might be willing to mouth all the proper sentiments, but his heart lusted for power. A lust that she did not doubt was shared by more than one of his conspirators.

Did he suspect as much, as well?

It seemed reasonable to suppose that he did.

"Yes, well, I am certain that you know best."

The narrow, handsome face tightened.

"I do know what you are attempting to accomplish."

"Really?" She shrugged. "And what is that?"

His sharp, humorless laugh echoed through the frigid air. "You could not convince me that you were a passing fancy that Edmond would happily toss to the wolves, so now you think to worry me into returning to St. Petersburg with fears of betrayal from those who I call brothers-in-arms."

Brianna did not bother to try and deny his charge. Regardless of whether or not he suspected she was deliberately stirring his instinctive distrust, she knew that her words were striking deep into his festering fear.

It was in the knotted muscles of his jaw, the restless tap of his fingers against his knee, the rasp of his swift, unsteady breath.

"Even you must admit that it is rather ironic to trust others who have come together in the name of disloyalty," she pressed, relentless. "Such a cause would hardly attract those of the highest moral fiber. Indeed, I would presume that such a disreputable purpose would be destined to lure only those utterly without conscience or scruples."

"I have been insulted on any number of occasions and in any number of languages, but never with such artful innocence." The dark eyes narrowed with a cold fury that warned Brianna that she had pushed too far. "Poor Edmond. You are a very clever, and dangerous, young lady."

Brianna turned to gaze out the window, barely noting the falling snow. Anything was preferable to meeting the fevered, nearly mad glitter in Viktor's dark eyes as she attempted to divert his anger.

"Hardly clever, considering that I have allowed myself to be taken hostage and that I am currently freezing to near death in a carriage that is no doubt destined to become stuck in a snowdrift long before we ever reach Novgorod."

She sensed him shift restlessly on his seat. The tension in the carriage was thickening with every mile they traveled away from St. Petersburg.

"You may take comfort in the knowledge that, if we do become stuck in a drift, then your lover will easily discover us and put a bullet through my heart," he mocked, attempting to disguise his growing agitation. "You will then be free to return to St. Petersburg and all the comfort you desire."

"Even presuming that Edmond would be willing to risk all to try to rescue me, how do you expect him to be able to follow us?" Brianna demanded. "Did you leave directions for him?"

Viktor made a sound of disgust. "Perhaps you do not know Lord Edmond Summerville as well I presumed. The bastard possesses an uncanny ability to haunt my every footstep. I cannot so much as sneeze without him knowing. There are moments when I wonder if he does not have some witchcraft at his disposal."

She was wise enough to hide her smile at his disgruntled tone. "If that is true, then why are you not concerned that he will overtake us on the road?"

"It will take him time to discover you have been abducted and yet more time to uncover our trail. Besides, I have ensured that my men are keeping a careful guard on the road. They have orders to shoot anyone who appears to be following us. With any luck, one of them will manage to…"

"No," she interrupted the taunting words, her head jerking toward her companion so she could send him a fierce glare.

Viktor's lips twisted as he held up a slender hand. "Forgive me. It seems that Edmond is not the only one afflicted with the pangs of love."

It would have been a great deal easier to deny his words, if her heart did not feel as if it were being brutally crushed at the mere thought of Edmond in danger.

Oh…God. She was such a fool. Such a damnable fool.

"What is to happen once we reach Novgorod?" she abruptly demanded, desperate to divert her painful thoughts.

Viktor glanced toward the window of the carriage, his expression hardening with determination.

"Actually I am growing convinced that there is no need to travel such a distance."

Brianna stilled, hope flaring through her frigid body. "Then we are turning around?"

He turned back to regard her with a mocking smile. "Not *we*."

"What do you mean?"

"It is enough that I have lured Edmond from the city." He shrugged. "There is a church not far from here. I will leave you there, bound and gagged, while I return to St. Petersburg."

Hope shifted to anguished fear as Brianna laid a hand against her lower stomach. She knew nothing of carrying a child. It was not something discussed in polite society, and certainly nothing her mother would share with her.

But she was intelligent enough to realize that such a tiny life would be a fragile thing that could be easily harmed.

"I will freeze to death," she breathed, not bothering to hide her terror.

"There is the hope you will be found by a priest, or even that Edmond will arrive, before such a tragedy befalls you."

"Please…you cannot…" Brianna bit off her pleading words as Viktor's eyes narrowed with disgust. It seemed entirely possible the heartless brute would simply toss her out of the moving carriage if she annoyed him.

She had thought she was so clever in convincing him that his companions were destined to betray him. She just assumed that if he returned to St. Petersburg, he would take her with him.

Fool, indeed.

"You are wise not to beg," he said, a grimness underlying his voice as he pulled the pistol from his pocket and once again pointed it at her heart. "I cannot bear a weepy woman."

Pressing herself even deeper into the corner of the carriage, Brianna tugged the blanket tighter and attempted to compose her frantic thoughts.

Somehow, someway, she intended to survive.

No matter what it might take.

CHAPTER TWENTY-FOUR

THE SMALL COPSE OF TREES had seemed a perfect location to await Boris's return. Not only was it close enough to the road to allow Edmond to keep a watch on the sparse travelers that dared the heavy snowfall and frigid temperatures, but it provided some protection from the brutal wind.

But very minimal, Edmond conceded, as he shivered beneath his greatcoat.

Vanya had, of course, attempted to make him take her carriage and outriders, even going so far as to warn him that Brianna would not be best pleased to be rescued on the back of his horse without so much as a blanket to ward off the frigid air.

Edmond, however, had been indifferent to the older woman's pleas and inevitable scolds. Once he had Brianna in his arms, he would worry about discovering a carriage and enough blankets to cover the Baltic Sea. Until then, all that mattered was catching up to Viktor Kazakov as swiftly as possible.

He muttered a curse as his horse shifted beneath him, the restless creature's breath turning to a mist as it hit the frozen air. Just through the trees, he could make out the vague silhouette of Boris, who had arrived just before Edmond had gone in pursuit of Kazakov and insisted on joining him. At the moment, his companion was interrogating the young peasant who was stationed outside the posting inn to assist with those carriages that became lodged in the snow.

It had been only a few minutes since Boris had left to question the servant, but his gut was twisted with sharp dread. With every beat of his heart, Brianna was slipping farther away from him. The smallest delay made him want to howl in frustration.

Unfortunately, the information he had received from the various individuals who had spotted Viktor Kazakov's flight from Vanya's house had only been able to lead him southward out of St. Petersburg. As much as he longed to charge like a madman through the snow and ice, he possessed enough of his shattered wits to realize he might cost Brianna her very life if his frantic haste made him lose her trail.

That he would not risk.

In an effort to distract his seething anguish, Edmond turned his attention back to the road that was barely visible through the heavy fall of snow. Nearly sixty years ago, the Empress Catherine had traveled this road on her coronation journey from St. Petersburg to Moscow. It was said that her sleigh was large enough to possess a bedroom and library, and that she tossed over a half a million silver coins to the crowds that lined the road.

The German Princess had understood the Russian people better than her grandson, Edmond ruefully acknowledged. The lavish procession and grand gestures of generosity had been a brilliant means to win the hearts of the peasants. Just as important, the spectacular displays she insisted upon were a subtle warning to the neighboring countries that Russia was a power to be respected, if not outright feared.

Alexander Pavlovich might bemoan the extravagant waste of the Imperial coffers, but he would never claim the love or loyalty that Catherine had so easily inspired.

A pity really. There were few rulers in the world that truly cared as deeply for his people as the current Czar. His sincerity, however, could not entirely compensate for his relentless doubt. Nor did it prevent his enemies from taking advantage of his weak rule.

Prepared for a wrench of guilt at the thought of Alexander Pavlovich and the knowledge he had abandoned his duty when he had left Herrick to deal with the traitors, Edmond felt nothing more than a vague hope that the older gentleman managed to bring an end to the conspirators.

After years of dedicating himself to the Czar and the Romanov rule, he realized that his loyalty now belonged utterly and completely to a tiny slip of a girl with emerald eyes and autumn hair.

Not a loyalty given to fill the aching void of his parents' death. Not a loyalty to try and give some meaning to his empty existence.

No, this was a warm, ceaseless devotion that had snuck up on him without warning. One that had nothing to do with the shadows that haunted him and everything to do with Miss Brianna Quinn.

His heart twisted with a savage pain as the image of her pale beautiful features seared through his mind. Thank God that Boris chose that moment to turn and weave his way back through the trees.

"Well?" Edmond impatiently demanded, not waiting until Boris brought his horse to a halt beside him.

The well-seasoned soldier tightened the woolen scarf that was tied about his lower face.

"Viktor's carriage was seen passing this way less than an hour ago. The servant is certain it turned to the left at the fork in the road. He remembers, because it nearly slid into the ditch and he had visions of a tidy reward for helping pull them free."

"Then he intends to head for Novgorod, not Moscow," Edmond muttered.

"Always presuming it is not merely a ruse." Boris cast a jaundiced glance toward the road nearly hidden beneath the thickening snowdrifts. "You do know that it is quite likely that Viktor Kazakov deliberately allowed his carriage to be seen fleeing St. Petersburg in a reckless enough fashion, precisely to attract attention?" he growled. "No doubt the bastard is even now hidden in some hired vehicle as he sneaks away."

Edmond was shaking his head before Boris finished speaking. "No, his entire purpose is taunting me into following him, so that I am unable to interfere in Grigori's plans. He will not risk trickery until he can be certain I am well away from St. Petersburg."

"You had best be right. If Viktor eludes us…"

"Enough! We will find Miss Quinn, make no mistake of that."

With a sharp jerk on the reins, Edmond urged his horse from the shelter of the trees and onto the road. Boris was swiftly at his side, his large body deliberately placed to offer as much protection as possible.

"As you say," he agreed, knowing better than to pursue his doubts.

Waiting until they were past the posting inn and the servants were busily attempting to sweep the gathering snow from the dirt road, Edmond cast a glance toward his companion.

"I must admit that you surprise me, Boris."

"Why?"

"I would have expected you to attempt to convince me to remain in St. Petersburg, so that you could assist in halting the traitors and be hailed a hero."

Boris snorted, his eyes darting from one side of the road to the other in constant vigilance.

"We have halted any number of revolutions, and I have yet to be hailed a hero. Damnation, I do not even recall a thank-you on most occasions."

That was certainly true enough. More often than not, only a handful of individuals ever knew that a looming disaster had been averted. Still, Boris had always been fiercely dedicated to hunting down conspirators and bringing them to justice. Perhaps even more dedicated than Edmond.

It was unlike him not to at least complain at being denied the pleasure of his favorite sport.

"I suppose I can always request that Alexander Pavlovich pin a medal upon your chest," Edmond said dryly. "He enjoys such formal ceremonies."

Boris did not have to pretend his horror. "God forbid."

Edmond carefully skirted a thickening snowdrift, recalling his companion's adamant refusal to be left behind when Edmond had announced his intention to follow Viktor Kazakov.

"You have not answered my question, Boris. Why are you so anxious to rescue Miss Quinn, rather than battling the traitors?"

Boris sent him an aggravated glare before grudgingly accepting that Edmond would not be diverted.

"Viktor Kazakov sent a thug to knock me over the head and then tie me in a cellar—is that not reason enough to pursue him to the gates of hell?"

"I did promise to return him to St. Petersburg, so you could enact your retribution."

"I prefer not to wait. The sooner I have my hands about his rotter of a neck, the better."

"Could it be that you did not trust my ability to capture the traitor?"

"Don't be a fool, Summerville."

"Then give me the truth."

The man heaved an aggravated sigh.

"For one thing, I happen to have become very fond of Miss Quinn," he growled. "For another…"

"Yes?"

"Janet sent me a letter before I left London, threatening to have me gelded if her beloved mistress suffers so much as a bruise while she is in Russia."

Edmond's muffled laugh echoed through the thick silence that blanketed the countryside. Boris was one of the most feared and respected soldiers ever to put on the Cavalry's gold-trimmed red tunics, but Edmond had seen how a mere glance from the spirited Janet could put the man on his knees.

"A potent inducement to rescue her."

There was a brief pause before Boris cleared his throat. "That is not the most potent inducement."

"Rather astonishing." Edmond glanced toward his friend. "I am almost afraid to ask what the most potent one is."

"You."

"Boris, I may be a demanding employer but I can assure you that I will never threaten to geld you," he protested.

Boris gave a slow shake of his head. "No, I could not bear what it would do to you if something were to happen to Miss Quinn."

Conversation ceased at the stark words, Boris intent on keeping guard, Edmond struggling to marshal the emotions that exploded within him. It was not the fear that something might happen to Brianna. He quite simply would not even consider the possibility. But more the knowledge that his entire existence now depended utterly on the happiness of the slender, beautiful woman.

They pressed on in silence, ignoring the relentless snowfall and brutal cold. Edmond kept their pace steady, knowing that Viktor Kazakov's carriage would be struggling to avoid becoming lodged in the snow. As much as it chafed him to plod along, they should catch up to Brianna within the hour, so long as he did not break his horse's leg and land him in a ditch.

He kept the thought foremost in his mind as his hands went numb from the cold and his eyes watered from the stinging wind.

"There is a carriage ahead," Boris at last called softly, pointing toward the distant shadow beside the road. "Is it stuck?"

"I do not know, but I intend to discover," Edmond muttered, slipping from his horse and tossing the reins around a nearby tree. "Remain here."

"Not bloody likely." Boris vaulted from his own mount, his expression grim with determination. "In the event you did not notice, there are a half a dozen outriders waiting just down the road."

"Fine. But for the moment, I merely want to ensure that the carriage is Viktor's and that this is not a trap."

Boris offered a sharp nod, and together they slipped along the edge of the road.

They had reached the back of the carriage when the door was pressed open and the vague outline of a slender woman wrapped in a blanket was pushed down the steps and onto the snow-covered path.

"Brianna," Edmond breathed even as Boris grasped his arm in a ruthless grip.

"Wait," Boris muttered next to Edmond's ear as Viktor Kazakov stepped out behind her, his hand pressed against her lower back. "He has a pistol."

Boris kept a tight hold on his arm as they watched Kazakov shove Brianna up a snowy path. Edmond frowned, his gaze briefly lifting toward the onion domes and kokochnik gables of the church. The wooden structure was like any other to be discovered across the Russian countryside. So why the devil had Viktor brought Brianna to this one?

"A church?" Boris muttered the same question echoing through Edmond's mind.

"He must intend to hide her there so that he can return to St. Petersburg."

"Then we need merely wait until he leaves. Unless..." Boris's fingers dug into Edmond's arm as he turned to meet Edmond's glittering gaze.

LIKE ALL RUSSIAN ORTHODOX churches, this one was built in a cruciform with the altar placed so that it faced the east. Pretending to stumble over the threshold, Brianna gave herself a moment to cast a quick glance about the small nave.

There were the usual lecterns with icons placed in honor near the front of the church, as well as rows of beeswax candles—a handful that were currently lit—and incense to honor both the icons and the deceased. Unlike European churches, however, there were no pews. The faithful were expected to remain standing in respect, and only the feast-day icon in the center of the nave cluttered the floor.

There was nothing ready at hand to use as a weapon, or even a place to hide, if she could manage to break free of her captor.

As if sensing her hesitation was more than just a bout of awkwardness, Viktor prodded her with the barrel of his pistol.

"Unless you wish to be tossed over my shoulder, you will

halt your dawdling," he warned, slamming the heavy wooden door shut behind them.

"I am not dawdling. My limbs are frozen."

He gave her shoulder a rude shove. "To the altar."

"The altar?" Brianna glanced toward the wooden Iconostas that separated the nave from the sanctuary. She knew little of Russian churches, but she was aware that the icon screen that possessed three doors to the altar was sacred. By ancient tradition, each door was reserved for specific church officials, and women were never allowed past the screen. "Are you attempting to have me struck down by God?"

Viktor frowned as he pressed her relentlessly forward. "You are an Orthodox?"

"No, but I would rather not tempt fate," she said, dryly. "Especially not when I have a pistol pressed to my back."

"No doubt a wise notion. If you do as you are told, you may perhaps live to witness history as it unfolds, after all."

Brianna stumbled through the Deacon's door, not having to pretend her lack of grace. She had long before lost any feeling in her feet.

"A pretty way of describing a bloody revolution," she muttered.

"It always takes blood to purify."

"I notice it's not your blood that is offered for the sacrifice."

"Of course not. It will be the tainted Romanov blood that will wash through the streets. Only then can our glorious empire rise and take its place in the world."

"With you as the emperor?"

"Perhaps."

"Charming."

Halting near the lavish altar, Brianna turned to watch as Viktor Kazakov stopped at her side. Was she to be shot and left to die alone? Or would the traitor possess enough compassion to simply leave her in the church while he returned to St. Petersburg?

Brianna was caught off guard when Kazakov reached beneath his greatcoat and pulled out a coiled length of rope.

"Kneel down," he commanded.

Brianna took an appalled step backward.

Viktor grasped her upper arm to jerk her back toward him. "As I said, if you do as you are told, there is no reason I must kill you. I do intend, however, to ensure that you are not allowed to raise the alarm before I am well on my way to St. Petersburg."

"You…you intend to bind me with that rope?" she rasped.

"Obviously you are as clever as you are beautiful," he mocked.

"Please…" She was forced to halt and clear her throat. "What if Edmond does not follow? With this blizzard, it could be days before anyone returns to this church."

Viktor reached out to brush a taunting hand over her cheek. "You possess a startling lack of faith in your lover, *ma belle*."

She jerked from his touch, her icy skin crawling with distaste.

"I have told you that he has pledged his life to the Czar."

"Now, that would be a pity," he said, deliberately uncoiling the rope as he took a step toward her. "No doubt, Edmond would be haunted for the rest of his life with the thought of your poor, frozen body lying on the altar, your beautiful eyes forever etched with futile hope as you awaited your savior."

"Have you ever thought of taking to the stage?"

The dark eyes flashed with anger at her barely concealed contempt.

"Kneel."

EDMOND ENTERED THE CHURCH with a skill he had honed over the past decade, slipping over the threshold and swiftly closing the door before a revealing draft could flicker the candles.

Pressed against the wall, he glanced about the empty nave, realizing that Viktor had forced Brianna through the Iconostas.

Why the devil would the man want Brianna at the altar?

Attempting to ignore the growing chill that spread through his body, Edmond cautiously inched his way toward the front of the church, the pungent scent of incense and beeswax assaulting his senses as he neared the wooden screen.

The chill deepened as he shifted to catch a glimpse through the narrow opening.

At first, all he could see was Viktor standing next to the altar, his profile hard with determination and a pistol in his hand. He took another step and he could see Brianna, her tiny body wrapped in a blanket and her face starkly white in contrast to the fiery cloud of hair that tumbled past her shoulders.

It was her expression that made his blood freeze in his veins.

That stubborn, defiant tilt of her chin and grim set of her lush, sensuous lips. She was about to do something incredibly, stunningly stupid.

Even as the thought slid through his mind, he watched in horror as she dropped her blanket and knocked the pistol from Viktor's grasp. In the same motion she turned and sprinted toward the back of the church.

"Brianna…no," he shouted as he charged toward Viktor, who was scrambling after the pistol that had slid beneath the altar.

He was just forcing his way through the door of the screen when Viktor wrapped his fingers around the handle of the weapon and lifted it toward Brianna's fleeing form.

Edmond heard the sharp crack of the pistol firing, the reverberation stabbing through his heart like a dagger. Across the church, he watched in helpless horror as Brianna halted and then, with a slow, graceful motion, slid onto the stone floor.

CHAPTER TWENTY-FIVE

No!

Edmond stumbled toward the tiny body, needing only to be at her side, so he could pull her into his arms and never let her go.

It wasn't until he was nearly upon her that he realized that Viktor was already standing next to her, his spent pistol tossed aside in favor of a lethal dagger.

"She lives, my lord, but stay back or I will finish my task."

"You bastard!" Edmond forced himself to come to a halt, a cold fury replacing his pounding fear. She was not dead. "Step away from her, Kazokov, or I will skin you alive and feed you to the wolves."

Viktor blanched at the stark sincerity of Edmond's threat, but with a determined bluster, he deliberately glanced toward the unconscious woman at his feet.

"I knew you would follow her."

"Really?" Edmond narrowed his gaze, his hand slipping into his pocket to clutch the handle of his loaded pistol. "And how were you so bloody certain?"

"I witnessed the two of you together in Vanya Petrova's garden." Viktor forced a mocking laugh that echoed uneasily through the shadows. "I must say that I have rarely taken such pleasure as I did in watching you regard Miss Quinn with such pathetic longing."

"Then you know that I will kill you for having dared to lay a hand upon her."

Viktor swallowed heavily, a thin sheen of perspiration upon

his brow despite the frigid air. "Toss me that pistol you have hidden in your pocket." He pointed the dagger toward the woman at his feet. "Carefully."

Gritting his teeth, Edmond removed the pistol and, bending downward, slid the weapon across the floor to his enemy.

"There."

"Very good." Clearly presuming he had managed to grasp the upper hand, Kazakov reached down to retrieve the pistol, pointing it directly at Edmond's heart as a smirk touched the thin features. "Do you know, Lord Edmond, I could become quite accustomed to giving you orders. Once I am settled in the Winter Palace, I may keep you near at hand to perform as my jester."

"The Winter Palace." Edmond did not have to feign his amusement. The only thing more pleasurable than strangling the life from Viktor Kazakov was revealing that his pathetic hopes to gain command of Russia were doomed to failure. "Do you truly believe that Grigori Rimsky will offer you rooms in the stables once he has grasped control?"

"How did you…" Viktor swayed in shock, his face ashen as he realized that Edmond had discovered the identity of the secret leader of the revolution. Then, with an obvious effort, he attempted to regain command of his shattered composure. "No, it does not matter. It is too late for you to halt the inevitable uprising. By morning, all of Russia will be throwing off the yoke of Romanov oppression."

A cold, mirthless smile twisted Edmond's lips. "There was no need for me to personally do the honors, Viktor. Herrick was quite pleased to take command of the situation. By morning, Grigori, your cousin, and any soldiers of the Semyonoffski Regiment who are foolish enough to join in your treacherous cause will be locked in the barracks to await Alexander Pavlovich's return."

"How?" Kazakov rasped, his usual conceit replaced with a growing air of desperation. "How did you know?"

"Fedor Dubov is an imbecile."

"I knew better than to trust the slack-witted fool."

Edmond shrugged, covertly glancing toward Brianna as she stirred on the floor.

"You have rolled the dice and lost, Viktor," he said, darkly. "There is nothing left but to accept defeat with a measure of dignity."

"Dignity?" Viktor stared at Edmond with undisguised loathing. "Oh, Summerville, you know better than to believe I shall go to hell with my head held high. I am quite willing to sacrifice anything and anyone to save my own hide."

"What do you want?"

"I want to escape this godforsaken country with my head intact," he said, his eyes darting about the shadows, as if the walls were beginning to close in on him.

Edmond arched his brows. "Surely you cannot be serious? You have committed treason. There is no place you can hide from justice."

"Oh, I will escape." Viktor licked his lips. "Because you are going to assist me."

"Am I?"

"You will, unless Miss Quinn was correct and you care more for your precious Czar than for your lover's continued survival."

Mon dieu. Did Brianna truly believe that he would allow her to die? That he would willingly sacrifice her out of duty to Alexander Pavlovich?

Then again, why would she not believe such a thing?

On the point of agreeing to whatever outrageous demand Viktor was about to make, Edmond stiffened as he realized that Brianna had managed to shift onto her side and was watching him with eyes that appeared far too large in her wan face. It was not the pain in those eyes, however, that made his heart lodge in his throat.

Instead, it was the sight of her hand reaching toward the dagger Viktor had left near his feet when he had replaced it with Edmond's pistol.

Christ. She was going to try to distract the man. And quite likely going to get both of them killed in the absurd attempt.

"Well, my lord, are you going to…" Viktor bit off his words with a sharp cry as Brianna managed to lift her arm high enough to stab the dagger into the back of his leg, just above his leather boot.

Not waiting for Viktor to realize who was attacking him, Edmond rushed forward. Wrapping his arms around Viktor, he drove them both to the stone floor.

They hit with enough force to crack Viktor's head against the floor, and levering himself upright, Edmond discovered that the blow had knocked Viktor senseless.

With a curse of disgust, Edmond rose to his feet and rushed to Brianna's side.

Kneeling beside her, Edmond's heart slammed against his chest at the sight of the blood that marred her night robe. She looked like a wounded flower with her vibrant curls spread over the floor and her skin so pale it appeared translucent in the flickering candlelight. It was the tightness of her fragile features, however, that spoke of the pain she must be enduring.

He hesitated in the act of reaching to draw her into his arms. Having been shot on more than one occasion, he knew the wound must feel like a hot poker being thrust through her shoulder. The last thing she needed was to be unnecessarily jostled.

He settled for gently brushing a stray curl from her ashen cheek.

"Is he dead?" she demanded, her voice strained.

"Not yet." He muttered a curse as she attempted to lift herself off the ground. "No, Brianna, do not move. Viktor Kazakov will never hurt you again. That much I promise."

With a groan she sank back onto the floor.

"Edmond…" She was forced to halt and clear her throat. "You should not be here."

Refusing to be offended by her rasping words, he shrugged off his greatcoat and carefully draped it over her shivering body.

"That is a fine thing to say to the gentleman who risked freezing his most priceless possessions, not to mention ruining a fine pair of boots, to ride to the rescue of his damsel in distress," he retorted, his tone deliberately light.

A hint of desperation rippled over her countenance. "No, you must return to St. Petersburg."

"I have every intention of returning, just as soon as I can arrange our carriage." He brushed a stray curl from her cheek. "For now, I beg you to be patient."

"No." She gave a shake of her head, wincing as the movement jarred her wounded shoulder. "I was only taken to lure you from the city. They are planning the revolt tonight."

"Shh." He pressed a gentle finger to her lips. "I know of their plans."

"Then you know that you must be there to halt them."

"That duty falls to another." He cupped her chin in his hand, capturing and holding her fretful gaze. "On this night, you are all that matters."

"But…"

Edmond placed his hand over her mouth at the screech of a door opening behind him. Still on his knees he turned, his pistol pointed at the dark figure that stepped through the side door.

"Bloody hell, do not shoot, Edmond," Boris muttered, shaking his head to rid himself of the clinging snow. "Although I would prefer a bullet in my arse to returning to that damnable blizzard."

"Are you not supposed to be keeping a watch upon Viktor's riders?"

With an encompassing glance that took in Viktor Kazakov's unconscious form and the wounded woman, Boris grimaced.

"I foolishly thought you might wish to know that they are currently standing near the front entrance arguing over whether they should enter the church to ensure that their master is well and hearty."

"Damn."

Edmond glanced down at Brianna's pale face and thick

crescent of lashes that had lowered to lie against her cheeks, as if she were too weary to keep them lifted.

Realizing they could not simply flee with Brianna so gravely injured, Boris drew his pistol and glanced toward the empty nave.

"How many times have I told you that a proper church should have pews?" he muttered. "Who knows when a gentleman might have need of blocking the doors?"

"I thought you wanted pews so that you could doze through the service."

"Well, there is that." Boris turned toward the sanctuary. "What of the altar? Is there anything there we can use to obstruct the door?"

"Not unless there is a key hidden among the gold and incense."

"So be it. Then we clearly have to kill them."

"I believe I have another suggestion." He glanced toward his loyal companion, even as his fingers unconsciously stroked through Brianna's curls.

"Well?" Boris prompted when Edmond hesitated. "What is this suggestion?"

"I need a distraction."

Boris frowned. "I can lure a few away from the church, but I doubt that I can convince all of them to follow me."

"They will if they believe that Viktor is commanding them to follow you."

"Perhaps. Unfortunately, he does not appear to be in the most cooperative mood at the moment."

"We shall see."

Boris watched in silence as Edmond moved to Viktor Kazakov and roughly jerked the heavy greatcoat from his body and tugged it on. He could not keep his skepticism to himself, however, as Edmond placed Viktor's hat on his head and wrapped the muffler around his neck.

"You believe a coat and hat will disguise you as Viktor Kazakov?"

"Trust me," Edmond murmured, gathering the blanket that

Brianna had dropped during her mad rush. With exquisite care, he wrapped it about her shivering body, careful to keep his own coat wrapped about her.

She moaned in agony as Edmond lifted her off the floor and cradled her against his chest with one smooth motion.

"Hold on, *ma souris,*" he whispered.

Boris stepped forward. "What do you need from me?"

"I want you to return to your horse. When I pull open the door and begin to shout, I want you to charge down the road making as much noise as possible."

Boris narrowed his gaze. "And you?"

"Once the outriders are in pursuit of you, I will carry Brianna to the carriage and command the driver to return us to St. Petersburg." Edmond lifted his head to halt Boris's words of protest with a fierce glare. "Among the confusion and the blizzard, the servants will easily mistake me for their master."

Swift to hide his doubt behind a wry smile, Boris pocketed his pistol and turned toward the side door.

"I suppose that it is just absurd enough that it might succeed."

"Or get us all killed," Edmond spoke the words they were both thinking.

"Then the sooner we discover our fate, the better. Give me ten minutes to slip back to my horse before you start your shouting."

"Boris," Edmond called softly. "As soon as you are away from the church I wish you to rid yourself of your pursuers and return to St. Petersburg."

A smile of anticipation touched the soldier's face. "You fuss over Miss Quinn and allow me to take care of myself."

"Boris…"

The door snapped shut, and Edmond carried Brianna through the nave to the front entrance.

Counting beneath his breath, he forced himself to wait until he was certain Boris had enough time to reach his horse. Then, pulling open the heavy wooden door, he swiftly stepped into the swirling snow, keeping his head bent downward.

"It is Summerville," he bellowed at the milling servants as Boris thundered past, his horse sending a spray of ice and snow in his wake. "Do not allow him to escape. After him, you fools. All of you."

A heartbeat passed during which Edmond barely dared to breathe. What if they suspected he was not Viktor Kazakov? What if…

The outriders scrambled as one for their horses and hurried after the fleeing Boris. Swift to take advantage of the chaos, Edmond waded through the drifting snow and, with an effort, managed to open the door to the carriage without dropping his precious burden.

"Return me to St. Petersburg," he barked at the driver who sat huddled on top the vehicle.

"What of Summerville?"

"Do not question me."

"I… Yes, sire."

CHAPTER TWENTY-SIX

THEY ARRIVED BACK IN St. Petersburg without incident, and after a short, brutal battle with Viktor's driver, he had arrived at Vanya's town house to discover that the older woman was wisely prepared for his return.

With a minimum of fuss, Brianna was whisked to her bed-chamber where the Czar's personal surgeon awaited her. There were a few awkward moments when the doctor had foolishly attempted to demand that Edmond leave while he treated his patient, but once he understood that he was more likely to be tossed headfirst from the window than to rid himself of the anxious nobleman, he had efficiently pulled the bullet from Brianna's shoulder and carefully cleaned the wound.

His deft fingers had lingered on the healing scar from Brianna's previous shooting, but contenting himself to a chiding gaze toward the hovering Edmond, the doctor had at last gathered his belongings and gone in search of Vanya.

Over the next hours, Edmond kept a constant guard on the slumbering maiden.

It was not guilt that made him unable to stray more than a few steps from her unconscious form, although he knew he would have to live with his aching regrets for all eternity. Or even concern that she would not recover. Already, a healthy flush was returning to her cheeks, and her breathing stirred the air with a steady rhythm.

No, it was quite simply an unbearable need to have her within his reach. If she were out of his sight, he feared she might disappear into the icy fog that cloaked the city.

On some level, he understood his fear was illogical. The doctor had warned that Brianna might sleep straight through until morning. And even if she were awake, she was far too weak to leave the bed.

That, however, could not ease the panic clutching his heart.

There was the sound of someone entering the outer chamber and the unmistakable scent of freshly baked bread filled the air, making Edmond's stomach clench with hunger. Throughout the day, Vanya had sent an endless parade of servants with trays to try and tempt him, even going so far as to personally deliver a warm plate of his favorite plum pudding; it had grown cold on the bedside table.

Now he waited in resignation for yet another lecture, his brows arching in exhausted surprise when a gaunt, silver-haired gentleman, rather than his concerned hostess, appeared in the doorway.

"How is she?" Herrick Gerhardt inquired.

Edmond's gaze skimmed over Brianna's pale profile, lingering on the thick sweep of lashes that lay against her cheek.

"So long as there is no infection, the doctor is confident that the wound will heal within a few weeks."

"Did he also claim that she cannot heal unless you are hovering about her like a mother hen?" Herrick demanded dryly.

Rising to his feet, Edmond rubbed the knotted muscles of his neck. "What do you want, Herrick?"

"I thought you might be anxious to know what occurred with Grigori and the others."

"Considering there are no pitched battles in the streets, I presume you managed to halt the revolution."

"Ah, well, if you have no interest…"

"Wait."

With a deep sigh, Edmond bent downward to place a gentle kiss on Brianna's brow. Straightening, he moved to steer Herrick back into the sitting room. Bypassing the tray that was set on a table near the porcelain stove, Edmond instead poured himself a large measure of brandy and tossed it down his throat.

"Tell me what happened," he commanded.

With a faint smile, Herrick moved to pluck the glass from Edmond's hand and firmly pressed him into the chair beside the tray.

"Eat."

"I am not hungry."

"Perhaps not, but you will do Miss Quinn no good if you collapse from starvation." Herrick pointed a finger toward the bowl of savory stew. "Now eat."

"Now who is behaving like a mother hen?" he muttered, even as he reached for the spoon.

He methodically consumed the savory stew and thickly sliced bread spread with honey, which did not offer the numbing warmth of the brandy, but did help to clear the thick fog from his mind.

At last pushing away the tray, he leaned back in his chair and regarded Herrick with a narrowed gaze.

"Tell me what happened."

The older gentleman allowed a grim smile to curve his lips. "Thanks to your warning, I managed to capture Grigori Rimsky before he reached his barracks."

"Does he still live?"

"There was a rather ugly brawl that included a busted nose and several broken bones, but he still breathes." The smile widened with anticipation. "At least until Alexander Pavlovich returns."

Edmond rose to his feet to pour another glass of the brandy. His entire body ached with weariness, but he could not allow himself to relax. Not so long as Brianna might have need of him.

"I never doubted for a moment you would manage to apprehend the villains without incident."

Herrick grimaced. "Actually, it was not entirely without incident."

Edmond stilled, warned by the edge in his companion's voice.

"What do you mean?"

"Unfortunately, even without their commander, a handful of the soldiers managed to disrupt the morning parade."

"How serious?"

Herrick heaved a deep sigh as he moved to peer out the window. "It would have been nothing more than a trifling annoyance if Prince Michael had not been in attendance."

Edmond set aside his glass with enough force to crack the crystal. His one comfort as the dangerous situation unfolded was the hope that they had managed to keep the heavy hand of the Romanovs from making matters worse.

Now that hope was to be dashed.

"What the devil was the Prince doing there?"

Herrick gave a rueful shrug. "I did not invite him, I assure you, but I could hardly command that he remain at the Palace."

Edmond shuddered at the mere thought of the unpredictable, highly emotional Prince reacting to the least hint of insubordination. Unlike Alexander Pavlovich, the younger royal had not yet learned the wisdom to be discovered in a tempered, thoughtful response to his subjects.

"Mon dieu."

"Exactly. His reaction was…" Herrick struggled for an appropriate word. "Excessive," he at last admitted.

"Tell me the worst."

"He allowed the General to have them stripped and beaten in front of the entire regiment and then dragged by the heels to the prison barracks."

"Did any die?" Edmond rasped.

"No, but the brutal treatment only inspired the other soldiers to resent his command. We were fortunate to keep the uprising to only a few of the Regiment."

Edmond scrubbed his hands over his face. Christ. He did not need to be within the barracks to realize that they would be smoldering with the resentment that could ignite the bloodshed they had struggled so hard to avoid.

"We both know that they will not forget, nor will they forgive. I fear we have only deferred the day of reckoning."

"Perhaps," Herrick grudgingly admitted.

"You do know, Herrick, most countries would run a great deal more smoothly if left in the hands of the commoners."

The older gentleman smoothed his features into an unreadable mask. No matter what his annoyance with Prince Michael, Herrick would remain stoically loyal.

"A wise gentleman would keep such thoughts to himself."

Knowing better than to argue, Edmond instead turned his attention to more pressing matters.

"And Viktor Kazakov?"

The smile returned to Herrick's lips.

"He was found in the church where you left him. Since the barrack prison was already filled, I believe he is currently locked in chambers at the Palace along with his cousin, Fedor Dubov."

Edmond gave a sharp bark of laughter, savoring the image of Viktor held prisoner in one of the luxurious rooms. It would be more galling than a damp dungeon.

"Ah, so he did manage to claim his chambers at the Palace. He will be so pleased."

"To be honest, he did not appear particularly pleased," Herrick said dryly. "Indeed, he was threatening all sorts of foul retributions toward you and your entire genealogy. If you desire, I can arrange a meeting so that you can rip out his tongue and put an end to his annoying boasts."

"I have far more important matters to attend to. I will depend on you to question Viktor and discover if there were any others involved."

"Of course." Herrick studied him for a long, searching moment, his expression oddly somber.

"Yes?"

"This woman…"

"Brianna," Edmond snapped.

"Brianna," Herrick readily soothed. "Is she more than a passing fancy to you?"

Edmond abruptly paced toward the stove, the rigid set of his shoulders revealing he was not pleased by the older man's question.

"You know that I never discuss my private affairs."

"And I would have no interest, so long as I presumed that the affair was…passing." There was another awkward pause. "If, however, you intend to keep Miss Quinn as more than your mistress, then you must consider not only her reputation, but also your own."

"Tell me plainly what is on your mind, Herrick."

"As much as you might wish to forget your duties to your Czar, they cannot all be ignored. The most important being the introduction of your future bride to society."

Bride.

A cold chill spread through his body. He had devoted years to convincing himself that he had been cursed. That destiny demanded he be alone, in punishment for having been the cause of his parents' death.

An irrational fear, perhaps, but one he could not overcome. Certainly not after he had watched Brianna nearly die twice in his arms.

"I will not discuss this!"

Herrick frowned, clearly puzzled by Edmond's sharp tone. "I understand that you are still worried for Miss Quinn's safety, but the traitors have been arrested, and the only danger now for the young lady is being revealed as your mistress before we can halt the ugly rumors. You know that Alexander Pavlovich will forgive any indiscretion, so long as it can be hidden beneath a vision of purity." He reached out to clap Edmond on the shoulder. "We must have Miss Quinn moved to a less…unconventional household and provide a guardian who is above question."

"She will remain here with me, Herrick."

"But…"

"Enough, Herrick." Edmond angrily turned to pour himself another brandy. "Brianna will never be my wife."

"And who the bloody hell ever said I wanted to be your wife?" a sharp female voice demanded from the doorway.

The glass slipped from Edmond's fingers as he swiftly turned to see Brianna leaning weakly against the door jamb.

With her slender body nearly lost amongst the folds of Vanya's robe and her hair tumbled about her wan face, she looked unbearably young and fragile. There was no mistaking, however, the wounded fury that flashed in her magnificent eyes or the stiffening of her spine as he took an instinctive step forward.

"Ma souris…"

He had no notion of what he intended to say as he hurried toward her swaying form, and in the end it did not matter. Offering him a glare that cut like a dagger, Brianna gathered her small reserve of strength and slammed the door in his face.

IF BRIANNA HAD NOT FELT SO weak and oddly defeated, she might very well have tossed a grand fit. There was, after all, any number of priceless figurines set about the room that would be perfect to shatter against the door. And if she managed to run out of ammunition, there was always the collection of marble busts that lined the bookshelves.

Instead, she turned the key in the lock and crawled beneath the covers of her bed.

Damn Lord Edmond Summerville to the netherworld.

How dare he shame her by pronouncing to the silver-haired stranger that he would never have her as his bride?

It was not as if she had been pestering him with pleas to become his wife. Or whining to have her shattered reputation restored. Or to even be assured that their relationship was more than a passing fancy.

For God's sake, she had not even told the annoying ass that she might be carrying his child.

And thank goodness for that, a tiny voice whispered in the back of her mind. The very last thing she would ever want was his guilt-ridden attentions, or worse, offers of money, when he so obviously was prepared to be rid of her.

Closing her eyes, Brianna struggled against the disappointment that threatened to drown her.

Nothing had truly changed, despite the fact that he had raced to the church to rescue her, and that he had put aside his duty to his country and his own fierce loyalty to Alexander Pavlovich to do so.

Or even though he had sat at her bedside throughout the night, his hand gently stroking through her curls as he whispered words of comfort in her ear.

She had been a fool to awaken with the warm sense of being utterly treasured. And even more a fool to force her aching body from the bed just so she could be closer to him. She would not make it all worse by allowing herself to be wounded by the realization that she was still no more than the woman currently sharing his bed.

The brave thought had barely passed through her mind when a fist impatiently banged against the wooden panel of the door.

"Brianna, unlock the door."

If she ignored him long enough, he would eventually disappear.

There was nothing more certain.

Nearly two hours later, she was proven right. Edmond did disappear. Or at least he halted the incessant pounding on her door and his demands that she allow him in.

Breathing a sigh of relief, Brianna pulled the covers over her head and concentrated upon the dull ache of her wounded shoulder.

Her morose mood was at last interrupted by a soft tap on the door followed by Vanya's voice.

"Brianna? Brianna, I come bearing gifts," she said. "May I enter?"

Brianna poked her head from the covers. "Are you alone?"

"Except for my maid."

"Just a moment."

On the point of attempting to struggle from the bed, Brianna was halted by Vanya's firm command.

"No, do not leave the bed, I have a key." There was the scrape of metal upon metal and then the door was being thrust open to allow Vanya to sail in, followed closely by a young maid with rosy cheeks and curious blue eyes. "Here you are, my dear." With an imperious motion, Vanya waved the maid forward, watching the girl as she settled the large tray across Brianna's knees before giving a hasty dip and scurrying from the room.

Brianna breathed deeply of the delicious aromas that filled the air. The faint queasiness that had returned over the past hour was not enough to put off her sudden appetite.

"Is that gingerbread?" She plucked off the linen napkin to reveal a bowl of broth and sliced bread, as well as a plate of freshly baked gingerbread.

"Still warm from the oven, although I was forced to promise Cook that I would ensure that you did not have a bite until you had finished off her famous chicken broth that she swears will heal any illness."

Obediently, Brianna reached for her spoon to sample the rich broth that slid down her throat and spread a welcome heat through her still-chilled body.

"It is very good," she murmured, polishing off the soup and a slice of the bread before reaching for the plate of gingerbread and leaning back in the mounds of pillows. As she savored her treat, she was aware of Vanya's concerned gaze.

"How are you feeling?"

"Weak."

"Are you in pain?"

"My shoulder aches, although I am unfortunately becoming rather accustomed to bullet wounds."

Vanya smiled, perching on the edge of the mattress. "It is not a habit that I would recommend."

"Neither would I." Brianna lowered her gaze to the plate of

gingerbread, deliberately hiding her expression from her companion. "Thankfully, I have every confidence that, once I return to London, my future will be a great deal more peaceful."

"London? You intend to leave St. Petersburg?"

"Of course. Russia is a beautiful, if rather frozen country, and you have made me very welcome, but England is my home."

Vanya shifted on the bed, clearly caught off guard by Brianna's firm insistence that she would be leaving.

"I can certainly understand your desire to return home, but surely Edmond will not wish to travel until you have completely healed?"

Popping the last of the gingerbread into her mouth, Brianna replaced the plate on the tray. Then, with a grim determination, she lifted her head to meet her companion's searching gaze.

"My travel plans do not include Edmond, Vanya." Her voice hardened. "Neither does my future."

With a frown, Vanya reached to grasp Brianna's fingers in a comforting grasp.

"Oh, my dear, I hope you do not blame Edmond for what happened to you? He could not possibly have known."

Brianna shrugged. She did not blame him for her abduction. At least not directly. He could not have known Viktor Kazakov would be so desperate.

But she did blame him for having forced his way into her life and her heart, only to leave both a shattered mess.

Something she had no intention of confessing to anyone. Not even this kind, understanding woman.

"Perhaps not, but I can assure you that I was never shot or kidnapped or attacked until Edmond insisted that I play the role of his fiancée."

Vanya arched a brow, her eyes questioning. "Actually, that is not entirely true, is it, my dear?"

"What do you mean?"

"Edmond did happen to mention that your stepfather attempted to kidnap you only days before you traveled to Russia."

"Good lord, I had almost forgotten," she breathed in genuine amazement. Thomas Wade and the fear he had once inspired seemed very far away. "Which only proves just how unnerving the past few weeks have been."

"And you blame Edmond?"

Brianna hid a rueful smile at the disapproval that Vanya could not entirely hide. The older woman might have come to care for Brianna, but her loyalty still belonged to Edmond.

"It is not a matter of blame."

"No?"

"It is…" Brianna heaved a deep sigh. "I just want to return to England and my quiet, uneventful life. That is what I have always wanted."

Vanya tightened her grip on Brianna's fingers. "And what if you carry Edmond's child?"

Brianna did not flinch at the blunt question. In truth, she had given the matter a great deal of thought over the past few hours.

It would be weeks before she could know for certain whether or not she was pregnant, but she intended to be well-prepared. She would do whatever was necessary, make any sacrifice, to ensure that she could create a warm, secure home for her child.

"Then I will choose a cottage in a small village where no one knows me," she said. "I have enough money to support a household and it will be a simple matter to pretend to be a widow."

"And what of Edmond?"

"What of him?"

Vanya stared at her with more than a hint of incredulity. "You cannot truly believe that Edmond will simply allow you to disappear to a small cottage? Especially if he discovers you are carrying his child?"

"Why would he not?" Brianna demanded, refusing to acknowledge the sharp pain that stabbed through her heart. "Our relationship was always destined to be a temporary affair, as Edmond has made painfully clear. No doubt he is already searching for another to take my place."

Vanya tilted back her head to chuckle with unexpected amusement.

"Good lord, Brianna, you truly are an innocent."

Brianna flushed with annoyance. "Not nearly so innocent as I once was," she pointed out tartly.

Vanya patted her hand. "My dear, may I give you some advice?"

"If you wish."

Vanya's lips twitched, as if she sensed Brianna was struggling to remain polite.

"I have never claimed to be extraordinarily wise, but life has taught me a few hard-earned lessons," she said in a soft, haunted tone. "The most important being that love is a rare and wonderful gift that you should never take for granted."

Brianna gritted her teeth against the tide of pain that slammed into her at the memory of Edmond's stark refusal to even consider her as his bride.

He could not have made his lack of regard more clear if he had etched it in stone.

"Edmond does not love me."

"Actually, I am not nearly so certain as you, but I do not refer only to accepting the love of others, but to allowing love to grow in your own heart." Vanya's eyes became misty with remembered pain. "In my fear and pride, I closed off my feelings for my daughter, not to mention a good and decent man who has offered me nothing but unwavering loyalty. Do not make my mistake, Brianna. Do not deny the emotions that fill your heart. That path leads only to regret."

Brianna determinedly ignored the faint chill at Vanya's dire warning, and instead concentrated upon the woman who clearly still mourned her past.

Unlike herself, Vanya possessed a man who loved her beyond all measure. A man who wanted nothing more than to have her as his wife.

"It is not too late, Vanya," Brianna insisted softly, not surprised when the older woman firmly pulled her hand free and rose from the mattress. "Mr. Monroe adores you, and I do not doubt he will forgive you if only you would give him the opportunity."

"But first I must forgive myself, my dear." A wistful smile touched Vanya's lips as she moved toward the door. "At least think upon my words. Edmond is pacing the floor outside. He is rather desperate to see you."

"No." Brianna gave a sharp shake of her head, only to wince in pain as she unwittingly jarred her tender shoulder. "No, I do not want to speak with him."

"Very well." Vanya heaved a faint sigh. "Just rest, my dear. All will be fine."

All will be fine?

Brianna shivered as Vanya stepped from the room and closed the door.

CHAPTER TWENTY-SEVEN

EDMOND LEANED WEARILY AGAINST the mantle as he waited for Vanya to leave Brianna's bedchamber. He could feel the rasp of his whiskers against his palms and knew that he must look nearly as bad as he felt.

He could not remember the last time he had slept, or eaten. Certainly not in the past two days. Still, he could not force himself to leave Brianna's chambers. Not until he had managed to...

To what?

His dark broodings were interrupted as the connecting door was thrust open and Vanya left the bedchamber. Edmond walked forward, but not swiftly enough. Before he was even halfway across the room, the wily woman had turned the key in the lock and tucked it into her pocket.

"How is she? Is she awake? Did she eat?"

Vanya gave a lift of her brows. "She is weak, but awake. And yes, she did eat."

"Then I will visit her."

He held out an imperious hand for the key.

"No, Edmond, she does not want to see you."

"Dammit, Vanya, I need to be with her."

Vanya skirted past Edmond's looming form to pour herself a small glass of sherry.

"Yes, you have made your needs quite clear, Edmond." Turning back to him, she regarded him with a disapproving expression. "In this moment, however, I am more concerned with Brianna's needs."

"She is upset. She does not know what she truly wishes."

"Actually, she seems inordinately certain of what she wishes, or more precisely what she does not wish. And that is to be in your company." Vanya narrowed her eyes with unconcealed suspicion. "What did you do to her?"

Feeling oddly defensive, Edmond shoved his fingers through his tousled hair. "I did nothing." He gave a vague lift of his shoulder. "She simply overheard me speaking with Herrick."

"Were you discussing another woman?"

"*Mon dieu,* of course not."

"I do not know why you appear so surprised," Vanya sternly chastised. "Brianna is convinced you are on the point of replacing her with another."

"Never."

"There must be some reason she is displeased with you," Vanya insisted. "What did you say?"

Edmond hesitated, strangely embarrassed to confess the truth.

"I was attempting to halt Herrick from arranging my imminent wedding."

"To Brianna?" Vanya demanded, her voice pitched low so that it would not carry to the adjoining bedchamber.

"Yes."

"And she overheard you refuse to have her as your bride?"

With a surge of restless annoyance, Edmond paced toward the window, not surprised that the panes were thick with frost. It was well past midnight and the night air was brutally cold.

"I have made no secret of my determination never to wed, as you well know, Vanya," he said, his voice harsh. "It has nothing to do with Brianna."

"No, of course not," Vanya said dryly.

Edmond turned back to glare at his companion. "Besides which, Brianna has informed me on half a dozen occasions that she has no desire to take on a husband or family, so why she should be so angry defies all logic."

Vanya waved aside his perfectly reasonable words. "A

female has no need to be logical, and in any event, there is no woman who would not be offended to have her lover proclaim to the world that he will not have her as his wife. It makes her wonder if she is somehow lacking."

"Which is precisely why I wish to speak with her."

"And what would you say to her, Edmond?" Vanya stepped forward, her expression troubled. "That she is convenient to trifle with when the mood might strike you, but not worthy enough to claim a permanent role in your life?"

"Would you prefer that I lie to her, Vanya? That I make promises that I cannot keep?"

"Why can you not?" She gave a wave of her heavily bejeweled hand. "Brianna is charming, beautiful, and obviously she brings you happiness. Any gentleman with the least amount of sense would be proud to call her his wife."

"I will not—" Edmond bit off his words, refusing to admit his reluctance to take Brianna as a wife was out of fear that some dreadful fate would await her. Vanya would think him a lunatic.

"You will not what?"

"I will never wed."

"Why, my dear?" With a frown, Vanya stepped close enough to place a hand on his arm. "It is obvious that you care very much for Brianna. Why are you so opposed to the notion of marrying her?"

"I will not discuss this, Vanya." He stepped stiffly away from her touch, his features hard with warning. "Not with you or anyone else."

"Fine." Shaking her head in disgust, Vanya moved toward the door leading to the corridor. "Then you will lose her."

"What did you say?"

"I said that you will lose her," Vanya readily repeated, pausing at the door to turn and stab him with a resigned expression. "Already, Brianna is planning her return to England."

"I am aware she desires to return to London so that she can meet with her solicitor and gain control of her inheritance," he said slowly. "I will accompany her once she is fully healed."

"She did not mention having you accompany her. Indeed, she was fairly determined that she would be returning alone, so that she could set up her household without interference."

"That is only because she is currently unhappy with me. Once she has recovered her temper, she will realize she is being ridiculous."

Vanya heaved a sigh. "Edmond, I love you as if you were my own son, but there are times when I want nothing more than to slap you. Let go of the past, before it is too late, my dear."

"This has nothing to do with the past!"

"Oh, Edmond."

With a last pitying glance, Vanya slipped from the room and disappeared down the corridor.

Left on his own, Edmond slowly sank onto a wing chair and allowed his heavy lashes to lower. Damn his supposed friends and their unwanted interference.

THREE DAYS LATER, EDMOND WAS forced to reconsider his arrogant assumption that Brianna would come to her senses and forgive him. The stubborn minx was determined to keep him at a damnable distance.

No matter how often he visited, she remained stoically aloof, her face wan and her beautiful eyes empty of expression.

It was almost as if it were merely her ghost that remained tucked beneath the heavy covers, while her essence had retreated so deep he could no longer touch her.

He had attempted every means to provoke a response from her. Teasing, goading, even bribery, but nothing could stir her from the strange lethargy. He might as well have been invisible for all the attention she offered.

Awakening on the fourth morning, he stormed into Vanya's breakfast room, which was hung with green damask and filled with charming Chinese vases and jade figurines. He was relieved that Monroe had been called to the Palace so he could speak with the older woman in private.

It was not often that Lord Edmond Summerville found himself at a loss, and his pride had taken enough of a beating without having his admission of defeat made public.

Vanya was seated on a birch settee next to a gilt table that was nearly hidden beneath the large tray of eggs and toast and delicately stewed eel. Attired in a rich brocade gown that had several large emeralds sewn into the bodice, her hair pulled into intricate curls to frame her handsome face, she appeared every inch the Russian noblewoman, an image that was only enhanced as she watched his furious approach with no more than a lift of her brow.

"Good morning, Edmond. Would you care for some tea?"

"No, I bloody well do not want tea," he snapped, the heels of his glossy boots clicking loudly on the polished parquet floor. "I want you to tell me why Brianna treats me as if I no longer exist."

"I cannot converse with you while you pace my floor like a caged beast," Vanya chastised. "At least have the decency to take a seat so I do not have to crane my neck."

"Dammit, Vanya, I am in no mood to be polite."

"Yes, I can see that." Sipping her tea, Vanya met his smoldering gaze with a faint smile. "Is she refusing to see you again?"

Edmond shoved impatient fingers through his hair. "She might as well. When I do visit, she treats me as if I am some vague stranger. Hell, I would rather she damn me to the netherworld than regard me with that perfected indifference of hers."

"She is still recovering, Edmond." Vanya slowly set aside her cup. "You must have patience."

The smooth explanation did nothing to ease Edmond's annoyance. Indeed, it only stirred yet another of his grievances.

"Is she recovering?" he demanded, his voice thick with disbelief. Vanya's lips parted, and he held up a slender hand. "Oh, I have heard the doctor claim that her wound is healing and that there is no infection, but I do not need to be a damned sawbones to see that she is far too pale and thin. When I cornered him this morning all he would say was that it was perfectly normal and that her appetite would return in time."

Something rippled over the lovely face. Some mysterious emotion that was gone so swiftly that Edmond could not fully capture it.

"We must trust his judgment," she said vaguely.

Edmond narrowed his gaze, sensing that there was more to Brianna's illness than he was being told.

"Actually, I have no need to trust anything the fool might have to say." A cold smile touched his lips. "I have called for Herrick's surgeon to examine her later this evening."

Vanya rose to her feet, an unexpected anger hardening her features. "Edmond, that is not at all necessary."

"It is my decision to make."

"No. It is Brianna's decision to make, and she is perfectly satisfied with the care she is being given. She will not thank you for your interference."

Edmond's suspicion that he was not being told the full truth of Brianna's condition was swept aside by a sharp pang of regret.

"She will not thank me for anything at this moment. She is…"

"What?"

"Slipping away."

Vanya's expression softened. "I did warn you, Edmond."

Edmond resumed his pacing. "She is doing this because I will not wed her?"

"I cannot say what is in someone else's heart, but I believe any woman with the least amount of intelligence would be wise enough to protect herself."

Edmond stiffened. "I would never hurt Brianna."

"Not intentionally." Vanya was swift to soothe. "But, my dear, I know you. You have enjoyed the attentions of dozens of women. Why should Brianna not be preparing herself to become nothing more than a fading memory?"

"Because I have no damned intention of making her into some fading memory."

Vanya clicked her tongue. "Of course you do. It is inevitable. And you are only upset because it was Brianna who chose to pull away before you could do so. Your pride is pricked."

"For God's sake, this has nothing to do with my pride." He pointed a finger at his hostess. "And I can assure you, there is no way in hell that I will allow her to escape me. Not ever."

Vanya regarded him with a searching gaze, her expression wary. "Edmond, what are you saying?"

The instinct to retreat from the intrusive question was near overwhelming. He disliked displaying his emotions as if they were a public spectacle for others to enjoy. He was beginning to accept, however, that revealing his feelings was going to be the least of the sacrifices demanded of him.

"I…" Grimly he forced himself to continue. "I care for Brianna."

Vanya was remarkably unmoved by his stunning admission. "We all care for Brianna," she said with a wave of her bejeweled hand. "She is a sweet, gentle child who has confronted the difficulties in her life with an amazing dignity."

"I do not think I would ever claim her as gentle," he said dryly. "She possesses the heart of a tigress, and she does not mind using her claws when necessary. Do you know, she blatantly blackmailed me when she forced her way into Huntley House?"

Vanya clicked her tongue. "My point is that caring for her is quite different from being devoted to her. She is…vulnerable and you could do considerable damage without ever meaning to harm her."

"I have just told you that I want her in my life."

"For now."

"Forever."

Vanya slowly lifted her brows, her expression skeptical. "Forgive me if I find your sincerity difficult to believe, Edmond."

"Why?"

"Because you refuse to make her your wife," Vanya replied, her expression accusing. "If you are truly dedicated to her, then you would want to make your relationship permanent."

"For God's sake, it is because I care for her that I refuse to put her in danger."

There was a long silence as Vanya attempted to comprehend his unspoken fears.

"The traitors have been captured, and so far as I know, there are no others that wish to abduct the poor girl." She offered a faint smile. "Of course, she may wish to flee once she is threatened with the prospect of facing the Romanov Court."

Edmond's features remained set in grim lines. Alexander Pavlovich and the numerous difficulties of negotiating the dangerous waters of the Russian Court were worries for another day.

"You cannot understand," he muttered.

"Not unless you explain, my dear," Vanya said, moving to give his arm a light squeeze. "Tell me why you hesitate. Does it have something to do with your parents?"

Edmond closed his eyes against the age-old pain that slammed into him. "They died because of me."

"No, Edmond. It was nothing more than an accident." The older woman patiently waited until Edmond forced open his eyes to meet her steady gaze. "It had nothing to do with you."

Edmond had heard the meaningless words too many times to take comfort in them. "They would never have been on their yacht that night if I had not been in trouble with the Magistrate."

Vanya's fingers tightened on his arm as she gave an impatient shake of her head.

"And who is to say that they would not have died in a carriage accident on the way to some social event? Or succumbed to the fever that ravaged Surrey only a few weeks later?" she demanded. "You are not God, Edmond, as much as you enjoy playing the role. You do not possess the power over life and death."

"You can say what you will, Vanya, but because of my decisions, they died. I will not have that happen to another."

"Another?" Vanya stilled, as if struck by a sudden, unwelcome realization. Then, without warning, she reached up to gently pat his cheek. "Oh, my dearest, what a heavy burden you have been carrying."

"If it is a burden, then it is one of my own making."

"No, it is not, and you have punished yourself long enough." With a brisk motion, Vanya took a step backward and squared her shoulders, as if preparing for battle. "Edmond, I knew your mother for near forty years, and I can tell you that the one thing she desired above all others was for her sons to be content in their lives." Her eyes narrowed with a stern determination. "To seek happiness is not betraying your parents' memory. Indeed, it is the only true means to honor them."

With jerky steps, Edmond moved to peer out the window. The thick clouds had at last parted to allow the morning sunlight to reflect off the snow with a breathtaking brilliance, making the streets appear to be dusted with diamonds. Farther away, he could make out the silhouettes of skaters and pedestrians that crowded the Neva.

There was something almost magical in the sight of St. Petersburg on winter's morning, but Edmond barely noted the beauty spread before him. Instead he forced himself to actually consider Vanya's accusation.

"I do not seek to punish myself," he at last said, more to reassure himself than to convince the older woman.

A good thing, since she was shaking her head as the denial was tumbling from his lips.

"That is exactly what you are doing." She deliberately paused. "And worse, you are punishing that lovely young lady who lies upstairs. She deserves better."

Edmond abruptly turned, for the first time forced to consider the notion that, in his determination to protect Brianna, he had actually managed to hurt her even worse. His heart twisted at the painful memory of Brianna's ashen countenance and wounded eyes just before she had literally and figuratively slammed the door in his face.

Ignoring Vanya's speculative gaze, Edmond slowly paced across the parquet floor, struggling to make sense of the chaos that ruled his mind.

What if…

The entrance of a maid brought his relentless pacing to a halt.

"Your guests have arrived," she announced.

"Thank you, Sophie, that will be all." As if sensing she had managed to plant the seeds of doubt in his mind, Vanya swept majestically toward the door, a satisfied smile curving her lips. "Just think upon what I have said, my dear."

Edmond watched Vanya sweep from the room before turning to glare out the window. He had sought out the woman for answers, not to be chastised as if he were a child. And to make matters worse, he could not dismiss the stinging reproach.

He remained lost in dark thought until the sound of heavy footsteps intruded. Turning, he found Boris at the door, his caped coat dusted with snow and his glossy boots thick with mud. With a flick of his hand, Boris tossed a brown-wrapped package toward Edmond, the scent of freshly roasted chestnuts filling the air.

Edmond caught the package with a grimace. He had sent Boris to purchase the treat in the hopes of tempting Brianna's appetite. A worthless task over the past days.

"Did you come across a bit of rancid eel in your breakfast this morning, Summerville?" Boris demanded, his arms folded over his chest.

"What the devil…you know very well that I detest eel, Boris."

"Then there must be some other reason for you to look so ill. Perhaps I should summon a doctor."

Edmond frowned. "I am not ill, I am annoyed. I cannot comprehend why women must complicate what should be a simple liaison."

"Take heart, old friend. My mother would tell you that if

a woman is not creating trouble in your life, then she no longer cares."

His stomach clenched in dread. "Damn."

Boris stepped forward, indifferent to the mud now marring the parquet floor. "That was supposed to offer you a measure of comfort. There is nothing wrong with Miss Quinn, is there?"

"Not physically. I have been assured that the doctor is satisfied she is healing in a suitable fashion." He managed a humorless smile. "You have no need to worry that Janet will be awaiting you in London with a sharpened knife."

Boris cleared his throat. "Actually, we have decided that once spring arrives, she will travel to Russia. The Czar has always wished for me to join his personal guard, and Janet will soon become accustomed to St. Petersburg. My only concern is whether St. Petersburg will survive Janet."

"You intend to wed?"

"She has not yet agreed to a formal arrangement, stubborn wench, but I have great confidence in my talents of persuasion."

"Good God."

Boris laughed at his shock. "Are you surprised because you assumed I would never wed or by the knowledge that there is a female willing to have me?"

"It never occurred to me that you would ever wish for a family."

"I doubt that it occurs to any man, until he encounters a woman who can reveal the pleasure to be found in such a commitment."

Edmond crossed to slap his friend on the shoulder, ignoring the hollow ache in the pit of his stomach.

"I shall miss having you at my side, old friend."

"Not if you have the sense to accept what is obvious to all."

"Christ, not you, too."

Boris studied him with a somber expression. "You have battled against the hope of happiness long enough. It is time to lay down your weapons and accept what the heavens have offered."

"It is not so simple."

"Yes, Summerville, it is precisely that simple."

IT WAS NEARING LUNCHEON when the door to the bedchamber was pressed open and Vanya entered, her smile not entirely hiding her concern as she crossed the room and perched on the edge of the bed.

Brianna swallowed a sigh as she pressed herself higher on the mound of pillows behind her. She knew her lethargy was worrisome to her hostess, but for the moment, she could not seem to battle her way through the cloud of fog that held her captive. She was certain, however, that it was a passing sensation, and that soon she would be back on her feet and prepared to confront whatever life might offer.

Unfortunately, she seemed destined to cause poor Vanya an inordinate amount of bother until she could shake off her lassitude. Something she would have given a great deal to avoid.

"Brianna, my dear, this simply cannot continue," the older woman chided.

Expecting the customary words of comfort, Brianna was caught off guard by the soft but unmistakable reprimand.

"I beg your pardon?"

Vanya folded her hands in her lap. "For your information, I have long been considered one of the most superb hostesses in all of St. Petersburg. Indeed, an invitation to my New Year's ball is the most sought-after ticket in town. Now, I begin to fear that having you fade to a mere wisp will destroy my reputation beyond repair. Already there are whispers that I am starving you."

"You know very well I adore your cook's creations. She is nothing less than an artist with gingerbread. I just am…not hungry."

Reaching out, Vanya grasped Brianna's hand in a tight grip. "Is it the babe? Are you queasy?"

Pain briefly stabbed through the haze that surrounded her. "There is to be no babe."

"You are certain?"

"I am bleeding."

"Oh, my dear." Vanya studied Brianna's pale features with

a hint of sympathy. "You know it is very possible that you were never with child?"

Brianna had, of course, considered the possibility. She'd had nothing to occupy her mind beyond brooding on the past few days. Oddly, it did not truly matter if there had ever been an actual child or not. She mourned the loss, regardless of the truth.

"Yes, I know."

"And no doubt it is for the best."

"No doubt."

Vanya sighed, her expression troubled as she squeezed Brianna's fingers so tightly her rings threatened to cut into her skin.

"Enough is enough, my dear. What can I do to please you?"

Surprising both Vanya and herself, Brianna shoved aside the heavy covers and moved to the edge of the mattress. Enough truly was enough. Ignoring the weakness in her knees and the twinge of pain in her healing shoulder, she shoved herself to her feet and charted a wobbly path to the window overlooking the garden.

It felt astonishingly refreshing to be out of the bed, despite the chill from the frosty panes, and with a pleased sigh, she sank onto the thick cushion of the window seat.

"Brianna?"

At Vanya's prompting, Brianna turned her head to meet the older woman's anxious gaze.

"I want to go home," she said, simply.

"Home?" Vanya appeared strangely baffled by the request. "To England?"

"Yes."

"But…" Giving a shake of her head, Vanya moved to sit next to Brianna on the window seat. "You must know such a thing is impossible. At least at the moment."

Brianna blinked at the blunt refusal. "Why?"

"Not only is your health far too delicate to undertake such a journey, but the weather will not improve for some months."

Months.

"I cannot remain here for such a length of time," she breathed.

"I fear you have little choice." Vanya directed a pointed glance toward the window that revealed a landscape layered with ice and snow. "Even the most seasoned traveler would balk at daring a Russian winter. You would be fortunate if the worst you suffered was being stranded at some uncomfortable inn, perhaps for weeks."

Brianna bit her bottom lip. Like any true Englishwoman she found it difficult to comprehend just how savage and unforgiving a Russian winter could truly be. Or perhaps she simply did not want to comprehend.

Her hands clenched in her lap as she tried to avoid the knowledge she was well and truly trapped.

"There must be some means for me to find passage."

Vanya smiled ruefully at the edge of horror in her voice. "Well, my dear, I must admit to being more than a trifle offended. Not only do you starve yourself until you are a mere wraith, but now you become hysterical at the thought you might be my guest for the next few weeks. Anyone could be forgiven for presuming that I am nothing less than a monster."

A rueful chuckle was wrenched from Brianna. "Good lord, no one would ever believe you have treated me with anything but utter kindness, Vanya. Far more kindness than I deserve." She reached out to pat her companion's hand, a lump forming in her throat. "If things had been different, then perhaps…"

"If Edmond had been different, you mean?"

"Among a great many things, including myself," Brianna muttered.

There was a brief hesitation, as if Vanya was considering her words. Then, sucking in a deep breath, she came to her decision.

"My dear, I think, if you will give him the opportunity, that Edmond will prove that he has changed," she said, ignoring the manner in which Brianna stiffened at the mere mention of his name. "Or at least, he has the potential to change with your assistance."

"Thank you, Vanya, but perhaps I should be allowed to speak for myself," a deep male voice echoed through the room.

CHAPTER TWENTY-EIGHT

IT WAS PRECISELY AS SHE HAD feared, Brianna realized as Edmond strolled into the room and her heart gave a familiar leap of excitement. Her deadened sense of unreality was crumbling to allow her raw, aching emotions to be exposed.

This was why she had to flee St. Petersburg.

Good lord, he had only to walk into the room for her pulse to pound and her body to tremble in anticipation of his ravishment. And when he smiled in her direction…her entire world seemed a brighter place.

The only way to salvage any peace for her future was to find the means to return to England and the life that she had planned for so long. That was surely preferable to allowing Edmond to become an even more vital part of her existence.

Perhaps sensing her sudden flare of distress, Vanya gently patted her hand before rising to her feet and flashing Edmond a stern frown.

"I shall allow you to speak for yourself only if you promise not to make a complete hash of it."

Edmond grimaced, thrusting a hand through his tousled hair. In truth, he appeared remarkably disheveled, with his cravat hanging loose to reveal the smooth column of his neck and his jaw shadowed with unshaven whiskers. If it were not so ridiculous, she would have thought he had slept in his current attire.

"I am not about to bind myself to such a promise. Not when history has taught me that my renowned skills in negotiation do not seem to impress Miss Quinn," he said wryly. "I do, however, believe I would prefer to knot my own noose as to have you do it for me."

"As you wish."

Moving forward, Vanya paused just long enough to pat Edmond on the cheek before sweeping from the room and closing the door behind her.

Taking advantage of the brief distraction, Brianna scurried back to the bed and tugged the covers over her shivering body. It was not the chill in the air, or even the lingering weakness that sent her diving beneath the blankets, but instead, an odd sense of vulnerability as Edmond regarded her with a gaze that was unnerving in its intensity.

Although Edmond did nothing to prevent her dive to safety, he prowled forward to peer down at her with a twisted smile.

"You really do look like the little mouse I have always called you, with your wide eyes and nose twitching just above the edge of the covers. Do you fear that I am about to pounce upon you?"

"I have learned not to try and predict what you might do."

"No doubt wise." Without warning he moved to sit on the edge of the bed, his slender fingers running a path of pure fire down her cheek. "So pale. *Mon dieu*. If you wish to punish me by not eating, you have succeeded, Brianna," he said huskily. "I have scoured all of St. Petersburg in an effort to discover some treat to tempt you, and yet each offering has been returned to the kitchen with barely a nibble."

Brianna managed to hide the flood of warmth at the realization that he had been responsible for those exotic delicacies that had been delivered on her tray.

"It was not my intent to punish you. Is there something you need, Edmond?"

There was a moment's hesitation before his voice floated softly on the air.

"You."

Her breath caught at the simple word. "I…" She was forced to halt and clear her throat. "I beg your pardon?"

Brianna expected him to laugh and brush aside his stark confession as a ridiculous jest. Instead, his fingers lightly traced her trembling lips as he regarded her with a somber expression.

"I need you, Brianna. I know that is not a particularly elegant or romantic declaration, but there it is." He caught and held her wide, disbelieving gaze. "I need you."

Lost in the dark beauty of his eyes, Brianna was finding it all but impossible to force her mind to function in a reasonable manner.

"For what?"

His smile was edged with self-derision. "For everything, it would seem. You are not the only one who has been unable to eat or sleep, *ma souris,* and while I have not yet taken to my bed, I have been unable to be gone from the outer chamber for more than a few moments unless I have set myself a task I hope will please you." His head turned to glance toward the hothouse flowers and small boxes of marzipan that had been arranged on her mantle when she had awakened that morning. "If I were observing some other gentleman mooning over a woman in such a pathetic fashion, I would be vastly amused."

She slowly shook her head, the pain of his rejection still brutally fresh in her mind.

"But you…"

"What?"

She tugged the blankets even tighter.

"You made it very clear that you consider me no more than a convenient body to warm your bed."

"Convenient?" His sharp, humorless bark of laughter echoed loudly through the room. "Miss Quinn, you have been by far the most bothersome, unnerving, intractable female who has ever crossed my path."

Stupidly, Brianna found herself offended by his mocking words. "I most certainly am not bothersome."

His lips twitched, but with an obvious effort he pushed aside his annoying amusement.

"My point is that I need only step out the door to discover a woman more convenient."

"Then why do you not do so?" she snapped.

"Because, you annoying wench, I do not want anyone else." He captured her lips in a brief, punishing kiss before pulling back to regard her with a glittering gaze. "I have not so much as glanced at another female since you forced your way into my home. And as for what you heard when I was speaking to Herrick, well…" His features tightened with self-disgust. "I suppose there is no excuse but the fact that I was being a ridiculous jackass."

Brianna grimly ignored the treacherous leap of her heart as she narrowed her gaze in suspicion.

"I will not argue."

"I am not surprised," he said, his eyes darkening with genuine regret as he cupped her face in a gentle grip. "Brianna, I am sorry that I hurt you. That was never my intention."

"I know your intentions, Edmond, and you have never attempted to deceive me."

"No, just myself," he muttered.

"What?"

With a grimace Edmond surged to his feet and paced toward the window, his shoulders stiffly angled and his hands clenched at his sides.

"I knew from the beginning that you were more than just another female I desired in my bed, but I was so determined to seduce you that I never allowed myself to acknowledge that I was the one being seduced." He pressed a fist to the frosted window, his head turned to reveal his perfect profile. "Not even when I was forced to accept I could not be far from your side without feeling as if an essential part of me was missing."

Bewildered by his husky words, Brianna sat upright, her brow furrowed at the mere thought that she could have such power over the man.

"Absurd."

"Absurd, but undeniable." He made a sound deep in his throat. "Why else would I have selfishly demanded that you remain in London with me, when it was obvious you would have been far happier at Meadowland with Stefan? And even when I did come to my senses enough to take you to Surrey, I could not leave you in peace."

"You came to my rescue," Brianna instinctively defended his rash return to Surrey, unable to forget the debt that she owed this man, no matter how aggravating he might be. "If not for you, then Thomas Wade would have…"

"Do not make me a hero, *ma souris,*" he interrupted, turning to regard her with a shadowed gaze. "We both know I should have left Meadowland once you were safe and allowed you to wed my brother, even if I would rather have cut out my heart. And I most certainly never should have demanded that you travel with me directly into the path of a brewing revolution. Hardly heroic behavior."

"You have never forced me, Edmond. I could have refused to accompany you."

He heaved a weary sigh, his gaze skimming over her tiny body, still hidden beneath the heavy covers.

"Could you?"

"I am not usually a spineless creature," she snapped, embarrassed to realize just how helpless she was behaving. "In truth, I am weary of lying in this bed like a coward."

"No, never that." With swift steps he was standing beside the bed, his hand reaching to touch her cheek. "Not even the staunchest spine could have survived what you have endured over the past weeks and not needed to recuperate. Especially when you were concerned that you had more than just yourself to care for."

It took a moment before Brianna was catching her breath in shock. With an unwitting movement she was pressing a hand to her empty stomach.

"You knew?"

"I overheard you speaking with Vanya just now."

"Are you relieved there is to be no child?"

"Relieved?" His eyes flashed with an emotion so intense that Brianna forgot to breathe. "*Mon dieu,* I can think of nothing that would give me more pleasure than to know that you carried my child."

Brianna had considered Edmond's reaction to the knowledge she was pregnant. She had envisioned telling him on a hundred different occasions. But not even her wildest fantasies had prepared her for the haunted yearning he made no effort to disguise.

"Oh."

Perching on the edge of the bed, Edmond reached to take her hand in his. "Of course, I would prefer that we are properly wed before the babe is born. Thus far, we shall be able to avoid the worst of the scandal by the simple task of taking our vows. It would be rather more difficult if you are carrying our child down the aisle."

Brianna stiffened. An awkward silence descended until she at last cleared her throat.

"Edmond?"

"Yes, I know." His smile was tight, almost as if he were as unnerved as Brianna by his astonishing words. "It is not a very charming proposal, but the truth of the matter is that I have precious little experience in asking a woman to be my wife, so I hope you will be patient with me."

"No…" A cold panic clutched her heart. It did not take a great deal of intelligence to realize Edmond felt obliged to offer for her. Or that he would be miserable if she were foolish enough to accept. "No, you do not want this, Edmond."

His eyes narrowed. "You are capable of reading my mind?"

"In this, yes."

Catching Edmond off guard, Brianna tossed aside the covers and slid from the bed. With a muttered curse he was at her side, his arm gently encircling her waist as if she were made of delicate crystal.

"Brianna, take care," he growled. "You are still weak."

She flinched as his words rubbed salt into her most vulnerable wounds.

"You pity me." She shivered from the cold that came from the pit of her stomach, not from the chill in the room. "That is why you believe you must propose."

"Pity you? Have I ever struck you as a man of great compassion, *ma souris?*" he taunted, his smile smug as she faltered beneath his blunt question. "Precisely. Whatever I do will always be what I desire, and what I feel will offer me the greatest gain. Or in this case, the greatest pleasure."

Gathering her courage, Brianna forced herself to pull away from his warm, comforting touch. She could not think clearly when her body was trembling with the joy of having him so near. And it had never been more vital in her young life that her wits be unclouded.

"Very well." She tightened her muscles, almost as if fearing a sudden blow. "If it is not pity that has prompted your proposal, then what precisely has occurred in the past three days that has altered your absolute conviction that you did not desire me to be your wife?"

With a ruthless determination, Edmond stepped forward, wrapping his arms around her waist and hauling her against his hard body.

"What occurred was a long overdue acceptance that you are a fever in my blood that I will never be rid of. A fever I do not *want* to be rid of."

A heady burst of heat flooded through her body, melting away that numbing cold that had held her in its grip for the past three days. Abruptly she realized just how much she had missed sharing her bed, her body, with this man. It was little wonder that she had been unable to shake off the gray lethargy. She had been denying herself the one thing certain to make her heart pound and her blood rush with joy.

"You have never made a secret of the fact you desire me in your bed, Edmond," she said, unable to completely disguise her pain. "That is considerably different from wanting me as your wife."

With a smile, he cupped her chin in his hand and forced her to meet his steady gaze.

"You are determined to make me say it, are you not?"

"Say what?"

"That I love you." His lips twisted at her stunned disbelief. "There. Are you happy?"

Brianna struggled to breathe, uncertain if she were more astonished at his blunt confession or the inelegant manner in which he had tossed the words in her face.

"Not when it so obviously makes you unhappy," she muttered.

"Oh, Brianna." His soft sigh was rueful. "It is not that it makes me unhappy. It has simply been difficult to put aside my fear."

"Fear of what?"

"Fear that I am destined to destroy anyone I love. After my parents…"

"Edmond," she interrupted his anguished words, her arms lifting to encircle his neck as she pressed closer to his tense body.

"No, allow me to finish," he whispered, his hand skimming up the curve of her back to tangle in her curls. "After my parents drowned, I blamed myself."

Her heart squeezed in sympathy. "It was nothing more than a tragic accident."

He absently rubbed his cheek against the top of her head, his whiskers tugging on the silky strands of her hair and his male scent clinging to her skin with familiar warmth.

"Logically, I understand that, but a part of me will always believe that, if I had not gotten into trouble with the Magistrate, they would still be alive." The fingers at the curve of her back tightened with a flare of painful emotion. "And that I do not deserve to care for another."

Brianna buried her face in the hollow of his shoulder, unable to endure the thought of the endless years he had punished himself.

"And now?"

"And now, I realize that I am far too selfish to deny my need for you. Perhaps I should be condemned to hell for my past, but I am desperately hoping that I am to be blessed instead." Pulling back, he regarded her with a wistful smile that could have melted a heart chiseled from granite. "Brianna, say that you will be my wife."

The heady, intoxicating joy that flooded through her body was nearly her undoing. She wanted to say yes. For all her bold determination to become a woman of independence, she was learning that being utterly alone was a rather high price to pay for peace.

"Brianna?"

She slowly shook her head, schooling her features to hide the longing that clenched her heart.

"I cannot answer in this moment, Edmond. I need time to think."

He stilled, his gaze boring deep into her wide, wary eyes. But instead of anger, his eyes slowly darkened and his hands tightened as a wicked smile curved his lips.

"If my words will not sway you, my stubborn beauty, then perhaps I can find another means to convince you."

With a soft tug on her curls, Edmond angled her head backward, his smoldering gaze lingering on the color blooming beneath her cheeks and the soft curve of her lips as they parted in silent invitation. Only when she arched restlessly against his hard body did Edmond at last lower his head and kiss her with a sweet yearning that made her heart melt.

He kept kissing her for a long time, one hand threading through her loose curls while the other splayed over the curve of her bottom. His lips moved lingeringly from her mouth to sweep over her face, nipping at her earlobe before he buried his face in her hair.

"Make no mistake, you will be my wife, Brianna," he said huskily, his breath hot against the curve of her neck. "I will never let you escape me. Never."

CHAPTER TWENTY-NINE

London, England
Three months later

LADY ABERLANE'S LONDON town house in St. James's Square was a long, narrow building with a profusion of Corinthian pilasters and marble floors and elegant Venetian windows. Despite the rigid elegance, however, the older woman had managed to create an atmosphere of comfort that instantly made Brianna feel at home.

Which would perhaps explain why she was still happily settled with the older woman rather than seeking out her own establishment, Brianna acknowledged, nibbling on a piece of toast as she awaited her hostess to join her in the pale blue breakfast room decorated with rare silver furniture.

When Edmond had grudgingly given in to her demands to return to England, it was at his insistence she stay with the noblewoman. He pointed out that Brianna was far too weary from the grueling journey to adequately deal with the tedious business of purchasing a house. And since she truly had been exhausted by the frozen, at times dangerous, travel from St. Petersburg to London, Brianna had not protested.

Now, however, she was fully recovered, and a part of her knew that she had no further reason to linger. Nothing beyond the pleasure of Letty's charming companionship and the incessant attentions of Edmond.

She had expected the gentleman to quickly weary of his

pursuit once they had returned to England. Not only were there any number of beautiful women to distract him, but her residence beneath Letty's roof meant that they were unable to exchange more than a chaste kiss. She, better than anyone, knew he was a man of strong passions. It would have been a simple matter for him to discover another to replace her.

But far from wearied, Edmond seemed more determined than ever to convince her that his attentions were sincere.

Each morning, a prettily wrapped gift was waiting her on the breakfast table, and every afternoon at the precisely proper hour, he called to pay his respects, always bringing her favorite pink roses until they threatened to consume Letty's front parlor.

It was…well, it was romantic.

Brianna barely managed to hide the idiotic grin that had spread across her face as Lady Aberlane swept into the room, her fluff of white hair pulled into a simple knot and her dark eyes snapping with excitement.

Taking the seat the footman held for her, Letty pressed her hands together and leaned forward.

"So, my dear, has it arrived?"

Brianna could not resist a bit of teasing as she reached for the nearby teapot. "Good morning, Aunt Letty. Will you have some tea?"

The older woman gave a flutter of her hands, ignoring the steaming brew that Brianna poured.

"Now, do not be so cruel as to leave me in suspense. You know how I look forward to your little baubles."

"Baubles?" Brianna laughed with rueful humor, recalling the emerald drop earbobs, the diamond bracelet, the sapphire necklace and a dozen other pieces of jewelry that had been delivered. "Only a ducal family could consider the gifts that Edmond sends to me as little baubles." To prove her point, Brianna pushed the velvet-lined box that sat next to her plate across the table. "That little bauble must be worth a fortune."

With a happy twitter, Letty tugged the lid off the box, her expression becoming one of stunned disbelief as she lifted her head to meet Brianna's suddenly wary gaze.

"Oh…my."

Brianna's pleasure at the brilliantly flawless ruby ring surrounded by diamonds faltered at the sight of her companion's strange reaction.

"I should return it." She wrinkled her nose. "Even to my untrained eye it is obviously far too generous a gift."

Letty cleared her throat. "It is rather more than generous, my dear."

"What do you mean?"

"This ring belonged to Edmond's mother." Closing the lid of the box, Letty slowly pushed it back across the table. "Indeed, it is an heirloom."

Brianna's heart slammed against her ribs, whether from panic or giddy excitement impossible to determine.

She should have suspected, of course. Such a perfect gem was not the sort of thing a man strolled into the shop to purchase for his passing fancy. For God's sake, the diamonds that surrounded the ruby could feed half of London for a year.

No, such an object was intended to be passed from one generation to another.

"Good lord, whatever is he thinking?"

Letty arched a knowing brow. "He is thinking that he desires his wife to possess his most prized possession."

"But…" Brianna licked her suddenly dry lips. "Surely this should go to Stefan's bride?"

"Stefan was given the Huntley jewels, as is only fitting for his position. Edmond was given his mother's property to pass along to his wife and daughters."

"His wife."

"Yes."

"He truly is the most stubborn, intractable man I have ever encountered," she muttered, her fond tone belying her words.

Sipping her tea, Letty watched her over the edge of the china cup. "He is not the only stubborn one, I think."

"You surely cannot be referring to me?"

"I may be old, but I am not yet entirely blind, Brianna. It is obvious that you love my nephew."

There was no point in denying the accusation. For all her determination to pretend indifference, even the most addlebrained fool could deduce she was utterly, completely and hopelessly in love with Lord Edmond Summerville.

"Yes, I love him."

Letty tilted her head to a puzzled angle. "Then why do you continue to refuse his proposals?"

Brianna shrugged. "At first, it was because I believed that he was only acting out of guilt and a healthy dose of pity. I could not bear the thought that he would eventually come to regret his impulsive proposal and blame me for his unhappiness."

"And now?"

"Now?" Brianna grimaced, a hint of color touching her cheeks. "I am embarrassed to confess the truth."

"Tell me, Brianna," the older woman urged.

Brianna hesitated before giving in to the inevitable. For all Lady Aberlane's sweet charm, she could be like a hound on the scent of a fox when she desired.

"To be honest, I am enjoying having Edmond dance attendance upon me."

There, it was said. Brianna squared her shoulders in expectation of Letty's anger. Edmond was, after all, her nephew and it was hardly kind of Brianna to toy with him as if he had no pride.

Instead, Letty merely gave a slow nod of her head. "Ah."

Her mild reaction only increased Brianna's guilt, and she could not halt her need to explain her less than commendable behavior.

"Because of Thomas Wade, I was never allowed a London season, or even so much as a soiree, as other girls enjoyed," she said, biting her lower lip. "I spent my days alone at home fantasizing about handsome gentlemen who never came to call."

"I understand completely, my dear." The older woman reached across the table to gently pat Brianna's hand. "You wish to be courted."

"I suppose that's rather silly, considering the circumstances."

"Actually, I think it is very wise. Every woman deserves to be properly wooed." Settling back in her seat, Letty offered Brianna an encouraging smile. "And in truth, it is probably best for Edmond as well."

Brianna's lips twitched as she recalled the smoldering glances and lingering touches that revealed that Edmond was far from satisfied with their platonic courtship.

In truth, she was not entirely satisfied herself. Oh, there was an undoubted pleasure in having Edmond dance attendance upon her, and to know that he could enjoy her companionship outside the bed. But the desire that pulsed between them was not entirely Edmond's, and the nights of lying alone in her bed were becoming near unbearable.

"I fear he would not agree with you."

"That is because he is accustomed to women falling over their pretty feet to capture his attention," Letty said tartly. "Edmond is a gentleman who appreciates having to fight for what he desires. And, my dear, he very much desires you."

"His desire is something that I have never doubted." Brianna glanced toward the box lying on the white tablecloth. "It is his heart that I seek."

"You have that as well," Letty assured her. "Never have I seen him so implacable. I do believe that he intends to spend the rest of his days sending you gifts and shadowing my doorstep if necessary."

Brianna's heart gave a painful jolt. The need that she had kept so tightly contained was threatening to break free and drown her in a dangerous tide of hope.

Even worse, she no longer desired to battle that hope.

"I did think he would be weary of it by now," she admitted, her voice so soft it barely stirred the air.

"No, my dear, his mind is set." Letty attempted to appear resigned, but managed only to look as satisfied as the cat that got the cream. "I quite suspect that you shall have to wed the poor man if I am ever to have peace in this house again."

Before Brianna could respond, a uniformed footman entered the room and performed a crisp bow.

"Lord Edmond, my lady."

"There…you see," Letty said with a knowing smile. "Please show him in, Johnston."

"Very good."

Resisting the urge to flutter like a nervous schoolgirl, Brianna covertly slipped the jewelry box into a pocket of her gown and turned to watch as Edmond strolled into the room.

As always, he managed to steal her breath.

Crossing the room with long, impatient strides, Edmond was at her side and lifting her fingers to press them to his lips.

"Good morning, *moya duska*," he said huskily, his voice tingling down her spine and making her toes curl in her slippers. With a last, lingering glance at the low bodice of her lavender silk gown, he turned to flash his aunt a questioning smile. "Hmm. Why do I feel as if I have just been dissected over the eggs and kippers?"

Much to her credit, Letty did not so much as bat an eye. "Tea, Edmond?"

"No, I thank you." His attention returned to a blushing Brianna. "I have actually come to invite Miss Quinn for a drive."

"It is rather early for a turn in the park," Letty pointed out before Brianna could reply.

"Then it is fortunate that we are not headed for the park."

"Where are we going?" Brianna demanded.

"It is a surprise."

She gave a lift of her brows, thinking of the magnificent ring now hidden in her pocket.

"I think there have been enough surprises for one day, my lord."

A slow smile of sheer temptation curved his lips. "Come, Brianna, I promise you will like this one."

"It does not include anything from the Crown Jewels, does it?"

His eyes twinkled with amusement. They seemed to do that a great deal over the past weeks. Something she would never have believed possible in the remote, fiercely grim gentleman she had first encountered at that Courtesan Ball.

"I fear not, the King is rather clutch-fisted with his family trinkets. It is well-known he would not even share them with his Queen."

"Good heavens, I would hope not," Letty said with a snort, her own lips twitching with humor. "That ugly little foreigner would have sullied them beyond repair."

"Spoken like a true Englishwoman, Aunt Letty. However, that ugly little foreigner did ensure that William Pitt increased the Prince's allowance and George was most anxious to get his hands upon the fortune."

"A pity he was not equally willing to get his hands upon her, or there might have been more than one child."

"*Mon dieu,* I brought Brianna here because I was convinced that you would be a proper chaperone, Letitia," Edmond chided, feigning shock at his aunt's words. "Obviously, I would have been better served to dump her in the stews."

Letty shrugged. "I merely say what everyone else is thinking."

"Yes, and you do so with such an innocent bat of your lashes that you are never given a proper set-down. 'Tis a talent that I have long admired."

The older woman gave one of the twittering laughs that so easily convinced others she was a bit of fluff.

"Really, Edmond, I haven't the least notion what you are speaking of."

"You know precisely what I speak of, you sly old fox." Edmond shook his head, but there was no mistaking his deep fondness for his aunt. "I can only pray that Brianna has not been entirely corrupted."

Letty turned her shrewd gaze toward the silent woman across from her.

"Oh, I believe Brianna possesses the spirit to decide whether she wishes to be corrupted or not."

"She does indeed," Edmond readily agreed, holding out a hand. "Well, my dear, will you join me?"

"I…" With a small nod, Brianna rose to her feet. For all her fears of the future, she did not want to end up like Vanya Petrova, bitterly regretting the decisions of her past. She wanted to reach out and grasp the happiness that was offered. "Very well."

EDMOND WATCHED IN SILENCE as Brianna slipped on her light cloak and charming bonnet decorated with satin ribbons and cherry blossoms. His heart clenched with a familiar ache at the sight of the early morning sunlight glinting off her fiery curls and brushing her ivory skin with a golden glow.

Just being near her was enough to lighten his mood and make the day seem a bit brighter, but for all his pleasure in being in her company, there was a part of him that felt growingly frustrated at the distance she kept between them.

He had been patient. He understood her need to be certain that his feelings were not driven by some ridiculous guilt and, more important, that he could be trusted with her fragile heart.

But the time had come to claim the woman who had stormed into his life and stolen his soul.

Refusing to believe that the butterflies in the pit of his stomach were actually nerves, Edmond led his beautiful companion down the steps and assisted her onto the waiting phaeton. Vaulting into the seat beside her, he took the reins from the groom and waited for the servant to leap onto the back of the vehicle before he set the matching bays into motion.

The early spring air was crisp, but the sun was warm and Brianna appeared content to enjoy the drive for several long moments. As he turned from Pall Mall onto St. James's Street, however, she at last turned her head to regard him with a hint of puzzlement.

"You do not intend to tell me where we are going?"

He smiled as he concentrated on weaving his way past a coal wagon. "I do not."

"Hmm." Surprisingly she did not press for more. "Aunt Letty mentioned that Stefan is in London."

Edmond shrugged. He had, in truth, been rather relieved to join his brother at his club the previous evening to discover that their relationship seemed none the worse, despite Edmond's crazed behavior.

Stefan not only was resigned to Edmond's determination to make Brianna his bride, but actually seemed pleased that his younger brother was so obviously caught in the coils of the beautiful young woman.

"There is some tedious bill or another up for vote in Parliament," Edmond said, slowing to turn the carriage onto York Street. "He devoted near three hours to boring me with the details last eve, but I must admit that I caught little more than taxes and angry tenants. Such tedious business goes quite over my head."

Brianna snorted at his offhand words. "Do you know, Edmond, your Aunt Letty is a mere amateur when it comes to playing the role of the silly aristocrat. You are the true master. I have seen you halt an entire revolution, if you will recall."

A ridiculous warmth flooded his heart at her instinctive defense. Surely it revealed that she possessed some feeling for him?

"Actually, I left the halting of revolutions to Herrick while I was in pursuit of my beautiful fiancée," he murmured softly. "I occasionally have my priorities in order."

She smiled, but her expression remained guarded. "I am rather surprised that you have not returned to Russia. Surely they have need of you?"

Edmond frowned, wondering if she were hoping to be rid of him. Not the most encouraging thought.

"When Alexander Pavlovich returns to St. Petersburg, I will return to pay my respects, but have written to inform Herrick that I will no longer be actively involved in Russian politics."

"Why?"

"Because I have more important duties that demand my attention," he said, turning to her with a smoldering glance.

"Duties, eh?" A hint of amusement brightened her emerald eyes. "Is that what I am?"

His annoyance faded beneath a blast of pure lust. Christ. If he did not have this woman as his wife and in his bed soon, he was going to become a stark raving lunatic.

"A most beautiful and tempting duty that I plan to tend to with exquisite attention," he promised, his voice thick with need.

She ducked her head, but not before he witnessed the answering flush of heat that stained her cheeks.

"Will the Romanov dynasty survive without you?"

With an effort, Edmond forced his attention back to the road. It would do his suit no good to overturn them in the gutter.

"In truth, I cannot say. Russia will always be a complicated mixture of tradition and enlightenment, of grandeur and wretched poverty, of effusive emotion and grim common sense. Perhaps such a country was not meant to have a comfortable crown to place on the head of their emperor."

She was silent a long moment before she reached out to lightly touch his arm.

"You will always love the land," she said softly.

He gave a nod. There had been a bittersweet pain in writing his letter of resignation. His duties to Alexander Pavlovich had given him a reason to crawl out of his bed each morning when he had been struggling through his darkest days, and he would never forget all that he owed his Emperor.

"And the people. But I am as much English as I am Russian, and I am no longer willing to play such dangerous games. Not when I at last have something to live for." With a sudden tug on the reins, he pulled the phaeton to a halt. "Here we are."

Brianna furrowed her brow as she studied the small but well-tended house.

"Is it not rather early for a visit?"

"Not at all." Edmond tossed the reins to the waiting groom and leaped onto the cobblestone street. Then, rounding the vehicle, he spanned Brianna's tiny waist and gently lifted her from her seat. "There is no one home."

Standing at his side, Brianna studied the whitewashed façade of the house with its garland-decorated pilasters and a fan window above the recently painted door.

"If there is no one home, then why are we here?"

"So I can give you your surprise."

She flashed him a baffled frown. "Edmond, you are being incredibly annoying."

"And you are dawdling. Come along." Taking her arm in a firm grip, he led her through the wrought-iron gate and up the wide steps. They halted at the door, and Edmond reached into his pocket to withdraw the heavy key. "Here. I think you should do the honors."

She blinked, staring at the key that lay in the palm of his hand.

"What do you mean?"

"I have given a great deal of thought to the perfect wedding present, *ma souris*."

"For goodness sakes, Edmond, you have already given me more than any woman could possibly desire."

He shrugged. "Mere trinkets that any man could purchase with enough wealth. This gift had to be special. Something that would prove that this is no bout of guilt or passing fancy. Something to convince you that all I desire is your happiness."

She regarded him with wide eyes, the pulse fluttering at the base of her throat the only indication she was affected by his words.

"And it is in the house?" she whispered.

Realizing she was too bemused to obey his bidding, Edmond unlocked the door himself and gently pressed her into the marble foyer decorated with matching satinwood chairs and a small cherry table with a vase of fresh pink roses.

"It *is* the house."

"You…" She shook her head in stunned amazement. "You bought me a house?"

Edmond smiled wryly. "Well, I will admit that I have great hopes that you will choose to live with me at Huntley House, or if you prefer, we can purchase our own town house. But since the first night we met, your one insistent, unwavering, at times aggravating desire has been to possess your own home, has it not?"

"Yes, but…"

Tossing the key on the nearby pier table, Edmond reached to grasp her trembling hands, his expression somber.

"I understand, *ma souris*. I understand what this house truly represents."

She gazed at him with wide, vulnerable eyes. "Do you?"

"Security," he breathed. "The absolute knowledge that you will never have to depend upon the whims and weaknesses of another. And that there is always a place where you can go to feel safe."

Without warning, tears rolled down her cheek. "Yes."

Unable to bear to see her cry, Edmond cradled her face in his hands and gently rubbed away the tears with his thumbs.

"So you see, even if you wed me, you will always have your own establishment to offer you shelter if you think I am being overbearing or annoying or…"

A tremulous smile curved her lips. "Or?"

He lowered his head to capture her lips in a soft, yearning kiss. "Or we simply decide to vary the location of our lovemaking," he whispered against her mouth.

For a moment she melted against his ready body, only to pull back with a sudden gasp.

"Edmond…the neighbors," she protested with a glance toward the open door.

Accepting that the moment was not yet ripe, Edmond stepped back. "Then let us inspect the house, *ma souris,* before we shock the good citizens of London."

Together, they moved toward the polished staircase to wander through the fully furnished rooms, a smile touching Edmond's lips at Brianna's unfettered wonderment. She looked for all the world like a child on Christmas morning as she inspected her domain, her fingers running loving hands over plain but solid English furnishings as if they were priceless treasures.

They had reached the master bedchamber when Edmond at last pulled her to a halt and turned her to meet his searching gaze.

"Well?"

"It's perfect." She heaved a deep sigh, her cheeks flushed with pleasure. "Did you truly purchase it?"

"I have made an offer with the owners, but I could not sign the final papers until I was assured you approved." He gave a tug on her hand, pulling her closer to his hard, desperate body. "Do you?"

With a smile as old as Eve, Brianna lifted her hand to trail her fingers along the line of his jaw.

"Do I have to wed you to get it?"

He sucked in a sharp breath, fiercely aware of the wide bed only a few steps away. *Mon dieu,* he would give the woman a dozen homes if it would allow him to place her on that mattress and end his torment.

"Will it make you agree to my proposal?" he demanded, his voice raw with desire.

"No."

Feeling as if he had just been punched in the gut, Edmond pulled back to regard her with a hopeless sense of despair.

"Brianna…"

She pressed her fingers to his lips to stop his pained words. Then, stepping back, she reached beneath her cloak to pull a small box from her pocket.

Still smiling, she opened the box to reveal the ring he had sent to her only that morning. His heart halted as she tossed aside the box and slowly slid the ring onto her finger.

"There is only one thing that will make me agree to your proposal, Lord Edmond Summerville," she said, tugging on his hand as she backed toward the bed. "And you cannot purchase it with your considerable wealth."

With a low growl Edmond had his arms wrapped about the teasing minx and tumbled them both onto the bed.

Later, he would teach her a lesson in nearly sending him to an early grave, but for now…ah, for now he intended to savor the woman who had given him something he never dreamed possible.

A future.

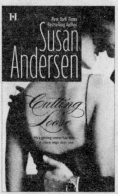

REQUEST YOUR FREE BOOKS!

2 FREE NOVELS
FROM THE ROMANCE/SUSPENSE
COLLECTION PLUS 2 FREE GIFTS!

YES! Please send me 2 FREE novels from the Romance/Suspense Collection and my 2 FREE gifts (gifts are worth about $10). After receiving them, if I don't wish to receive any more books, I can return the shipping statement marked "cancel." If I don't cancel, I will receive 4 brand-new novels every month and be billed just $5.49 per book in the U.S. or $5.99 per book in Canada, plus 25¢ shipping and handling per book plus applicable taxes, if any*. That's a savings of at least 20% off the cover price! I understand that accepting the 2 free books and gifts places me under no obligation to buy anything. I can always return a shipment and cancel at any time. Even if I never buy another book from the Reader Service, the two free books and gifts are mine to keep forever.

185 MDN EF5Y   385 MDN EF6C

Name   (PLEASE PRINT)

Address   Apt. #

City   State/Prov.   Zip/Postal Code

Signature (if under 18, a parent or guardian must sign)

Mail to **The Reader Service:**
IN U.S.A.: P.O. Box 1867, Buffalo, NY 14240-1867
IN CANADA: P.O. Box 609, Fort Erie, Ontario L2A 5X3

Not valid to current subscribers to the Romance Collection,
the Suspense Collection or the Romance/Suspense Collection.

Want to try two free books from another line?
Call 1-800-873-8635 or visit www.morefreebooks.com.

* Terms and prices subject to change without notice. N.Y. residents add applicable sales tax. Canadian residents will be charged applicable provincial taxes and GST. Offer not valid in Quebec. This offer is limited to one order per household. All orders subject to approval. Credit or debit balances in a customer's account(s) may be offset by any other outstanding balance owed by or to the customer. Please allow 4 to 6 weeks for delivery. Offer available while quantities last.

Your Privacy: Harlequin is committed to protecting your privacy. Our Privacy Policy is available online at www.eHarlequin.com or upon request from the Reader Service. From time to time we make our lists of customers available to reputable third parties who may have a product or service of interest to you. If you would prefer we not share your name and address, please check here. ☐

BOB08R

SILHOUETTE

SPECIAL EDITION™

NEW YORK TIMES BESTSELLING AUTHOR

DIANA PALMER

A brand-new Long, Tall Texans novel

HEART OF STONE

Feeling unwanted and unloved, Keely returns to Jacobsville and to Boone Sinclair, a rancher troubled by his own past. Boone has always seemed reserved, but now Keely discovers a sensuality with him that quickly turns to love. Can they each see past their own scars to let love in?

*Available September 2008
wherever you buy books.*

Visit Silhouette Books at www.eHarlequin.com   SSE24921

ROSEMARY ROGERS

77247   A DARING PASSION   ___ $6.99 U.S. ___ $8.50 CAN.

(limited quantities available)

TOTAL AMOUNT	$	_____
POSTAGE & HANDLING	$	_____
($1.00 FOR 1 BOOK, 50¢ for each additional)		
APPLICABLE TAXES*	$	_____
TOTAL PAYABLE	$	_____

(check or money order—please do not send cash)

HQN™

We *are* romance™